BLADES OF SHADOW

RYAN KIRK

WATERSTONE
MEDIA

For Dwight

PROLOGUE

Isau hid in tall grass as those who sought his life followed the road. He and his companion had left the road earlier, anticipating this very moment. Three hundred paces and more of empty grassland separated the parties, and still the sight of their white robes flapping in the breeze sent his heart racing.

Isau stared until his eyes ached, watching the slow movement of the monks. If those white-robed figures sensed him, they'd immediately turn and charge this direction, and the chase would continue.

The monks never failed to avenge their dead.

Eventually, they would have to fight.

At times, when Isau's feet cried out for mercy and his legs fought against the idea of taking another step, he wished for that fight. Even now he wondered if their discovery wouldn't be for the best. If nothing else, a battle would stir his companion to action.

He risked glancing at the enigmatic man who had so recently become the center of his life. While Isau maintained his vigilant watch, the man was sprawled out in the grass, arm flopped over his eyes to protect them from the glare of the sun.

Just looking at the man made Isau want to kick him. When they had first met, Isau thought him a hero. "Why are we hiding?" he whispered.

The man unshaded half his face, revealing one dark, uninterested, eye. "Because the monks are chasing us." He spoke normally.

Isau's eyes darted fearfully toward the road. The monks walked on, apparently oblivious to the fact that those they pursued were less than a league away. "Do you want them to hear us?"

The lone eyebrow that Isau could see arched. "If they can hear us this far away, they aren't even human."

Isau forced himself to take a deep breath. Arguing with him was as wise as getting in a fistfight with a stone wall. "We should fight!" he insisted.

"You mean you want me to fight."

Isau almost protested, but he was old enough to know that despite his dreams of martial prowess, he would be little help. He pushed his disappointment aside to focus on his new companion. "You did before."

"Because they left me no choice."

Isau remembered that day. He thought of it constantly. It hadn't been long ago, a half-moon at most. They'd been surrounded by four monks, and Isau thought for certain that he would die and rejoin the Great Cycle. The monks were the strongest warriors in the land. Even hardened soldiers turned away from duels with them.

But Eiji, the man beside him, had cut all four down without blinking.

Isau recalled every moment, every clean cut Eiji had made. As they walked, when he thought Eiji wasn't watching, he would re-enact the battle. The monks never blocked so much as a single attack. They died, their white robes stained with their own blood for once.

When Isau looked down at Eiji now, he had trouble believing the man who killed the monks and the one now trying to nap were the same man. It felt as if one night, while he slept, the true Eiji had wandered off and an imposter had taken his place. Eiji was a warrior of incredible skill, but he chose to hide instead of attack.

Isau often wondered if Eiji was actually a coward.

He didn't want to believe so. There must be something else to Eiji's actions, something Isau didn't understand. But the belief didn't make the endless days of running and hiding any easier to bear.

Eiji had saved him. When family, friends, and neighbors had all turned their backs on Isau, this stranger had risked his own life. In the whole history of Isau's days, he'd never experienced the like. Not only had Eiji rescued him that day, he'd promised to escort him someplace safe, someplace where Isau could live without having to fear the monks.

The promise seemed too good to be true, but what other choices did he have? To refuse was to commit a slow suicide.

He didn't want every day to be like today, chased across the vast prairies of the Western Kingdom by monks who wanted nothing more than to kill him. Refuge from this endless pursuit meant the world to Isau.

And Eiji seemed as good as his word. Their progress was slow, but they neared the border of the Western Kingdom. Though the monks respected no boundaries, crossing the border would still hinder their pursuit. The crossing was risky, but necessary. Isau didn't believe Eiji would bring him this far just to abandon him now.

The monks finally wandered beyond Isau's sight, but still Eiji didn't stir.

"They're gone," Isau reported.

"I'm thinking," Eiji said.

Isau tried to wait patiently, but his attempt didn't last long. "And?"

"That's the same group that's been on our tail for the last few days. When they realize they passed us, they'll stop and wait up ahead for us."

Isau eyed the wide prairie. "It's not as though we can't walk around them."

"True, but they've likely guessed our direction by now, and they'll find us again. The monks are nothing if not relentless."

"So what? I thought the only safe crossing was this direction."

Eiji sat up and rubbed his eyes. "The safest by far, yes, but not the only." He stood up. "Come, we're heading north. There's a bridge crossing there."

"With guards?"

"The kingdoms don't usually leave them undefended."

"They'll know who we are."

"And you're the one who wants a fight, aren't you?"

Isau's stomach felt like ice. He imagined them fighting soldiers, but in his imagination, they always lost. Fighting four monks was one achievement, but an entire detachment?

Impossible.

Eiji's tone softened. "We're far more likely to walk past guards than monks." He held up a hand. "And although I would prefer keeping our dispute between us and the monks, I still think the bridge is safer."

Isau shook his head. "I don't like it."

Eiji grinned. "Neither do I. But it's the best idea I can come up with."

Isau rubbed at his eyes, as though hoping he would soon wake from a horrible dream. When his efforts failed, he sighed. "Fine."

Eiji stood and began trekking north. Isau watched for a moment and then followed, wondering if he'd just made the choice that would lead him to his death.

1

"How many people have you killed?"

Eiji glanced down at Isau, not certain he had heard the question correctly. Then he returned his gaze to the abandoned fields surrounding them. More than a day had passed since they had last seen another living person.

He yearned for a town then. Even a village would do. Just so long as it had a place where he could drink.

And where enough people wandered the streets that the boy wouldn't ask such questions out loud.

He knew the answer, because after every kill he made a thin slice across his left forearm. If he lifted the long sleeves of his tunic, he'd be able to count every one, seven parallel lines.

The practice hadn't started intentionally.

In the fight that led to his first murder, his opponent had made the first cut across his forearm. To this day, it was the closest he'd come to rejoining the Great Cycle. The wound, although not deep, hadn't closed for days.

A bad omen, if one believed such nonsense.

It only seemed fitting that the others he killed also leave scars. Physical ones, to match those no one could see.

"Too many," he answered.

Like many of the young, Isau didn't understand. He had grown up on the stories, just like everyone else in the Three Kingdoms. But they weren't cautionary tales for him. To Isau, gifted with the sense, he only heard a promise of power. To a young farmhand who toiled from sunrise to sunset in the fields, whose stomach had never known the drowsiness of a full meal, that power was especially intoxicating, far more alluring than even the strongest drink.

Eiji imagined that Isau dreamed of revenge. Given the state he'd found the boy in, betrayed by his own family and neighbors, it would be a wonder if he didn't.

But revenge was nothing more than selfish pleasure. It only lasted for a moment. When the moment ended, the absence remained.

But how did he tell that to a boy who hadn't yet completed his eleventh cycle?

For a while, Eiji hoped his answer would satisfy Isau's curiosity.

Perhaps he underestimated Isau. The boy possessed a sense of honor that would have been admirable in an adult. He told himself that honor was the reason why he'd saved the boy in the first place. That and the fact the boy was gifted.

"But how many is that?" Isau asked.

"More than none," Eiji replied.

Isau was young, but he possessed a wisdom beyond his cycles, and he was old enough to catch the cold tone in Eiji's voice. Some questions his savior wouldn't answer. Isau let himself fall a few paces behind Eiji, silently voicing his displeasure.

More than anything, the boy hated when he was treated like a boy.

Eiji didn't mind the silence. The border quickly approached and he wanted to be prepared.

They reached the bridge later that afternoon.

The crossing over the fast-moving water was old, the stone worn by the passage of countless carts and untold cycles of storm and wind.

The stone towers on both sides of the river, though, were newer additions. The stone of each was different, mined from different quarries. Those towers hadn't been worn down by anything, far too young to show the ravages of age. They stood, the windows above looking like watchful eyes on the road below.

They were yet another part of the legacy of the Great War. The Kingdom, once whole and united, had been split in three. This bridge, which had once served to connect the lands of two houses, now served as a barrier passed by very few.

Troops dressed in green patrolled the area surrounding the tower Eiji and Isau approached. Eiji saw little to concern him. The guards' uniforms were ragged, and their patrol patterns were sloppy. Had he been alone and the night moonless, Eiji could have reached the bridge unobserved without problem.

But he wasn't alone.

Isau, he found, made almost every part of life more difficult.

The presence of the troops brought Isau once again closer to Eiji. Eiji saw how the boy shook out his hands, then wiped their sweat off on his trousers.

He spoke softly. "We'll be fine."

He wouldn't admit he felt the same. On his own, he had

options. But Isau cut off many of them. Their best hope was a clean border crossing.

Hopefully, news of Isau and Eiji hadn't spread this far yet.

Eiji counted the guards. Six patrolled the grounds surrounding the tower, with another eight stationed at the ground level of the tower around the thick gate. Six archers patrolled the top of the tower. Several had arrows nocked, their eyes following Eiji and Isau's every movement.

The guards seemed wary, but not alarmed.

Eiji stopped several paces in front of the guards at the gate. One of the guards held out his hand, too lazy to even ask for papers out loud. There was no recognition in his eyes as he studied the two travelers. Eiji relaxed, just a little. Word hadn't reached the crossing yet, making their long days on the road worth it.

But word would spread. It always did. And maybe then the guard would remember they had come this way, and one of the monks would have another footstep to track across the Three Kingdoms.

There was nothing to be done for it, though. Eiji had given his word to Isau, which made this necessary. Eiji would have to hide in the Northern Kingdom for several moons, at least, but he supposed he was willing to pay the price. It was worth doing at least one good thing in his life.

They passed the first tower with ease. The guards didn't care much who was leaving their lands, and if they weren't yet on the lookout for a man and an unrelated boy, they had no reason to delay the travelers.

Entering the Northern Kingdom would be more challenging.

The blue-uniformed guard who took their papers proved to be far more cautious. He studied the papers closely, and Eiji could do nothing but hope that the amount he'd paid for the forgeries would be enough. The guard looked at the two travelers. He tilted his head to one side as he studied them, and Eiji fought the urge to go for his sword. Isau was doomed if he did.

"You two are merchants?"

That was what the papers claimed. Few besides diplomats and merchants crossed the border, and Eiji would never pass as a diplomat. He nodded. "Yes, sir. Selling medicines."

"He's not your son?"

"No, sir." That much was obvious. Eiji and Isau didn't look anything alike. "I've never started a family, and I needed an apprentice."

The guard chuckled. "You should be thankful. Extra mouths to feed mean more shifts standing at this bridge no one's trying to cross."

Eiji forced a smile.

"He's a bit young to be an apprentice, isn't he?"

"For most trades, yes. But his smaller hands are useful in the preparation of medicines, and he has a sensitive nose I find useful in identifying mislabeled herbs."

"Is that so? What do you smell now, boy?"

Eiji grimaced. Isau had grown less tolerant of disrespect on the road, a problem they'd had to deal with more than once. The child was already starting to think of himself as a nightblade, somehow superior to everyone else.

"That you need a bath," Isau answered.

Eiji swore to himself. He'd leave the child here, tied to another tree, if that attitude doomed their crossing.

The guard glowered for a moment. He stared at Isau, who stared right back, defiant in that way only a child can be.

The guard cracked first, laughing to himself. "Too much wit for his own good, too."

"You don't know the half of it." Eiji glared at the boy.

Isau looked studiously at the ground below.

The guard handed back their papers and waved them through. Even as they walked away, though, Eiji felt as though the archers had drawn their bows and aimed at his back. He imagined he could feel the point, itching in that place just below the shoulder blades that was difficult to reach, where the arrow would strike.

He didn't relax until the tower was far behind them.

He paused only once to look back. They'd escaped the Western Kingdom, which was no small feat. His eyes traveled over the now-foreign land, expecting at any moment to see a group of white-robed figures on horseback chasing after them.

But no one came. The grasslands remained empty.

They were safe, at least for now.

Eiji turned back and looked at the land ahead of them.

Now came the hard part.

2

They reached a small village not long after the sun had set for the day. Eiji had been here once before, though he'd been traveling the opposite direction. Two cycles had passed, though, so he doubted any here remembered him. He did little to stand out.

He remembered a cozy inn where the quality of the ale far surpassed the quality of the rooms. This close to the bridge, he imagined the ale drew more merchants than most would expect. Drunk guests rarely complained about poor bedding.

Neither he nor Isau had slept in a bed for nearly a moon. They'd had to move fast, and they largely kept off the roads, to better avoid the monks searching for them.

The border wouldn't stop the white-robed hunters, but it would slow them down. Different monasteries controlled this land.

Now that they were safely in the Northern Kingdom, it was time for a bath, a full night of rest, and as much ale as his stomach could handle.

The moon above cast the village in dull grays. No

torches were lit to keep the darkness at bay, and even from a distance, the village looked less welcoming than it had in his memories.

But the past two cycles had been difficult ones. Food remained scarce, and there were always rumors of war rumbling throughout the countryside.

The inn, fortunately, still stood. And if no torches lit the street outside, the inside was bright and warmed by a crackling fire. Heads turned as they entered, but quickly returned, none of the other guests noticing anything worth their attention.

Eiji studied the others closely. Nice, if dirt-stained, clothing identified the merchants. The rest, gathered in groups, appeared to be locals similarly attracted to the ale. No one paid them any particular attention.

Eiji and Isau took a table near the center of the room. It was hardly ideal, but few were open.

The presence of so many in such close proximity pressed against Eiji's sense. He felt the lives of those surrounding him, a lightness and a pressure that was his sense exploring the room. Out in the open fields, his sense freely roamed. Here, he reined it in. Too much information for too long could drive a nightblade mad.

Before long, the innkeeper set two large bowls of rice and vegetables before them, accompanied by a mug of ale. Isau attacked his food with the vigor of a master swordsman fighting a strong opponent. Eiji drank the mug of ale in a few gulps, catching the innkeeper's attention with a gesture. He let his food rest for a while, allowing the ale to work its magic.

After so long on the road, the drink hit fast and hard.

Eiji welcomed the fuzziness in his mind. The details he worried about constantly slipped from his grasp, leaving behind only an easy contentment. Perhaps life wasn't all suffering, as he often believed.

Isau noticed Eiji's behavior, of course. The child was sharp, as nightblades often were. The sense was information, and those gifted with it missed little, no matter their age. Eiji's momentary pang of guilt quickly faded, though, unable to find a foothold in his slow thoughts.

Eiji ate as he drank the second mug of ale, balancing his inebriation with a skill he couldn't have imagined possessing three cycles ago.

As his masters used to say, though, practice leads to perfection.

Oh, how they would look down on him now.

But like guilt, regret found no home in his thoughts. The simple meal filled the holes in his stomach, and the two went off to find baths and their beds.

Despite Eiji having the advantage of two drinks, Isau still fell asleep first, as he did most nights.

Eiji envied the boy. His ten cycles hadn't been easy ones, but to the boy, the world still possessed a simplicity Eiji had never known. Isau's hands were already callused from a lifetime of labor, and his back scarred from beatings, but he'd known the course of his days. He woke, worked, and slept. His world was filled with sharp distinctions and absolutes.

Day and night.

Right and wrong.

Life and death.

Eiji wondered how long the boy's worldview would hold. How long would it be enough?

Once Isau's gift had been discovered, the boy had expected death. Then Eiji had appeared, a fortuitous coincidence. Now Isau's days were once again simple. He woke, traveled, and slept, eager to train his newfound gift so that he could take revenge on those who had destroyed his life.

Isau knew his future.

Eiji wished for such certainty.

Despite his racing thoughts, though, sleep eventually found Eiji. His sleep, thankfully, was dreamless. When it wasn't, he was haunted by a singular nightmare he couldn't escape, no matter how many leagues he put between himself and the island.

He woke to Isau shaking him, eyes wide with fear. "They're here."

Eiji sat straight up. "They" could only mean monks. But how had they been discovered so fast?

The answer to the question would have to wait. Eiji closed his eyes, extending his sense. He grimaced at the effort. Between the number of people sleeping nearby and effects of the drink, extending his sense felt like wrestling a wild animal.

But he still felt the monks easily enough. Those with the sense appeared different than others. Their lights burned brighter.

As near as Eiji could tell, these two were strong enough to notice, but not so strong he needed to worry. If it came to a fight, he would most likely win.

Despite Isau's desires, he didn't want to draw his sword. He'd already earned the ire of the monasteries. If he harmed more of their order, he'd have dozens of monks chasing him endlessly throughout the Three Kingdoms.

Eiji came to his feet and glanced out the window. Two monks were passing through the town on horseback.

He cursed. The monks weren't paying any attention to the town. They were just riding through. Their meeting was nothing but poor luck.

"Pack up," he told Isau. "We'll be leaving soon."

He followed his own advice, a process that didn't take long. He flung wet clothes into his pack and cinched it tight, watching the window the entire time. If he had any luck at all, the monks would ride by without noticing either him or Isau.

But it was hard for gifted to hide from the gifted.

The riders pulled up to a stop in front of the inn. They spoke to one another, though Eiji couldn't make out the words. Then they dismounted and hitched their horses. They entered through the inn's front door, swords in hand.

Isau watched with Eiji. "What do we do?"

Thoughts weren't coming quickly enough. Eiji squeezed at his temples, regretting his choices the night before. Outside, he heard one of the horses neigh.

And then he had it.

Eiji took out his purse and laid enough gold pieces upon his bed to cover the cost of the room and the food from the night before. Isau stared in mute disbelief.

Their debt paid, Eiji returned to the window and opened it. He gestured for Isau to slide out.

Eiji followed the boy, closing the window behind him just as the innkeeper unlocked the door to their room. He heard shouts from the monks, but they were already in the street. He ran toward the horses, Isau less than a step behind him.

Eiji didn't think there were many horses in the small village. The monks had just left behind the best means of escape. He threw Isau on top of the first horse, then unhitched both animals. For the first time since he'd been rescued, Isau's worry was plainly evident. "I don't know how to ride."

A small part of Eiji sympathized. Horses looked majestic

from a distance, but when you were on top, all you could think about was the sheer amount of muscle underneath you. But they didn't have time for lessons.

"It's easy," Eiji said as he put the reins into Isau's hands. "Don't fall off." Then he slapped the horse into motion.

He climbed onto his new horse just in time to see the monks barge back out of the inn. He kicked his steed into motion, chasing after Isau.

They left the shouts of the monks behind them.

3

The monks posed a problem.

Eiji and Isau were gifted criminals, and Eiji suspected it wouldn't be long before their names and likenesses were known throughout the Western Kingdom. But he'd hoped crossing the border would give them time and allow them to breathe.

Encountering a random pair of monks was one of the most rotten pieces of luck imaginable.

Now the pursuit would begin again, not just because they were gifted, although that was justification enough, but because they'd stolen horses from the monasteries.

And no one stole from the monasteries.

He cursed himself, more than anyone.

If he'd just left Isau tied to that tree, none of this would have happened. He'd still be in the Western Kingdom, searching for a legendary nightblade.

He wouldn't be hunted through two of the Three Kingdoms.

They rode at a steady clip throughout the day. Isau grew more comfortable in the saddle. They rode east, toward the sunrise, avoiding main roads. It wasn't the direction they needed to go, but Eiji didn't want the pursuing monks to guess their final destination.

Isau's growing comfort in the saddle turned to enjoyment by early evening. He kicked his horse into a gallop, hooves thundering across the farmland, long hair whipping behind him.

Eiji preferred his pace steady, so he contented himself with watching the boy.

As a young farmhand, Isau had probably never dreamed that someday he might ride a horse for countless leagues in a foreign kingdom. Such dreams brought only despair to children tied so closely to the villages and land of their birth.

In this moment, with a warm sun on his face and the sound of Isau's laughter ringing in his ears, all seemed right with the world.

Eiji held on to such moments.

He knew they wouldn't last.

They couldn't last.

Within the next moon, they would reach Highgate. Eiji would hand Isau off to others better suited for the task of raising the child.

Then, assuming he lived that long, he would begin the long journey back, once again searching for Koji.

Seeking his own answers.

Eiji called a halt just before the sun kissed the horizon. The boy reluctantly brought his horse to a stop and they made camp.

Eiji showed Isau how to tend to the horses, but afterward they fell into a familiar routine. Isau built the fire and Eiji prepared their food. He'd hoped to replenish their supplies in the last village, but their hasty departure meant they were low on goods.

Fortunately, Isau never complained about Eiji's meals. He was grateful to be fed regularly, which said enough about his life before the two had met. Although, to be fair, regular meals were a gift for many these days.

As Eiji cooked the food, Isau fidgeted. He sat, then stood. He paced back and forth, then attempted to sit once again.

Eiji didn't ask. If Isau had a concern to voice, it was his responsibility to speak.

Isau broke when Eiji offered him a bowl of food. The boy accepted the food, but didn't touch it.

That spelled trouble. Eiji suspected Isau could eat a full meal in the middle of a battlefield.

"You should train me, now," Isau said.

Eiji met the boy's defiant gaze. This wasn't the first time the request had come up, but Eiji hadn't been ambiguous in his refusal. He respected Isau's tenacity, but it didn't change his answer.

"No," he said.

He braced himself for the deluge to come.

"Why not?" Isau asked. "You've told me that other nightblades start training when they are even younger. And I can help. If more monks find us, I could fight them with you."

"I don't plan on fighting any monks."

"Why not?" Isau almost yelled the question.

Ahh. That, then, was the true heart of the problem, the real answer Isau needed.

"You're stronger than them!" Isau shouted, losing control of his tightly held emotions. "When we saw those monks outside my village, and you killed them, it was easy for you. They never blocked a single cut! Why are we running? Why not fight?"

Isau's words resurrected memories Eiji kept burying. They played as a series of moments seared into his nightmares.

Finding Isau, captured by the monks, tied to a tree in the center of his village, a child beaten by adults.

Leaving the village behind with Isau in tow, the hope of finding Koji still burning in his heart.

Watching the monks as they rode up on horseback, leaving him no choice.

The look of surprise on the first monk's face as he realized he'd picked a fight with a warrior far stronger.

The blood and bodies on the ground, the too-familiar burst of sickening exhilaration.

Followed by the sinking knowledge that Koji had once again slipped through his grasping reach.

The moments flashed through his memory, striking quick as lightning, leaving him reeling in their wake. He took another bite of food and slowed his rapid breath.

"Why do you keep running?" Isau asked again. This time the question was quieter, the boy's anger spent.

Isau looked to him as a hero. The boy believed Eiji could fight the monasteries and win. That belief made Eiji want to turn to his old masters, to show them they had been wrong about him. Eiji hoped Isau never looked at him any other way.

But he would. Eiji could never be the hero Isau believed him to be.

"Strong as I am," Eiji said, "a warrior can only fight so many battles. Some are worth fighting, like the one that occurred after I freed you. Those monks left me no other path. But there was no need this morning."

Eiji saw Isau didn't understand. In the boy's mind, any battle you could win was worth fighting.

Hopefully the masters on the island would teach him different.

But Isau had earned something, Eiji supposed. He pulled his weight and rarely complained about the difficult conditions of the road. Some basic lessons would prepare the child for what was to come. And Isau was right. On the island, the others his age had already started their training. Many his age were already dangerous warriors in their own right.

But on the island, the harm one could do was limited. Here, the consequences of wrong action were far greater.

Isau deserved some trust, though.

"I will teach you empty-handed techniques starting tomorrow," Eiji said.

He regretted the concession as soon as the words left his lips.

But the smile on Isau's face made the decision worth it.

4

They rode the horses for three more days. Eiji gradually angled them northeast. It still wasn't the shortest path they could have taken, but long days in the saddle now led them closer to the port that was their final destination.

When Eiji judged it safe, they returned to the road, selling the horses at the first village they came to. They allowed the villagers to purchase the horses for far less than they were worth, making Eiji and Isau local heroes. They left with gold in their pockets and goodwill pushing them on.

After two more days of walking east, Eiji finally turned them north. He'd observed no signs of pursuit, and their trail would be cold enough.

They were safe, for now.

Isau bemoaned the loss of his horse. In the few days they'd had together, the boy had become fond of the beast, going so far as to speak to it each night before sleep.

In response, Eiji offered even more training. When they

woke in the morning, he demonstrated empty-hand techniques as well as some wielding a knife.

Isau's commitment to his training impressed Eiji. Most young blades on the island didn't show half the dedication his ward did. When the boy arrived, he'd still be well behind the others his age, but Eiji suspected Isau would catch and surpass many of his peers in short order. Every time Eiji called a rest during the day, Isau remained on his feet, practicing what he'd been taught that morning.

Combined with a natural physical aptitude, Isau advanced faster than Eiji expected, at least in the martial forms.

The boy's slow development of his sense frustrated them both. Isau's sensitivity impressed Eiji, but he struggled to focus, to push away the superfluous signals that limited his range and ability.

Eiji guessed the mental aspects of the sense would come with maturity and desire. Right now, Isau only wanted to learn how to fight. Once he learned to integrate his martial skills with his sense, though, he would open up new doors and pathways he wouldn't be able to resist exploring. After all, it was only when one integrated martial skill and the information from the sense that a nightblade was born.

That was a lesson the Three Kingdoms willingly forgot. Their monks might fashion themselves the nightblades of old, but with every passing cycle, that belief wandered further from the truth. True, the monks were skilled fighters, but their innate fear of their gift prevented them from integrating their abilities with their martial arts. They limited themselves.

The days passed easily enough. They risked an inn one night, and when the evening passed without incident, Eiji decided it would be safe to stay in one every few nights.

Every day they ate up the distance between them and Highgate.

When the monk found them, it caught Eiji completely by surprise.

He and Isau were enjoying lunch in a small tavern. Fish from a nearby stream filled their stomachs, and a perfectly fine local ale occupied most of Eiji's attention.

Eiji felt the presence of the monk before Isau, but it was still too late. He'd let down his guard and relaxed behind a facade of anonymity. In the crowded tavern, his sense didn't extend all that far, anyway. The monk reached the entrance before Eiji could even warn Isau. When the door opened, Eiji saw one of the most intimidating men he'd ever encountered silhouetted in the afternoon sun.

The monk was dressed in the white robes of his order, but he filled the entire doorframe, from top to bottom and side to side.

Despite his size, when he stepped into the tavern, the man moved with the grace of a predator.

Eiji swore under his breath.

The monk's eyes traveled quickly over the crowd of now-quiet patrons, settling without question on Eiji. His eyes narrowed and he stepped forward.

Eiji swore again, this time loud enough for Isau to hear. With his back to the door and his attention completely captured by the meal in front of him, the boy still didn't realize the trouble behind him.

Isau looked up from his fish. "What—"

His words were cut off as his own sense caught the monk behind him.

Indecision froze Eiji's hand. A fight inside the tavern risked many lives. And monks always traveled in pairs, meaning at least one remained outside, waiting for them.

Besides that, Eiji wasn't even sure he could defeat this monster of a man.

But what choice did he have?

Before Eiji could draw, the man reached the table and pulled up a chair. It squealed in protest as he settled his weight on it, but the tension in the room immediately dissipated as other customers realized no fight was imminent.

Eiji wasn't so certain. Yes, the monk appeared relaxed, but he looked like a cat resting on a perch overlooking its prey.

The monk waved at the barkeep, ordering a beer loudly enough that everyone in the village probably heard.

Eiji would never have a better chance to draw, and he didn't believe the monk's easygoing facade.

But he was curious.

Every monk he'd met before attacked without preamble.

Only after he'd taken a long sip did the monk turn his attention fully to Eiji. He offered the nightblade a small bow. "Name's Itsuki."

Eiji, raised from birth to be respectful, returned Itsuki's bow, matching its depth. "Eiji."

The enormous monk turned to Isau, his gaze inviting a response. The boy glanced between both men, then swallowed hard. "Isau," he said.

Itsuki offered Isau a short bow, which wasn't returned. If Itsuki took any offense, he didn't show it.

The monk took another long sip of his beer, apparently content to drag the moment out. Then he spoke. "I'm a hunter for the monasteries. One of the best they've got, and that's nothing more than a fact."

Eiji didn't doubt it. This man put the others of his order to shame.

Isau asked the question Eiji was too proud to voice. "How did you find us?"

Itsuki's smile was wide and welcoming. "It wasn't too hard to do, not when you've been at it as long as I have. I knew you headed east after stealing those horses, and I figured you might take a bit of a turn to the north. So my partner and I, we asked around, asking questions at every village I thought you might pass by."

"No small amount of effort," Eiji said. Most monks were determined, but even mounted, Itsuki and his partner had covered an enormous amount of ground.

"Well, I've long believed that if you're going to do something, it's worth doing well," Itsuki replied. "And sure enough, I found your horses, sold far more cheaply than what they're worth, I might add. I think our stablemasters would be angered to learn that."

Isau interrupted again. "What did you do to them?"

Itsuki shook his head. "Nothing. Those villagers need the beasts more than the monasteries do. The way I see it, I never did find those horses."

Eiji raised an eyebrow at that. He couldn't imagine another monk choosing not to take the horses back. Most monks wouldn't even have paid, leaving the townspeople without the beasts or their hard-earned coin.

Itsuki turned his attention back to Eiji. "The villagers said you'd continued east on foot, but I suspected you'd turn north eventually. So my partner and I repeated the process, asking after you in every village for leagues."

He paused, basking in the glow of his success. He leaned over to Isau, causing the boy to flinch away. "You see, Isau, you spend your days in this land trying to hide. But you're alone. I, on the other hand, have the whole of the Three

Kingdoms helping me. And that makes your efforts pointless."

The monk's last words were aimed as much at Eiji as they were Isau. And they struck true.

"How did you know we would head north?" Eiji asked.

Itsuki took another pull of his beer. At this rate, there couldn't be much left. "Because you're going to Highgate."

Eiji tried to control his expression, but knew he failed when he saw Itsuki's grin grow broader. "It's where all you blades trying to escape go."

Eiji almost drew his sword then. That secret, more than any other, he would die to protect. And this monk knew it.

Itsuki waved his hand. "Relax. I'm the only one who's figured it out. Everyone else seems to forget what happened after the Great War, and as there are fewer and fewer of you making the journey every cycle, I imagine the knowledge will soon be lost to time."

Eiji wasn't convinced.

"Besides," Itsuki said. "I don't care."

Eiji relaxed, but only a fraction. "Why not?"

"Because gone is gone. The method doesn't matter much to me."

The two men stared at each other.

"So what happens next?" Eiji asked.

Itsuki finished the last of his beer. "Your choice. If you wish, you can return to the monasteries with me."

"Or?" Eiji again tensed for a fight.

Itsuki kept grinning, as though he'd expected the response. "Or you can continue on to Highgate. You put yourselves on one of your ships and never come back."

Itsuki stood up. "But just know, I'll be watching you. If either of you attempt to remain in Highgate, or return to the

Northern Kingdom, I'll kill you before you even know I'm there."

Eiji supposed it wasn't a good time to mention that he'd been exiled from the island. He couldn't board a ship if he wanted to. So he just nodded. "That's a generous offer."

"It is, isn't it?" The enormous monk took one last look at the two criminals. "Well, I'll be seeing you."

"Why not just kill us?" Eiji couldn't restrain his curiosity.

"Because I wanted to meet you. You didn't draw on me the moment you noticed me, which is a far cry better than most of your kind. And all you've done is steal some horses. If you're leaving, I'm happy not to have more blood on my hands. As I said: 'gone is gone.'"

Itsuki turned to the barkeep. "Put my drink on my friend's bill."

With that, he was gone, leaving Eiji with more questions than answers. He laid enough coins for the food and drink on the table. It was time to go.

Beside him, Isau whispered, "He's going to be really upset when he learns that you've also killed four monks."

Eiji agreed. Which made their haste all the more important.

5

When they left the tavern, Isau spotted Itsuki at a teahouse down the street. The man raised a teacup, so small in his hands Isau was surprised it didn't break just from being held. Isau wondered what it would be like to be hit by those meaty fists.

He didn't want to find out.

He hated all monks. They had destroyed his life once already. But he hated Itsuki most of all. He was an egotistical fool who lorded his strength over others. If any monk deserved to suffer, it was that one.

If Eiji thought the same, there was no way of knowing. The nightblade also noticed the monk, politely nodded, and led them out of the village heading north. At a fast pace, Highgate was only three days away.

Isau waited until they had left the town, then spoke. "We can't trust him."

"Why not?"

"He's a monk."

Eiji was silent, then said, "That's it?"

"Do you need more reason?"

Eiji chuckled a bit at that. "I suppose not." A short pause, then, "I do trust him, though. At least, mostly. He could have killed us both, and apparently he has no trouble tracking us."

"Maybe he just wants to see where you go."

The nightblade slowed at that. "I'm worried about that, too." Eiji stopped completely. "But from what he said, I think he already knows enough." He paused, and when he spoke again, his voice revealed a wound Isau didn't understand. "And he's right, I think, about the blades. The Three Kingdoms just wants to forget. You're right to be worried, but I think we will be fine."

Eiji resumed their walk, and Isau followed. He chewed over Eiji's words, wondering if they were making the right choice. But one thought became the center of his attention. "Why do you think Itsuki is right?"

"About what?"

"About the Three Kingdoms wanting to forget the blades."

Eiji looked off into the distance. "I think all they want is to put that part of history behind them. They would rather act as though the blades never existed."

That hurt Isau. He didn't want to be forgotten. He wanted to leave something behind that lasted longer than he did. But it wouldn't be in these lands. "I can't wait to be on the island. I'm tired of being chased."

Eiji nodded. "I also dream of a day where I can lay down my head and not worry about someone coming to cut it off. You will like it there, I think."

Something in the tone of Eiji's voice caught Isau's attention. He wrinkled his brow. There had been an emphasis, however slight, on the "you." And the nightblade only dreamed of a day where he would be safe; he didn't plan for it. Isau made the connections quickly enough. "You're not coming to the island with me, are you?"

After a long pause, Eiji shook his head.

"Why not?"

Eiji smiled, but to Isau, that smile contained no joy. "I'm not allowed to return."

Isau stopped walking, forcing Eiji to stop, too. Eiji gestured for him to continue. "Come, we can talk while putting more distance between us and Itsuki."

Isau dragged his feet, not really believing they were losing Itsuki. "Why can't you return?"

Eiji bit his lower lip. Isau tried to remember what the nightblade had said about the island and realized that for all they'd spoken about the place Eiji had grown up, Eiji never talked about his own past. He'd only talked about what the island was like. He'd been avoiding the subject. After all the leagues they'd put behind them, it was the only explanation.

"I killed one of the elders of the island," he confessed.

Eiji looked anywhere but at him. Isau stopped in his tracks, but Eiji didn't even notice. A few steps later, he realized Isau no longer followed him. Eiji looked up at the sky and took a deep breath.

Eiji had killed a nightblade elder?

Isau now questioned everything he thought he knew about the blade.

What kind of man was he traveling with?

Eiji turned and faced the boy. Isau clenched his hands into tight fists, the knuckles turning white. His breathing came in short, quick bursts. "Why?"

Eiji didn't answer for a long time. "The blades on the island disagreed about an important question. I led a group of young blades who wanted to return to the Three King-doms. But once you're on the island, you can't leave. I tried to break that rule, and a fight ensued. In that fight, I killed an elder."

Isau stared daggers at him, forcing him to continue.

"I never meant to hurt anyone. But I did. After, I surrendered."

"Why didn't they kill you?"

"Many wanted to. But there were many blades who agreed with me. Killing me would have made the problem worse. So the elders granted my wish. They sent me to the Three Kingdoms, and I'm never allowed to return home."

For the first time since his confession began, Eiji met Isau's stare. Isau stood there, glaring, hurt and betrayal mixing together.

"Then why send me there?" he finally asked. "I thought we would go together."

"Because it is what you said you wanted," Eiji replied. "It is a good place. You'll be able to train and learn how to use your skills. You'll become a nightblade. At night, you'll sleep easy, and in time you will start a family. None of that will happen if you remain in the Three Kingdoms."

"If it's so wonderful, why did you want to leave?"

Eiji grimaced. "I didn't want those things."

"What do you want?"

"Back then, I thought I wanted to make a difference. I wanted to make the Three Kingdoms a better place."

Isau left no stone unturned. "And now?"

"Now I don't know."

They stared at each other. Isau wasn't sure he'd ever felt so angry. Somehow, the betrayal stung even worse than his family's. His family had only done what any family would in their situation.

Isau had thought Eiji was better than that.

Eiji then asked a question Isau didn't expect. "So, will you have me escort you to the island, or is this where our paths diverge?"

Isau's eyes widened. Would Eiji really leave him here, on his own? Looking into Eiji's eyes, he believed that he might.

Isau supposed he had a choice, but it was really no choice at all. If he remained in the Three Kingdoms alone, he would be dead within a moon. Especially with that monk behind them.

"Take me to the island," he said, his decision less certain than in the past.

Eiji nodded and resumed their trek toward the sea.

Isau stared at the nightblade's back and swore he would never look at him with respect again.

6

The companionship between Isau and Eiji wasn't completely dead, but it had been mortally wounded, and its death throes lasted for days.

Isau's regular stream of questions slowed to a trickle.

At first, Eiji enjoyed the peace. He told himself it was for the best. The sooner the boy forgot him, the better off they would both be.

But he soon came to miss the boy's curiosity.

They stayed at inns every night now. At least once a day, Eiji caught sight of Itsuki, somewhere far behind them. Whenever their gazes met, the monk would bow, a grin stretching from ear to ear.

Eiji saw little point in hiding, so they moved in the open. Their pace quickened, Isau unwilling to stop for any rest. The boy took the lead now, and with every step it felt as though Isau ran away from him.

Eiji considered apologizing, or attempting to explain further. Simplifying the story for Isau's ears might have been a mistake.

But this was for the best.

It would make the parting easier.

And he deserved the boy's scorn.

His first real combat, his first kill, had been against his own elder. A woman who had helped raise him since before he could walk.

And when he cut her down, he had loved it.

Six more kills later, he understood the feeling was a natural reaction of the body. He'd felt it to some degree every time he'd been forced to defend himself. The sensation was never as strong as the first time, but always there.

The knowledge didn't erase the horror of that moment.

After, when the first cut on his forearm hadn't healed, a part of him had hoped that it never would. He wanted to bleed, to be reminded of what he'd done.

His skin had knitted back together eventually, but other, deeper wounds never healed.

And all it took was a look from Isau to tear the scabs off and rip them wide open again.

He reminded himself that the boy would be dead if not for his actions, but it did little to ease his troubled thoughts.

When Highgate came into view, it was a welcome relief. Eiji looked forward to leaving Isau at the docks. Granted, he'd have to figure out what to do about Itsuki afterward, but he welcomed that problem.

Though they still had some daylight remaining, Eiji's caution prevented him from simply marching straight to the docks, finding the ship, and leaving Isau there. They stopped at an inn on the outskirts of town, in a seedy area that saw little honest trade. Those that proclaimed themselves merchants hid inside their shops behind thick doors that kept their business from prying eyes and ears. Children with quick feet and a light touch darted around those who dared walk the streets unarmed, emptying pockets and purses with ease.

Isau's eyes were as wide as a full moon, and had Eiji not been near, the boy would have lost everything, including his shirt, within five blocks. They passed by a brothel, Isau staring without even a hint of shame at the women who invited passersby inside.

Eiji sometimes forgot how little of the world the boy had seen. Before his rescue, Isau had been tied to a small farmstead, where the longest journey he'd ever taken was to the village less than a league away.

Eiji rolled his shoulders as they settled into their room at the inn. He detested Highgate, and this section of the city more than any other. He hated the filth and the naked greed, the constant scrabbling for coin as though nothing else mattered. The quicker he left Isau behind and left the port, the happier he would be.

If he could find a safe inn with good ale after, so much the better.

Two problems prevented Isau's quick departure, and both began with Itsuki.

Even if Itsuki knew the blades used Highgate as a connection to the Three Kingdoms, Eiji didn't want to be the one who led the monk to the actual ship. Perhaps the point was moot. If Itsuki wanted to find the ship, he could. The gifted couldn't hide from the gifted, not for long. Still, the point of honor remained. The problem was exacerbated by another detail Eiji hadn't shared with Isau. He wasn't just exiled. If the other blades so much as saw him approach the ship to the island, their orders were to execute him.

Second, Eiji still hadn't figured out how to evade Itsuki once he left Isau behind.

The delay at the inn was thus necessary. In the morning,

he would head north, toward the docks, and scout the situation. There wasn't always a ship docked here, so it was possible they might have a bit of a stay before them. Hopefully Itsuki would understand.

They ate a quiet meal before the evening rush of customers began. Though the beds were clean enough, the inn didn't exactly attract a wholesome crowd. Eiji planned on being locked within their room by the time the evening became rowdy.

Isau fell asleep as soon as the sun dropped below the horizon, but as usual, sleep evaded Eiji with the skill of a master swordsman. His worries piled on top of one another, and underlying them all was the open wound of his past actions.

How much longer could he keep running?

Eventually he admitted defeat in his quest for sleep. He rolled out of the bed, moving softly so as not to disturb Isau.

Eiji left the room, locking the door again behind him. Isau's snoring never varied.

A few moments later Eiji sat downstairs, a mug of ale in hand that tasted as though it was mostly piss. As he'd expected, half the crowd here looked like they would stab him for coin, and the other half wouldn't even blink in surprise.

He put his drink down when he felt the presence of another blade nearby.

Strong, too.

He turned around in his chair, but saw nothing. The presence came from outside, more than a block away.

The energy was one of the strongest he'd felt in a long time. Maybe ever. It was hard to tell amongst the crowd at the inn.

That very crowd protected him from detection, at least a little.

He stood up and left the inn. A single blade that strong and alone was an opportunity. Maybe it was a friendly face from the island, someone whose skill had blossomed in Eiji's absence. Maybe the blade would help him get Isau to the ship.

It was worth a look.

As soon as he left the crowd, his sense sharpened. The other blade wasn't just a block away, but two. Their strength unsettled him. No one he knew had reached such a level on the island. And he didn't think anyone could have in the intervening cycles.

Could it be Koji, here?

The odds were impossible, but who else except the legendary nightblade had such strength?

Curiosity and hope led him deeper into the filthy back streets of Highgate.

Eiji walked through narrow passages, stepping over a woman passed out against a wall. A few people walked the streets, but not many. The shadows here held too many threats. The wise were inside, doors and windows tightly locked.

A single scream pierced the night.

No one nearby reacted. If anything, they kept their eyes lowered and walked faster, away from the sound.

Which had come from where Eiji sensed the other blade.

He ran.

Ahead of him, his sense of the blade grew stronger.

Then Eiji sensed the blade's movement. They sprinted away from Eiji's approach.

He came into a small square, catching a brief glimpse of

dark clothing as someone turned a corner. It was the other blade. Eiji could sense the energy coming off the fleeing warrior with ease.

But a still figure lying in the middle of the square caught his attention. It was a woman, most likely from a brothel, considering her clothing.

Eiji glanced between the corner where he'd last seen the blade and the figure on the ground. Cursing, he approached the figure to see if she needed help.

He reached out to her with his sense, but he felt nothing.

He kneeled down next to her. At first, he saw no visible signs of violence. There was no cut, no blood anywhere. Her eyes were wide, frozen in an expression of horror that captured the last moments of her life.

A closer examination revealed red marks around her neck.

Before he could investigate further, Eiji felt another presence approach.

But this one was familiar.

Itsuki.

Eiji looked at the dead body beneath him, swore, then ran.

7

E iji ran, but no one pursued. He paused, six streets away, extending his sense. Lives surrounded him, their energies quiet as families slept or relaxed, oblivious or willfully ignorant to the excitement beyond the walls of their homes. But he sensed no nightblades and no monks.

Eiji caught his breath, walking aimlessly in any direction except that of the inn. The slums of outer Highgate transformed, block by block, into friendlier neighborhoods.

The details made the difference. Houses still stood shoulder to shoulder, overflowing with families that had far more members than rooms. But the streets were wider and cleaner. Well maintained, if worn, storefronts welcomed customers.

Those who lived here might lack the affluence of those closer to the center of the city, but most could meet their needs. Passing militia patrols kept the peace, watching Eiji with wary eyes but giving him no trouble.

When the moon was high, Eiji proceeded back to the

inn, often glancing over his shoulder to ensure no one followed. He neither sensed nor saw any threats.

If Eiji had enjoyed cities, he would have lived in one. The press of people limited the range of his sense, but it affected all the gifted. His presence was also harder to sense in the crowded streets. Despite the warrior's unbelievable strength earlier tonight, if they hadn't been within three blocks of the inn, Eiji never would have noticed them. Cities hid blades better than anywhere else in the Three Kingdoms.

The thought gave him comfort. Tomorrow, he and Isau would switch inns, just to be safe. But he could lose Itsuki here, then return to the open lands he preferred.

The close spaces of the city felt too much like another prison.

Eiji wasn't surprised to find Isau still snoring softly when he returned. He watched the boy for a moment, trying to absorb some of the peace Isau radiated.

With a yawn, Eiji retired, optimistic about the day ahead.

He fell asleep as soon as he lay down.

But he woke with a curse.

His tirade woke Isau, who grumbled at the long, uninterrupted string of swearing. "What?"

Then the boy sensed it, too. He sat up straight in bed, all attention.

Eiji's stomach jittered and he looked around the room, as though some answer might be written on the walls.

How had Itsuki found them again?

Eiji rubbed at his eyes, the events of last night crashing into his memories. Itsuki had found the body, and if Eiji had sensed the monk, Itsuki had sensed him standing over it.

Eiji swore again, unable to articulate his frustration any better way.

Isau, though, looked frozen to the spot.

Eiji climbed out of bed, then gestured for Isau to relax. "If he was here to kill us, he would have already. Lock the door behind me. I'll return soon."

Eiji hoped having a simple command would break Isau out of his terror. Long experience had taught him that when afraid, the quickest way to restore calm was to focus on finishing the next task.

He took his own advice, leaving the room and forcing himself down the stairs to the common room. He didn't believe Itsuki was here to kill them, but the monk's presence didn't bode well, either.

The enormous man had a table all to himself, and he sipped at what appeared to be tea, although given the quality of drink here, Eiji wasn't sure he would have trusted this particular establishment for a cup. Itsuki smiled when he saw Eiji, as though greeting a long-lost friend. He gestured to the spot across the table, which Eiji took.

"I didn't kill her," Eiji began.

"I know," Itsuki said.

Eiji's next words died on his tongue. He'd been prepared to defend himself.

Itsuki's smile never faltered, even as he sipped at the tea. The proprietor approached and asked Eiji if he cared to break his fast, but Eiji waved him away.

Itsuki knew Eiji hadn't killed the woman. And he had found the inn without problem. Granted, sufficient effort would have sufficed in the latter case, but Eiji suspected that wasn't the explanation. "You're remarkably well informed."

"I am."

"I don't suppose you'd share your secret? It's proving vexing."

That ever-present smile grew wider. "I'd rather not. It's far more entertaining to keep you guessing."

"Do I also have to guess at the reason you're here?"

"Not at all. I want to know what happened last night."

Eiji leaned back. Itsuki defied expectations at every turn. "I had trouble falling asleep. I came down for a drink. Not long after, I sensed another blade, stronger than any I've felt. I was curious, so I went to investigate."

Itsuki nodded for him to continue.

Eiji did. He ended the story at Itsuki's approach.

"And you saw nothing more than a glimpse of the blade?" Itsuki's eyes studied him, missing nothing.

"Barely even that."

"Why didn't you chase them?"

Eiji fought his desire to raise his voice at the monk. "Because there was a woman on the ground who might need help. I wasn't going to ignore her."

"Most of your kind would."

Eiji forced himself to take a long, slow breath. The monk had a way of crawling under his skin, tormenting him with his calm smile and apparent omniscience.

"Will you be leaving soon?" Itsuki changed the subject.

"Soon. As early as I am able to arrange it."

"But not today?"

"Maybe. I don't yet know how long it will take. We can't just swim."

"Delay too long and I might not give you the choice."

Eiji took note. Itsuki showed remarkable tolerance for a monk, but it wasn't mercy, nor some secret appreciation of blades.

Itsuki hated him.

Only because he was a blade.

This monk was just better at hiding it than most, and less insistent on violence as a solution.

But none of that meant Eiji could relax around him.

"As soon as we can leave, we will," Eiji reassured the monk.

"Good." The monk finished his tea, then gestured to the innkeeper. "Add this to my friend's room, please!"

Itsuki stood. "Don't try to switch inns. I'll know, and it will do nothing but make me suspicious. And neither of us want that."

With that, the monk left, leaving Eiji again with only more questions and the bill.

8

E iji tracked Itsuki with his sense as the monk left the inn. Itsuki paused briefly in the street, then turned toward the heart of Highgate. Within moments Eiji could no longer sense him.

Itsuki complicated matters. Eiji had to assume that whatever he did, Itsuki somehow observed it. He believed it far safer to overestimate an enemy than make the opposite mistake.

Someday he needed to learn how Itsuki discovered all that he did. No one had followed him last night. He was certain of that.

And he hadn't sensed another monk, not for nearly a half-moon. There was no monastery near Highgate. Eiji assumed Itsuki traveled with a partner, as the monks tended to, but he'd neither seen nor sensed anyone else from Itsuki's order.

A storm cloud hung over his thoughts as he returned to the room, unlocking the door with his key. Isau eyed him warily.

Eiji told the boy everything, from the murder the night

before to his conversation with Itsuki. Isau absorbed the information with surprising calm. "What do we do next?"

"I need to visit the docks to see if a ship is there. Then we can decide on our next steps."

"I'm coming with you," Isau announced.

"No, you're not. If something happens, I have more options alone."

"You're not leaving here without me."

"Yes, I am."

"I can cause more trouble than you can handle," Isau said.

That made Eiji pause. Isau, unlike Itsuki, was probably bluffing. Trouble for Eiji meant trouble for Isau. But he respected the ultimatum. A moon ago, the boy never would have had the courage to threaten him.

A moon ago, though, Eiji could do no wrong in Isau's eyes.

Still, that courage deserved recognition.

"Fine. But keep track of where we are. If anything happens, you run back here and lock yourself inside this room. Do you understand?"

Isau nodded, and they began their journey down to the docks. Their route reversed the direction Eiji had traveled the night before. The slums faded, replaced by busy markets and crowded streets. Eventually the crowds thinned as they neared the center of Highgate. Here the streets were even wider and the buildings taller, casting long shadows.

The two travelers skirted around the heart of the city. The low quality of their clothing would attract unwanted attention in the nicest neighborhoods.

The quality of Highkeep's architecture deteriorated the farther they got from the center. Towering buildings became squat huts, and squat huts eventually turned into the giant storage halls near the docks.

Throughout their journey, Eiji kept an eye out for anyone who followed them, anyone who paid them more attention than they deserved. But he noticed nothing out of the ordinary.

And yet, with every corner they turned, Eiji expected to see Itsuki leaning against a wall, just watching as they passed by.

The docks were less busy than Eiji expected. Only a few ships were berthed, and those that were saw little activity. As his eyes traveled over the ships, though, he kicked at the ground.

The blades weren't here.

Because why should his luck change?

Beside him, Isau unintentionally drove the dagger of disappointment deeper. "I don't sense any blades."

"You won't. The ship isn't here."

"Why not?"

"It isn't, always. The island has two, although I suspect more are hidden. They have to sail back and forth, and one doesn't leave the island until the other arrives."

"We have to wait?" Isau's voice sounded close to cracking.

"Not more than a few days."

Isau mastered himself with a visible effort. Eiji gave him a moment, using the time to study the horizon and the docks one more time. No ships approached, and he was certain the blades weren't here. He didn't like it either, but for a reason he didn't care to mention to the boy.

If the ship wasn't here, it meant the blade he'd felt last night wasn't associated with the island.

Which meant more trouble.

He swore softly. Isau heard him, but probably suspected the curse was at the delay.

They turned around, retracing their steps. Eiji treated Isau to a nicer meal of fish caught fresh from the sea. The boy threw himself into the meal with reckless abandon, his worries fading with every bite.

Eiji wasn't so callous as to believe he wouldn't miss the boy when he was gone. He enjoyed Isau's love of simple pleasures and his straightforward manner. But the boy would be much happier on the island. He was used to living his life on a small plot of land, so the invisible walls of his prison wouldn't bother him the way they had Eiji.

But he would miss the companionship and Isau's boundless curiosity. Though Eiji had only seen twenty-three cycles, he'd stopped asking why, and hadn't even realized as much until he'd escorted Isau the many leagues between his village and Highgate. Isau's constant questioning made Eiji realize how much he had left to learn.

It was for the best, though. The Three Kingdoms were no place for a blade, especially not a young one.

Rescuing Isau had been little more than an impulse. Eiji had just seen and ignored too many indignities heaped upon the gifted, and Isau was the weight that tipped the scales of his anger. He'd certainly never intended to escort a child halfway across the Three Kingdoms.

But he was glad he had.

By the time the food was finished, Isau seemed back to his old self.

They continued toward the inn, the weight of the meal settling comfortably in their stomachs. With nothing but time on their hands, they wandered more than they had on the way to the docks. Isau's curiosity, and his grateful belly, finally caused the wall he'd built between them to crumble.

He asked questions about currency, trade, and the incredible variety of goods sold on the street.

Eiji was embarrassed to admit he didn't know the answers to most of Isau's questions. In many ways, he was as new to this land as Isau. The difference was that he was less comfortable asking questions, his pride restraining his curiosity. The boy might have known only long days of labor, but Eiji had grown up on an island where blades did little but train.

Exploring Highgate with Isau made Eiji feel a bit like a child again, the world filled with mysteries and opportunity.

Eventually their path brought them back to the outskirts of Highgate. Isau's questions faded. He was less curious about the dilapidated structures and seedy streets.

As the questions slowed, Eiji's focus on their surroundings returned.

Before long, he discovered an unwelcome surprise.

Another blade was on the road.

Eiji held out his arm, stopping Isau in place. Isau looked offended, but then his sense caught the other blade.

The blade possessed a shadowy aura, but strong.

Not the warrior from last night, though. Not that strong.

Eiji picked the figure out without problem. They leaned against a wall about three dozen paces away, features hidden by a deep hood. Even though Eiji couldn't see the blade's face, he was sure their eyes were staring right at him.

It was only instinct, but that had always been enough for him.

He didn't know this blade, but the warrior was a threat.

Eiji spoke to Isau, his eyes never losing the nightblade before him. "You remember how we talked about running to the inn?"

He sensed the boy's nod.

"Do that, now. If I'm not back by nightfall, find Itsuki."

"No!"

"If I'm not around, he's your best chance of surviving. Do it!"

Isau hesitated for a moment, then ran.

The other nightblade made no move to follow. They just pushed off the wall and walked toward Eiji.

And Eiji saw they had their hand on their sword.

9

The warrior's stance left no doubt in Eiji's mind.

He faced an experienced foe.

The other blade stopped six paces from Eiji, far enough away to prevent a quick, killing attack. Eiji shifted his back foot, ready to draw.

The few passersby on the street trickled away into alleys or homes. Those who lived in these neighborhoods possessed a sense of their own, a constant vigilance. No threats had been issued, nor steel drawn, but they recognized the danger all the same.

Within the space of a few heartbeats, the street was abandoned except for the two blades. New visitors who turned onto the street saw the two and immediately scurried along alternate routes.

The voice that came from beneath the hood was that of a woman. Eiji had suspected as much. Though her loose-fitting robes concealed much of her identity, something indescribable in her stature and movement had alerted him. "Who are you?"

Her sense spread from her like shadowy wisps of smoke.

They wrapped around him, taking his measure. Invisible to the eye, his own sense responded to her gifts in kind.

"Eiji," he said.

"Why are you here, Eiji?"

"Passing through."

"We don't simply pass through Highgate. Why are you here?"

There was something odd about the woman's abilities. He sensed the power of her gift and her physical strength. But for all her might, she seemed... insubstantial, as though a breeze might blow her away like a cloud. He'd never sensed anyone quite like her. "That's not your concern."

She stood still for a moment. "It's the boy, isn't it? He's untrained, yet full of promise. You seek a ship."

Eiji didn't answer.

"Will you give him to me?"

"What?" Eiji frowned. "No. He's not mine to give."

"A shame." The woman turned to leave.

"Who are you?" Eiji asked.

She gave no answer, her pace already quickening.

He had too many questions. Their meeting wasn't coincidence, and her strength reminded him of the blade from the night before. He didn't think the mysterious blade had been Koji, but he needed to know, needed something certain to act on. The woman held some of his answers.

He'd barely taken two paces when he sensed her movement.

Even with the warning, her speed caught him by surprise.

She was fast.

Instinctively, Eiji stepped back, his own sword clearing its sheath as she advanced.

When she paused her advance, he halted his retreat. He

still couldn't see her face, but he could sense some of her attitude, reflected in her energy. Her actions were cold and rational. "Don't follow me," she warned.

"Who are you?" Eiji repeated.

Her silence was his only reply. She turned and stepped away again, but Eiji refused to let her leave without answering.

When he followed, she attacked.

He sensed her moves a moment before she made them, her intentions clear.

She led with a flurry of cuts, her sword flashing as it sought his flesh.

Eiji evaded two cuts and parried another. He didn't mind giving up ground to keep himself safe. Many of his peers considered such retreat disgraceful, but in Eiji's mind, any fight you walked away from was a victory.

It had been cycles since he'd dueled with another nightblade.

Against those without the gift, strategy was simplicity itself. Avoid the cut and respond with one of your own. With the advantage of the sense, little else was needed.

But against another nightblade, a duel was as much a mental battle as one decided by strength, speed, and martial skill. The blade who sensed intent further into the future always had the edge.

After another pass, Eiji guessed the ultimate outcome of this fight.

The woman was faster, and her sense was stronger. Her sword drove him back and back some more.

She would have killed most of the masters on the island.

Her sword slapped his away and a spinning kick caught him in the side of the head. He tumbled and rolled, returning to his feet with his sword's deadly point still held between them.

But she didn't pursue. She sheathed her sword. "I have no desire to kill a blade."

Eiji stumbled after her as she walked away. She stopped again, and this time he saw her shake her head.

"Who are you?" he asked for the third time.

She appraised him silently for a long moment. "Stubborn, aren't you?"

"So my masters always told me."

Some sound emanated from deep in her throat. Perhaps a chuckle, perhaps a growl of frustration. Even though he sensed her attack, his doubt of its veracity made him sluggish to respond.

She leaped at him, not even bothering to draw her sword. Even he couldn't lose such an exchange. He brought his sword to bear, the tip pointed at her chest.

She swung her arm, just as his sense had warned, and steel met steel.

Eiji barely had the time to understand she wore bracers underneath her loose clothing. Then she was inside his guard and her cold palm was on his forehead, driving him back.

Still dazed from the kick, Eiji lost track of his feet and fell backward. She followed him down, shoving his head the entire time. Stars exploded in his vision as the back of his head slammed into the hard-packed dirt of the street.

She didn't give him a moment to recover. Her fist slammed into his face, once, twice, three times. Then she stood up and kicked him, hard, in the kidneys.

Eiji groaned and curled into a ball, grateful when he sensed her walk away.

He swore through gritted teeth when she returned.

Through his one open eye, he saw that she was holding his sword. He didn't even remember dropping it. She towered over him, bringing the sword to his neck. "Don't try following me. If I see you again, I will kill you."

She ran his own sword lightly against his exposed skin, drawing blood. Then she tossed it away and kneeled next to him. She slapped him twice gently across the cheek.

The blows weren't heavy, but his head already felt as though it was filled with rattling stones that dreamed only of escaping the tight confines of his skull. Each movement made him want to vomit.

"Do you understand?" she asked.

"I do," he croaked.

She slapped him twice more, harder, making his vision blur. "Good."

Eiji closed his eyes. He sensed her walking away, this time not to return. Slowly, people began to trickle back to the street. The danger had passed.

But no one offered to help him up.

10

E ventually, Eiji found his feet. His head pounded, every heartbeat a fresh wave of suffering.

She hadn't even landed that many blows, but he felt the echoes of each. Those on the street passed him by, flowing around him like water avoiding a rock in a stream. No one met his eye. He might as well not exist.

Eiji didn't bother brushing himself off. Every movement brought pain, so he moved only as much as necessary. He retrieved his sword and returned to the inn, where even the innkeeper studiously ignored him, as though Eiji's troubles were a disease that might be catching. The blade stumbled up the stairs, pausing halfway up to regain his balance.

Fortunately, the boy was safe. Eiji sensed him in the room. He unlocked the door and nearly fell in, the world spinning around him.

"Eiji!"

Isau ran to the nightblade and helped him to the bed. Eiji wouldn't say it out loud, but he was grateful for the assistance. It had seemed a very long ways away.

Isau brought water and tended to Eiji's wounds.

The boy displayed an uncommon skill at the treatment of wounds. His small fingers moved with deft surety, the boy's talent reminding Eiji that Isau's early life had been anything but easy.

Eiji didn't protest. He stared up at the ceiling, wincing at Isau's efforts.

"What happened?"

"She didn't want to answer my questions."

Isau looked at the extent of his injuries. "I don't think she liked you much."

"She's not the first."

Isau finished doing what he could, and Eiji thanked him. Then he closed his eyes.

He'd suffered plenty of defeats in his life. His cycles of training were rife with examples. Even once he'd passed his trials and become a full nightblade, he lost to some of the better swords on the island. But he'd never been beaten with such ease, such precision.

His cuts weren't always the cleanest, but his defense, that was a skill he relied on. His intuition, combined with the sense, allowed him to withstand most attacks, to wear down opponents until they made a mistake.

No one beat him that easily.

And in the back of his mind, another thought clawed for purchase. The woman hadn't even been as strong as the blade the night before.

He'd always been able to rely on himself.

There was a comfort, knowing he could move through the world, immune to most threats. He could defeat almost every warrior and monk in this land without difficulty. Bandits didn't frighten him in the least.

But that woman made him feel small.

Eventually, he fell to sleep, reliving his defeat in his dreams.

11

Isau watched Eiji rest, forcing himself to remain awake.

He knew he didn't understand everything. Eiji still confused him. But he understood enough. The night-blade planned on abandoning him soon, just like everyone else. Sure, Eiji cloaked his deeds in noble words, but the actions were still the same.

Eiji didn't want him.

Neither had his parents.

It had taken the discovery of his gift for him to see the truth. Growing up, he'd become all too familiar with the phrase "another mouth to feed." Though Father had never said so directly, the threat had always been understood. Isau needed to work hard enough to earn his food and bed, meager as both were.

So he had. He'd worked the fields from dawn to dusk, and he cared for his siblings when they were injured.

Life had been hard, but Isau had always believed his efforts would be enough. He'd believed in his family.

Until the day of his discovery.

It didn't surprise him that his family abandoned him. Such was the fate of all gifted in the Three Kingdoms.

But he'd at least expected to see sorrow on their faces that day.

And he'd found none.

Eiji came awake with a groan, clutching his head in his hands.

The sudden movement, after a night of mostly inactivity, startled Isau out of his depressing reverie. Conflicted as he was about the nightblade, he was grateful Eiji had regained consciousness. He rubbed the weariness from his eyes and took a step toward his reluctant savior. "How are you feeling?"

Eiji groaned again. "Like a horse kicked me in the head."

Isau allowed himself a hint of a smile. "Considering the condition you came here in, I'm surprised you don't feel worse."

The nightblade sat up in the bed and looked out the window. "How long?"

"All night, and about half the day."

Eiji's gaze turned to him. Once, such a look might have caused him to avert his eyes, but no longer. He met the warrior's stare with his own. "You've been watching over me the entire time?" Eiji asked.

Isau nodded. "When people suffer head injuries, it is not uncommon for them rejoin the Great Cycle after falling asleep. I felt that remaining awake was the only prudent way of ensuring your survival."

Eiji looked like he was about to argue, but then closed his mouth. Instead he gave Isau a small bow of his head. Even that movement seemed to cause him a fair amount of agony.

Isau appreciated the gesture, though. More than once

he'd been tempted to leave the difficult nightblade behind. It was far better to abandon than to be abandoned. "What are we going to do now?"

"We're going to make sure that we're ready for whenever the next boat arrives. As soon as it does, I want you on it."

Isau tried not to wince at Eiji's words. "And what about you?"

"What about me? I'll find my way out of this. I have before, and I'll probably have to again."

"She beat you with ease."

Eiji's glare was hard. "No need to remind me. I don't plan on crossing paths with her again."

Isau knew that his suggestion would likely fall on deaf ears, but it didn't stop him. Eiji wasn't a simple man, but Isau had grown used to his company. He didn't want to leave Eiji if another option existed. "Use me. I know that I've just started training, but even you say that I am better than you expected. I know I can't beat her on my own, but if I help you, I am sure we can win."

Eiji shook his head. "I appreciate your offer, but that's not how fighting together happens. You would just get in my way."

After everything, hearing such a casual dismissal felt like a body blow. "But I want to help. I want to be with you when you fight your enemies."

"I don't plan on fighting my enemies," Eiji said.

Isau's anger erupted. "You're a coward," he spat. "You can't run forever."

His insults had no effect on Eiji. "You might be surprised. The Three Kingdoms is a large place. If I keep my head down there's no telling how far I can go."

"Your brilliance hasn't stopped everyone from finding you lately."

"And that's because my movements are predictable, because of you. If you say that you want to help, the best thing you can do is leave. Then I don't have to worry about you anymore."

And that was that. Isau knew that even if they continued the argument, it would always come back to this. Eiji didn't want him. Eiji could live better on his own. He'd said as much with his actions for days now, and he'd just confirmed it with his words.

The bitterness rose in his throat, and Isau spoke before he considered his words. "Sometimes, I'm not even sure why you saved me."

Eiji lay back down in bed and closed his eyes. He looked exhausted. "Sometimes, I wish I knew the answer to that myself."

12

E iji woke with a start. He sat upright in bed, cold sweat trickling down his back.

The vision of her faded slowly from his memory, and he pressed his palms tight against his eyes, as though he could squeeze out the nightmare.

But if that technique worked, he would have been free of this memory a long time ago.

Though his eyes were open, taking in their quiet room, he only saw her in those last moments before she joined the Great Cycle. Her eyes haunted him. First wide, reflecting her surprise that their duel had gone too far. Then they had softened, disappointment and forgiveness somehow held in equal measure.

Eiji no longer knew how truly his nightmares reflected the reality of her final moments. Forgiveness hadn't been in her nature, yet it was upon that look that his dreams always ended. It was that final act that caused his hands to shake even today.

Life would be easier if she had hated him, if she had

snarled a curse with her last breath. And maybe she had. He didn't trust his memories any longer.

Across from him, Isau stirred to wakefulness. The boy rubbed at his eyes and groaned. "You feel like a thunderstorm," he said.

At times, Eiji forgot just how sensitive the boy was. Isau currently lacked the training and focus to make much of his incredible ability, but the tendrils of his sense were thin and yet strong as wire. It was a gift, that if nurtured with care, could become one of the most impressive on the island. Isau would go from being a farm boy no one noticed to one of the most skilled nightblades in the world.

All Eiji had to do was get the boy there.

They were interrupted by the sense of someone approaching their door. Whoever it was, they weren't gifted. A soft knock on the door came a few moments later.

Eiji rolled out of bed and opened the door. One of the inn's staff stood outside, fidgeting with a folded piece of paper. She handed it to him.

"I'm sorry to disturb you. She told me to give this to you."

"Who?"

"A woman, dressed in one of the finest cloaks I've ever seen."

Eiji opened the note. The message was short, written with a quick and delicate hand.

The ship you wait for has arrived.

Eiji looked around, as though they were being watched. It couldn't have been the woman he'd fought. Her cloak hadn't been fine. Who else knew they were here?

"Can you describe this woman?" Eiji asked.

The poor girl shook her head. "She wore her hood up, so

I didn't see much of her face, and she left as soon as she placed this note in my hands."

Eiji swore. Another mystery with no easy answer.

"Thank you," he said as he shut the door. He pressed his forehead against the wood, willing his mind to come up with some possible answer.

None came.

Isau had watched the entire exchange, and Eiji answered his unspoken question. "Someone else knows we're here and why. And we need to visit the docks again."

"How can you be sure it isn't some sort of trap?" asked Isau.

"I'm not," Eiji replied, "but it would be an odd trap. We would have most likely gone down to the docks today anyway, and they're large enough that we aren't walking into some confined space. I'm not sure what advantage the note would give anyone."

To be safe, though, the two of them took a different route to the docks today.

"So why the note?"

Eiji grimaced. "I wish I knew."

All he knew was that the note worried him, and he wanted a drink more than anything in the world. He hadn't necessarily expected escorting Isau would be easy, but he had thought it would be simple. Now at least three people knew of them and their destination. Eiji didn't know how they knew, but each created a new complication.

Whatever the case, their path today still took them to the docks.

"What do you dream about?" the boy asked, the question unexpected.

It wasn't the sort of question Eiji would have typically answered. But perhaps it was exactly what the boy needed, the knowledge that would cool his desire to fight. "I have nightmares from the fight in which I killed my master."

"What happened?" The judgment Eiji had feared wasn't present in the question. Only curiosity.

"I attempted to leave the island with a group of my friends," Eiji began. He'd never told this story out loud. "But our plans weren't as secret as we thought they were. A group of masters intercepted us and a brief fight ensued. Most of my friends quickly surrendered. None of us had any desire to fight another blade.

"But I was angry and stubborn. I refused to surrender and our duel went on far longer than it should have. My master had the better of me, but she held one of her cuts. Instead of recognizing my defeat, I made one last move. I think she sensed it, but she didn't believe it. She didn't believe I would make a killing cut."

Eiji couldn't even look toward Isau as they walked. "I cannot forget that moment, nor am I sure I want to."

Isau's voice remained free of judgment. "Is that why you were searching for Koji?"

Eiji nodded. "Among the blades, Koji is known mostly for his incredible strength. But I read the histories, the complete ones that most ignore. He is perhaps the strongest blade that ever lived, but he made horrible mistakes. I want to know how he kept going."

They walked in silence for a while. Some part of Eiji was glad to have shared his quest with someone, even if it was just a young boy from the Western Kingdom. Another part regretted it. He'd enjoyed Isau looking up to him, and it was hard to confess his failures.

"I always assumed you just wanted to get stronger," Isau said. There was something in his voice Eiji didn't recognize, an emotion he couldn't quite put his finger on. But the story seemed to have affected the boy, somehow.

Eiji felt the tension ease between the two of them. The wall that Isau had built finally cracked.

When they reached the docks, it only took Eiji a moment to see that the note they had received was true. A new arrival was berthed not far from where he and Isau stood in the shadows. The ship's lines were familiar to him, as it was the very ship he had come to the Three Kingdoms upon.

His stomach sank, though, when he saw the first face near the ship. Though he didn't wear the black robes of a nightblade, his posture gave him away as he walked a simple guard route. It was a man he knew well, named Kosuke, who had, two cycles ago, argued strongly that Eiji be killed after his attempted escape. The two blades had never been friendly, and if Eiji approached him with Isau, Isau would never reach the island.

So they waited, and eventually another face appeared above deck. This blade was a young woman, and although she hadn't joined Eiji's ill-fated rebellion, they had always gotten along well. She spoke briefly with Kosuke and then left the ship. Eiji watched her for a moment and pointed her out to Isau. Their best chance of success was letting the boy take the lead.

Eiji smiled at Isau. "Time for you to introduce yourself to a proper nightblade."

13

The nightblade's name was Harumi, and Eiji sent Isau to her with specific instructions. Harumi would be skeptical of meeting a stranger on the docks, but she'd sense Isau's gift. Hopefully it would be enough to entice her to a meet.

As soon as Isau took off toward the nightblade, Eiji left by a different route. Even being this close to the ship made his pulse rise. The storm of emotions beating inside his chest made focusing on the task at hand nearly impossible.

There were days when Eiji dreamed of returning to the island. It hadn't been all bad. Not even close. He'd felt safe there, and welcomed into a community of others like him. He hadn't realized how much that meant until he'd sacrificed it. The days when he focused on what he'd lost were the days he often ended the night in a tavern, senseless in every meaning of the word.

The ship was a reminder that home wasn't far away, but also a reminder he could never return. Harumi might not kill him on sight, but many nightblades would.

When he had put several large storage halls between

himself and the ship, he relaxed. His focus returned and he extended his sense.

It didn't take Isau long to appear at the meeting point with Harumi in tow.

It took even less time for Harumi to notice Eiji, recognize him, and draw her sword. She sprinted at him.

Eiji didn't let himself react. He kept his arms loose and at his side, hands well away from his weapon. He knew Harumi. She wouldn't kill him.

At least, he hoped she wouldn't.

Her sword stopped less than a hand's width away from his heart, the tip steady. "Give me one reason why I shouldn't kill you for breaking your vow!"

Eiji stood frozen, not out of fear, but out of a healthy respect for self-preservation. The depth of Harumi's anger surprised him, and a single wrong move could very well result in a sword piercing his chest. He also didn't think she would respond kindly to him pointing out he hadn't broken his vow. He hadn't been seen by anyone in sight of the ship. "The boy."

She hesitated. "What about him?"

"I want you to take him to the island."

For a long moment, Harumi didn't move. Then she withdrew her sword and sheathed it.

"Who is he?"

"Isau," said the boy, reminding them both he was a part of the exchange.

Together, Eiji and Isau gave a brief retelling of the story that had brought them this far. Harumi listened. Her eyes narrowed at parts, but she made no further move to kill him, so Eiji maintained high hopes.

When they finished, Harumi looked between the night-blade and the boy, clearly deciding if she should believe their story or not. Fortunately, the boy's gift was easy enough to sense. No matter how Isau came to be here, he deserved to be on the island as much as anyone else. Which brought Eiji to the ultimate question. "Will you take him?"

Her forehead wrinkled, then she stared at her feet. Eiji held his breath.

Finally, Harumi gave a small nod.

That small gesture lifted an enormous weight off Eiji's chest. He took the first deep breath in what felt like two moons.

Isau would be safe.

"I'll need to speak with the others," Harumi warned. Her eyes met Eiji's. "It's best if no one knows the boy has any link to you."

Her tone gave him pause.

"That bad?"

"Worse." She sighed. "You've broken us, Eiji. More than anyone wants to admit. Between the violence, your ideas, and the disagreement over your punishment, I've never seen the blades more divided. There are still those who petition the council every moon to send blades after you, and the movement is growing in popularity. Many believe your blood will heal our divides. Others defend you and wonder if maybe you didn't have a point."

Eiji didn't know how to respond. He'd always imagined that the island would have largely forgotten him by now.

The knowledge that his actions had so divided his community cut deep. Though he'd disagreed with the council, he never wanted to hurt others. He just wanted a freedom denied to him.

But nothing he could say would make any difference.

Still, something had to be said. "I'm sorry."

Almost meaningless, perhaps, but it was all he could do.

She nodded, accepting his apology but not letting it touch her. "I'll talk to them. I'll leave you out of it. Make sure he understands, too. Meet me right here again at sundown. I'll take the boy then."

Eiji agreed, as did Isau. If the boy had any uncertainty, he showed nothing.

With that, they separated. Harumi returned to the ship, and Isau and Eiji once again began the long journey to the inn. Eiji decided getting a place so far away from the docks hadn't been the wisest choice.

His thoughts wandered as they did.

He couldn't stop thinking about the island, his family, and friends he'd left behind in a previous life.

Given the severity of Harumi's reaction, he saw little point in lying to himself. His actions had destroyed what he loved. Maybe, once Isau was safely away, Eiji would fall on his own sword.

The thought was short-lived. Perhaps he was too much of a coward. But he didn't want to return to the Great Cycle.

No, what he had to do, more than anything, was find Koji. Koji knew of these burdens and had gone on to great deeds. He would have answers.

Bringing Isau here had been a kindness, but perhaps it was still a mistake. He should have kept searching for Koji. He'd been so close.

Distracted as he was, it was Isau who noticed something first. "Do you sense that?"

Eiji paused, closing his eyes and focusing on his sense.

It took him several moments, but he did.

Another nightblade.

But faint.

Isau glanced up at him. "I only sensed something for a moment, but it felt as though it was moving away from us."

Eiji tried again, and this time he felt nothing. Had the presence felt familiar, or was his imagination running away from him?

He only wondered for a moment. After so many mysteries, there was no point in worrying about another. They would return to the inn, pack Isau's goods, eat one final meal, then return to the ship.

Whatever was happening in Highgate felt too large for Eiji, and the truth was, he didn't care. Once Isau was safe and he'd evaded Itsuki, he planned on finding a quiet corner of the Three Kingdoms and drinking so much he forgot the past.

14

Isau and Eiji made the journey to the docks one last time. Their afternoon had featured a quick meal, devoured too quickly, as usual, by Isau. Afterward, they'd packed his bag and left the inn as the sun began to fall toward the horizon.

Eiji stopped Isau outside a smithy, victim of an impulse too strong to deny. He stepped in, the boy following on his heels. Eiji browsed for a moment, then purchased a small dagger. When they left the shop, Eiji held it out to Isau.

The boy looked at him, eyes wide. His hands snaked out and grabbed the knife, a smile growing across his face.

"Something to remember me by," Eiji said.

Isau bowed deeply. When he straightened, Eiji saw his eyes were glistening. "I've never thanked you."

Eiji shook his head. "Don't."

There was no need to make this harder. By dawn's light, the boy would be sailing toward an island where he'd never have to look over his shoulder again. Eiji gently guided him forward.

They'd barely made it a block before Isau tried again. "I'll tell them all what you did for me."

Eiji sighed. They'd spoken of this, too. "Don't. At best, it will make your life more difficult. At worst, they might also exile you, if what Harumi says is true."

"But they'll never know."

"You will."

"It's not right."

"Life rarely is." Eiji saw that the subject bothered Isau. The boy had a firm idea of justice, and it wasn't easy for him to let the matter drop.

Isau stopped them again before they reached the docks. Despite Eiji's protests, he went down to his knees and bowed until his forehead touched the dirt of the street.

Eiji's heart swelled. He would miss the boy. There was no doubt of that.

Isau stood back up. "Thank you, Eiji."

Eiji returned a respectful bow. "You're welcome, Isau. May your strength grow with the cycles."

There wasn't any more to be said, and the sun was reaching the time of their parting. Both looked at the horizon at the same time, recognizing how little time remained between them.

Sudden uncertainty gripped Eiji's heart. Isau never complained and carried his weight. He was a liability in a fight, but Eiji was a master at avoiding those.

Eiji considered what a future with Isau might be like. They could wander the land together. Their gifts would prevent any stability, but they would have each other. Eiji could raise Isau as the son he would never have. A wise nightblade couldn't risk raising a family in the Three King-doms, and Eiji couldn't return to the only place in the world where he could.

Eiji shook his head at the thoughts. They were selfish. Oh, the boy would be grateful enough at first, but in time, he would decide a life of itinerant wandering wasn't for him. He had grown up a child of the land, after all, and he would want to set down roots.

The island could be home for him. The parting might hurt, but they would each be happier in time.

They arrived at the location of the meet first, but Harumi arrived before any further doubts could find purchase in Eiji's mind.

She looked the boy over, then glanced at Eiji, as though this still might be some sort of trick.

Her posture made it clear she wanted to end this as quickly as possible.

Eiji agreed. A clean break was best.

"I have permission to bring him back to the island. We'll leave on the first tide," Harumi said.

Eiji nodded, then squatted so he was eye to eye with the boy. Isau made no effort to hide his tears. "You'll like it on the island. And I'll think of you often. I'll always wonder how strong you became."

"When I'm older, I'll come back for you," Isau said.

The brave promise of a young boy who didn't know better.

He wouldn't dash the boy's hope, though. "If you do, I will be delighted to see you again," Eiji said as he stood back up. "But I will not hold you to that."

He tousled the boy's hair, not sure what else to do. Isau glared, then tentatively embraced him. Eiji returned the embrace, then stepped away.

"Let's go," Harumi said.

Eiji offered him one last bow. Isau gave a short nod, then followed Harumi without looking back.

They turned the corner, and just like that, it was done. For the first time in almost two moons, he was alone once again, as he had been for cycles before.

It was time to find Koji.

To forget Isau, Eiji imagined his next steps. Everything he owned was already in his pack. He could escape the city tonight and put Highgate behind him. Then, if he hadn't lost Itsuki, he would do so in the tall mountain peaks of the Northern Kingdom.

Once again, the world was completely open to him.

That feeling of freedom collapsed a few moments later.

He heard the clang of steel against steel before he sensed anything. Distracted by his thoughts, he hadn't paid any attention to the sense of yet another blade nearby. There was a single yell, loud and sharp, and then silence. One of the auras pushing against his awareness faded rapidly.

Harumi.

Eiji dropped his pack and ran, straight toward her. As he closed the distance, he resolved the feeling of the other nightblade's aura. He recognized her. The nightblade from the street. The one who had beaten him with such ease.

He'd underestimated her the first time, but he wouldn't again.

By the time he reached Harumi, it was already too late. The fight was over, and Harumi was on her knees, her head slumped at an unnatural angle. Eiji raced to her, seeing the blood spilled all down her chest. Another two steps revealed the blood came from a cut at her neck.

If she'd lost that much, she was already dead. Her body just didn't know it yet.

Eiji came to a stop and kneeled beside her. He pressed his hand to the cut as though it would make a difference.

Her eyes looked at nothing, but they focused, just for a moment, on him. Her lips moved, but no sound came out.

Her blood, warm against the cool air of the docks, spilled through his fingers and down his own shirt.

"I'm sorry," he said, because what else was there to say?

Isau.

Where was Isau?

He looked around, but Isau wasn't nearby. Eiji extended his sense, but he only felt one other life, one approaching quickly.

For a moment, he thought it was Isau, but the aura was too strong.

Isau was gone.

Taken by the woman.

When Eiji opened his eyes, he saw Kosuke nearing, then saw the recognition on the other nightblade's face.

Eiji looked down at Harumi's body, then down at himself, covered in her blood.

Kosuke wouldn't be inclined to listen to an explanation.

Eiji swore, stood up, and ran. Footsteps pursued him, shouting after him, calling him a coward and demanding a duel.

He didn't stop.

He wouldn't allow the blood of another one of his brothers or sisters to fall tonight.

One was already too many.

15

Harumi's corpse didn't slow Kosuke's pursuit in the slightest.

And why should it?

The nightblade knew his friend was dead. His sense told him she had already rejoined the Great Cycle.

Which left Kosuke free to pursue Eiji through the streets of Highgate.

Eiji ran, feet slapping softly against the road, breath coming out in quick, even exhalations.

This wasn't his first time being chased.

The Three Kingdoms had taught him valuable lessons.

One was that speed was only one of two deciding factors in a chase. The other was will.

It didn't matter that Kosuke considered Eiji a blight upon the honor of the blades, nor did it matter that he believed Eiji had killed another nightblade. Kosuke's will to exact revenge couldn't match Eiji's desire to stay alive.

Eiji wouldn't rest until he was as far away as he needed to be to ensure that his heart still beat when the sun rose.

Kosuke, inevitably, would give up when the pursuit became too difficult.

At least, Eiji hoped and expected as much.

Hiding wasn't an option. Even if Eiji broke Kosuke's line of sight, he couldn't find some dark corner and hope the nightblade would run past. They would still sense each other. This only ended one of two ways: either enough distance opened between them that Eiji could lose himself in the city, or one of them was too injured, or worse, to continue the chase.

Eiji hoped for the former.

Kosuke, however, seemed set on the latter, and he was fast enough to catch Eiji before Eiji could flee too far.

Eiji sensed the cut a moment before Kosuke drew his sword. Eiji stopped and reversed direction. He lowered his weight and thrust his shoulder into Kosuke's right arm. Kosuke, of course, had sensed Eiji's move, but he committed to drawing his sword. Once the decision was made, the outcome was determined by speed. Was Kosuke's draw faster than Eiji's tackle?

Kosuke's blade extended about three quarters of the way out of the sheath when Eiji crashed into his arm.

Kosuke had enough presence of mind to angle his sword so that the impact slammed it back into its sheath. He grunted as he and Eiji collided.

Eiji's momentum carried him two steps beyond Kosuke. He backed up a few more. If Kosuke had caught him once, it stood to reason he would again.

"I didn't kill her," Eiji said.

From the fire burning in Kosuke's eyes, Eiji saw it didn't matter one bit.

Eiji searched his memory. Had he been stronger than Kosuke on the island? He thought so.

But that didn't matter now. Kosuke had done nothing but train for the last two cycles, constantly sharpening his skills against talented blades.

Eiji had wandered the land, only drawing his sword when necessary.

So Eiji ran.

He sprinted away from Kosuke and cursed as he sensed the pursuit closing once again.

They left the large storage halls behind them, running into a more crowded and ramshackle area. The streets grew quiet as evening fell, but a handful of people remained, finishing up their last errands of the day. They turned in shock as Eiji and Kosuke tore past them, but no one had time to do more than stare after the two.

Eiji twisted into a slim passage between two buildings just as Kosuke came close enough to swing again. The passage was so narrow Eiji had to shuffle sideways, but it prevented Kosuke from using his sword.

He emerged from the other side and broke into a full run again, but Kosuke still pursued.

The chase had already gone on longer than Eiji expected. A reasonable warrior would have given up by now.

Eiji considered charging through a house but decided against it. The idea might work against a city guard, but against Kosuke it was pointless. Breaking line of sight wasn't enough. He needed distance, and a fair amount of it.

So he ran, and Kosuke ran after him.

If only Kosuke would give him a chance to think.

That was it.

Eiji's eyes darted left and right, searching for terrain he could use. He found a pile of used barrels near a house, and Eiji put on a burst of speed, pulling ahead of Kosuke just as the vengeful nightblade once again closed and cut at him.

Eiji leaped onto the barrels, then jumped from them onto the rooftop beyond.

In terms of getting away from Kosuke, it did little to nothing.

But as Eiji had hoped, Kosuke didn't follow onto the roofs. Eiji had the advantage of higher ground he was willing to fight for, and the roofs, again, didn't hide Eiji from Kosuke's sense. As they were more difficult to traverse, Eiji hadn't done himself many favors.

But he had given himself time.

Kosuke stood below, trying to glare hard enough to melt the roof underneath Eiji's feet.

Eiji didn't seek to bargain. It hadn't gone well the first time, and he didn't expect Kosuke to respond much better to a second attempt. Alone, there was little he could do but fight.

He was just about to resign himself to crossing swords when the idea occurred to him.

He wasn't alone.

Of course.

He looked around, taking note of where he was. When he was confident he knew which direction he needed to travel, he sprinted up the roof and down the other side, dropping down and running away.

The run over the roof gave him a small amount of room to work with, but it wasn't long before Kosuke was on his heels again.

A part of Eiji almost admired the man's persistence.

They ran through the poor neighborhood, moving into nicer areas of town. Eiji aimed for the center of Highgate.

The streets were too quiet.

He swore. Where were guards when you needed them? They were always around when he wanted privacy.

Finally, he sensed some, a group of six on patrol. He ran to them, and when he skidded to a stop before them, he didn't need to fake his relief. "There's a man after me with a sword!"

If any of the guards noticed that Eiji also wore a sword at his side, no one spoke a word. Many men carried them in the Three Kingdoms, but few were any good with them. No doubt the guards would just think him another merchant pretending to be a warrior.

Kosuke turned the corner moments later. He slowed to a stop as he assessed the new situation. The six guards stood between them, but for a moment, Eiji feared Kosuke might be angry enough to charge forward anyway. He braced himself for a fight.

"You're a coward!" Kosuke roared as he turned and ran.

The guards pursued, but Eiji knew they wouldn't catch him. There was no hiding from a nightblade, but the same gifts made blades nearly impossible to find if they didn't want to be.

Eiji didn't waste the opportunity. There was a chance that Kosuke would circle around and try to track him again. He needed to be well gone by then.

Eiji ran into the night.

16

Isau's return to consciousness was bumpy. The back of his head hurt, far worse than it ever had when his father had cuffed him for disobeying directions. Fortunately, when he opened his eyes he found himself in a dark and quiet room.

He stared at the ceiling for a moment, allowing memories to wash over him.

He had been with the nightblade, Harumi. She'd seemed kind enough, even though they hadn't known each other. Her aura had been smooth, like a lake on a still day.

She'd been nothing like Eiji. Even when they ate, Isau sensed Eiji's presence as a storm, chaos and uncertainty covered in dark clouds.

Harumi had noticed the attacker first, but Isau felt them, too.

The other nightblade had moved fast, faster than Isau thought it was possible to move.

Harumi drew her sword, but her cut was blocked by the attacker's arm. Eiji had heard the clang of steel on steel, but he hadn't understood how that was possible. Then the attacker had grabbed Harumi by the throat, lifting her into the air with one arm.

That wasn't possible, either.

Harumi had fought back, driving one of her knees toward the attacker's chin. But Harumi's assailant blocked the attack with their free hand.

A hand emerged from the attacker's robes and a knife glinted in the last of the sunlight. A smile opened on Harumi's throat, and Isau felt the life bleed from her.

Isau watched Harumi's feet kick, but then his attention was drawn upward. Something was happening, something he didn't have the words for.

Harumi was becoming weaker and the attacker was becoming stronger.

The attacker had turned to him, and he'd sensed the blow, a shifting of the attacker's aura. And then his world went black, and he woke up here, still in darkness.

Groaning, Isau sat up. He was on a bed, even more comfortable than the one he'd had in the inn, and that had been one of the nicest he'd ever known.

He frowned at the detail.

He stood up. Balance proved more difficult than he'd expected. The absolute lack of illumination robbed him of sight, and his head felt light. He reached out with his hands, surprised to find a cold stone wall after only a few paces.

A little more searching revealed a door. Isau tested it.

It opened without problem.

Isau glanced back at the room he'd been left in, now visible from the faint light of the hallway. As far as rooms went, it wasn't much. The walls and floor were bare. A chair sat near the foot of the bed, an unlit lantern beside it, but otherwise, the room was empty.

He turned his attention to the hallway, then froze.

He'd never been anywhere like this.

The walls were tall, the ceiling so high even an adult wouldn't be able to reach. Paintings covered every surface, and lanterns flickered in both directions.

He had to be in a castle. How and why were questions he had no answers to, but such opulence could only belong to a noble.

As his focus returned, he sensed someone else in the house. Someone powerful.

He didn't truly understand his gift yet. He could feel things others couldn't, but he wasn't sure how to turn those feelings into the skills of a nightblade. Eiji could have told him more details about the presence below, but all Isau knew was that the presence felt cold.

What had happened to Eiji?

The nightblade had left him to Harumi. Had he been attacked, too?

Isau wasn't sure. He was on his own.

The idea didn't scare him like it once had. The last two moons had taught him hard lessons, and Eiji had confirmed the worst truth: a person was always alone. Even in a room filled with others. Friends and family would leave you when you needed them most.

He could try escaping, but why bother? The nightblades wouldn't take him to the island anymore, not after Harumi's death. He supposed he could beg on the streets, the way he saw some do, but that held no appeal.

And anyway, someone had carried him to a castle. He wanted to know why, and he wanted to know the person who had done so.

If their aura was cold, what did that matter? Eiji had been a storm, and he'd never hurt Isau.

At least, not in the ways one could see.

Isau explored the castle, finding wonders around every corner. But he always chose the path that led him closer to the power he felt. He descended a long staircase, taller than anything he'd seen before.

He came into a room that was warmer than the rest of the castle. A fire crackled in a stone fireplace, and a woman sat on the floor in front of it. This room was different than the others in other ways, too. Weapons adorned the walls, of a variety Isau had never imagined. There were no paintings here, and no furniture.

Without turning, the woman gestured for Isau to join her. It surprised him at first, because he thought he'd been moving quietly. But then he remembered, if her aura was so strong, she could sense him. She'd known from the moment he woke, and she'd let him explore her castle without escort.

He found himself comforted by her trust.

Isau accepted her silent invitation, sitting down far enough away that she couldn't attack without warning.

In the light of the fire, he saw her clearly for the first time. She was young - far younger than he'd expected. She barely looked old enough to be an adult. She had long hair and dark brown eyes that held his.

He didn't ever want to look away.

With an effort, he tore his gaze away from hers. She wore something on her wrists, metal bands that protected most of her forearm. Those were what she had used to block Harumi's sword.

Though he'd expected as much, it confirmed that this was the attacker from the docks, the one who had killed Harumi.

"My name is Yua. It's a pleasure to meet you," she said.

"Thank you. I'm Isau." He didn't know what else to say, but if she was polite, he could be, too.

"Would you like to stay with me?"

The question made him feel uneasy, but he couldn't say why. She seemed kind enough now. She had hit him, but she'd brought him here and put him in a soft bed.

"Why?"

"I want you to stay with me, so I can show you how to use your gift so that no one can hurt you again."

Isau wasn't certain, but what else could he do? Eiji was probably already out of the city or hopelessly drunk. He'd intended to leave as soon as they parted ways.

Isau didn't have anyone else, and the girl wanted to help him become stronger. He couldn't see the harm in that.

He nodded, and the girl smiled.

17

W hen Eiji stopped to catch his breath, he found that he had run to the other side of Highgate. He stood in the same district of the city where he and Isau had rented their rooms the previous nights.

Isau.

Eiji didn't allow his break to stretch too long. After a few moments, he continued walking, with no particular destination in mind. He didn't dare risk remaining in one place long enough for someone to find him.

Several ideas, each more absurd than the one before, warred for his attention. Isau needed him.

But a wild reaction did no one any good, either.

He wandered and wondered.

The most reasonable conclusion, based on what he had sensed and his brief investigation of the scene of Harumi's murder, was that Isau had been taken by the mysterious nightblade.

But why?

Eiji imagined half a dozen reasons, several of them too horrific even to contemplate.

He didn't know, though, and guessing didn't help.

So what did he do?

He swore at himself for the thought, but for several long, tempting moments, he considered turning his back on the whole problem. By morning he could be long gone, and he could let the pieces fall where they would. He didn't owe Isau anything. He'd already escorted the boy halfway across the Three Kingdoms, which was far more than anyone had ever done for him.

Across the street, an old woman swept the street in front of her house. She glared at him as he passed, as though she was privy to his thoughts and also found them repugnant.

But what could he do? If the boy was still in Highgate, it would be a nearly impossible search. Even with the gift, Eiji would have to be close to sense the boy, and he had no doubt that as he searched for Isau, Kosuke would be scouring the streets for him.

He could only think of one person who might be in a position to help.

He shook his head.

The boy was going to owe him for this.

LEAVING HIGHGATE WAS SIMPLE ENOUGH. Eiji frequently explored his surroundings with his sense, and he was certain no one followed him.

Which meant Itsuki probably wasn't far behind.

He walked until the moon was high in the sky, then found a welcoming copse of trees. He stumbled into them and worked himself into a position that, if not comfortable, was close enough. His back was against a wide oak, and his sword was propped up against his shoulder. Should he need to, he could be on his feet with a sword in hand in the span of a heartbeat.

His training on the island had been brutal, but he'd mastered the use of his sense, even as he slept. How many nights had he spent sleepless on the island, waiting for another student to sneak up on him? The lesson wasn't one he'd learned easily.

True sleep evaded him, but he rested, drifting in and out of consciousness. His sense remained alive, though, warning him of anyone approaching too close.

His nightmares visited, as they did whenever his sleep was restless. Harumi's final moments blended with his fight against his master. It seemed as though the same blood ran through both memories.

Eiji opened his eyes, transitioning from rest to wakefulness in an instant. The sun rose on the horizon and the air was still, promising an unusually warm day. Eiji closed his eyes for a moment and gently knocked the back of his head against the tree.

Then he sighed and stood up. His body protested, muscles aching. He still hadn't fully recovered from the beating he'd received in the street, and he'd layered on a chase that had lasted far too long. But true rest wasn't his anytime soon.

He returned to the road and walked until he came to a small inn nestled in a cluster of tall pine trees. Eiji entered the inn, studying the guests in the common room. No one paid his entrance any particular attention, and nothing in the room caused the hairs on the back of his neck to rise in alarm.

Eiji took a seat, then, with a smile, ordered breakfast and tea for two.

Not long after the meals arrived, Itsuki stepped through

the door. Eiji gestured to the meal, still steaming. Itsuki shook his head, but a hint of a grin cracked his angry expression. He sat down. "I must be getting predictable," he said.

"I just assumed you'd be hungry after chasing me as far as you had."

Itsuki dug into the food with relish. "I told you that if you returned to the Northern Kingdom, I would kill you." He took another bite of food. "I'm a man who keeps my word."

"Isau's been kidnapped."

The food paused, just for a moment, halfway between Itsuki's bowl and his mouth. "Tell me."

So Eiji did, leaving out details about the ship and Harumi.

By the time he finished the story, Itsuki had finished his meal. The monk looked at the bowl in front of him, then at Eiji. "You left Highgate to make me approach you, didn't you?"

Eiji nodded.

"Clever." He paused. "But what you nightblades do to one another isn't my problem."

"Of course it's your problem. A master and an apprentice blade are killing and kidnapping citizens. And I don't believe you think blades fighting against blades isn't a cause for concern. Not if you know anything about history."

"What would you have of me? You want me to help you find the boy?"

"I do."

Itsuki laughed, but bitterly. "I won't."

Eiji was about to protest, but Itsuki cut him off with a glare. "I told you, don't confuse my generosity with sympathy. Do you know what my father did for a living?"

Eiji's mouth hung open, not following the rapid change of subject.

"He was a soldier during the Great War. Mother always said he wasn't very good with a sword, but it was money and it supported us. He was in the lines when the blades made their final push out of the valley of Stonekeep."

Eiji didn't have to ask what happened. In that final retreat, the blades had largely destroyed the ability of the Three Kingdoms to wage war. The blood spilled over a single night would fertilize the valley for generations.

"You can probably imagine what came after. The cycles of famine nearly killed us more times than I can count. But my mother survived, up until the day they discovered her son was gifted. That was the only burden she couldn't bear. She took her life as the monks took me away."

He looked at his hands. "You call the sense a gift, but it is anything but. It doesn't belong in this land." He looked up and met Eiji's eyes. "You don't belong in this land."

Itsuki stood up. "Enjoy your meal. When you're done, I'll be waiting for you outside."

Itsuki left some coin on the table, enough to cover both their meals.

"As I said, I'm a man of my word."

18

I sau had never met a woman like Yua. That first night, they didn't speak much, but something about her aura calmed him. They stared into the fire, entranced by the dancing flames that burned the logs down to coals.

When the fire died, Yua escorted him back to his room. Though questions threatened to burst from Isau with every step, he reined them in. Her silence, although welcoming enough, didn't invite questioning.

When she escorted him back to his room, she lit the lantern for him and asked if he needed anything else. When she seemed satisfied that he was comfortable, she left without a word. He followed her with his sense, an easy enough task in this otherwise empty castle. She slept on the floor above, and Isau wondered just how tall this building was. Where he grew up, nothing had been more than a single level.

He didn't know what to make of recent events. People who hit you didn't then invite you into their homes. Experience had taught him that well enough. But everything about

Yua defied his expectations. He'd watched her in front of the fire, and nothing about her seemed to fit. She was a mystery he expected he could spend his whole life trying to solve.

Yua moved with the same easy grace that Eiji did, but she lacked the muscular frame of the nightblade who had saved him from his village. She certainly didn't look strong enough to pick Harumi up with one hand.

He supposed it was rude to question one who was so generous. In the morning, perhaps, she would be more talkative and answer his questions.

Isau didn't realize how tired he was until he laid his head down. He fought against sleep, hoping to decide what he should do next, but it was a losing battle.

He woke to the tantalizing smells of breakfast being prepared.

He rolled out of bed smoothly, feeling better after a full night of rest. His nose led him downstairs to the kitchen, where Yua cooked with practiced efficiency.

If it tasted half as good as it smelled, he was in for a treat.

She set a bowl down in front of him, and he barely remembered to say thanks before digging in.

The food tasted exactly as good as it smelled. Isau was certain he'd never eaten anything half so delicious. He stared at Yua. He hadn't expected cooking to be among her skills. Eiji's had been barely passable, and Isau had welcomed every inn and tavern they stopped at.

Isau had never understood love, but as he watched Yua pile another helping in front of him, he thought he might have his first clue.

Yua watched him eat with a blank look on her face. She had barely started on her own food, her bites a third the size of Isau's. It was no wonder she was so thin.

He took a deep breath. Putting down his food was one of

the hardest things he'd ever done, but he needed to ask his questions, and now seemed as good a time as any. "You said that you would train me to become a nightblade?"

She finished her bite, the process agonizingly slow. Isau fought the urge to ask the question again. "No," she answered. "Not a nightblade. Something more."

Something more than a nightblade? Had the idea come from anyone else, Isau would have laughed. But she wasn't jesting, and Isau knew she'd already beaten two nightblades with ease.

Had he stumbled upon something even greater?

"What's more than a nightblade?"

"We have no name for it, but I am apprenticed to one who has learned the secrets of true power. He wants you to learn from him, as well."

As he often did, Isau imagined the faces of his friends and neighbors in his home village, the ones who had turned against him as soon as they learned he was gifted. He remembered the way they hunted him, and when they found him hiding in the fields, beat him and tied him to a tree, turning their backs as he'd cried for help.

No one would turn their back to him again.

It all seemed too good to be true, which meant it probably was. "Why me?"

She held his gaze then, and he sank into those eyes. Her aura was cold, yes, but her eyes told a different story. There was concern there, hidden deep. "Because your gift is special," she said.

Her words sent a flood of warmth through him. No one had ever told him anything half so kind.

Even Eiji, who had been with him for the past few moons, hadn't given him such an affirmation.

Though Eiji had never said it, Isau knew the nightblade

had viewed him as a burden, something to be packed off and sent away as soon as possible. In that, Eiji hadn't been much different than his parents.

He would always be grateful to Eiji for saving him, but right now, he could think of no one more perfect than Yua. "Really?"

"Of course." Her voice was soft and even. "You have the gift, and a strong one. Any blade could tell that. But do you know what really makes you special?"

He shook his head.

"You see truth. I can see it in your gaze."

He didn't understand.

"Was the nightblade you were with your friend?"

Isau considered for a moment, feeling the weight of Eiji's dagger still in his pocket. Eiji had been kind enough, and Isau was grateful for all the nightblade had done. But Eiji had wanted to send him away. Friends didn't do that. The understanding hit him like a fist to the stomach. "No."

"And did you really want to go to the island?"

That question was easier to answer. He'd been willing, because Eiji said he would be happy there, but he hadn't really wanted to go. He just didn't want to be chased anymore. Here, around Yua, that seemed as clear as day. Why had he ever let himself be convinced? "No."

She smiled, and Isau was convinced it was the most beautiful sight he'd ever seen, better even than a colorful sunset. He'd do anything to see that smile again. "See," she said. "Even though they try to persuade you, you always see to the heart of the matter. You don't belong on the island. Your gift isn't one to hide, to keep locked away in a land far away that no one will ever see. You belong here, where you can use your strength to make a difference."

She was right, of course. Every word she said was perfect.

"How do I start?" he asked.

"By meeting my master," she answered. "He's waiting for you."

19

Eiji took plenty of time to finish his bowl of food. Perhaps, if he waited long enough, Itsuki would give up and wander away without a fight.

He laughed to himself.

The monk would grow roots before he let Eiji leave here alive.

He wished he could say he was surprised by Itsuki's hatred.

But he'd wandered this land for cycles, and this was far from the first time he'd seen the same. The blades' true history was a bit different than the stories told here, but despite the ambiguities, some details remained certain. The blades and their misguided ambitions were most, if not all, of the reason the Kingdom had divided in three.

The actions of his predecessors echoed down through the cycles. War and famine had brought the Three Kingdoms to the brink of extinction, and although they now crawled forward, the wounds of history hadn't scarred over yet.

Itsuki was just another man who had suffered, the same as thousands upon thousands of others.

That, more than anything else, was what Eiji hadn't understood on the island. They had taught him, in his lessons, how blades were viewed in the Three Kingdoms. But he had been an idealist.

He'd imagined a future in which the blades returned to the land. Maybe they wouldn't have been welcomed with open arms, but with time and effort, Eiji had believed those who remained in the Three Kingdoms would forgive them.

He hadn't understood the depth of the wounds the generation before him had left.

Now he knew better. The blades wouldn't return. Not in his lifetime, and maybe not ever.

Some crimes would never be forgiven.

Eiji ordered another bowl of breakfast.

Let Itsuki wait.

He planned on dying on a full stomach.

Eventually, Eiji once again stared at an empty bowl. As far as last meals went, he had to admit he'd hoped for something better. But it was passable, and far tastier than anything he'd have made on his own.

He took a deep breath and set his shoulders.

Much of what he'd been taught as a young nightblade revolved around the acceptance of death. The blade who truly welcomed their death gained the freedom to fight without fear. Paradoxically, the warrior most prepared to lose was the one most likely to win.

Eiji also knew that something existed beyond death. He'd sensed it himself, the life force escaping from the body to join the Great Cycle. He had the benefit of knowing the long-held belief was actually true.

But he still didn't want to die.

He stood and left another coin on the table.

Itsuki waited for him outside. The monk had found a clearing on the other side of the road where they would have room to fight without disturbance.

Eiji sighed. There wasn't a cloud in the sky, and the day was already uncomfortably warm. Then he stepped across the road and entered the clearing.

Itsuki drew his sword in a smooth, practiced motion.

He'd been trained well. Eiji saw it in the small details, from the warrior's impeccable balance to his grip on the hilt of the sword. The monk was every bit as skilled as Eiji had suspected.

Eiji didn't draw his sword.

"Scared?" Itsuki taunted him.

But Eiji sensed the uncertainty in Itsuki's aura. His intent wavered, if only for a moment.

"No," Eiji lied. His heart threatened to beat out of his chest. But not for the reasons Itsuki suspected.

"Then draw your sword, and let's finish this."

Eiji forced his smile down. He supposed that to most, Itsuki's threats would terrify. But Eiji sensed Itsuki's intent, and it conflicted with his words.

It was a thin hope to hang his life on, but only a warrior prepared to lose his life could win.

"No," Eiji said.

"Then die!"

Itsuki's approach and cut were almost as perfect as any Eiji had ever seen. Fighting Itsuki would be a challenge, but it wasn't one Eiji accepted.

He remained still.

He doubted, especially for Itsuki's first two steps. The monk's intent solidified, and Eiji feared that his gamble had failed.

But then the monk took another step, and he finally understood that Eiji would not draw against him.

Itsuki's aura shifted, a sudden storm bursting to life within his once-clear intent.

The monk's sword stopped less than a hand's width from Eiji's neck.

Eiji breathed softly out.

"Draw!" Itsuki commanded.

"I won't fight you," Eiji said.

The moment stretched over several heartbeats. Eiji sensed the battle within the monk. Itsuki huffed, then shifted position.

Eiji sensed the blow, an elbow aimed straight at his nose. He angled his head and the elbow passed by his ear.

But he'd let Itsuki well within his guard, and the monk made full use of that advantage. Itsuki pummeled him with knees and elbows, finishing the sequence with a back kick to Eiji's stomach that sent him stumbling several paces away.

Eiji remained standing, but Itsuki hit like a kicking horse. The world spun around him. Slowly, he straightened up, wincing at the injuries, new bruises layered over the ones still healing.

"Draw!" Itsuki shouted again.

When Eiji made no move, Itsuki sheathed his sword and switched to hands and feet, every part of the combinations landing with devastating force.

A spinning kick snapped his head around and he crashed to the ground. He landed hard and swore.

Above him, Itsuki was breathing hard, as though this was harder for him than Eiji.

Eiji groaned, then pushed himself to hands and knees.

A powerful kick to his ribs sent him back to the ground clutching his torso.

"Stay down!" Itsuki commanded.

Eiji laughed as he struggled back to his knees. He couldn't say why. He just found the entire situation humorous.

When Itsuki didn't kick him again, Eiji made his way to his feet. His balance was unsteady, but he remained upright.

"You are," Itsuki said between breaths, "without a doubt, the most frustrating man I've ever met."

Eiji laughed again, clutching at his side. If his rib wasn't broken, it was at least bruised. "It's been said before."

"If I help you find the boy, you'll both leave?"

Eiji nodded. That, too, was a lie, but one he would figure out later. Perhaps, if it came to it, he could ask to return to the island and be executed there.

"Then let's find Isau," Itsuki said.

20

A fter breakfast, Yua informed Isau that she needed to complete a few errands before they could leave. He asked to join her, but she shook her head. He was about to complain, but her next words stopped the words on his tongue. "You're too valuable to risk in the streets of Highgate."

He realized it wasn't that she was trying to hide her actions from him, but that she was trying to protect him.

How could he argue against that? He felt honored that she would consider him so important. He bowed to her, and she promised to return soon.

With little else to do, Isau explored the castle. The building was the largest he'd ever been in, and in time, the emptiness of the place started to make his stomach quiver. The home he'd grown up in with his parents and siblings could have fit within some of the rooms here. His sense confirmed that he had this place all to himself.

Eventually, he returned to his small room, shut the door, and curled up on the chair.

He waited for Yua to return.

She was as good as her word, returning well before Isau expected. As soon as he sensed her, he ran to join her.

She allowed him to follow her to her own room, where she quickly packed her belongings. Isau noticed that she didn't grab any of the clothes from the chests scattered around the room.

That made him examine the room more closely. One of the chests was open, and it contained clothes as fine as any he had ever seen. But they didn't seem like clothes Yua would wear. In their time together, he'd only seen her wear a dark cloak and a simple tunic and pants. She dressed like a peasant, and these were the clothes of a noblewoman.

Yua didn't give him time to ask. By the time she finished packing, Isau sensed more lives near the front of the building. Yua didn't appear surprised, though, so he said nothing.

He followed her to the front, where they stepped into the light of day. For the first time, Isau looked at the castle from the outside.

He was disappointed to see that it wasn't a castle at all. It was instead a large building, lacking fortifications of any kind. As Isau examined his surroundings, he saw that the building he'd been in was hardly unique. Their home wasn't even the largest he saw.

This, then, must be near the very center of Highgate. It was one of the only parts of the city Eiji hadn't taken him to. The nightblade had been too worried about attracting attention.

Yua had no such concerns.

The lives Isau had sensed were those of a carriage driver and a servant.

Isau stared, open-mouthed, as Yua handed her pack to the servant, who loaded the pack into the carriage.

Yua stepped up on the mounting block, only to stop

before she climbed into the carriage. She turned around, a quizzical look on her face. "Are you coming?"

"That's for us?" Isau could barely form the words.

She smiled, and any concerns he had faded. "Of course. How else would we travel?"

Then she climbed into the carriage and beckoned for him to follow.

Isau did, and the servant closed the door behind them.

Without further ado, the carriage lurched into motion. Isau stuck his head out the window, watching as the servant went into the house they had just left.

The inside of the carriage had cushioned seats, and Isau sank into them.

His sloth didn't last long, though. Curiosity brought him back to the window, and he peered out as Highgate passed them by. Some parts of town seemed familiar, but everything looked different from the height of the carriage.

When he wasn't looking out the windows, Isau glanced at Yua. She sat on the cushions with her eyes closed, her aura far steadier than the carriage.

To her, this was nothing special.

Isau shook his head. He swore that no matter how many times he rode in a carriage, he would never take it for granted. He thought of the endless leagues he and Eiji had walked to reach Highgate, the time and effort the journey had taken. When they had stolen the horses, it had been an incredible luxury. And those were nothing compared to this.

Before long, they left Highgate behind. The road stretched out before them, but they ate incredible food and Isau watched the scenery pass. Yua asked Isau to tell her about himself, and he did. At first, he told the short version, because he knew that adults didn't like it when you talked about yourself for too long.

But Yua again defied expectations. She interrupted often, asking questions until Isau laid out his entire life before her. He felt his cheeks flush as he told of his time growing up on the farm. He hoped Yua wouldn't think less of him for being a farmer. He spoke of his parents and the long days, the hunger that never seemed to fade.

Then he spoke of the discovery of his gift, and the subsequent hunt by the monks.

Yua asked him many questions about his rescue, and it seemed to him she was also curious about Eiji. Unfortunately, Isau couldn't answer her questions about the nightblade's skills. At the time, he'd been too surprised by everything to pay close attention, and he hadn't seen Eiji fight since then.

When he finished his story, ending with him in Highgate, she nodded. "My master will be very pleased to meet you," was all she said.

The journey stretched on, and Isau lost track of how far they traveled. The carriage rarely stopped except to exchange horses, and he and Yua both slept through the night as the carriage rumbled along.

The next day, the carriage began to climb into the mountains, and to pass the time, Yua helped Isau develop his sense. Many of her lessons on mental focus seemed very similar to Eiji's, but unlike the nightblade's lessons, Isau found he had no difficulty focusing on hers. She was an excellent teacher. Within a day, he was picking up details in auras he hadn't been able to before. Whenever he impressed her, she would smile briefly, and he would redouble his efforts.

Eventually, though, the carriage came to a halt.

They found horses waiting for them, and Yua led the way deeper into the mountains.

Growing up in the Western Kingdom, Isau had never seen mountains. On his journey with Eiji, he'd seen one mountain range far to the east of their path, but that was as close as he'd come.

He decided that mountains terrified him. The paths they led their horses on were narrow, with drop-offs that spelled death if they fell. Land wasn't meant to be this rugged.

Yua, of course, navigated without a hint of fear. Her aura didn't so much as flicker, and Isau took courage from that. If she wasn't frightened, he wouldn't be, either.

They continued their lessons as they rode, and Isau was certain he was already stronger than he'd ever been. He dreamed of the warrior he'd become. Perhaps soon he'd be stronger than Eiji.

With a start, he realized that was the first thought of Eiji he'd had in some time.

It didn't bother him in the slightest. He felt drawn to Yua, as though she was the one he had always been meant to follow. Eiji had only been an intermediary.

They crested a ridge just as the sun kissed the mountaintops to the west. Even after several days of wonder, Eiji had to stop to study the view below them.

A village lay less than a league away, nestled in a deep valley and hidden from the world.

"What is this?" he asked.

"This is my master's kingdom," Yua answered. "And you will meet him tonight."

21

While Eiji recovered from his beating, Itsuki wandered off into the grove of pines surrounding the inn. He gave no reason for his disappearance, but Eiji could guess.

Itsuki emerged from the trees with someone a step behind him. It was a woman, and something about her tickled Eiji's memory. But if they'd ever met, Eiji couldn't remember it.

Even though they hadn't been introduced, Eiji knew he saw before him Itsuki's mysterious partner.

The two of them stopped a few paces away, and Eiji realized the woman wasn't gifted.

Itsuki laughed at his blank look. "Eiji, meet Chiasa. She's my partner, and one reason why I've been able to find you no matter how hard you try to hide."

"She's not a monk." He realized he was stating the obvious, but his mind couldn't move past the fact.

"There are drawbacks to monks hunting blades," Itsuki explained. "By working together, we negate those disadvantages."

The arrangement was perfectly reasonable now that it was in front of him. Itsuki's gift gave him all the same advantages a nightblade enjoyed, but Chiasa wouldn't even raise an eyebrow. She could get close to a blade without arousing suspicion.

And then Eiji remembered where he'd seen her. On the night of the first murder, when he'd glimpsed the powerful nightblade. He'd stepped over a poor woman in the alley.

That had been Chiasa.

She'd been outside the inn, watching the entrance.

And he'd walked right past her.

He nodded. That was how Itsuki had known Eiji wasn't guilty of the murder.

Perhaps he should be thanking Chiasa. She might be the reason he still lived.

Their partnership impressed him. How many blades had fallen into the same trap in the cycles these two had worked together? Eiji might have crossed paths a dozen times with Chiasa, but without the gift, he'd never paid her any attention.

Itsuki's partner had a bow strung over her shoulder and a look that said she knew how to use it. Eiji frowned as he looked from the bow to where she'd emerged from.

He swore to himself.

She'd been watching the duel, too. Most likely with an arrow nocked and ready to release.

He met Itsuki's eyes. "Would she have killed me if I'd drawn my sword?"

Itsuki smiled. "Only if you had bested me."

Eiji was doubly glad he hadn't drawn against the monk. Focused as he had been on Itsuki, he never would have sensed someone drawing a bow fifty paces away.

"So, what next?" Eiji asked.

"If you want Isau, we need to return to Highgate," Itsuki answered.

"He'll be hard to find, even with the three of us working together," Eiji remarked.

Itsuki's smile never left his face. "We know where he is."

Eiji shook his head and blinked rapidly. "What?" Mentally, he had braced himself for a task that took days, if not longer.

"We know where he is," Itsuki repeated.

"How?"

Itsuki's smile grew even broader. "I could tell you, but it's much more entertaining to watch you figure it out."

Eiji glared at the monk, and Itsuki chuckled.

"I thought I was the most frustrating man in the world," Eiji said.

Chiasa laughed. Eiji looked to her. Her eyes never rested, wandering constantly over their surroundings. She only met his gaze for a moment, and she smiled.

For the first time, Eiji realized she wasn't unattractive. He'd been too distracted trying to place her earlier to actually pay her much attention. She was tall for a woman, almost at height with him. Her dark hair was braided down to her shoulder, but it was her perpetual grin that drew most of his attention. One corner of her mouth was always slightly turned up, as though life was a joke only she understood.

"I like him," she said.

Itsuki snorted. "Great."

The monk returned his attention to Eiji. "The woman who took Isau took him to a home near the center of Highgate, one owned by a noble who rarely visits."

"Then what are we waiting for?" Eiji asked.

Itsuki grinned and gestured back toward the road. "After you."

Eiji shook his head and led the way. Itsuki followed, but Chiasa didn't.

"She'll be along in her own time," Itsuki said, answering Eiji's unspoken question.

Not long later, Eiji turned around, but he didn't see Chiasa. He stopped and searched, and Itsuki spoke. "You won't find her."

Eiji glanced at the monk. The enormous man shrugged. "It's what she does. If she's following you, you'll never notice. No one ever has."

Eiji stared, determined to prove Itsuki wrong.

But he couldn't.

According to every sense he possessed, no one was behind them.

"It's hopeless," Itsuki said as he resumed walking. "Come, the faster we can get you to Isau, the faster we can get you two on that ship."

The monk set a demanding pace, and although Eiji's body protested at first, he welcomed it. Thoughts of what had befallen Isau plagued his mind. He had no idea how he would get the child on a ship to the island now, but that was a problem he looked forward to solving when the boy was safe again.

They returned to Highgate and Itsuki wasted no time, leading them straight to the center of the city. This was where those who made their wealth from trade lived, in houses larger than anyone could ever need. After two cycles of walking through the Three Kingdoms, seeing the suffering of so many, the mere presence of the houses offended Eiji.

But why had Isau been taken here?

Eiji's battered and disheveled appearance drew the attention he dreaded, but Itsuki's white robes provided answer enough. Even the frequent guard patrols in the streets avoided them.

Such was the power of the monasteries, and growing with every passing cycle.

Itsuki stopped them about a block away from the house he pointed out as their destination. They stood behind the corner of another house, watching their target from a safe distance.

"You know he's in there?" Eiji asked.

"As of last night, yes."

They were too far away to sense into the house. From where they stood, it looked abandoned. But it could have held several guard units comfortably within.

"I'm of a mind to charge in," Eiji said to the monk.

Itsuki grimaced but nodded. "I'm afraid I agree with you."

"Chiasa?" Eiji asked. He hadn't seen a hint of her since the clearing.

"She'll support us." Itsuki didn't seem inclined to say any more.

Eiji tested his sword. It slid smoothly from the sheath. He was exhausted, and his ribs still hurt from where Itsuki had kicked him earlier in the day.

But Isau needed him.

He nodded to Itsuki, and the two warriors walked side-by-side toward the house.

Eiji almost felt sorry for anyone who opposed the two of them working together.

Almost.

22

I sau followed Yua into the secluded valley. It wasn't long before they ran into a patrol, a group of four young men walking a narrow path that overlooked the town. The men all bowed deeply to Yua, who barely nodded in return.

The small exchange surprised him. Even here, Yua was treated with deference and respect.

And she had cooked for him, and personally escorted him here.

He felt the gazes of the young men on him. They weren't gifted, and he suspected they looked upon him with jealousy. His chest tingled at the thought. Someday, they would bow to him.

He could hardly wait.

This late into the evening, the streets were largely quiet. Isau sensed the lives within the dwellings, gathered around tables for the evening meal.

Isau thought it was the most peaceful place he'd ever been.

Yua led him to the center of town.

Isau guessed their destination quickly enough. The building was the tallest in town, and the only one surrounded by a wall. It wasn't nearly as large as the house he'd woken up in back in Highgate, but somehow, Isau was more impressed by it.

He couldn't sense houses. No one could. Stone and lumber weren't alive, so they remained invisible to his gift. But all the same, every sharp line of this building spoke of strength and stability. Though it only stood two levels high, it towered over him as he approached.

If Yua felt anything similar, her face didn't betray her. She led him through the front gate, guarded by two men. Both were nightblades, their auras strong.

At the least, they were gifted. Yua hadn't appreciated being called a nightblade.

Because they were something more.

As soon as they stepped into the courtyard, Isau could sense him. His strength was enormous, glowing as brightly against his gift as the sun did in the sky. He grimaced.

"You'll get used to it," Yua said. "It's not always this strong, but he's probably training."

She opened the front door and Isau stepped again into a new world.

There was money here, just as there had been in Highgate. But this was a quiet wealth, one that didn't need to shout to draw attention to itself. The house was minimally furnished, and Isau couldn't spot so much as a speck of dust anywhere.

Yua led him past a large room with a raised dais, where Isau imagined her master received most visitors. He'd seen a similar room once when he was younger, in the home of their local noble.

Instead, they settled in a small room. Yua promised she would return in a few moments, and then she disappeared.

Isau missed her immediately. The presence of the master was like a weight on his sense. He'd never felt such power before.

Maybe someday, he would have a power like that.

He smiled at the thought.

Yua was as good as her word. She reappeared not long after leaving, carrying a tray filled with a teapot and cups. After she settled, Isau felt the master's presence fade. Despite himself, he breathed a sigh of relief. The air now seemed easier to breathe.

Isau's heart beat faster as he sensed the master's presence nearing their room. Then the door slid open and he was before them.

His face fell when he saw the master. At first glance he seemed nothing special. He possessed an average build, and wasn't physically imposing in the least. Isau had expected and hoped for a man who looked more like Itsuki.

But the strength emanating from the master defied description.

Yua bowed all the way down, with her head to the floor. Isau hurriedly followed suit.

"Rise, apprentice, and introduce us."

Isau wasn't sure about proper etiquette, but he also lifted his head.

"Master, this is Isau. Isau, meet Master Ryota."

Isau bowed again. He could feel Master Ryota's sense run over him. It was overwhelming, like being crushed underneath a boulder.

"You've done well, Yua."

"Thank you, master."

Yua poured them tea, but Isau was afraid to grab his cup,

certain he would spill, either over himself or over the pristine floor. Yua's hands didn't shake at all as she poured the drinks.

It was the bravest thing he'd ever seen.

Master Ryota interrupted his thoughts. "What do you want, Isau, more than anything?"

He answered without hesitation. "I want to be strong, master."

A hint of a smile played upon Master Ryota's lips. "Everybody wants to be strong. But what are you willing to sacrifice for the strength I offer?"

Isau didn't know, but he couldn't give that as his answer. "Anything, master."

"The answer of a child," Master Ryota said. "Would you allow me to strike you, now, as hard as I could?"

Isau gulped, but nodded.

"I didn't hear you."

"Yes, master."

"Would you go days without food?"

"Yes, master." He'd gone days without eating much before. That one wouldn't be much of a challenge.

"Would you kill the nightblade you traveled with?"

Isau hesitated. Eiji had done him no harm. Did Master Ryota want blind obedience, or did he want a child who did what was right? Isau didn't dare think for too long. "No, master."

Master Ryota didn't respond, and Isau knew he'd given the wrong answer.

When his master spoke again, the voice was grave. "Would you kill those who have chased you through the land?"

That question, at least, was easy. It was no more than he had dreamed about. "Yes, master."

Another pause. "Then you are welcome here. Our training is the most difficult you will ever experience, but if you survive, you will know a strength most only dream about."

With that, Master Ryota stood up. He looked to Yua. "Show Isau to his rooms. He'll need his rest for tomorrow."

Yua bowed, and Master Ryota left the room.

Once he was out of earshot, Isau asked the question he'd been too afraid to voice with Master Ryota nearby.

"What happens tomorrow?"

She smiled, and the fears that had built up within him vanished.

"Tomorrow you begin Master Ryota's training."

23

E iji didn't sense any lives within the building as they neared. He hoped he was wrong, and that he didn't sense Isau because the home was enormous, and they were in the middle of Highgate. But his hope died a little more with every step.

The front door was locked, but Itsuki broke one of the windows with his elbow, ignoring the curious stares of those on the street. When they saw his white robes, they turned and hurried away as though they weren't witnessing two armed men breaking into a house in the safest neighborhood in town.

Eiji wondered what it would be like to pass through the world like Itsuki, so confident in his place, so sure he would never be hunted for his gift.

If the price wasn't so high, Eiji might have considered joining the monasteries.

But he refused to hunt down the gifted, to force them to choose between a life of forced service and death.

Itsuki entered the house first, minding the broken glass.

He signaled that the house was safe, and Eiji followed him inside a moment later.

Eiji had never been in a structure this large. He paused, awestruck despite the task before them.

Itsuki moved deeper into the house, and Eiji followed.

They both knew the truth, though.

There was no one here.

This close, they both would have sensed any life.

Eiji had little desire to explore. The rooms felt cold, as though they had trapped an unnatural chill. Shadows jumped even though the light from the windows remained constant. Eiji wasn't superstitious, but he didn't like this house. Something within him, even deeper and more primal than his gift, responded to this place.

He feared what he might find. Hopefully Isau had simply left the mansion, but far darker possibilities haunted Eiji's imagination.

Itsuki moved through the rooms quickly. Armed with their sense, they didn't worry about assailants hiding in shadows or corners.

Eiji followed, drawing strength from the large man's efficient efforts.

Every new room and hallway revealed nothing but more mysteries. Many rooms were small and sparsely furnished. All had a bed, a chair, a lantern, and nothing else.

In contrast, the halls were covered in paintings, scenes that Eiji identified as being part of the history of the Kingdom.

On the top floor they found one master room, but though the bed was softer, and the room possessed a greater amount of furniture, it didn't feel like a true bedroom.

Itsuki's thoughts mirrored Eiji's own. "This isn't a home," he said. "No one lives here."

Eiji finally found the words he was looking for. "It feels more like a wayside rest, or a private inn." That thought led to another. "It's a perfect place to hide blades, at least for a time."

Itsuki nodded. "Right in the middle of the city, where monks rarely travel. Even if one passed by outside, I'm not sure how many of my brothers and sisters would sense a blade within. Most would keep their gifts close in the streets."

Though he suspected the feeling was foolish, Eiji's stomach twisted into more knots with every door they opened. He still worried that in one they would find Isau's body, as cold as the rest of the house.

But the last door Itsuki opened revealed a room just as empty, and as pristine, as every other they had been in. Eiji let out a long sigh of relief.

The two warriors returned to the ground floor, where Itsuki unlocked the door and stepped out.

The monk waited in front of the house, and before long Chiasa appeared. Eiji blinked. Where had she come from? The two spoke rapidly, and before long, Chiasa was gone again, commanded by Itsuki to learn what had happened. She vanished from his sight, even as he watched her.

"How does she do that?"

Eiji had muttered to himself, but Itsuki overheard. "She has gifts all her own."

Eiji shot the monk a glare. "That's not an answer."

"Her story is hers to tell, not mine."

The moments passed like small eternities. Isau was gone, and Eiji couldn't imagine how they would track him down.

Which left Eiji bereft of options. He could never return to the ships, but Itsuki wouldn't let him leave the city, either.

Chiasa returned before Eiji solved his conundrum. Her report was brief. "They left this morning by carriage. I didn't follow it too far, but they were heading out of town."

Itsuki nodded, as though this was exactly what he had expected, and he wasn't dismayed at all. "Good. We'll pursue." He turned to Eiji. "This is where our journey together ends."

Eiji's confusion must have been evident. Itsuki explained. "The pursuit of Isau is now my responsibility. If he wishes to return to the ships, I will do so, in honor of the agreement we made. If he wishes to join the monasteries, I shall allow that, also."

"But—" Eiji trailed off. He wasn't quite sure what to say.

Did he really want to pursue Isau? He'd done everything he promised, which was more than he had ever owed the boy in the first place.

He banished the thought quickly. Perhaps he had no obligation, but he still felt honor-bound to ensure he was safe.

Chiasa read his emotions perfectly. "He's not going to leave."

She turned and walked away, leaving Itsuki and Eiji to argue.

Itsuki shook his head. "You're leaving on the first ship."

Off to the side, Eiji couldn't help but notice that Chiasa had put about ten paces between them and was unslinging her bow. She didn't seem perturbed in the least to be readying it in the middle of Highgate. It didn't help his concentration.

With an effort, Eiji returned his focus to Itsuki. He wanted to find Isau, but finding Isau might also be the only way for him to remain alive. "I won't leave without the boy. I promised I would get him on that ship, and I won't break my word."

Itsuki's hand hovered near his sword, a perfect metaphor for the monk's indecision.

Eiji pressed further. "You're dealing with nightblades stronger than most. You'll need help your monasteries can't provide. I'm willing."

For several heartbeats, Eiji wasn't sure which direction Itsuki would choose.

Then the monk's hand moved away from his sword. "I really don't want to travel with you."

Eiji chuckled. "You're not my first choice of companions, either."

"Then let's get to it," Itsuki said. "The longer we wait, the harder he'll be to track."

24

Isau woke early the next morning, feeling better rested than he had in ages. He wasn't sure if the mountain air, filled with the scent of pine, or the fact that he planned on sleeping in the same place for several nights had eased his troubled mind.

Before Eiji, Isau had dreamed of a life on the open road. He had listened to stories of heroes who traveled from town to town, solving problems with their wit and martial skill. That life called to him.

But the storytellers had left out the rigors of travel. They didn't weave legends around sore feet, rumbling stomachs, and rain-drenched mud paths. Eiji had introduced him to all those experiences and more.

Now he was grateful to have a place of his own where he could rest his head. Here, Yua had said, he could rest easy. The monks didn't travel here.

They had given him a small house, a gift he still didn't actually believe was real. Yua had told him Master Ryota had people constantly expanding the village. She wouldn't say why, but it seemed strange to Isau that one would build houses when there was no need.

Regardless, they'd given him his own house, one nearly as large as the one he'd grown up in. But he didn't have to share. It was his alone. His father had toiled in the fields endlessly for the right to live in the house they'd had. That work had been what broke him. Here, Isau had to do nothing more than show up to receive this gift.

He'd never been given anything that was just his. His clothes had belonged to his older siblings, and what toys they had were shared among all. Except for the dagger Eiji had given him, he supposed. But a dagger didn't compare to a house.

He got dressed in the new clothes that had been provided him. He left the dagger on the dresser. When he stepped out of the house, he shut the door carefully behind him, as though he was leaving a shrine.

They served all meals for the younger students in a common hall. Yua had told him why, but the reason escaped him now. All he remembered was the location of the hall, which he probably could have found from the smell alone.

When he entered the hall, he looked around, his heart sinking when he saw that Yua wasn't there. But there were plenty of others, all of whom were gifted. His sense came alive, and he was filled with sudden energy. He felt like he could run for leagues without stopping.

Despite his desire for movement, he froze. He was in a room full of strangers and didn't know what to do next. He could smell the food, and saw the others eating, but didn't know how to get the food. And if he figured that out, where would he sit? Everyone here knew one another.

Fortunately, he didn't have to solve his problems alone. A group of boys, who all appeared to be around his age, stood up from their table and greeted him. They introduced themselves and showed him how to get food and what rules he needed to follow. After he had filled a bowl to the brim, they made space for him at their table.

He forgot their names almost as soon as they spoke them. He would learn them in time, but for now he allowed himself to be overwhelmed. They asked him how he had come to be there, and he told them his story, which they listened to with rapt attention.

Through it all, he felt the gifts of everyone surrounding him.

Here, he wasn't alone.

Perhaps they weren't a family by blood, but as he broke his fast he thought this group reminded him of his family on one of their rare happy days.

While he ate, Yua came in, her aura dominant among the others. Their eyes met across the room, and Isau knew she had been looking for him, ensuring he was getting along well. She saw him with his new friends, gave him a little smile and nod, then left again.

Isau smiled from ear to ear.

Soon after, their meals finished, his friends led him to the large square in the center of town. They showed Isau where to stand, and he waited for whatever would happen next.

He noticed, as he waited, that not everyone in town was in the square to practice. Men and women shuffled around the perimeter, many carrying heavy loads. Though it was difficult to be sure in the crowd, none of them seemed gifted.

When he had a chance, there were many questions that he wanted answered.

Before his questions could run away with him, Master

Ryota appeared. He stood in front of the assembly, looking them all over with a stern eye. He nodded once in approval.

Then training began.

Master Ryota's methods of training were different than the limited training Eiji had given him. Those had been small lessons, fit in between long stretches of traveling. Master Ryota clearly intended to keep them here for some time. He had them jump, rotate, and run in place until everyone had broken a light sweat.

If anything, Isau worked too hard. Every time Master Ryota's eye wandered over him he redoubled his efforts until his hair dripped. He wanted to be worthy of the gifts Master Ryota had given him.

After, wooden swords were distributed and Master Ryota went through a handful of techniques. The weapon quickly grew heavy in Isau's hands, but the instruction was relentless, and Master Ryota made it clear he accepted nothing less than the best one was capable of.

Following the final technique, the assembly broke into smaller groups, and Isau once again joined the boys he'd met over breakfast. An older student led them through a practice tailored just for them. These moves were simpler than the earlier ones, but Isau already worried about how he would feel come evening. His body was used to hard work, but this was beyond his current endurance.

Master Ryota went from group to group, offering advice and giving the instructors guidance on their next lessons. He singled Isau out for a few moments, providing suggestions to his newest recruit.

The sun was high in the sky when they took a break. Isau lay down, exhausted, next to the other boys. They were more conditioned to the training than he was, but they still collapsed next to him in the shade of a building. One of the boys offered a ladle of water from a nearby spring. Isau sipped greedily, careful not to drink more than his share.

As they rested, the boys spoke with one another. They talked of the training, each of them focused on improving. They included Isau as though he'd always been one of them, listening to his insights with polite attentiveness.

Their words buzzed in his ears as he looked around. Similar groups were scattered around the square, and the village itself seemed to be alive with energy.

This was what he had always wanted.

Eiji thought he'd have to go to the island and hide from the world for this.

But the nightblade had been wrong.

Paradise was here, and Master Ryota had more money and power than Eiji could ever imagine.

And he had welcomed Isau with open arms.

For the first time in his life, he finally thought he understood what home was.

25

After Chiasa updated Itsuki, she disappeared once again.

For partners, Eiji reflected, the two of them were rarely found together.

But their results couldn't be argued with. They'd tracked him and Isau across the Northern Kingdom without difficulty. Eiji hoped that feat hadn't been a fluke, and that they would be equally successful tracking Isau again.

He didn't like what little they had learned from Chiasa. A carriage implied money. Mix in fugitive nightblades with a nasty murder habit, and Eiji couldn't imagine a scenario in which Isau wasn't in trouble.

Itsuki wasted no time in returning to the road. Eiji's feet protested. The sun was falling, and he'd been walking to and from Highgate for most of the day. Given his restless sleep the night before, his body demanded a break.

But Itsuki and Chiasa took no rest. They were consummate hunters, and their prey were the gifted.

Itsuki led him to a stable, where the monk acquired

horses for them. No money was exchanged, leading Eiji to believe there was some prior relationship here.

Eiji and Itsuki rode side by side as they left Highgate. Eiji glanced over at his new companion, still coming to terms with the fact that this morning Itsuki had wanted to kill him.

Of course, the monk probably still did.

But no one could guess by looking at him. His constant friendliness was a mask concealing the killer underneath. Eiji forced himself to remember that.

Only one road led out of Highgate. Less than a league outside the city it branched in several different directions, but if the carriage had left town, they knew where their pursuit began.

As they neared the edge of the city, Eiji stopped Itsuki. "Do you sense that?"

The feeling was faint, barely noticeable over the late-day dying bustle of traffic entering and leaving Highgate. But a nightblade waited near the exit of the city.

A few moments later, Itsuki nodded. "A friend of yours?"

"You might be surprised to know I don't have many friends here."

Itsuki grunted at that.

Eiji could guess the blade's intention well enough. After Kosuke had lost him in the streets, he'd ordered his fellow blades to seal the city. He anticipated Eiji running.

But Eiji couldn't tell Itsuki the truth. If he did, it wouldn't take long for Itsuki to realize Eiji couldn't return to the island, imperiling their temporary partnership.

Eiji breathed a sigh of relief when Itsuki decided not to change course. In Eiji's experience, most monks would charge after whoever they sensed, but Itsuki remained focused on one task at a time. No doubt, though, he would return. Perhaps he'd permit blades on the docks, but no further.

They left town, and Eiji never spotted the blade. Whoever watched the road never pursued them. But if Eiji had sensed them, it was likely they had sensed Eiji and Itsuki as well. His former friends from the island would be less than pleased to see him keeping company with a monk.

But there was nothing for it. He seemed to be developing a knack for collecting enemies.

He feared Kosuke would follow him into the Northern Kingdom and seek revenge for Harumi's death. But at the moment, it was one worry among many. He would deal with it if the time came.

Chiasa was already waiting for them where the road branched, sitting atop a horse of her own. A small collection of businesses had been built here, taking advantage of the traffic that had once come from throughout the Three Kingdoms.

Their meeting, as with all meetings involving Chiasa, was brief.

"There was someone near the road in Highgate, watching from a rooftop," she said.

"A nightblade," Itsuki confirmed.

Eiji didn't interrupt the partners. Both were remarkable. He couldn't guess how Chiasa had spotted the blade, but neither of them missed much of anything. It was no wonder they tracked the gifted so effectively.

Chiasa pointed to a road that led southeast. "The carriage went that way."

Eiji supposed she had spoken to the business owners at the intersection. Perhaps there was even some agreement already in place to watch the road and share information. Such practices hadn't occurred to him before now, but it helped explain how Chiasa and Itsuki knew so much. They didn't rely just on themselves, but on a whole web of informants.

How wide did that web spread?

"Inn tonight?" Itsuki asked.

Chiasa nodded. "He looks dead on his feet."

It took Eiji a moment to realize they were talking about him. But before he could protest, Chiasa left again. She took off down the road, disappearing among a caravan getting a late start out of Highgate.

"Come on," Itsuki said. "We'll rest tonight."

The sun had barely set below the horizon when Itsuki pulled to a halt outside a nondescript inn. They handed their horses off, and Eiji wasn't surprised to find Chiasa waiting for them, an ale already in hand.

"Their carriage passed through this morning," Chiasa said. "They switched horses here and continued on."

Eiji shook his head. Someone was spending an enormous amount of money to take Isau away. But where to, and why?

He had no answers, but he resolved to look for them in the bottom of a mug of ale.

When he didn't find his answers in the first mug, he decided to search another.

He didn't find answers there, but his tongue was sufficiently loosened that he felt comfortable asking his new companions questions he would have normally avoided. His most pressing questions were aimed at Chiasa. "What did you do, before you hunted blades?"

"A little of this, a little of that."

Eiji shook his head. His interest wasn't idle, and he wouldn't be so easily turned away. "Someone took the time to train you well, so you weren't a thief. But beyond knowing what you aren't, I couldn't say."

Chiasa glanced at Itsuki, who gave a shrug. She returned her gaze to Eiji, studying him. "Let me ask you a question first. Why are you here? Itsuki tells me that you've been trained in the old styles, the same as him, which means you probably weren't born in the Three Kingdoms. So why return?"

Eiji slowly spun the mug of ale in his hands. "I believed the blades could return to the Three Kingdoms to put right the wrongs we had done."

Not the full truth, perhaps, but a truth all the same.

"And now?"

"Now I don't know. I didn't understand how deep the wounds we created were. I had thought to help, but now I suspect the best we can do is leave the Three Kingdoms alone."

Itsuki grunted his agreement, but Chiasa's eyes held his.

Finally, she nodded. "You know of Lady Mari?"

Eiji did. In the Great War, she had led the Northern Kingdom, then known by its house name: Kita. Politics had forced her into marriage, but she still ruled side by side with her husband, and if rumors were true, she made as many or more decisions for the Northern Kingdom than her husband did.

"Lady Mari has always understood the power of information," Chiasa said, "and also understood how easily a woman could be underestimated. Not long after her reign began, she trained specially selected women, providing them with a unique set of skills. I am a member of one such cohort."

Eiji noted the use of the present tense. Chiasa still

served the Northern Kingdom. He looked between his two companions. A unique partnership, then.

"How did you two come to work together?"

Chiasa smiled at that. "Itsuki doesn't play well with other monks, but his skills are unsurpassed among monasteries in the Northern Kingdom. Lady Mari heard of the dilemma and suggested the partnership."

That cast Itsuki in a new light.

Eiji had noticed that Itsuki's techniques were unlike those taught to most monks, but perhaps his differences with the others went even deeper than technique and training. His behavior was certainly different enough.

Chiasa finished her ale with a long pull. "Good night, gentlemen."

Eiji watched her go.

Beside him, Itsuki chuckled. "She'll kill you if you even try."

"What—?"

"If I noticed, she certainly has. It's a small wonder you aren't already bleeding out on the floor, but don't take that as encouragement."

Itsuki finished his own beer. "I'll see you upstairs." The two of them were sharing a room. "Don't be too late. It will be an early start tomorrow."

With that, Eiji was alone, and he noticed his ale no longer tasted as delicious as it had before. He gulped the last of it down and followed Itsuki upstairs.

26

After a few days of training, Isau wasn't sure how he found the energy to even roll out of bed in the morning. But he did, pulled by his desire to please both Master Ryota and Yua.

Already his days had fallen into a familiar rhythm. He woke early in the morning and broke his fast. He preferred to eat with the boys who had first welcomed him, but they encouraged him to meet with other students, as well.

Despite his initial reluctance, he did speak with the others and found them all to be welcoming. He'd never been in a place where everyone was as kind as they were here. It seemed, at times, to be too good to be true.

He decided it was in no small part due to their shared purpose. Everyone here respected Master Ryota. As Isau learned the stories of his new friends, he realized his own wasn't that unique. In one way or another, every person here had been rescued by Master Ryota and brought here to train.

They had all come from similar situations and they all trained for the same reason: to learn Master Ryota's secret techniques and bring about his vision of the future. Division died among such similarities.

The kindness at meals wasn't matched in the merciless training sessions, though. When they sparred, no one pulled punches. Master Ryota usually encouraged students of similar skill levels to practice together, but twice now he'd matched older students against younger, reminding them that not all fights would be fought between evenly matched opponents. The older students didn't hold back, either, and Isau had the bruises to prove it.

The group had a quick break for lunch, which was little more than a snack. Then came the part of the day Isau dreaded.

All afternoon they trained their gifts.

The morning was dedicated to the physical, the afternoons to the mental.

Unfortunately, here Master Ryota's lessons weren't much different than Eiji's had been.

Only longer.

Master Ryota's presence, as well as Yua's, helped keep Isau focused, but he struggled. He'd never considered himself particularly intelligent, and Master Ryota demanded a level of attention and focus no one had ever asked Isau for before.

The afternoons crawled by, and Isau gladly welcomed the end of the mental sessions. Their days concluded with light movement that prepared them for the next day.

After the evening meal, some students spoke with one another, but most returned to their own houses, collapsing into bed.

The days were difficult, but Isau experienced a certain satisfaction at the end of each one. Every day felt like a trial, but with each day he survived, he came closer to gaining the same strength his master possessed.

The fifth morning of training posed a new challenge.

After the demonstration of a now-familiar technique, Master Ryota called Isau to the front of the assembly.

He'd never been called before, and although he stood in front of a group of familiar and kind faces, his heart pounded in his chest.

"Why are you here?" Master Ryota asked.

"I want to be as strong as you," Isau replied.

He'd hoped his answer would earn some acknowledgment, but there was none. "And why do you wish to be as strong as me?"

Isau considered for a moment. "I want to stop those that would hurt us."

To this, Master Ryota nodded. "A noble thought. But my secret techniques require a perfection of will that few attain. Do you understand?"

Isau didn't, but he nodded anyway.

"To master my techniques," Master Ryota said, "there cannot be even the smallest grain of hesitation. No weakness can remain within you."

He turned to the class. "As is traditional on the fifth day, one's commitment must be tested."

The entire assembly bowed.

Isau's fingers went cold. For the first time, he wanted to be anywhere in the world but here.

But no one else appeared surprised. They had all passed this test, and he could, too.

"Yua!" Master Ryota called.

From the back ranks, Yua hurried forward, standing beside Master Ryota as indicated.

"You respect Yua, do you not, Isau?"

Isau nodded.

"You would even call her a friend?"

Isau gulped, then nodded again. He didn't know if Yua thought the same of him, but he knew he would do anything for her.

"Yua is one of my prized students, Isau. Do you know why?"

"She is very strong," Isau guessed.

"She is, but she is prized because she possesses the will necessary to shape the future of the Three Kingdoms." Master Ryota turned to Yua. "If I asked you to bite through your tongue, right now, and so bleed to death, would you?"

"Gladly," came Yua's instant reply.

A shiver ran through Isau's body. He believed her. She would do it with a smile on her face.

Master Ryota turned to the two students standing off to the side. "Bind her!"

Isau's whole body froze as he watched the students bind Yua tightly. One wrapped a leather strap around her ankles, and another tied her wrists tightly behind her back. She submitted to the treatment without question, without even the slightest change in her neutral expression.

When they were done, the students returned to the line. Master Ryota stepped away from her.

"Isau, I want you to beat Yua. As hard as you can."

Isau opened his mouth to protest, but the words wouldn't form. She was defenseless. Tied as she was, even he could defeat her without problem.

Isau shook his head. He would fight those who sought to harm him, but Yua had shown him kindness. She had cooked for him and escorted him here, to a new home. How could he strike her now, bound as she was?

"This is your test, Isau. I need to see your will."

Though Master Ryota didn't say, Isau understood the stakes. If he failed, he would be thrown out of the community. Perhaps he'd be killed. He imagined Master Ryota didn't let people simply leave.

For a moment, he wondered if perhaps the test of will was to disobey, to do what was right.

Another moment of reflection convinced him that wasn't true. Master Ryota had been disappointed when Isau said he wouldn't hurt Eiji.

And the truth was revealed in Yua's eyes.

She wanted him to obey.

She grew more disappointed with every moment that he didn't.

He couldn't stand to see that look in her eyes.

Growing up, when he didn't do as his father wanted, his father lashed him. Right now, Isau would have welcomed that pain. He wanted to be made to do this.

Master Ryota provided no easy excuse. If Isau made the choice, it would be entirely his own.

"You're running out of time," Master Ryota said.

Isau looked again at Yua. It was her gaze, more than Master Ryota's threat, that pushed him forward.

With a loud yell, he stepped forward and drove his fist into her stomach. She didn't even flex against the blow. Her only reaction was a sharp exhale of breath as he knocked the wind from her lungs.

"Not just a single punch!" Master Ryota yelled. "Beat her!"

Her lips close to his ears, she whispered, "Do it."

Something broke inside him. His stomach, twisted in knots, relaxed, and his heart pounded in his ears. He struck at her, punching again and again, his fists unopposed. When he stepped back, she stumbled, and he lashed out at her face.

He felt the tears running down his cheeks, but he couldn't stop. Everything stuffed deep inside him came rushing out.

One of his blows flung her to the ground.

"Don't stop," Master Ryota said.

He didn't.

Isau kicked and kicked, tears blurring his vision until Yua was nothing more than a dark stain against his vision.

He only stopped when he felt strong hands on his shoulders.

"Enough," Master Ryota said.

His master gestured to the line, and Isau returned, wiping the back of his hand across his eyes.

He felt nothing at all, like a jug filled to the brim with water had been poured out.

The same two students who had tied Yua came to her aid, but Isau couldn't watch. He couldn't bring himself to look at what he had done.

The students carried Yua off, and when Isau finally looked up again, he saw the pride on Master Ryota's face.

"Welcome home, Isau," he said.

As one, the rest of the assembly bowed, not to Master Ryota, but to him.

"Welcome home," they repeated as one.

27

T he next morning, they resumed their pursuit.

In many ways, Eiji felt as though he was being escorted through the Northern Kingdom. Itsuki, for understandable reasons, requested that Eiji always remain in sight, which he had no problem acquiescing to. Until they found Isau, they were all on the same side.

Chiasa served as their way finder. She scouted ahead, interviewing witnesses and tracking the location of the carriage. Fortunately, such carriages were rare, especially as they traveled farther from main roads. Chiasa had little difficulty following the trail.

The farther they traveled, the more Itsuki's frown deepened. When Eiji asked him why, Itsuki gestured to the mountains climbing ahead of them. "We approach the lands of Tomiichi. He has forbidden monks from entering."

"He has such authority?"

"Much of the gold and iron ore mined in the Northern Kingdom comes from this area. It provides Tomiichi a certain—latitude—not afforded other nobles."

"I'm surprised the monastery submits to such authority."

Itsuki shrugged, but the gesture held layers of meaning. Indifference, yes, but a resignation and frustration as well. Eiji chose not to press the matter. Someday, he wanted to unravel the relationship Itsuki had with the monasteries, but not today.

"Do you know why he would forbid monks?"

"He claims it is because he wishes the gift completely banished from his lands. Every cycle, he collects all the young people in his domain and brings them to his house on the border for testing. Few gifted are ever found, and those that are immediately join the order."

Eiji's hand tightened on the hilt of his sword.

He didn't argue. He liked Itsuki, but the monk believed in the monastic system. Eiji didn't understand how a man could inflict the same wounds on others he'd endured himself as a child.

Eiji didn't understand why the gifted children born today had to suffer for the crimes committed by the gifted many cycles ago.

They traveled on in silence, and Eiji gave the large man more space. Over the days of travel, Eiji had become familiar with Itsuki's aura, and he detected the subtle shift. The monk was preparing for a fight.

Eiji didn't envy Tomiichi the challenge coming his way.

But Eiji was also thrilled their pursuit proceeded as smoothly as it did. The carriage made it easy.

The carriage also implicated Tomiichi, if Itsuki's claims were accurate. The noble no doubt enjoyed a surplus of wealth, even in these trying times. He would be one of the few in the Northern Kingdom who had the coin to afford the carriage and horses.

Tomiichi's mistake was to think Isau wouldn't be pursued.

Eiji's hand ran up and down his sword's hilt. He hadn't harmed anyone since rescuing Isau from his village. He'd defended himself from the woman who'd stolen Isau, but other than that, he hadn't even drawn his sword.

His hand moved from the hilt to his left arm. The tips of his fingers ran over the scar tissue from the seven cuts. No matter how much time passed, his dreams were still often filled with vivid memories of his previous kills.

They felt like a weight he had to pull with every step.

Another day of pursuit brought them to Tomiichi's lands. His home, easily visible from a distance, made the enormous dwellings near the center of Highgate seem like servants' quarters. Walls of stone towered over the surrounding lands, and Eiji whistled softly. He hadn't seen any of the castles of the Lords of the Three Kingdoms, but he suspected this house had to be among the largest in the land.

The grounds surrounding the house were crawling with guards. Though none of them were gifted, Eiji never would have approached the house without Itsuki's company. As he often did, he searched for Chiasa but didn't see her. For the first time, the fact strengthened his resolve. Itsuki's complete trust in his partner wore off on him. He appreciated having someone, hidden in the distance, protecting him at all times.

Itsuki displayed no hesitation. He walked straight to the grounds, asking for Tomiichi when they were stopped by the first guard they came across. Eiji noted that the guard didn't seem to have the same respect for monks that most in the Three Kingdoms did.

The guard escorted them to the home, although in his head, Eiji was beginning to think of it as a castle. They were made to wait in a receiving hall like common peasants.

Eiji kept expecting some reaction from Itsuki, but he remained disappointed.

Some time passed before Tomiichi entered. Eiji's first glance didn't impress him. The noble was tall, but almost sickly thin. Malicious eyes glittered over a sharp nose, giving Eiji the impression of a hawk looking down on the world below for prey.

Tomiichi barely bowed, only offering the slightest dip of his head to the monk.

Eiji kept his eyes straight ahead, though the effort was difficult.

Tomiichi's every action insulted Itsuki's pride. Yet the noble, clearly incapable of defending himself, shunned even basic decency. He trusted his money to protect him.

"What do you want?" Tomiichi's voice was high and nasally.

"We seek a carriage that passed through here a few days past," Itsuki replied. The monk's voice was even and slow, betraying nothing of his feelings. Even the man's aura, strong to Eiji's sense, was steady.

"I cannot help you. No carriages have passed through here for at least a moon," Tomiichi said.

"There are reliable reports one entered your lands," Itsuki answered. "Perhaps it escaped your notice. I would like permission to enter your lands and pursue."

"Never." Tomiichi didn't even consider the request for a heartbeat. "Are you not aware that the gifted are not allowed anywhere beyond these very rooms?"

"I am. The carriage that passed onto your lands was carrying two gifted I have been hunting. I assumed that if you knew the truth, you would welcome my search."

"And again, there has been no carriage. I keep a sharp eye on my holdings, monk, and I can assure you nothing of the sort has happened. You should be more thorough in your investigation, and you can be certain I will report this failing to your abbot."

For a single heartbeat, Eiji thought Itsuki would attack. The monk's aura shifted, but it never coalesced into movement.

Itsuki bowed, and Eiji followed suit. They said their farewells and left the castle.

Eiji wasn't half as calm as Itsuki. Their options for pursuing the boy had just been destroyed.

But Itsuki didn't seem disturbed, which Eiji hoped meant he had a plan. So Eiji followed his lead, at least for now.

Once they were safely out of hearing, Eiji spoke. "He's lying."

"Of course he is," Itsuki said. "But it was important to try, first."

"We're going into his lands?"

"We are."

"He didn't strike me as a fool. He'll know we'll try. He'll be expecting us," Eiji said.

"Then we move quietly," Itsuki replied. "He's hiding something from the monasteries, and I intend to figure out what it is."

Isau's failure during mental training that afternoon was complete. His mind, restless at the best of times, was a stallion that wouldn't be tamed. His thoughts turned endlessly to Yua. When training ended, Isau asked his friends for directions to her house. Then he ran, their knowing looks at his back.

He was surprised to find that her home was smaller than his, and older as well. Though the village wasn't large, Isau hadn't visited this part of it yet. Many laborers lived here, their energies weak compared to the gifted he spent the rest of the day with.

Why was she here? Hurried as he was, the question nagged at him.

As he approached her door, he felt her familiar cold aura wash over him. Her energy felt strong and healthy.

Isau skidded to a stop just in front of her door and knocked.

"Enter."

He did, surprised to find Yua up and about, cleaning her small place with a rag and soapy water.

Isau blinked. She should have been in bed, healing from what he'd done. He didn't deceive himself about his strength, but he knew he'd hurt her badly enough that she shouldn't be cleaning. She shouldn't even be able to.

Isau fell to his knees and pressed his forehead against the floor. "I'm sorry! Let me do your chores so you may rest."

She actually laughed, the first time he had heard the sound. It was the most delightful he'd ever heard. "Stand up, Isau."

He almost didn't. He didn't deserve to face her, but he also couldn't deny a request from her.

Isau straightened, then stood. He kept his eyes on her feet, though.

She reached out and lifted his chin, her fingertips sending a tingling feeling through his face. She gave him no choice but to look in her eyes.

"I'm proud of you," she said. "And as you can see, I'm fine."

She was. Isau knew well the effects a beating had on a person. She wasn't simply pretending to be healed. "How?"

"Balance." When she saw that he didn't understand, she explained. "I can't say much, but I can say that Master Ryota's secret techniques require knowledge of both healing and combat. After your trial, he came to me personally to provide healing."

"He's a dayblade, too?" Isau knew of the legendary healers. Though their use of the sense made them healers instead of fighters, they'd been driven from the land with their nightblade brethren after the Great War.

She smiled. "He's neither dayblade nor nightblade. As I've said before, he's something more."

A feeling of awe passed over Isau, but it couldn't find

root in his mind as he looked at Yua. "I didn't want to hit you."

"Which is exactly why it was your trial." She squatted down so they were the same height. "Master Ryota knows that there will come times where we will be forced to take actions we don't like. We've all gone through our own personal trial, every single one of the gifted here. You're one of us now."

"What was yours?"

Her smile faded. "In some ways, it was similar to today's. But instead of binding me, he put two knives in my hand and had another student punch me over and over."

"Why?"

"Because when I came here, I fought over anything. I would fight if someone looked at me the wrong way. My trial was learning how not to fight."

Isau didn't understand. "But why so harsh? There must be a better way."

She shook her head. "Here, Master Ryota will train you to be a true warrior. Your skills, once you graduate, will know no equal in the Three Kingdoms. But just as he trains you to wield a sword, he will shape you into a weapon for his own use. Our role isn't to question, but to follow."

Isau frowned. He wasn't sure if he liked the sound of that.

He couldn't hide his reaction from Yua's study of him. "You don't approve?"

"What's the point of becoming strong, if you're just going to follow someone else's orders?"

"True freedom," she answered.

"What?"

"Freedom is found in surrender. That's another lesson I've learned here."

"I don't understand."

"Someday you will. I appreciate you checking on me, but as you can see, I'm fully healed. I'll return to training tomorrow."

Isau bowed and was about to leave when he noticed the presence approaching the door. Distracted as he'd been by Yua, he'd lost his awareness of his surroundings.

Master Ryota approached. He was already too close to the door for Isau to leave unobserved. Isau wasn't sure he wanted to see his master at the moment, but he had no choice in the matter.

Master Ryota entered without knocking. In a single glance he took in the room and his two students within. Somehow, Isau knew he didn't need to explain his actions. In that one moment, his master had understood the purpose of Isau's visit. Fortunately, he didn't seem perturbed in the least.

Both students bowed deeply.

Master Ryota focused his attention on Isau. "I'm proud of you today," he said. "I know I asked you to complete a difficult trial, but you fulfilled it beyond my expectations. I see a great future ahead of you."

At the compliment, Isau's doubt melted away. Master Ryota was a man worth serving.

Their master turned his attention to Yua. "Are you in condition to fight, if need be?"

"Yes, master."

"Good." Master Ryota glanced at Isau, appraising his new student. "Have you ever been underground?"

Isau shook his head. He'd dug some deep holes, but he'd never truly been underground.

"Then you're in for a treat. Yua and I have a task we must

attend to, but your company would be welcome. You can learn one of the secrets of our land, if you wish."

Isau bowed to hide the flush of pride in his cheeks. Master Ryota trusted him with a secret! "I'd be honored, master."

"Good. Then come with us."

Master Ryota addressed Yua as he turned to leave.

"Bring your sword, too. There's a good chance you're going to need it tonight."

29

They waited until nightfall to cross into Tomiichi's lands again.

Fortified with a bit of rest and a full meal, they snuck through wooded land about half a league to the south of Tomiichi's castle. Chiasa had scouted the route earlier, while Eiji and Itsuki's attempt to gain Tomiichi's permission failed.

Geography limited their options. Tomiichi's castle commanded a view of the only gentle entrance to the mountains beyond. Their approach through the woods involved scrambling up and down steep slopes, but the only alternative required them to fight their way through a considerable force.

Unfortunately, the moon rose above them in a perfectly clear sky. Still, what darkness remained served as their ally. Itsuki even changed out of his white robes, the first time Eiji had seen that feat accomplished.

Chiasa led the way, but for once she remained close enough for both Itsuki and Eiji to see her.

Eiji admired the coordination between them. Chiasa,

even if she lacked the gift, remained as aware of her surroundings as a mountain cat. What little she missed, Itsuki's sense caught. Between them, not even a field mouse could hide.

Their movement also impressed him. They seemed to have a window into one another's thoughts, naturally choosing spacing and routes that altered as their needs changed. Nightblades on the island usually trained to fight alone, which made the partnership between the monk and the scout seem almost otherworldly. He'd never imagined such coordination was possible.

Truthfully, Eiji felt as though he had little to contribute. He followed close behind Itsuki, his own sense searching for threats behind them, but he suspected he only slowed the pair down.

Their earlier suspicions about Tomiichi's preparations were quickly confirmed. Guards patrolled the paths in large groups and were posted around the grounds at natural chokepoints. The three invaders flitted from shadow to shadow, their progress slow but consistent. Their combined awareness ensured no guard approached too close.

Only once did Eiji fear he would have to draw his sword. An oblivious pair of guards had passed within fifteen paces of Chiasa's position, and she'd had an arrow nocked and ready to release. Those guards never knew how close they'd come to rejoining the Great Cycle.

Eventually they passed the worst of the patrols. Eiji wasn't sure what Tomiichi hoped to accomplish. His lands were enormous, and he couldn't possibly protect them on his own. But he seemed committed to the attempt.

Eiji didn't know many specifics about how the Northern Kingdom was governed, but it seemed unusual that Lady Mari would allow some of her most valuable lands to be protected by a single noble's forces. Why wasn't one of the Northern Kingdom's armies stationed here?

For all the time he'd spent in this land, he still didn't understand. Somedays, he wasn't sure he ever would.

Their pace quickened as the need for stealth diminished. Chiasa remained on point, and Eiji realized she was leading them in an enormous arc. He wasn't sure why until she stopped at a well-worn road. She gestured for them to join her.

The two hunters conferred quickly.

"If he was still in the carriage, this is the only road we've found it could travel on," she said.

Itsuki looked back toward Tomiichi's castle, a small beacon of light in the distance now. He rubbed at his bare chin for a moment, then nodded. "A hundred paces. They'll be watching the road."

Chiasa rolled her eyes. "We've done this before."

Itsuki grinned, his teeth shining in the moonlight. "I was telling him," he said as he gestured toward Eiji.

"Then you should speak slower," Chiasa said.

Eiji pretended the comment hurt.

Chiasa laughed softly and melted back into the woods.

Itsuki clapped him on the shoulder. The large monk barely knew his strength. Eiji worried for a moment his shoulder joint would pop out of its socket. "I think she likes you."

Then the monk was off, and Eiji could do nothing but follow.

Again, Chiasa and Itsuki's suspicions about Tomiichi's guard placements proved correct. They made their way around two fully manned and alert guard posts.

The moon was high in the sky when they found the carriage.

It had been left in a small structure, most likely designed for this very purpose. It matched the description of the carriage they'd been following to the smallest detail.

Unfortunately, multiple paths led away from the building, each to a different section of the mountains beyond. Itsuki and Chiasa studied the ground, but each of the paths looked to have been traveled recently.

After their brief examination, they looked to one other.

"What do you think?" Itsuki asked his partner.

"Make him choose," she replied, nodding to Eiji.

"Why me?" Eiji didn't have the slightest clue which way they'd taken Isau. The other two were the ones who hunted the gifted.

"Any of us would only be guessing," Itsuki said. "But this way we can blame you if we waste our time."

"But what if I'm wrong?" Eiji glanced up at the moon. They didn't have all night.

Itsuki shrugged. "Then we return and follow another path. And then we do it again, until we find him."

The monk made it sound like the leagues of walking ahead of them weren't an issue in the least, and Eiji was reminded of the persistence that made Itsuki so dangerous.

"Fine," Eiji said. "Then we go that way." He pointed down a random path.

"Works for us," Chiasa said, and began following the path.

Eiji regretted his choice not long after making it. The path had seemed flat at first, but quickly ascended through a series of switchbacks that forced them to gain considerable elevation quickly.

He saw Chiasa stiffen, then lower herself to the prone position as soon as she gained a ridge. Itsuki paused, waiting patiently for her signal, which eventually came.

They joined her at the ridge, looking down into a valley below.

Eiji needed a few moments to find what had alarmed Chiasa.

Movement, far below, a shadow rippling through the sparse trees. They were far enough away Eiji couldn't sense the person at all.

As Eiji watched, he became more and more convinced this patrol wasn't the same as the guards they'd passed earlier. This warrior blended with the shadows and didn't use torches to light the surrounding area.

"I think it's a blade," Chiasa said.

Eiji frowned. He couldn't sense the warrior, so he couldn't tell one way or the other. He wanted to trust Chiasa, but what would a blade be doing here?

Itsuki's questioning glance at Eiji implied he was wondering the same thing. Eiji shook his head.

But if Chiasa was right, their lives had just become far more complicated. Patrolling blades made stealth nearly impossible.

Off in the distance, Eiji thought he heard the clang of steel on steel. He closed his eyes, and a few moments later, he heard it again.

The others heard it, too. "We need to get closer," Itsuki decided.

Eiji swore and glanced back the way they'd come. Every step forward increased the odds they'd have a fight on their hands. He liked Isau, but he wasn't sure the boy was worth this much trouble.

Itsuki and Chiasa, though, showed no hesitation. They crawled down the slope together, not even taking the time to ask him his opinion.

Eiji looked longingly back. Of course, if he left now,

they'd pursue him. He had a choice, but it wasn't much of one.

He crawled after them.

They kept close to one another, never more than a few paces apart.

About halfway down the valley, Eiji sensed another presence. He gestured the group to a stop. The presence was faint, some ways away. But there was no mistaking the strength of it.

Chiasa's guess had been correct.

Blades couldn't sense the same distances. That ability had some correlation with both mental strength and training. Eiji was fairly certain his sense extended farther than Itsuki's. But if Eiji could sense the other blade, they ran the risk the other blade could sense them. Eiji's range was hardly unusual in a trained nightblade.

Itsuki gave Eiji a questioning glance.

"Nightblade," Eiji confirmed.

They remained still. Eiji closed his eyes and pushed his sense as far as it would go. The other warrior's presence remained faint, and after several long heartbeats, it began fading.

Eiji exhaled slowly, then nodded to his companions. They resumed their journey, first to the bottom of the valley and then up again to the next ridge line. Itsuki placed Eiji in the front of the column, and he followed game trails up the side of the next ridge.

Their going slowed even further. Every hundred paces or so, Eiji threw out his sense to seek others. He found little, though.

Upon the next ridge line, the sound of steel against steel rang clearly. But it wasn't a battle, as Eiji had expected. In the next valley, fires burned brightly despite the lateness of the hour, and hammers rang out as they pounded molten steel into weapons.

Eiji had no words. There were enough forges below to supply every army of the entire Northern Kingdom. But this was no army village. Not if blades patrolled the outskirts.

What had they stumbled on?

Before they could decide on their course of action, horns blew from both their left and right. Below, a bell began to ring.

Both Itsuki and Chiasa looked at Eiji, as though he somehow knew the cause.

He didn't, but he suspected that somehow, they had raised an alarm.

Then he felt them. Pursuers came on them from all directions.

Nightblades.

And they were ready for a fight.

30

I sau followed Yua and Master Ryota as they left the village. The sun had already fallen below the peaks, and it wouldn't be long before the sky turned dark. Neither Yua nor Master Ryota carried torches. They climbed a narrow trail leading from their village.

In the few days he'd spent training under Master Ryota, Isau hadn't thought much about life beyond the walls of the village. So he stopped and stared when they climbed into the next valley and another village appeared. The buildings here were far more worn down than those in Master Ryota's village. They were built with lumber instead of stone, and most looked to be in serious need of repair.

The homes and streets were crowded, too. Even from a distance, the town burned brightly against his sense.

"This village also belongs to Master Ryota," Yua said. "Those who live here work deep underground."

They didn't pass through the village, but went around it. He could feel the people below staring at him, and his own gaze kept returning to the shacks. This didn't seem like a place he wanted to live, and he was more grateful than ever for all that Master Ryota had done for him.

They continued to climb until they reached an opening carved straight into the heart of the mountain. The entrance was roughly square and supported by thick wooden beams. When Isau peered in, nothing but darkness greeted his curiosity. A creeping dread seized his stomach. Before, going underground had sounded like an adventure, especially accompanied by Master Ryota and Yua.

Now he wasn't so sure.

"Why are we here?" Isau asked.

"One of the men working in the mines died late this afternoon," Master Ryota replied. "Some of the others have stopped work, so we need to speak with them."

Master Ryota found a lantern and lit it. He stepped into the cave, ducking low so he didn't strike the wooden beam wedged across the top of the entrance. Even Yua was almost too tall to walk upright.

They walked slowly, largely because Master Ryota couldn't stand straight as he walked. Isau took one last, long look behind him as they turned a corner. Then the exit disappeared from sight and the tunnel seemed to clutch him even tighter in its grip. Isau hugged his arms to his chest, though the cave wasn't any colder than the air outside.

The tunnel angled down, sometimes sharply, but often gradually. Branches led off in different directions, but Master Ryota remained in the main tunnel, always leading them deeper.

Isau imagined the weight of the mountain above them. He'd helped his father and brothers move boulders out of their fields before, and even those no larger than him took several of them working together to move. He couldn't comprehend the weight of the rock above, but he easily imagined the mountain collapsing, either crushing him beneath its weight, or worse, trapping him alive.

His breath came in short gasps.

The wooden supports didn't bolster his confidence. Everyone knew stone was far stronger than wood. What was wood doing holding up a mountain?

Yua turned back to him. "There's nothing to fear. Our people work down here every day."

He wanted to believe her, but hadn't Master Ryota just said that a man had died down here?

Regardless, he swallowed the lump of fear in his throat. He tried an exercise Master Ryota had shown him where he focused on his breath. In time, he was able to reshape his inhalations and exhalations into a longer pattern. As he did, the sensation of fear decreased.

Time lost all meaning in the tunnels, but Isau didn't think they'd been traveling for too long before they came upon a large chamber, the first space lit by lanterns. A group of gaunt men, caked with grime, sat within in silence. When Master Ryota entered, they looked up with empty eyes.

Yua stopped near the edge of the chamber and held out her hand to prevent Isau from entering as well.

He grimaced. The chamber seemed so spacious after the tight tunnels. There, he thought perhaps he could breathe freely for the first time since entering the mines.

But her aura was even colder than usual, and Isau noticed her feet were positioned in a combat stance. She was ready to draw her sword. He frowned, then took a step back so he wasn't in her way. She nodded her appreciation.

Master Ryota came down to one knee and spoke softly. "What happened?"

"It was Naoyuki, master," one of the men replied, his

voice dry and cracking. "He discovered a fresh vein, but dug too far without reinforcing the walls."

A moment of silence followed. Master Ryota hung his head, as though in grief, but Isau didn't feel it reflected in his energy. If he had to rely on his sense alone, he would have said Master Ryota was impatient, or perhaps even angry. He assumed his sense was confused, though. A man had died. Of course Master Ryota was saddened. Isau promised himself he would pay better attention during his afternoon training so he wouldn't make the same mistakes when it mattered.

"He's still down there?" the master asked.

"He is, master. There's too much stone."

"Why haven't you started to free him?"

"His spirit is angry, master. All of us feel it. It's trapped here, far from the sun."

Isau's eyes widened at that. Could it be they were too far from the surface for the man's spirit to rejoin the Great Cycle? He'd never heard such a belief, but that didn't mean it was untrue.

Just in front of him, Yua's posture shifted. Her weight settled a bit lower.

Though Isau couldn't say why, he was certain they were at a moment of crisis.

Master Ryota's voice was as calm as ever, though. "I understand. I can act as a path for his spirit to rejoin the Great Cycle. But I will need your help."

The men shared glances with one another, and the one who had been speaking kneeled before Master Ryota. "What must I do, master?"

"Nothing much," Master Ryota answered. "But you knew Naoyuki. I will work through you to release his spirit. You'll feel a bit weaker for a while, but that will be all."

The man nodded, and Master Ryota laid a hand on the miner's shoulder. Isau extended his sense, wondering what Master Ryota was about to do.

Isau didn't know anything about spirits or the Great Cycle, but he felt the transfer of power from the miner to his master. Not much, but enough he noticed it.

Then Master Ryota released his grip. "Do you feel the difference?"

The miner looked with awe upon Master Ryota. "I do, master." He pressed his forehead to the rough stone of the chamber floor. "Thank you!"

Isau frowned again, but he knew his questions would be answered later. He couldn't say for sure what had just happened, but he saw Yua's stance shift into one that was more relaxed.

Their farewells took some time, but Master Ryota left the miners with instructions to dig out the body and return to work. If necessary, they were to recruit more people to speed the process along. The miners agreed and promised it would be done. Isau thought they looked at Master Ryota as though he were a living shrine.

Neither Yua nor Master Ryota explained what had transpired as they left the tunnel. When they finally emerged from the tight tunnels, all Master Ryota uttered was two words: "Superstitious fools."

Before he could say more, a messenger ran up to them, panting heavily with sweat pouring down his face. "Master! Gifted intruders. They were sensed just outside the village of smiths."

Master Ryota's face hardened. "The students have been alerted?"

"Yes, master."

"Good. I'll return with you." Master Ryota looked at Isau,

then spoke to Yua. "Take Isau. Keep him safe. We'll surround them and tighten the noose. Intercept them, if you can."

Yua nodded.

Isau had more questions. But they didn't give him time to ask. Before he could form a single question, Yua tugged on his arm and pulled him down the mountain.

Then they were running together, toward the invaders.

Isau only wished he had a sword.

31

I tsuki didn't waste time with unnecessary questions. He didn't ask how they had been surrounded, nor did he ask how many neared their position.

Instead, he asked the one question that mattered, one Eiji dreaded. "Will you draw your sword now?"

Eiji met the monk's gaze. Itsuki knew. It was as if the monk had a window to his heart, understanding the conflict that tore at him.

Nightblades approached from every direction, and every heartbeat Eiji didn't answer was one in which the net closed tighter. But Itsuki made no move to escape, waiting for Eiji's answer.

These were blades. He didn't want to fight. There were far too few of them already.

"Us or them," Itsuki said.

Eiji swore. He was never saving a child again.

But he'd seen enough of these mysterious blades to know they unsettled him. Itsuki was at least a force he understood.

He grimaced. "I'll fight."

Itsuki nodded. "Good." He looked one last time at their surroundings. "We head north, then back west."

"Why?" Eiji asked. The quickest route to safety was straight west, the direction they'd come from.

"Because they'll expect us to head west," Chiasa answered for Itsuki. "And because he hasn't yet figured out what's happening here."

Eiji glanced between the two of them and shook his head. Had the monastery been formed entirely of partnerships like this one, the Three Kingdoms would be a very different place.

Itsuki took the lead, asking Eiji to act as their rearguard.

There wasn't any point in stealth. Like in Highgate, the chances of hiding from another gifted were slim. Instead, Itsuki aimed for a weak point in the tightening net, then ran for it.

Eiji's world became a blur of moonlit trees and gray shadows. He ran, focusing on his sense, which would warn him of danger long before his sight would.

The ring of enemies closed faster as they sensed the invaders running. Eiji couldn't be sure, but he suspected that nearly twenty enemies surrounded them.

It wasn't long before Eiji saw the blades converging on them. The battle had become a footrace. They were trying to escape the net before it closed.

And it was closing fast.

Itsuki reached a pair of defenders before the blades behind Eiji caught up. The fight was over within two heartbeats. Itsuki moved like water, his cuts somehow perfect even though he ran at his full speed. The blades in front of him parted, both clutching fatal wounds.

Chiasa launched an arrow that caught another approaching blade in the chest.

Then they were through the line.

Eiji only caught a glimpse of the blades as he ran past them. They were young.

Too young.

He frowned, but there was no time to wonder. The remaining blades had coalesced into a mob behind them, and now they wanted revenge.

Eiji focused less on his sense. He knew what he would find. He put everything into running, slipping around trees and pushing as hard as his legs could carry him. They felt heavy, as though weighted with stones. His breath came in labored gasps.

But if he stopped, they would swarm.

So he ran, finding a place inside himself he'd only discovered a few times in his training, a second burst of energy that kept him sprinting away from his pursuers.

He didn't know how long or how far he ran. Chiasa and Itsuki remained in front of him. But when he explored with his sense, he found that their pursuit had slowed.

Eiji didn't dare slow down. He feared that if he did, he would never run again.

But maybe they were safe.

The blades seemed to be breaking off.

Itsuki still led the way. He ran fast, but it was no longer the full sprint they'd needed to escape the others.

Their trail paralleled a ridge line, though they were well below the ridge itself.

Above, Eiji suddenly sensed another presence, this one as strong as the entire group that had been chasing them put together. He swore, knowing who stood on the ridge. The blade who had killed the woman in the streets of Highgate.

Itsuki also sensed him and slowed to a stop. He looked

up to the ridge, where the moonlight silhouetted a lone figure watching them.

The monk didn't even give Eiji enough time to argue. He turned to Chiasa. "Get out. I'll meet you."

Then he was gone, tearing up the ridge with the grace of a gazelle. "Itsuki!" Eiji yelled, but the monk ignored him and was soon out of sight.

"We need to go after him," he told Chiasa.

"He ordered us to leave."

"He'll die," Eiji said. But the heat had gone out of his voice, his rationality restored. What was he saying? He didn't want to run up the ridge to fight that blade. He should be thanking Itsuki for distracting the blade long enough for them to escape.

Chiasa gestured toward the west. "We head that way. You take the lead."

Eiji looked one last time up the ridge. He saw Itsuki, now halfway up and not slowing a bit. He cursed the monk, he cursed Isau, and he cursed himself. Then he turned to the west.

Until a thought crossed his mind. He glanced at Chiasa. "You're not going to shoot me in the back, are you?"

Chiasa shrugged.

He stared at her until a hint of a smile played upon her lips. "Probably not," she said.

Eiji swore again, then took off at a trot. He wanted nothing more at that moment than to find a corner at some local tavern and drink until oblivion overcame him.

The moon was falling when Eiji sensed two more blades. These were coming from even farther north, and they were moving to intercept him and Chiasa.

Eiji slowed to a stop as they came to a clearing. "There's a pair of gifted ahead of us."

Chiasa nodded, then melted back into the woods, far enough away that Eiji could barely sense her.

As the two gifted came closer, Eiji realized who they were.

Isau.

And the woman who had attacked him in the streets of Highgate.

They were walking side by side. Eiji's mouth went sour.

Isau and the woman stepped into the clearing opposite him. The woman wore no hood, and Eiji was surprised how young she was. She'd seen less than twenty cycles.

"Eiji?" Isau's eyes were wide.

"In the flesh."

"Why are *you* here?"

"I chased you."

Isau gave him a blank look. "What?"

Had the boy lost his wits? "I came here for you."

The boy still looked confused, but the young woman next to him had no such problems. She dashed forward, and Eiji saw the sword at her hip.

She didn't draw it, though.

But Eiji had learned his lessons from the previous fight well enough. He stabbed straight ahead, then ducked, anticipating her attack.

Sense, steel, and speed collided. She deflected his initial blow but wasn't fast enough to respond to the lowered shoulder that followed. The knife that had appeared so quickly in her hand cut through the space where his head had been a moment before.

Eiji slammed into her, his legs churning in an effort to unbalance her. They went down in a tangle of arms and legs, which suited him just fine.

The woman was no stranger to grappling, though.

Before he could pin her, she had twisted around, clutching an arm and wrapping herself around him. Somehow, she ended up on top of him, knife raised for a final strike.

Eiji grimaced, knowing he'd lost again. His arms were pinned.

The moment came too fast for him to even reflect on his life.

Then the woman looked up. She dove off him less than a heartbeat before an arrow split the air where she'd just been.

Eiji hadn't even sensed Chiasa's attack. His enemy's gift was stronger than his.

The woman charged Chiasa, but Eiji's ally already had another arrow pulled to her cheek. Eiji rolled to his feet and chased after the woman.

Chiasa's aim shifted slightly, then she released.

The woman clearly expected it, though. She dodged as she sensed Chiasa's intent. But Chiasa had aimed slightly to the woman's side. When the young woman dodged, as expected, it brought her close to Eiji.

Eiji grinned viciously. Chiasa was *good*.

The woman realized her mistake, twisting in mid-stride to defend against Eiji's cut. His sword caught her against the bracers and flung her to the ground. He followed, fully intending to put an end to this fight for good.

"Yua!"

The voice was young.

Isau.

Eiji looked up to see his young ward running toward the woman.

The woman scrambled to her feet, making full use of Eiji's single moment of distraction. She ran across the clearing.

"Eiji!" Chiasa yelled at him, and when he turned, he realized he was between her and Yua. He stepped out of the way, but by then, Yua had reached the safety of the other side of the clearing.

Only Isau and Eiji remained in the clearing. "Come with me, Isau," Eiji called. "We'll get you out of here."

But Isau didn't come. He stood, rooted as a tree. The boy turned his head to where Yua had crashed into the trees, then looked back at Eiji.

Eiji took a step forward, but Isau looked like prey, ready to startle if he took another step. He stopped and held out his hand.

For a long moment, the world held still.

Then Isau shook his head and ran after Yua.

Eiji flinched, as though he'd been slapped. He stared at the gap in the trees Isau had disappeared into, imagining him coming back, grinning, saying that it had all been a joke.

But he sensed the boy running away.

Chiasa came up behind him and laid her hand gently on his arm. "We need to go."

Eiji continued staring at the woods.

Then he turned his back on the fleeing pair and ran.

32

Isau sat in a corner and hugged his knees tightly to his chest. He'd never experienced Master Ryota's anger before, and it was among the most terrifying experiences he'd ever lived through.

Back home, his father had often lost his temper, his ferocity whispered about behind his back through the surrounding area. He shouted, screamed, and beat them with his fists. Those times had scared Isau, too, but he'd found ways to cope. He knew to avoid his father when his breath reeked of ale, knew all the places where his father wouldn't find him. And if that failed, he knew that if he could endure the blows they wouldn't last long. His father's temper was like lightning. It built over time, erupted in one spectacular flash, then vanished, leaving destruction in its wake.

All of which was unlike Master Ryota.

There was no hiding from this. Master Ryota's energy burned brighter than the sun, blinding in its intensity.

His master didn't shout, but there was no need. Every

gifted person in the village knew. Isau wasn't certain he could move his limbs even if he wanted.

Even Yua appeared uneasy. She paced the other side of the room, waiting for their audience. He didn't know how she stood against the onslaught.

Master Ryota wasn't even that near. He remained among the dead.

That, too, seemed unreal. Some of the students he'd been training with just that morning were dead. Isau had seen the bodies. But he felt nothing.

They'd been killed by Itsuki.

Despite their loss, Isau couldn't focus on his friends. He should be grieving, but another memory consumed him.

Eiji, reaching out his hand.

Eiji had come back for him.

The nightblade who had wanted nothing more than to be rid of him had returned. He'd crossed who knew how many leagues, just for Isau.

Isau didn't understand.

Eiji didn't want him.

Eiji had traveled into danger to rescue him.

The two facts clashed in his mind, warriors matched in skill, battling an eternal struggle. For a moment, one would gain the upper hand, but as soon as the advantage was won, the other fact would undercut it.

Both couldn't be true. But both were.

Master Ryota's aura moved. Eiji sensed it approaching, crushing his thoughts until all that remained was the master's presence.

When Master Ryota slid open the door separating this room from the hallway, Isau almost cried. It was too much. His master took one look at him, and with a deep breath, controlled the massive strength flowing from him.

He turned first to Yua. "What happened?"

"We intercepted them. Eiji and a female archer I've never met."

"Working in tandem?"

Yua nodded. "An interesting strategy, and effective. Alone, either would be easy to beat, but they protected one another well. Victory was uncertain."

For a long moment, Master Ryota didn't respond. His aura was more subdued, but the anger remained, a fire burning brightly underground. When he finally spoke, his voice was softer than Isau expected. "In the future, Yua, I hope you will stand your ground with more certainty, but your decision today was correct. I underestimated our foes."

"The monk?" Yua asked.

Master Ryota's aura flared for a moment, then faded again. "We fought. His skill was–uncommon–for a monk. But when I broke his sword, he fled. I pursued, but he jumped from the ridge."

Yua's eyes went wide. "That fall..."

"Is far, yes. But I sensed him as the current swept him downstream. For the moment, he lives, although I ordered several students to pursue." Master Ryota turned his attention for the first time to Isau. "And him?"

"They came for him. He chose to remain," Yua said.

Master Ryota crossed the room in three strides. He squatted down next to Isau. "Why?"

Isau couldn't think. He tried, but all he could do was stare at Master Ryota, his mind as barren as the walls of the room. "I don't know."

Isau glanced over at Yua. He didn't want to disappoint her, but he didn't know the answer. It had been what he wanted, but he couldn't say why.

Master Ryota missed nothing. He saw Isau's eyes

wander to Yua, and he nodded, as though Isau had answered the question well. He stood up, and Isau welcomed even the slight lessening of the man's attention.

"I see," Master Ryota said.

"What are your orders?" Yua asked.

"Even if they were here for Isau," Master Ryota answered, "they know more than can be allowed. I suspect they'll slip through Tomiichi's units without problem, which means we need to advance our plans."

"It's soon," Yua said.

Master Ryota nodded. "Too soon, but I see little choice. If Lady Mari brings her forces to bear against us, we won't survive. We must act before they do."

"What would you have of me?" Yua asked.

"Visit Chiyo. Tell her it's time."

Yua's eyes glowed, and she leaned forward. "It's now?"

Master Ryota nodded again. "It is."

Yua kneeled and bowed. "I'm honored, master."

"Thank you. I will let the others know in the morning. If tonight has demonstrated anything, it is that we still require more preparation. I shall use the time of your travel to ensure no weakness remains."

Master Ryota paused, then once again turned to Isau. "Take him, too. I believe he will flourish under your personal tutelage. And if the monk and Eiji are after him, perhaps it will distract them."

"A slim hope."

"Perhaps, but there is nothing lost by having him travel with you."

"How much should I teach him?"

"Everything, if he is ready."

"Everything?" Yua sounded uncertain.

"There's no time, and little to lose. Use your best judgment."

Yua bowed again. "I look forward to our next meeting, master."

"As do I, Yua. Don't fail in this. We depend on Chiyo more than I'd like, especially now."

Master Ryota looked to Isau once more. "I believe in you. You'll travel with Yua on a very important task, and she will continue your training. When we meet next, I expect you to be nearly as strong as me."

Isau nodded. He wouldn't do anything to disappoint Master Ryota.

Then the master was gone, his aura receding, finally allowing Isau to think again. His thoughts, such as they were, were simple. He was entrusted with a very important task, and he'd spend his days with Yua. He was pleased with both.

"Come," Yua said. "We must rest. Tomorrow we will prepare and leave."

"Who is Chiyo?" Isau asked.

Yua smiled, but there was no warmth in it. "The world's greatest assassin."

33

C hiasa pulled Eiji down.

There, at the limits of their sight, a patrol of guards walked through the trees. Unlike most units, this one carried no torches. Had Chiasa not been alert, Eiji might have walked straight into them.

"Focus," Chiasa growled.

Eiji tried, but his mind was a raging river, powerful and turbulent, carrying him wherever it pleased. He tried focusing on his breath, but even that technique failed.

Isau had left him.

After all this pursuit, the boy had simply turned around and left. The ungrateful brat.

He and the archer lay concealed by the forest's undergrowth. Now that they'd stopped running, he finally had the chance to think.

And he wished he didn't.

Isau's betrayal hurt.

It did worse than hurt.

It tore into his heart, revealing a latent darkness residing there.

Time and time again, he had tried to help.

He once thought he could return the blades to the Three Kingdoms, to set right the wrongs of his ancestors. That had ended in blood. He'd thought to save the boy from the monks, which had required him to kill once again. And now he'd chased the boy halfway across a kingdom, only to reveal Isau as a traitor.

Never again.

Let the world burn, for all he cared. He'd lost his family and friends, but he still had his strength. That would be enough to build a new life here in the Three Kingdoms.

Yes, he was done with trying to change the world.

With that realization, his focus returned, as cold and sharp as the sword he carried.

The guards continued on, passing less than fifty paces away, never realizing how close they came to their ends.

Because he would kill, now. Without hesitation. He knew it.

Chiasa whispered to him after the guards vanished into darkness. "This will be a lot easier if I know I can count on you. Can I?"

He met her eyes. "Yes."

She saw beyond his words and nodded. Without comment, she returned to her feet and gestured for him to lead the way.

The sky had just started to show the first light of morning when they were certain they were out of Tomiichi's lands.

Chiasa found a small grove of trees in which they could rest. It was far enough out of Tomiichi's lands they didn't need to worry about pursuit, but still afforded them a view of the road, some ways away. She unstrung her bow and began studying her arrows.

"What happens next?" Eiji asked.

"Itsuki and I have established places where we can meet. We'll head to the nearest one and wait."

"That's it?"

She shrugged. "He makes the decisions. I'm just support."

"What about me?"

"Not sure." She paused and smiled, giving the arrow she was holding a meaningful look. "I have some ideas, though."

Eiji grunted. "Seems rude."

Chiasa shrugged again.

"You could just let me return to the ship."

Chiasa found a nice position to lie down in and she closed her eyes. Eiji noted she kept her hand close to a dagger. "You're not going back to the ship. You never meant to."

Eiji's mouth moved, but no words came out. How did she know that?

Chiasa smiled, her eyes still closed. "Itsuki knows, too."

"Then why haven't you killed me?"

She shrugged a third time. "I think he likes you. Clouds his judgment."

"And you?"

"I'm just waiting for you to fall asleep."

Eiji shook his head. He'd never met a woman like Chiasa before, mostly because he was fairly certain others like her didn't exist.

Then she was asleep, as though she didn't have a care in the world, as though she didn't possess even an iota of fear about sleeping next to a nightblade she'd just threatened to kill.

Eiji shook his head. Probably because she didn't.

As the sun came up and warmed Eiji, it melted his

resolve to remain awake. He was exhausted, both from the mental and physical strain of the evening. He was fairly certain Chiasa jested, but it was hard to tell. He supposed there were worse ways to die.

His fight against exhaustion couldn't be won, though.

Eiji laid his head down, and a few moments later, he also slept.

HE WOKE to Chiasa shaking him. He came alert instantly, cursing himself for surrendering so easily to sleep. The fact he still drew breath surprised him.

He followed her finger.

The carriage, the same one they'd tracked for countless leagues, was leaving. Eiji glanced up at the sun. It was past midday, but not by much.

"Can you sense it?"

Eiji closed his eyes. At this distance, it seemed unlikely, but if the one blade was within, perhaps he would sense them.

He received nothing, though. He opened his eyes and shook his head.

Chiasa swore but took no action as the carriage passed in front of them. As much as she might desire to know who was inside, there was no way to find out. They were still on foot and the carriage was making good time.

"New plan," Chiasa decided. "We follow that carriage."

Eiji groaned. "No."

She raised an eyebrow.

"I don't want to. We chased that contraption all the way here, trying to find Isau. We found him, and he made his desires clear. I'm done."

He'd half-expected Chiasa to get angry at him, but

instead she watched him with those eyes that missed so little. Then she smiled again, and a shiver passed through him. "You can come with me, or I actually will kill you in your sleep. I've done it before, to other blades. I can't let you go free."

He didn't doubt her.

But even though a part of him was frightened by her, another found her company inexpressibly exciting. Fighting her was an option, but he found he didn't want that.

He sighed. "Fine."

Her smile widened. "And you can lead the way. I don't trust you behind me."

Eiji groaned but stood up.

"Now get moving," Chiasa commanded. "That village was working hard enough to forge steel for an entire army, and I'm certain Lady Mari has no idea. So we need to find out what's happening before it comes to pass."

34

The carriage was, in Isau's opinion, as close to paradise as he could come. While he had fond memories of his journey to Master Ryota's village, they quickly paled in comparison to the new ones made as they traveled to visit Chiyo.

Before, Yua had been his escort.

Now he was a student of Master Ryota.

Now they trained.

Yua, like all of Master Ryota's senior students, demanded nothing less than perfection. Unlike the others, she didn't yell or berate him when he erred. She didn't need to. One look from her was all that was needed for Isau to redouble his efforts.

She also allowed him to be more casual than training in the square allowed. In that place, Isau had always felt a tension, an unspoken command that he abide by the formal behaviors of a training hall. When it was just him and Yua, she encouraged him to display both his frustration at his failures and his pride at success. So long as his effort didn't wane, she didn't mind.

Isau found he progressed more rapidly under Yua's careful eye than he had in Master Ryota's village. At first, he believed it was because Yua was a better teacher, but when he said as much, she disagreed.

"Any student would progress faster under individual instruction," she said. "And they would progress fastest of all if they could train directly under Master Ryota. But I appreciate your kindness."

And then she smiled, and all was right with the world.

He paid less attention to their surroundings than he had on the way into the village. Mostly, he wasn't interested. Yua and training dominated his thoughts.

Still, he knew they were moving quickly. They didn't have a relay system of fresh horses set up for this trip, but they still covered impressive distances every day. For a child who had never wandered much more than a league from his home, Isau couldn't believe how expansive the Three Kingdoms was.

At night they slept in the carriage, making themselves as comfortable as they could in the cramped space. Some part of Isau wished for a full bed, but he reminded himself it was still more comfortable than sleeping out in the open as he often had with Eiji.

He still thought of the nightblade on occasion. But his thoughts lacked the vigor of that night when they'd met in the clearing.

He didn't understand Eiji. The fundamental conflict remained: Eiji hadn't wanted him yet had come back for him. Trying to reason out why only confused Isau, so in time, he'd stopped worrying. He'd learned to be content without answers.

Yua only ordered the carriage to stop at larger villages, where she would quickly procure more supplies and then return them to the road. They never slept anywhere near a village, opting instead to pull far off the road as evening came.

Though Yua never explained her behavior, she didn't need to. Isau understood that they were minimizing the chances of running into monks. It was little different than what Eiji had done as they traveled to Highgate.

They didn't run into any trouble until the third day. The carriage slowed to a stop and their driver called out. "Smoke ahead."

Both Yua and Isau stepped out of the carriage, Isau grateful for the opportunity to stretch his legs.

A plume of dark smoke billowed up ahead, rising into the cloudy sky. The smoke made the clouds appear even more ominous. There would be rain soon.

The source of the fire was hidden behind a rise, so they climbed back in and rode for a brief period until a small village came into view. Though the village was still distant, they could see the source of the inferno was a small home on the outskirts of town. It had already collapsed.

Isau focused on the villagers he could see. None of them, so far as he could tell, were doing anything to stop the fire. They watched, as still as trees.

One problem with the carriage, Isau decided, was that it wasn't able to leave roads as easily as someone walking on foot or traveling by horseback. Yua looked at the fire and the crowd, then nodded to the driver. "Take us through."

They climbed back into the carriage, but they hadn't even reached the village when Yua called for a stop. "Do you sense that?" she asked.

He closed his eyes and focused on his sense, but it was nowhere near as developed as hers was. He shook his head.

"Monks," she said.

Isau's heart pounded faster in his chest. If true, he knew why the house was burning. He'd heard plenty of stories, but he had also been a part of one. Memories of being pursued, caught, and beaten flashed across the back of his eyelids, vivid and intense as if they had just happened yesterday. "We should go around," he said.

He felt her hands grab his. He opened his eyes and stared into hers.

"No," she said. "We don't leave any gifted to the mercy of the monks."

With that, she stepped out of the carriage. Isau noticed she left her sword behind. It didn't concern him. She always carried several daggers. Even he had two. One had been the gift from Eiji, the other given by Yua on the eve of their journey.

"Remember," Yua said, "most monks aren't trained very well. They don't sense as well as we do, and their martial skills aren't as developed as most believe. You're strong now, and I'm behind you. You have nothing to fear."

He wished he could more easily believe her words. But his palms still sweated, and he had to wipe them off on his pants over and over.

Isau felt the heat coming off the burning building, even though they stood over two dozen paces away from it. A few villagers still watched the flame, but most had gathered in the village square. Isau couldn't sense them yet, but he saw the two white-robed warriors standing in the heart of the commotion.

As they neared, Isau heard the cries of the small crowd, the delight they took whenever the monks struck whoever had lived in the burning house.

He froze. Those sounds were still too familiar. He'd heard them himself, back when they had discovered him. It was the sounds of friends and family applauding the pain and suffering he'd endured. It was the sound of an entire village laying the blame for every misfortune on the shoulders of the gifted.

He wanted to run. He wanted to put as much distance between himself and this unfolding tragedy as possible.

But Yua stood at his back, preventing escape. He couldn't run, not with her watching.

Isau turned to her. "What should we do?"

Her aura chilled him, and she shook her head. "The question is, what will you do? Once you get closer the monks will sense you. But they are hurting a gifted, the same as you were hurt. You've told me you want to protect our kind. So, what will you do?"

Isau knew what answer she wanted.

But he wasn't sure he could.

Yua stood there, waiting for him. She wouldn't move until he did.

Another harsh cheer rose from the crowd behind him. It snapped something inside him.

Isau growled, turned on his heel, and drew his dagger.

They were all going to pay.

35

Eiji and Chiasa collected their horses from the farmer they'd left them with, then resumed the pursuit. Chiasa left a note for Itsuki at the first village they passed. She gave Eiji no chance to read it.

Eiji considered the act pointless. If Itsuki was still alive, which seemed unlikely, there wasn't any good way of leaving a trail for him to follow. Not when Chiasa didn't know their ultimate destination.

But he said nothing. The partnership between the monk and the archer had already surprised him more times than he could count. Perhaps they had some way of communicating over long distances, too. He wouldn't put it past them.

As before, Chiasa inquired after the carriage in the village, and they followed. It sounded like they were almost a full day behind, with the carriage heading west.

Chiasa acted as though nothing was wrong, but Eiji saw through her facade easily enough. She kept glancing back toward Tomiichi's lands, as though she expected Itsuki to gallop up behind them at any moment.

He didn't have the heart to remind her just how strong of an opponent Itsuki had chosen to fight.

If he had cared more, the mystery of that opponent's identity would have tormented him. Though Eiji had only heard legends of Koji's strength, he imagined it had to feel something like that man on the ridge. But Eiji was certain that wasn't Koji.

Koji would be old by now. Still dangerous, but he had seen at least sixty cycles. And everything Eiji had learned in his pursuit told him that Koji was a wanderer. Not a man who surrounded himself with forges and protective nobles.

When he caught himself considering possibilities, he shook his head.

None of this was his problem anymore.

All he had to do was worry about himself.

He brought his horse beside Chiasa's. She cast him a sidelong look.

"How did you come to Lady Mari's attention in the first place?" he asked.

When Chiasa glared, Eiji's horse shied away.

Eiji was just about to give up when Chiasa answered. "I didn't come to her attention. I applied to be a member of her guard. But while my archery was superb, I never acquired the skill with the sword necessary to defend her. But she didn't want to waste my talents, so here I am."

As far as stories went, it wasn't much of one. Eiji knew there was more she wasn't sharing, but it was easier to catch a fly in hand than get details from Chiasa.

"Why did you apply to be a guard? That doesn't seem like a usual choice for a woman in the Northern Kingdom."

Eiji wasn't sure she would answer, but fate never gave her a chance. In the distance, Eiji felt a presence. He cursed.

"What?" Chiasa asked.

"A nightblade on the road."

Her bow was in hand within a heartbeat. "How far?"

Eiji closed his eyes. "Two hundred paces, maybe. And approaching."

Eiji pointed in the direction of the blade. At the moment, they rode through open grassland, and the blade must have been concealed by tall grass.

Chiasa slid off her horse and handed the reins to Eiji. "Distract them."

Then she was gone, hiding in the grasses herself. Eiji tracked her presence for a while, but she soon disappeared with distance. Even though he couldn't sense Chiasa, he felt more comfortable just knowing she was around.

He wasn't sure he'd ever felt the same about anyone else.

Eventually, the nightblade emerged from the grass ahead. Eiji squinted, surprised to see who it was.

Her name was Kaiya, and like Kosuke, she was from the island. From the glare she aimed at him, he suspected she held no love for him.

She stopped about two dozen paces away.

Wind swirled on the road, kicking up a pile of dust in a small cyclone that quickly faded.

"Eiji."

"Kaiya."

"It's been a while."

"It has."

Eiji contemplated running. He was on horseback and Kaiya on foot. If not for the fact he'd be leaving Chiasa behind, he would have. He had no desire to fight with those he'd grown up with.

But Kaiya's presence deep in the Northern Kingdom didn't bode well for him. Still, this might be the only chance he had to explain himself. A slim chance, but better than nothing.

"I didn't kill Harumi."

Kaiya didn't react, and that was when Eiji knew just how much trouble he was in.

"I have no quarrel with you, Kaiya."

She drew her sword. "Where is the woman you rode with?"

"Probably behind you, with an arrow aimed at your back if you attempt to cut me down."

Kaiya shook her head. "Your lies won't save you."

Back when Eiji had lived on the island, the ships had been crewed by nearly a dozen blades. Given the timing, the only way Kaiya could be here was if she had been on the same ship as Harumi.

Which meant Kosuke himself had given the order to kill Eiji.

Kaiya stepped forward. "Let's finish this."

He wasn't sure how he'd been found, but it wasn't Kaiya that worried him at the moment.

Blades would never travel through the Three Kingdoms alone.

There was at least one more blade out here.

And he couldn't sense them.

36

Isau's world sharpened as he stepped into the crowd. His sense illuminated the near future, capturing the intent of every person gathered to cheer on the atrocity before them. He slipped between the shifting bodies, his sense identifying gaps a heartbeat before they existed.

Behind him, a man reeking of ale swung a meaty fist at his head. There was no rational reason. The man was angry and Isau was a target who wouldn't fight back.

Isau sensed the blow, though. Compared to the strikes he'd been learning to evade the past fortnight, this was slow and clumsy. He tilted his head to the side and the fist breezed past his ear. The drunk man stumbled forward into a man even larger, setting off a confrontation.

Isau didn't care. Most of his attention remained fixed on the energies of the two monks ahead of him. A third aura, slightly stronger than most, was the child the monks had come to collect.

When no gap opened in the last line of onlookers, Isau made one, lowering his shoulder and pushing through. His sense of the crowd faded as he focused entirely on the scene before him.

The monks should have sensed him by now, but he didn't think they had.

Isau stepped boldly into the gap between onlookers and participants, and everyone became aware of him. He felt their attention shifting from the monks to him.

They saw nothing but a child, but he would show them. The gifted would no longer be hunted and hurt by their own families and neighbors.

He quickly deciphered the scene before him. Two monks stood over the curled-up body of a man. Each carried a staff. The man on the ground looked to have seen twenty-some cycles, and the cause for his suffering stood behind him, frozen in fear.

A young girl, no more than four or five. Her energy was the stronger one he had sensed a moment ago.

The man stretched out an arm to grab one monk's ankle. He croaked something but sounds no longer reached Isau's ears. His world was too rich in sights and intents.

The monks ignored the father's pitiful attempts at restraining them, instead looking up in unison as Isau broke from the crowd, their eyes wide. They both turned toward him, but to Isau, their movements seemed slow.

The nearest monk was a woman, younger than the father lying helpless on the ground. She brought her staff up and thrust one tip at his face.

As with the drunk man before, Isau sensed the attack. He knew the line of her strike, and knew that if he moved his head to the side, she would respond by snapping the staff's tip across his face.

Isau didn't think. Instinct and training took over, a knowledge inscribed deep within his body. He shifted his head to the side, and as he expected, the monk turned her thrust into a swing, hoping to catch him in the side of his head. But he was already ducking, still moving forward, breaking inside her pathetic excuse for a guard.

Dagger in hand, he stabbed at the monk. The weapon slid into her stomach with ease.

The monk stopped moving, and Isau didn't understand why. His cut was fatal, but it wasn't immediately so. He pulled his dagger out and spent a moment fascinated by the blood dripping down the edge.

Isau stabbed again, then once more. The monk's defense had completely broken, and stabbing into her didn't seem any different to him than stabbing into the dummies filled with hay Master Ryota made them practice with.

The monk fell. She wouldn't get up again.

He felt weightless, as though he could leap into the sky and never return. Never again would he have to share space with those who cowered in fear.

That was one monk who would never terrorize anyone, ever again.

The second monk was older than the first. When his first efforts to escape from the father's grip on his ankle proved unsuccessful, he jabbed at the man's forearm with his staff until the grip loosened.

The second monk's movements looked as slow as the first's.

This was what he had feared for so long?

These monks were weak.

Still, the second monk had learned from the failure of his partner. He knew his return to the Great Cycle loomed, so he fought cautiously. He extended his staff almost like a sword, keeping the length of the weapon between him and Isau.

The monk gave up ground willingly, preventing Isau from easily closing.

But the monk never noticed Yua, who appeared behind him. Isau couldn't see the fatal blow, but he sensed it well enough. Yua stabbed a dagger between his ribs, cutting open the monk's heart with practiced ease.

A complicated exchange happened then. The monk didn't die the way the first one had. Yua had her free hand on the back of the monk's neck, and energy passed between them. But when it was over, the monk was dead, and Yua's aura felt more powerful than before.

Questions sprang to life, but Isau knew that this was neither the time nor the place. His momentum had carried him past the father and gifted daughter, so he turned back to them and the crowd.

As he did, the crowd scattered, some screaming as they rushed to their homes.

As though mere walls could protect them.

The daughter had broken through the fear that held her in place and now knelt next to her father. Tears fell down her face.

When Isau took a step toward her, she cowered, shrinking into a small ball, holding onto her father's hand as though it were an anchor.

Isau stopped, confused. He and Yua had freed the family. But the girl feared him just as much as she had the other monks. "We came to help," he said.

The girl wiped her eyes on her sleeve, then stared daggers at him. "Get away!"

The vehemence in her voice knocked him back a step.

He felt Yua's cold presence behind him, and he found comfort in it. Her hand rested on his shoulder. "The girl is of no use to us. Her gift isn't sufficient."

"Get away!" the girl screamed again. "Get away!"

Not sure what else to do, Isau obeyed. His whole body felt numb, but his legs still propelled him forward. He walked past the girl and her father, taking some satisfaction at the sight of the girl scrambling away from him.

Then he and Yua left the village behind, the only evidence of their passing the bodies of the two monks in the village square and the blood that dripped from the tip of Isau's dagger.

37

The silence of wild grasslands had always held a special place in Eiji's heart.

Growing up on the island, the sounds of the ocean had always been nearby. It wasn't until his exile in the Three Kingdoms that he experienced the quiet of wide open spaces.

There were types of silence. One could be found underground, and yet another in the heart of a dark wood. But the grasslands were a paradox. The silence felt expansive, as though he would never hear another sound again. And yet it held him close and comforted him.

Until today.

Kaiya wouldn't be alone. But he couldn't hear or sense her ally. Chiasa, too, had been swallowed by the tall grass that surrounded the road.

He should run. He could turn the horse around and ride off.

But neither Kaiya nor the others would abandon their pursuit. If Kosuke had marked him for death, it would never end.

Kill or be killed.

All too often with the nightblades, those were the only options that remained.

Besides, he was done running. He was tired of living in fear. The monks were bad enough, but they were usually easy to avoid. He didn't think he could so easily evade the blades he'd grown up with. Their desire for vengeance was too strong.

He dismounted and strode forward, ready to fight.

The temptation during battle was to allow his sense to focus on one object. The reaction was natural, but it made one vulnerable. Kaiya was the distraction. He was supposed to focus on her. The real attack would come from another direction, after they were engaged.

He hoped Chiasa would protect him, but he couldn't predict what she might do.

Kaiya waited for him, sword ready.

"I don't want to fight." The words sounded weak, even to his ears. But it was worth trying once more, at least.

She made no response.

Before either of them could make the first move, a scream erupted to Eiji's right. It was the sound of a young man who had just been injured.

Eiji hid a smile. He didn't know how Chiasa managed to surprise a nightblade, but it sounded like she had.

Now Eiji knew where the other nightblade was, and he knew Chiasa was supporting him. That was more than enough.

He leaped forward, drawing his sword as he charged at Kaiya.

His attack caught her off guard. She'd underestimated Chiasa, and her plan had fallen apart before it even began.

Still, she reacted in time, scrambling out of the way as she deflected his powerful cut.

Eiji's momentum carried him past her, but he slid to a stop and reversed direction.

Kaiya fought for balance, stumbling back as she dodged and deflected his cuts.

Eiji maintained the pressure. He had little confidence in his abilities against the blades who had continued their training on the island, and his only answer was to keep attacking, to never give Kaiya a moment to regain her balance and counterattack.

Off in the grass, another scream died with violent suddenness. It left no room for interpretation.

Some part of Eiji felt a twinge of sorrow. The one message he'd been fed almost every day growing up had been that there weren't enough blades left in the world. Extinction was a real concern. As children, they'd been taught that no matter what else might occur, they were to always remain allies with one another. So long as the blades were unified, nothing could stop them.

As an adult, he knew that for the lie and wishful thinking it was. But it was still very much a part of his beliefs. He wanted the blades to be whole.

They never should have drawn their steel against him.

The death of her partner startled Kaiya. She left herself open, and Eiji kicked straight forward, his heel catching her in the chest and knocking her off her feet.

Eiji didn't pause. He followed, stomping on her arm hard enough to make her release the sword.

He held his sword to her chest then, causing her to cease her struggle.

Kaiya glared at him.

"I told you," Eiji said. "I don't want to fight. I didn't kill

Harumi, and all I want is to be left alone. Tell that to Kosuke. None of you will ever see me again, and no one else needs to die."

She didn't respond.

"Will you tell him?"

For a few moments, he thought she might actually choose death. Finally, she nodded.

Eiji stepped back and sheathed his sword. He put enough distance between them that he didn't need to worry about her surprising him with another attack.

Kaiya didn't look like she believed him, but frankly, Eiji didn't care. They still had the horses and could ride away. Hopefully, the fact he hadn't killed her would lend his claim some credence among the other blades. It was the best he could hope for, at least.

Kaiya rolled over and grabbed her sword, then came to her feet, still wary. For a moment, Eiji worried that she might try attacking again.

Then she sheathed her sword.

"I'll pass along your message," she said. "But I do not think he will listen."

Then her eyes went wide.

As did Eiji's.

An arrow had punched its way through her body, the arrowhead emerging from her chest. Kaiya looked up at him, betrayal written across her face. Her lips moved, but only a trickle of blood came out. Then she fell forward, the life gone from her body.

Well behind them, Chiasa already had another arrow fitted to her bowstring, as though she expected she might need to use it on Eiji.

For a long moment, he felt nothing.

Then he stormed toward Chiasa, finding new combinations of curses never before uttered in the Three Kingdoms.

Chiasa weathered the storm impassively. When Eiji got within twenty paces she suddenly brought her bow up and pulled the string back.

Eiji stopped in his tracks. At this distance, he wasn't quite sure he could dodge as soon as he sensed her intent.

"She was a nightblade in the Three Kingdoms, an offense punishable by death," Chiasa said, her voice emotionless.

Eiji clenched his fists, wanting to argue all the reasons Chiasa was a fool, but knowing nothing he said would make a difference. Chiasa was like the arrows she favored. Once launched, she flew straight until she killed her target.

"Your pacifism will get you nowhere," Chiasa continued. "Now, are you with me, or not?"

Eiji well knew the consequences to his choice, but he was still tempted to say no, just to test her.

But he didn't think her arrow would miss.

"I'm still with you," he said.

She lowered the bow. "Good. Then let's find that carriage before they can unleash more mayhem."

38

After a league of trying, Yua finally declared that further training was foolish.

Isau's desire was as strong as ever, but his focus kept slipping like a fish through his grasp.

When he closed his eyes, he saw his knife sliding into the monk. When he opened them, he heard the sound of the girl screaming at him to get away. Neither would be banished, no matter how disappointed Yua became.

He'd expected her to push him, to demand the same effort he'd given throughout the past few days. But after a number of failed attempts, she allowed him space. They rode for half the day in awkward silence.

Isau chose to keep his eyes closed. Remembering the fight with the monk disturbed him less than the girl's screams.

He hadn't thought taking life would be so easy. After all of Eiji's warnings, Isau had expected more. But the monk had been hurting the girl's father. Whether the girl recognized it or not, Isau had saved her.

In time, the power his memories had over him faded.

He wanted to succeed at Yua's training, but at times he wasn't sure he was capable. When the others described how the sense felt for them, Isau wondered if he was somehow broken. He understood their descriptions, but none seemed to match his own experience. What if he couldn't do what Yua asked of him?

The worry ate at him, gradually overcoming his most recent memories.

Tentatively, he opened his eyes once again, pleased that he had silenced the echoes of the girl's screams. "I'm ready to train now."

Yua nodded and leaned forward, so that her face was close to his. "How did you feel when you killed the monk?"

Isau bit his lower lip. He knew the true answer, but worried how Yua might respond. Her question, like one of Master Ryota's, was a test. He didn't know the right answer, though, so he was left only with truth. "I didn't really feel anything."

Yua smiled widely at that, brightening Isau's entire day. "Then perhaps you are ready for your next challenge. Tell me, do you know the difference between nightblades and dayblades?"

Of course he did. "Nightblades are warriors. Dayblades are healers."

"But do you really know the difference between them? Do you know why some become nightblades and others dayblades?"

Isau didn't.

"All gifts come from the Great Cycle," Yua said, "but they manifest in different ways. A nightblade's gift is less refined than a dayblade's, but it extends farther and better captures the energy of an individual. That makes it useful for a warrior to master. In contrast, dayblades can sense subtle patterns invisible to most nightblades. But their sensitivity limits the range of their gift and is more harm than help in combat."

She paused, studying him to see if he understood.

"Master Ryota's secret techniques are based in the combination of the two sets of skills," Yua said. "That is why few have been able to learn them. But you have promise."

Isau's heart beat faster at that. "What do I need to do?"

"First, you must learn how to heal," Yua said.

Isau cast his eyes down. "Really?"

Yua nodded, then drew out one of her daggers. She held it to Isau's palm, and he didn't flinch away. She drew it quickly across, leaving the smallest of cuts.

Isau grimaced but left his hand in place.

She put her hand over his. It was cool and strong, like steel. Then she closed her eyes and Isau felt the healing begin. His palm tingled, then stung as though he was being cut all over again. The sensation passed quickly, and when he looked down, the cut she'd just inflicted on him was gone.

Had it not happened to him, he wasn't sure he would have believed it.

Yua leaned back. She closed her eyes for a moment, then answered his unspoken question. "I'm fine. But even simple healing takes extraordinary effort."

While Yua recovered, Isau stared at his hand. He'd heard legends about dayblades, but they'd never seemed as real to him as those of the nightblades. Their gifts were no less incredible, though.

Yua opened her eyes, then removed the bracer from her

left arm. She bared the top of her forearm and extended it to him. "It's easier when you learn from someone else's energy. Most dayblades can't sense their internal energies. Put your hand on my arm."

Isau only hesitated for a moment. He'd never been this close to Yua. He obeyed.

"Now," she instructed, "sense the energy flowing through my arm. It will be hard, but I want you to keep trying. Focus like you've never focused before. I've felt the nature of your gift, and I believe you can do this."

He closed his eyes, pleased that the image of the monk had faded. He brought his attention to his gift. As expected, Yua's aura overwhelmed everything else. He was certain it had gotten more powerful since the village.

"Don't focus on my aura," Yua commanded. "Dive deeper. Focus only on me, on my arm."

She was right. Pushing past her aura was difficult. But this was Yua, and she had invited him closer. He focused, imagining himself diving into her aura. In many ways, it felt the same as when he quested long distances for the feeling of another. Except somehow, this seemed easier, more natural.

The carriage rumbled along, and still he felt nothing but her aura.

With anyone else, he would have given up.

But he persisted.

There were moments when he thought he almost had it, when he sensed details he never had before. But when he reached for them, they disappeared.

"Relax," Yua said.

He tried. The next time he felt details beginning to resolve, he didn't chase after them. Isau took a deep breath, and then there they were. He sensed Yua in a manner he never had before. He felt the beat of her heart, the flow of energy to and from her core.

"Well done," she said.

Then he felt a wrongness appear, a shifting of energy that didn't belong.

"Can you heal me?" she asked.

Isau knew, instinctively, what must be done. The energy needed to flow the same way it once had. If he could simply manipulate the flow of that energy, he would heal Yua.

But when he tried to nudge the energy onto a correct path, he found that he couldn't. A wave of exhaustion passed over him, as though he had run for days without stopping. He tried one more time, but it was no use. He might as easily have moved a mountain. Though he didn't want to, he let go of Yua and slumped back in his cushions.

He opened his eyes and saw her arm. She'd done nothing more than prick her skin, but it had felt like so much more. He hadn't even been able to heal that.

"Rest now," Yua said. "Though it may not seem like it, you did more than I've ever seen a student do on their first attempt. That you still had the energy to try to heal is remarkable."

At first, Isau didn't understand what she meant. But then he looked outside and saw that the sun was falling. He thought he'd only been trying to heal her for a little bit, but that was a lie.

Yua didn't need to tell him twice. Isau let his body relax and less than a heartbeat later he was asleep.

He woke the next morning to the carriage jolting to a stop. He blinked, surprised at how lethargic he felt. In front of him sat a full breakfast, prepared by Yua.

"Eat up," she said. "This is as far as the carriage can take us. From here we walk."

"To where?"

"To our destination," Yua said. "Chiyo's village of assassins."

39

Chiasa was a wolf hunting her prey. They rode at a steady but demanding pace, but her questions kept them close behind their quarry. She spoke to all they passed, and from the answers they received, Eiji knew they gained on their enemies.

For all her friendliness to others, little was left for Eiji. When her gaze passed over him, he shivered. He couldn't help but remember the arrow through Kaiya's heart.

The two hadn't been friends. But he'd known Kaiya, and he'd let her go. He'd given his word.

Chiasa had made him a liar. She'd known his intent, and she still shot Kaiya in the back.

His cold silences didn't bother Chiasa. She continued forward with a singular purpose. Eiji didn't know why she didn't kill him.

When they rode, she usually remained behind him, ready to strike. When they rested each night, he feared he wouldn't wake in the morning. Every sunrise was a surprise.

He considered killing her. Though she was wary, no one could remain on guard day and night. Opportunities presented themselves, but he never took them, no matter how often he imagined the outcome.

Eiji spent their long silences planning. Chiasa pulled him deeper into her world, but he had no desire to live there. There would be a chance to escape, a chance to live free. He just had to wait for the right moment.

Then they encountered the village. It was one of the larger ones they'd passed, but from a distance it appeared deserted. Thin wisps of smoke rose from a home near the edge of the village. But it was as quiet as the surrounding plains.

Tragedy carried its own weight, a feeling that remained the same no matter the manner of loss. Eiji felt it here, and he looked at the wide and empty grasslands with undisguised longing. Better to pass this village by.

They would find nothing worth searching for in there.

And yet, by necessity, their path would carry them through the center of it.

They found the bodies. White-robed, but stained with blood and caked with the dirt from the village square. Perhaps there was meaning to be made from their appearance, but Eiji couldn't find it.

The bodies could rot, for all he cared.

Two less monks weren't a reason to weep. They were barely a reason to slow down.

Chiasa went from door to door until she found someone willing to answer their questions, though Eiji saw little point. This work had been completed by whoever rode in the carriage, and it had been carried out with brutal efficiency.

Eiji studied the bodies, already swarming with flies. He wondered if the villagers would find the courage to move the monks, or if they would rather endure the stench that would soon waft through open windows. One had been stabbed repeatedly in the front, but there were no other signs of struggle. She possessed no bruises or cuts on her arms.

The other had been stabbed in the back.

And who could sneak up on a monk? They lacked the training Eiji had grown up with, but they still possessed the gift.

It hadn't done them any good, though.

Chiasa returned. "They discovered a gifted here. The father fought for his daughter, and a crowd had gathered. A young woman and a boy came through. The boy killed her," Chiasa said, pointing to the monk who'd been stabbed multiple times, "and the young woman killed him."

Yua and Isau.

Eiji turned away from Chiasa. His stomach felt sick, and he thought he might lose the last meal he'd eaten. He clenched his fists and stared at the sky, as though his answers were written in the clouds.

He swore that he wouldn't weep. But the dead monk was his complete failure.

He sensed Chiasa step closer.

"This was why I wanted him to leave," Eiji said. "No child should have to carry murder in their past."

She didn't respond.

"Which way did they go?"

Chiasa pointed to the road, and Eiji led them out of town.

His emotions stormed within him, leaving nothing but torn scars across the fields of his heart.

As they rode, Eiji looked down at his hands. Was the blame his? Had he not saved the child from the monks, Isau would have been tortured and killed. Not a pleasant ending, but an innocent return to the Great Cycle. He would be reborn, hopefully in better circumstances.

Had he ruined not just the boy's life, but his future as well?

"Eiji."

He ignored Chiasa, hoping she would leave him alone.

His hope, of course, was in vain. She blocked his way. "We need to talk."

"Then talk."

"What will you do, when you find them?"

He thought of a dozen lies but knew she wouldn't believe a single one. "I don't know."

"Isau's gifted, and a murderer." Chiasa's voice hardened. "The law is clear. Will you stand with him, still?"

The rest went unspoken. But Chiasa made her intent known. If she didn't trust him, it wouldn't be long before he, too, had an arrow in his back.

He could kill her now. The thought was becoming uncomfortably comfortable. He didn't want to make another cut on his arm, but at the same time, it would solve many of his problems. Perhaps it would solve enough problems to justify a lifetime of nightmares.

His sword remained in its scabbard, though. "I won't make you a promise I can't keep."

Chiasa's aura was unsettled. She had no hesitation about killing, and had every reason to end his life, but she restrained herself.

Maybe someday, she would tell him why.

Chiasa swore and turned away from him, leading them away from the village, now haunted by the memories of the dead monks. Eiji suspected, though, it wouldn't be the last violence they would see before this journey ended.

40

In many ways, Isau could almost believe he was back at home. Farmland stretched as far as his eye could see in every direction. Now that the clatter of the carriage was behind them, he felt as much as heard the expansive silence, broken only by soft sounds of the occasional breeze through the wheat and their footsteps.

Sometimes it surprised him he didn't miss home more. Perhaps there wasn't much in it to long for, but it had been all he'd known.

But he didn't miss it at all.

He'd much rather follow Yua through a battlefield of corpses than his father through a field of corn. He'd much rather carry a bloody dagger than a scythe.

This was what he had always been meant for.

In a way, he'd really been born on the day Eiji stole him away from everything he knew.

The trail they followed was no road, not even wide enough for two to travel abreast.

Yua stopped at a rock painted white. She raised her hand and made a series of gestures. Isau tilted his head to the side. Yua remained still, and Isau was about to ask her what she was doing when he heard the clear, piercing cry of a hawk off in the distance. Yua resumed their journey.

"Tell me," Yua asked, "do you sense anyone near us?"

Isau paused and closed his eyes, throwing out his sense the way Yua had taught him. "No."

"Neither do I, and there's a lesson in that."

Isau looked back at the white rock, now receding with every step. "That was a marker," he observed.

"Well done. Chiyo's village cannot easily be approached by stealth. Though you won't see them, these fields are crawling with assassins in training. Few come close enough to the path to sense, but if one doesn't know the appropriate signs, arrows would rain down on us before we made it a dozen more paces."

Isau looked up, even though the sky remained perfectly clear.

He thought, briefly, of the monks in the village they had passed not long ago. Though gifted, they were distracted and confident, and because of that, he'd been able to walk right up to them. "The gift doesn't make us invincible."

She glanced back at him and favored him with one of her rare smiles. "It doesn't. And more gifted die because of that misunderstanding than any other. These assassins aren't like us, and yet, if they chose, they could kill us with ease. Always remember that."

The thought unsettled him. In the stories he'd heard growing up, the nightblades were always nearly invincible, able to change the course of entire wars.

But strength and invincibility were two very different qualities.

Isau considered the skills of the assassins. They seemed useful. "Is it possible for them to train us?"

"Master Ryota has been asking Chiyo for just that favor. She hasn't accepted yet, but if our plans come to fruition, I think it likely we would one day train side by side."

The trail bent and without warning they emerged from the farmland into a cleared area. Directly ahead lay a village.

Isau's face fell when he caught the first glimpse of Chiyo's village. In his imagination it was a walled city, crawling with dark-robed assassins. Instead, it appeared much like the village he'd grown up near. It looked like every other small village that dotted the Three Kingdoms.

Yua must have noted his disappointment. "Also remember that appearances can be deceiving. Say little, here. This is, without doubt, one of the most dangerous places in the Three Kingdoms, although they will do their best to convince you it is a place like any other."

A young woman, somewhere in age between Isau and Yua, greeted them with a smile and a polite bow. "Mistress Yua, it is a pleasure to see you once again."

Yua returned the bow, and Isau followed her lead. "This is Isau. He is my apprentice."

His heart skipped a beat when Yua claimed him as such.

The young woman didn't introduce herself, but turned and led them into the village. She stopped outside a nondescript house and gestured for them to enter. "She is waiting for you."

Inside, Isau immediately noted two facts. First, the woman before them was nothing like he expected.

Chiyo, he assumed, had seen about forty cycles and had the first streaks of grey appearing in her hair. She smiled at them as though she was the matriarch of a family inviting her grandchildren over for tea.

Isau blinked rapidly.

Chiyo appeared almost matronly, but her aura was unlike any Isau had ever felt. It was gelid, making Yua's seem like a warm summer day in comparison. Not strong as a blade's, but potent, nonetheless.

"Welcome," she said.

Yua bowed deeply, and again Isau followed suit.

"It is time," Yua said when she straightened up.

Chiyo's eyes narrowed. "So soon?"

Yua nodded, and Isau caught a flicker in Chiyo's aura, an excitement. Her expression never changed, though. "Very well. Will you stay the night?"

"If we may."

Chiyo nodded. "We will speak again in the morning. I will have information for Ryota."

Yua bowed again, and Isau clumsily followed. He was still trying to wrap his head around Chiyo, but already their audience was at an end.

He'd expected something more—dramatic—he supposed.

When they were back on the street, Isau couldn't contain his questions. "We traveled all this way for that?"

Yua nodded. "There could be no other way."

Isau didn't even know what question to ask first.

Yua turned away from him, looking around the village. "Remember this moment, Isau. As little as it may have seemed to you, it was the moment the fall of the Three Kingdoms began."

41

They found the carriage.

They almost missed it. It was parked in a small village, less than a dozen homes all built around a bare patch of dirt. The carriage sat between two houses, apparently abandoned.

Chiasa and Eiji rode past, feigning ignorance. When the archer glanced his way, Eiji shook his head. He sensed no one gifted nearby.

They found a nearby farm where a man was willing to watch their horses for coin. Then they returned on foot, using the tall grass for cover.

Chiasa found a hidden position that afforded them a view of the village. Eiji lay down a dozen paces away from her, staring at the sky. The falling sun illuminated the bottoms of the clouds, casting them in gorgeous pinks and grays.

He'd stopped pretending to aid Chiasa, so as exhaustion crept over his limbs, he let it take him, and he drifted off into what he hoped would be a dreamless sleep.

He woke to the warmth of the sun on his face, and the sense of Chiasa walking away from him.

Eiji sat up, blinking away the sleep in his eyes. He must have been exhausted to sleep so long.

It didn't take him much time to determine what had happened. A man was at the carriage, and from Eiji's brief study, it appeared as though he was cleaning it. Chiasa stalked toward the man.

She had left him behind. For the first time since Highgate, he was alone.

He glanced off in the distance and extended his sense, expecting a trap. But if there was one, he couldn't sense it.

He would never have a better chance to leave this all behind. She wasn't paying him any attention. He could take both horses from the farmer and be gone. He could hide, maybe for a cycle or two, then rebuild his life.

His future unspooled before him, a promise of peace.

So why didn't he run?

He looked back to the village as a howl of pain carried over the plains. Chiasa hadn't even bothered with conversation. She'd led with the point of her arrows, as she often did.

Eiji gripped his sword.

Did he always have to choose the path of the fool? Was he somehow cursed to repeat the same mistakes over and over? His freedom beckoned, right behind him.

He stepped forward.

He sensed the people within the village, but no one elected to check on the injured driver. Eiji noted it. These were people familiar with trouble, people who chose willful ignorance over involvement.

Another howl. Eiji shook his head when he came upon the scene. Chiasa had stabbed an arrow into the man's shoulder. The man tried to scramble away from her, but her first arrow had caught him in the leg. No doubt, it had been intentional. Chiasa bent over the man, slapping away his futile attempts at defending himself.

Chiasa's foot found the man's side, then she stabbed the arrow into his other shoulder.

Eiji hurried.

How long would people suffer because of the gifted?

Chiasa caught sight of him when he was about twenty paces away. He tried to keep his approach natural, as though he was only coming to join her. He wasn't sure if she believed his posture, but the man chose that moment to try to escape again.

She returned her attention to the driver.

So she didn't see Eiji's blow at all.

His kick caught her in the side, sending her sprawling. Before she could recover, he was there, a sword under her chin.

She froze but smiled at him. "Wondered when you were going to turn."

"You're a monster."

"I never claimed I wasn't."

Behind him, the man tried to get to his feet. Eiji twisted his head, not daring to move his sword. "Don't move. Who were you transporting?"

The man glared at them but said nothing.

"He works for them," Chiasa spat. "You won't get any answers by asking."

Eiji ignored her.

And the other man ignored Eiji. He crawled away.

Eiji swore, then chased the man down. He was their best lead to finding Isau. A foot on the man's ankle pinned him in place.

But of course, Chiasa was up in that heartbeat, an arrow nocked and pointed at Eiji.

Eiji swore. "Really?"

Chiasa shrugged. "Get him to tell you where they went. Otherwise I kill you, then go back to asking him directly."

Eiji extended his hands in supplication, but they had no effect on the archer. So he turned to the driver. "You heard her."

The man groaned. "They're visiting a small village north of here. There's a footpath out of this village that leads there. And I hope you find them." He laughed bitterly.

Eiji raised his foot off the man's ankle and glared at Chiasa. "There."

Just then, Eiji sensed another person approaching, and fast. Chiasa's interrogation had taken too much of his focus. The person came skidding around the corner, by all appearances oblivious to what was happening. "Riders!" the man shouted. "I've already sent a—"

He skidded to a stop when he saw what was happening to the other man. Surprise was quickly followed by confusion.

"What—" he began.

Unfortunately for him, he'd come to a stop right next to Eiji. The nightblade lashed out with his fist, catching the man across the jaw with enough force to send him crashing to the ground.

Eiji's eyes met Chiasa's. If these men had been surprised by the riders, there was only one reasonable conclusion, no matter how unlikely.

"Blades," Chiasa confirmed.

Eiji nodded. They needed to leave this village, and the road, now.

"Kill them," she commanded, gesturing with her bow to the men on the ground.

"What? No."

"Them or you. It's time to choose a side."

The distance was perfect for her. At this range, even if he felt her intent, it wouldn't give him enough time to dodge. And if he moved first, he had little doubt she'd release the arrow. "No."

He sensed her intent, but there was nothing he could do. There was too little time, even for a nightblade.

He cursed the world as she released her arrow.

42

I sau's hopes for an interesting evening were quickly dashed. The same young woman who had led them into the village escorted them to an empty house. Yua, clearly familiar with the routine, started a small cook fire.

Isau quested with his sense, hoping to find something of interest. But the village felt much like any other. He could sense others nearby, walking between houses or sitting within them. But there were no large gatherings, no training he could find.

"You'll not find anything," Yua confirmed, sensing his attempts with her own gift.

"Don't they train like we do?" He imagined this village as a dark mirror of Master Ryota's. Back home, they would probably be gathering for the evening meal right about now.

She shook her head. "We train in a group so that Master Ryota can more easily train us all. Chiyo's method is different. Here, apprentices train singly under masters, and not much is done in the village proper."

Isau looked down at the floor.

"Don't worry," Yua said. "If everything works as it should, soon, you'll also be able to train directly under one of their masters. It'll be much more useful than attempting to sense their training from a distance."

He supposed Yua was right, but he still would have liked to see their training. He wanted to compare it to what he imagined.

They ate in comfortable silence, then retired for the evening early. Isau didn't realize just how tired he was until he lay on the bed. The carriage, although nice, still didn't compare to a real bed.

He woke to activity in the streets.

Both Eiji and Yua had tried to train him in the ways of keeping his sense alive while he slept, but he'd never mastered the art. Still, he couldn't miss this.

People hurried back and forth, far more than he'd felt in the village before going to sleep. It was the most movement he'd sensed since he got here.

For all the activity, though, there was little noise.

He sensed Yua moving through the rooms.

Isau rolled out of bed and called to her. "What's happening?"

"I'm not sure, but be ready to leave."

That was easy enough. They'd left most of their supplies back with the carriage, so getting ready mostly meant rubbing the sleep from his eyes and securing his two knives to his hips.

A knock sounded at their door a moment later. Even though the head assassin wasn't gifted, Isau could sense who it was. Her aura, as before, was unmistakable.

Yua bowed as she opened the door. "Mistress Chiyo."

Isau almost didn't recognize the woman. The mistress of

assassins' face was transformed from the last time they had met, as cold now as her aura. "Were you followed?"

Though Yua's face betrayed nothing, Isau sensed the shift in her energy. Yua was prepared for this confrontation to turn violent. Against the woman reputed to be the most dangerous of assassins, that didn't bode well. "Not that we noticed, no."

Chiyo's glare didn't soften, but Yua met it. Isau cast his eyes to the ground, feeling small. The moment stretched, but then Chiyo spoke quickly. "Six warriors on horseback were noted by our scouts on the main road. They approach the guardian village as we speak. Two are women and carry swords."

"Blades?" Yua asked.

"So we believe."

Yua's confusion clearly convinced Chiyo. Isau wanted to ask questions, but it was not his place. Besides, Yua didn't know the answers either.

Chiyo handed Yua a letter, sealed tightly. "Inside is everything your master needs to know. We'll abandon this village, but our agreement still holds."

"You'd leave your home?" Isau blurted out.

He regretted his outburst immediately. Both women gave him hard stares.

Chiyo answered. "We have no home. This village wasn't ours when it was built, and in time, we will take another."

Yua bowed. "If we brought any of this upon you, I apologize. Regardless, I will pass on this information to my master, and I look forward to meeting you soon in Stonekeep."

Chiyo offered a slight bow of her head in response. "Your safe departure will be vital. Most of us are scattering and will reach Stonekeep in time. But I'm leaving a contingent here to deal with the blades. Another group will guard your departure."

"We're ready," Yua said. "Have you heard any word from the guardian village?"

"None yet, but I expect we will have a bird from them shortly, informing us of the riders. They may yet pass us by, but better to be safe."

"Then we will see you soon," Yua said.

Chiyo nodded one last time, then turned and walked to her next errand. It was the first time Isau had seen her move, and he was impressed by her deadly grace. Even in the midst of chaos, she walked with a confident step, easily avoiding passersby as they ran from one place to another.

Yua turned to Isau. "Ready?"

He nodded, and she led them out.

The village was a scene of controlled disorder. People ran back and forth, but they all moved with purpose. No one shouted, and no one seemed particularly worried. It was almost as if abandoning the village was a regular occurrence.

The same young woman who had escorted them earlier met them on the outskirts of the village. "Stick to the path," she said. "We're anticipating that if they approach, they'll use the fields for cover, and we've prepared some surprises for them, especially if they're on horseback. You'll have archers covering your retreat."

"Thank you," Yua said.

Without further word, they were off, walking away from Chiyo's village and into whatever trouble awaited them next.

43

The arrow sped past Eiji, burying itself deep in the heart of the man who'd been cleaning the carriage. Frozen in surprise, Eiji didn't even react fast enough to stop the second arrow, which killed the new arrival to the scene. By the time Eiji moved, Chiasa had a third arrow nocked, drawn, and pointed at him.

Her speed was incredible.

"What will it be?" she asked.

Eiji cleared his throat and stared hard at the ground.

What he really wanted, more than anything, was to be far from this place and these decisions. Unfortunately, that wasn't one of the choices Chiasa offered.

"I'm with you," he said.

He wasn't sure he believed it himself. But it was the only decision that didn't lead to an arrow embedded in his chest.

He was a coward.

"Look me in the eyes. Swear it."

Eiji took a deep breath, then raised his gaze to hers. Her eyes were hard, but he thought he saw something else there. Hope, perhaps?

She wanted him on her side.

Or maybe he was just deluding himself.

"I'll fight by your side," Eiji said. "I swear it."

The promise slipped past his lips easier than he expected.

Chiasa's posture relaxed and she slowly released her tension on the bow. She gave him a slight nod, then slung her weapon back over her shoulder and went to pull the arrows out of the men she'd shot. "We need to leave. We'll follow the footpath and hope your friends don't find us."

Eiji wasn't convinced of the wisdom of her approach, but he suspected there would be no arguing with her. They were just as likely to get caught between two forces that wanted to kill them as they were to evade the pursuing blades.

They found the trail heading north with little difficulty, and Chiasa ran. Eiji followed, his stomach rumbling, reminding him he hadn't eaten in far too long.

Somehow, he didn't foresee Chiasa stopping for sustenance anytime soon.

They put the village with the carriage behind them. Eiji tried to extend his sense while running, but he didn't sense the presence of blades in pursuit.

Eiji figured they'd run at least a league when Chiasa suddenly slowed and crouched down. The trail they followed was narrow, surrounded by farmland.

"Do you sense anyone?" Chiasa asked.

Eiji closed his eyes and cast out his sense. As near as he could tell, they were alone. He shook his head.

Chiasa bit her lower lip as her eyes darted around. Eiji wasn't sure what she sought. This low, all they could see was a few rows of wheat and the open sky above. "Something's wrong."

Had he been accompanied by an average warrior, Eiji

might have dismissed her concerns. But Chiasa had proven herself repeatedly in the days they'd spent together. If something bothered her, Eiji would stake his life on it. "Should we leave the trail?"

Chiasa considered for a moment, then agreed. "Follow me and stay low."

She led them about fifteen paces off the path and began following a gap in between rows of wheat. They stayed low, moving slowly so as not to disturb the crops by their passage.

An arrow punched through the space between them.

Eiji swore and closed his eyes.

But nothing else happened. The expected follow-up arrows never fell.

When he opened his eyes, he saw that Chiasa had turned around and was studying the shaft, stuck deep in the dirt between them. She glanced in the direction the arrow had come from, but she wouldn't see anything. Not through the countless rows of crops.

A soft wind blew across the tops of the wheat.

The silence of the open plains caused his heart to beat faster.

Why did Chiasa remain? Another arrow could deliver their end at any moment.

Eventually, she turned back in the direction of the path, waiting. When another breeze rustled the top of the wheat, she slipped through a space in the rows. Then she waited for another strong breeze and repeated the process. Eiji mirrored her actions as best he could, clumsy and oafish beside her smooth movement.

With every movement she looked into the sky, and he fought the urge not to look himself.

On one such check, her eyes widened. She reached out and pulled at him.

He risked a glance back, then swore again as he saw half a dozen arrows arc into the air. He stumbled after her, trying to both run and stay low at the same time. As much as he wanted to watch the flight of the arrows, he kept his eyes fixed on the ground in before him. A heartbeat later, shafts hissed through the tall grass behind him.

Never having gone far from the path, it didn't take them long to reach it again. As soon as their feet hit packed dirt, Chiasa turned north and ran, still remaining low.

After a few dozen paces, she slowed.

"Those arrows came from over a hundred paces away," she said. "I think they're prepared for blades."

"Who?"

They'd been following Yua and Isau, not a small army.

Chiasa shrugged her shoulders. "I'd like to know that, too. They're good archers, and observant, too. Even you weren't moving the wheat that much." She looked around. "Do you sense anybody yet?"

He closed his eyes, then shook his head.

His sense still told him they were alone, and yet they were hunted by archers. The dissonance between those two truths worried him more than he cared to admit. He wasn't used to not being able to sense the dangers around him.

She gestured toward the north. "Nothing to do but continue on."

He couldn't help but ask the obvious question. "If we're expected, wouldn't it be more reasonable to retreat and fight another day?"

Her answering smile was grim. "There are probably blades behind us."

Eiji cursed. He'd forgotten about them already. "You're going to be the death of me."

"One can hope."

Without waiting for further argument, Chiasa continued north.

Eiji shook his head but followed. They both kept an eye on the sky for more arrows, but none came.

Eiji was the one who stopped them next. He reached out and grasped Chiasa's arm. She looked at him, a question in her eyes.

Eiji swallowed. "There are two blades approaching."

Chiasa's eyes narrowed. "From behind us?"

He shook his head. "From the north." He paused, because he recognized at least one of the auras. It was strong and cold.

"I think it's Yua and Isau."

44

I sau and Yua hadn't made it more than a few hundred paces from the village when she stopped him. She closed her eyes. "There's a blade out there, alone." She scrunched her face as she focused. "No, the blade is with someone else."

Isau and Yua realized the truth together. "Eiji," they said in unison.

Isau wanted to ask why Eiji was here, but there was only one reason.

For him.

But why? Isau had made it clear how he felt when they ran into one another in the woods. He chose to follow Yua, and his decision had only been reinforced in the time since. He'd learned more in a few days with her than he'd learned in all the days he'd traveled with Eiji. And she promised even more.

Yua stared at him, and he busied himself with checking his daggers. She would want to know why Eiji continued his hopeless pursuit, and he had no answers for her.

Isau closed his own eyes, throwing out his sense to see if

he could find the man who had saved him from his village. He felt nothing, though. Eiji remained too far away, and too weak, for him to sense.

"Will you fight him, if the time comes?" Yua asked.

Isau's hesitation was answer enough.

"No matter," Yua decided. "He's in our way. We'll go through him."

Isau thought she sounded excited by the prospect. Even though she'd retreated the last time they'd met.

Master Ryota's words came back to him. Their master had absolved Yua of her retreat, but she wanted a second chance. She wanted to return to Master Ryota and offer her victory over the rogue nightblade as an apology.

Off in the distance, Isau watched a small flight of arrows launch into the sky, landing near where the path led. His heart beat faster and he felt sweat form on his palms. Eiji was fighting the assassins. Would the nightblade even live long enough for Yua to face him?

Yua's pace never faltered. The archers hadn't killed Eiji. If they had, she would have sensed it.

Soon they were close enough that Isau sensed Eiji. Compared to Yua, his former companion felt weak. If they met again, the conclusion seemed certain.

Isau caught sight of another flight of arrows, but this one wasn't aimed where he sensed Eiji. Isau frowned but didn't think much of it. He didn't understand the ways of assassins.

Yua snapped him out of his wandering thoughts. "I'll walk near the path, but not on it," she said. "I'm not going to make myself an easy target for that archer. Keep walking along the path until you meet them."

He knew he was the distraction, but for Yua, he didn't mind.

Isau followed her instructions, and it wasn't long before a bend in the trail revealed Eiji.

Isau thought the nightblade looked tired. He hadn't shaved in forever, and his hair was a matted mess.

The two stared at each other for a moment, neither speaking. Though nothing but empty space separated them, Isau imagined a wall between them now. He'd outgrown his onetime companion.

Isau drew his dagger, the one that Yua had given him. He sensed her still, moving through the wheat, approaching Eiji. He'd killed a monk. If he killed Eiji, he would be truly free.

Eiji didn't reach for his sword.

The nightblade stepped forward. "We can still make this right," he said.

Eiji's words grated against Isau's thoughts. Eiji believed that everything that had happened since they separated had been a mistake. But Isau knew the truth. "It is right," he replied.

He'd always been meant to be with Master Ryota and his students. For the first time in his life, he was home. Why couldn't Eiji understand that?

That Eiji considered Isau's decision a mistake made the nightblade his enemy.

Isau snarled and charged.

Eiji drew his sword, but it wasn't because of Isau.

Yua broke from the wheat, and their swords met. The two blades passed and then passed again. A shallow cut opened up on Eiji's arm. Next to one another, the differences were stark. Yua was stronger, faster, and more confident.

The best that could be said about Eiji was that he was still standing after two of Yua's passes.

Isau slowed his charge. If he got closer, he would only hinder Yua's own efforts, which were more than sufficient.

Eiji slid to the side, nearly disappearing into the first rows of wheat. Yua followed suit less than a heartbeat later, into the wheat on the opposite side of the path.

An arrow flew down the trail, missing Isau by less than a pace.

It had been intended for Yua.

The blades both emerged from the wheat, but now, Yua refused to pass Eiji.

Isau thought he understood. If she passed Eiji, the archer would have a clean shot at her. Eiji and Yua fought for a moment, but neither gained a substantial advantage. The archer, once again, prevented Yua from fighting at her best.

Isau decided he should focus on the archer. If he got close enough, he could finish her and leave Yua free to fight Eiji with her full attention.

But before he moved, he heard the thunder of hooves.

Six horses charged the scene of their battle. The blades had their swords drawn and shouted cries Isau couldn't make out.

Isau froze in place. What good could he do against mounted warriors?

The first rider was a young man Isau had never seen. He waved his sword above his head, as though the birds in the sky were his enemy. As foolish as the man seemed, though, he would still tear through the battle with undeniable force.

Isau saw the moment the fight changed yet again, destiny spinning like a child's top.

One heartbeat, the rider was pushing fast toward them, then he shouted and tumbled forward. Isau sensed the life leave the rider in an instant.

The other riders pulled up short, and Yua cursed.

She ducked back into the grass and ran from Eiji.

Isau frowned. What had happened?

The riders turned their horses until they were riding on the path. Yua emerged from the wheat close to him and pulled him back toward the direction of the village.

Isau glanced back. Eiji and the archer were chasing after them, and behind them came the remaining five blades.

A sharp pull on his wrist reminded him to pay attention where he was running.

He didn't know what had happened, but he knew that once again Yua had chosen to run from Eiji, and this time they were being chased back to a village filled with assassins.

45

C haos.

Eiji's world narrowed to the sight of Isau and Yua running ahead of him and the overwhelming presence of blades behind him.

Some small part of him, honed by cycles of relentless training back on the island, shouted at him. A narrow focus killed more blades in combat than any other single enemy. But his body possessed its own mind, one that seized control of his actions.

He'd sensed the blades behind him, but he'd misjudged their speed. They had ridden like all the angry mobs of the Three Kingdoms were behind them, and he imagined that thoughts of vengeance for their fallen friends drove them far past the bounds of caution.

Eiji knew nothing but confusion. He didn't know why archers remained comfortably beyond the range of his sense, lobbing arrows into the air after him. He didn't know how the blades had found him so quickly.

All he understood was that those who wished him dead surrounded him.

The death of the horse and rider caught him by surprise. He'd seen the moment, glancing back to check on his pursuers, though it took him several more to understand.

The villagers must have built an abatis near the path and hidden it within the tall grass. No other explanation was reasonable.

But what village took such measures?

His legs carried him toward the village even though his mind protested. This place was not as it seemed.

But he needed shelter from the archers, and narrow spaces to prevent too many blades from striking at him at once. He feared his choice, but the alternatives were worse.

He was about twenty paces behind Isau and Yua when they reached the outer ring of houses in the village. Chiasa had started this footrace behind him, but she turned out to be faster, and was now a couple of paces ahead of him.

Eiji slowed once he entered the village, keeping close to Chiasa. He pressed himself against a wall, glad to be safe from the archers in the fields.

His relief was short-lived.

He sensed the attack before he saw it. The next house over, a figure emerged from the shadows and threw a knife.

Eiji was already moving, sliding to the side, his reaction saving his life. The knife sliced through the space where he'd just been, embedding into the wall behind with a terrifying *thunk*. It didn't take much to imagine that sound being the sound of his death.

Eiji started to shout at his assailant, but the figure had crossed between two houses and was gone again. Eiji sensed them circling around, just in time to sense the danger behind him.

He spun and drew his sword. Steel clashed against steel as Eiji deflected the attack aimed at Chiasa's back.

Like the first figure, the second one also ran past, uncon-
cerned their attack had failed.

Chiasa gave him a quick nod of appreciation, but he saw
the question on her face that was reflected on his.

What was this place?

These weren't villagers as Eiji understood them. Those
attacks had been precise and well executed. Against anyone
but a nightblade, they would both be dead.

They'd stumbled into something.

"We need to keep moving," he said. He sensed their
assailants, circling around him and Chiasa, waiting for
opportunities to strike. Behind them, but closing fast, the
remaining blades neared the village. The abatis hadn't
slowed them much.

Ahead, a house caught on fire, the flames spreading with
unnatural quickness.

But he and Chiasa weren't close enough for the fire to
threaten them, and the blades were even farther away.

Why were these people lighting their own homes on
fire?

He followed his own suggestion, pushing Chiasa gently
forward. She had her bow ready, but no targets appeared.

Eiji took the lead. Here, his sense provided more protection than Chiasa's well-developed intuition. Smoke gently
wafted through the streets, and up ahead, another house
caught fire.

Eiji nearly froze. His fears demanded that he both
remain in place as well as keep running.

This village was a death trap.

Distracted, he almost didn't notice the presence
approaching. "Above us!"

There was nothing he could do. The figure who passed

overhead was beyond the reach of his sword. Chiasa swung her aim up, but even had she had more warning, there was little chance of her hitting such a target. A shadow passed over them and a knife appeared, as if it had always been there, in Chiasa's upper right arm. The weapon had missed embedding itself in her head by less than a hand's width.

The impact caused Chiasa to involuntarily release her arrow. The shaft sped into the sky, but it would harm no one.

Chiasa cursed. "Give me a moment."

Eiji approached her as she leaned against a wall and pulled the blade from her arm. She examined the edge and the wound.

"Not poisoned, at least," she said through gritted teeth.

She tore a strip from her clothing and wrapped her arm. Eiji almost offered to help, but knew it would be refused. Now that they weren't running, he took the opportunity to expand his sense further.

There weren't as many people in this village as he would have expected, but then again, nothing in this village met his expectations.

A few people continued to circle, and one even passed in sight of them. It was a young man, and he paused for a moment to study the pair. He made no move to attack, and a moment later was gone.

The young man not attacking worried Eiji more than an assault would have.

Off in the distance, he felt two stronger energies collide. One, he'd come to sense, was Yua. Her aura was unmistakable.

The blade she fought against quickly died, and Eiji swore he felt Yua's strength grow.

The blades weren't an organized unit anymore. Whether by choice or by the attacks in the village, they had become separated, and a single pair approached his and Chiasa's position. He glanced at her. She awkwardly tied a knot around her arm using her left hand and her teeth.

"We should be going soon," he said. The blades couldn't be more than a house or two away. As near as he could tell, the murderous, well-trained villagers were leaving the nightblades alone.

The smoke grew thicker, and Eiji wondered just how many of the homes surrounding them had been lit on fire. If the villagers weren't careful, it wouldn't be long before the whole village was up in flames.

"I'm good to move," Chiasa said. She had a long knife in her left hand.

Eiji frowned. "Can you fight left-handed?"

"Not well," she admitted.

"Perfect," he muttered.

A group of villagers had gathered just to the east of their position. The blades came from the south. Eiji pointed to a gap between houses that would take them north. Chiasa gestured him forward, and Eiji once again took the lead.

The sense had many limitations, Eiji reflected as they turned the next corner, and one of them was that it only worked on living creatures. It didn't, for example, let him know when he was walking into a dead end, as he did now.

For whatever reason, a cluster of houses had been built so close together they were touching. He and Chiasa would have to turn around and try again.

Then he noticed that each of the houses surrounding them was smoking, so much so that the alley itself was filling with dark clouds.

But when they turned, two blades blocked their exit. He didn't immediately recognize one, but his stomach dropped when he saw the other.

"Hello, Eiji," Kosuke said, just as the house behind Eiji started to spout fire. "It's been a long time."

46

Even Yua's presence wasn't enough to assuage Isau's fears. Her expression never changed, but from her hurried step, he believed that even she was worried about the arrival of so many uninvited visitors.

Again and again, it seemed as if nothing went to plan. This should have been nothing more than a quick meeting between Yua and Chiyo.

Instead, Eiji and that woman were here, and they had brought other blades with them. With every clash of steel and shout of alarm, Isau saw his chances of training with the assassins slipping away. They would never trust him after this.

Eiji had saved his life once, but now seemed determined to destroy it.

Yua led them deeper into the village, turning corner after corner.

It seemed foolish to Isau. After all, Eiji could sense them. The other nightblade was close enough even Isau knew where his former companion was.

He suspected that if it seemed foolish to him, there was

more to it than he understood. He extended his sense, wondering what he had missed.

To his surprise, he quickly discovered he had been a fool. Though his sense was dominated by Eiji's presence behind them, when he focused, he noticed the assassins swarming around the village. Yua wasn't trying to lose Eiji by taking this twisting route—she was trying to bring him into contact with as many assassins as possible.

And she was succeeding.

Isau hoped that someday he would be as calm and effective as Yua. Even in the midst of this mess, her actions were carefully considered. He never should have doubted her.

Soon Yua circled back to where the path entered the village.

Isau sensed the blades ahead of them, but said nothing. Yua's gift far surpassed his own, and he suspected she was plenty aware of them.

When she drew a knife, he knew his guess had been correct.

When they were about a house away from the blades, Yua stopped without warning. Then she swore under her breath.

Isau noticed a moment later. The remaining blades had separated, and a group was running their way.

Yua didn't have enough time to shout a warning. Three blades appeared in the space between houses, and when they saw Yua, they all attacked.

The narrow width of the alley probably saved Yua's life. The three blades were crammed in tightly, and in the alley, Yua's knife gave her more freedom of movement than the longer swords. But even though she was faster and more mobile, there was little she could do against three trained blades.

Yua gave up ground, backing closer to Isau.

He turned and ran, expecting her to follow a step or two behind him.

He turned one corner, then another, then realized Yua wasn't behind him. The clash of steel on steel let him know the battle was still being fought.

Smoke drifted into the alley, dark and noxious. Isau coughed and quested forward with his sense.

Two blades ran toward him.

Isau swore, turned, and ran deeper into the village.

The blades followed.

The chase, he quickly learned, was hopeless. He might be fast for his age, but against the far longer legs of the adults, he had no chance.

He cried out in despair, but no one came to his aid. He couldn't sense Yua anymore.

Isau thought of the monk he'd killed in the village square.

If that had been so easy, perhaps he was running for no good reason.

Isau drew his dagger and spun around, launching himself at the blade closest to him. But when he attacked, the nightblade was no longer there. Isau stumbled, off balance, but his momentum carried him far enough away from the blade to put him out of reach.

He sensed the blade approaching for the attack, knew where the man's sword was going to cut. He raised his dagger, just as if he'd been practicing in Master Ryota's village square.

The impact of steel on steel numbed Isau's entire arm, but he held onto his weapon. The blade frowned, then attacked again. Again Isau got his dagger positioned correctly. This was just like training.

He could fight and win.

Then Isau's sense exploded as the blade attacked with a quick flurry of strikes, far faster than anything he'd been expected to defend against in training. Against such an onslaught, all Isau could do was give up ground. In the corner of his vision, he saw the second blade circling around, ready to attack from the side.

In that moment, Isau knew he was lost for good. His skill wasn't nearly sufficient to stop two true blades. As near as he could tell, it wasn't even sufficient for one.

Then the relentless attack stopped, the sword suddenly dropping from his assailant's hand.

At first, Isau thought that Yua had finally arrived to rescue him, but he couldn't sense her.

Then the nightblade fell forward, and Isau saw that two arrows had embedded themselves deeply in his back. Isau looked up and saw a pair of assassins on the roof of a house across the way. They gestured north, then vanished behind the house.

The second blade had frozen in place, but Isau knew the surprise would quickly wear off. He ran, following the directions of the assassins.

A vicious grin spread across his face.

He might not yet be strong enough to fight all his battles on his own.

But thanks to Master Ryota and Yua, he wouldn't have to.

He wasn't alone anymore.

47

S ome fights were doomed from the start.

With Chiasa unable to draw her bow, Eiji faced two blades of considerable skill alone.

No thoughts of a heroic last stand polluted his mind. He realized, now, that he enjoyed playing at being a hero far more than actually being one. As Kosuke and the other nightblade advanced, Eiji focused on the unfairness of it all.

All this, just because he'd done one good deed.

If he somehow survived, he'd not make that mistake again.

Fire blossomed in the houses behind him, and the blades blocked the exit ahead. Chiasa would fight, but armed only with a knife in her off hand, the only question Eiji had about her was if she could last a single pass. He doubted it.

There was a freedom in inevitability, though.

Forced into a fight he didn't want, with no hope of victory or peace, he only saw one choice.

Eiji drew his sword, not because he meant to defend himself, but because he wanted these blades to hurt.

Steel met steel, and the first exchange saw Kosuke and his partner driven back three paces.

Eiji pushed forward, indifferent to the sharpened edges that sought to slice his flesh into ribbons. His own sword moved without thought, deflecting, countering, and cutting at his enemies.

He suspected the blades were faster than him. His sword never came close to ending either life.

But the blades no longer charged forward, even when he gave them the space to do so. Their confident strides had transformed into wary glances, and when they advanced, it was one tentative step at a time.

Eiji greeted them again, and their second exchange ended with no clear victor.

He was running out of time, though. The heat built behind him, already to the point where the warmth was uncomfortable. Simply surviving had never been enough for this fight.

And it had never been what he wanted, either.

Eiji attacked, a vicious grin stretching from ear to ear as he imagined the look on Kosuke's face when the nightblade fell to Eiji's bloodthirsty sword.

The third exchange began, and the unpleasant truth revealed itself.

Eiji wasn't enough.

He remained unharmed, a feat he would have been proud of days ago, but the growing fire behind him didn't care. He wasn't fast enough to dislodge the blades from their position at the mouth of the alley. The pair held their ground, content to let the fire do their work for them.

The only way to victory required a sacrifice of blood. If he let a cut through, perhaps it would give him the opening required to strike one of them down.

It was far from perfect, but what else could he do?

He broke away, putting four paces between him and the blades. Every step made the skin on the back of his arms burn worse. The air became too hot to breathe. But he wanted to treasure just a few more breaths before he made his final attack.

He'd accomplished nothing of note in his short life. All he had to list as his accomplishments was a failed rebellion and a boy who'd disowned him. Eiji swore. Perhaps on his next trip through the Great Cycle he would do better.

A man could hope, at least.

"Eiji!"

The voice was sharp, and feminine, but scratched on the edges. He'd forgotten about Chiasa. He turned in time to watch her leap into the inferno of a building. In two steps her figure was swallowed by flame.

What fresh madness was this?

He looked closer and saw what she must have seen. The fire had burned through the walls. He couldn't see to the other side from where he stood, but perhaps Chiasa had found a way out.

At least, she didn't seem like the type of woman who would sacrifice herself to the flames.

The house she had run through groaned, the sound of an old man stretching before his final rest. The fire licked at the remaining supports, consuming with insatiable hunger.

Almost certain death by fire, or very certain death by steel?

Eiji ran toward the maelstrom of flame.

Any chance of survival was better than none, but even more than that, he didn't want Kosuke to have the pleasure of defeating him. If today marked his final day, he wanted to die on his own terms.

Eiji took one last deep breath, the air burning his throat. He swore he felt his skin blister, but he charged forward, through the same gap Chiasa had a moment earlier. He heard Kosuke scream his name, the blade's frustration rending the air.

That alone made this worth it.

He heard a crack over the sound of the flames, and a large beam fell in front of him. Eiji leaped over it, the fire from the beam reaching out to caress his legs. His eyes watered, blurring the sight in front of him.

Was that dark spot ahead an opening?

With no other options, he ran for it.

More cracks, all around him.

The death throes of a burning house.

The building began to collapse on top of him.

48

Smoke clouded Isau's vision, obscuring anything farther than two houses away. Only the bright orange lights of homes catching fire broke through the gloom.

When the assassins decided to leave a village, they really left.

His heart pounded in his chest.

His momentary confidence had faded like a wave crashing upon the shore, receding back into the sea.

Despite the directions, he hadn't come across aid.

He was alone. His sense confirmed it. He'd switched directions as the fires spread, and now he was lost, surrounded by fire. No one came for him. No one called his name, and if they did, he wouldn't hear it over the growing roar of the flames.

None of this was right.

Yua should have come back for him. She was his master. His safety was her responsibility. But if he couldn't sense her, it was likely she was already out of the village.

He would have given anything for just one more moment within her cold aura.

Would she even mourn his loss?

Somehow, he didn't think so.

The smoke caused tears to fall from his eyes.

He didn't want to die.

Two figures emerged from the smoke, both running with swords drawn. Too late, his sense identified them as nightblades.

Why hadn't he sensed them earlier? Both were strong. And yet Isau hadn't noticed them.

Had this village also taken his gift?

Both men were looking around, as though searching for something they had lost. Something valuable.

Isau wondered if anyone would ever search for him with such intensity.

They weren't here for him, but then Isau and one of the men locked gazes, and the man's look changed.

Isau knew that look, and knew he should fear. He'd seen it on his father's face, more than once, the nights he came home smelling more of alcohol than the fields he'd worked all day.

The nightblade couldn't have what he most wanted. But Isau was here, and small, and the nightblade was thinking that perhaps Isau's demise would be reward enough.

It was the look that preceded violence against one who couldn't defend themselves.

The blade attacked, followed by his partner.

Armed with nothing but a dagger, Isau had no chance fighting them. But their longer legs would catch him easily enough if he ran.

So he stood his ground, weapon in hand.

He'd run often from his father, but he refused to run from these blades.

It was time to show someone he wasn't as helpless as they thought.

49

Eiji dove through the small gap as the building collapsed behind him, a wall of flame exploding overhead. It scorched his clothing but vanished too quickly to do any lasting harm. He lay in the dirt for a moment, wondering if it wouldn't be better to close his eyes and just rest.

He could let the fire take him.

A hand clutched at his shoulder, pulling. He heard swearing, although distant. His head felt as if it was underwater.

The hand lacked the strength to pull him to his feet, but it wouldn't let him rest. He swatted at it, but it refused to let go.

Eiji groaned and pushed himself to hands and knees. He coughed, then coughed again. The smoke hung thick around him, embracing him, clouding his vision.

Chiasa was yelling, and suddenly all his senses returned at once.

"We've got to get out of here!" she shouted.

Eiji nodded and stumbled forward. Smoke filled his

nose and throat, and all he wanted was one deep lungful of clean air.

The whole village was alight. Dark smoke filled every corner and blocked the sun. Eiji saw the fires, burning down homes with unbelievable speed. Soon, this village would be nothing more than a smoldering ruin.

Supporting each other, the two warriors made for the outskirts of town. Eiji wasn't sure what new nightmare he would find there, but anything was better than the endless flame and smoke within the village.

After a dozen steps, the fog in his mind cleared enough for him to use his gift again. The village was largely empty, although he would have been surprised had it been anything but.

There were three gifted one house over, though, fighting with one another.

Eiji stopped, almost sending Chiasa to the ground.

One of the gifted was Isau.

Getting involved would take Eiji deeper into the village, the opposite of where he wanted to go. Isau had left him behind once. It was time to return the favor.

Chiasa pulled at him, and he saw she was considering abandoning him just as he was Isau. Without the gift, she had no idea of the fight happening less than thirty paces away. But her look solidified his will.

He let her go. "I'll find you, if I can."

Without waiting for a response, he tore away from her, circling around yet another burning house to approach behind the two nightblades attacking Isau.

It was Kosuke and his partner, because who else would it be? The Great Cycle kept slamming them together until a victor emerged. The nightblades fought together, swords cutting at Isau.

The boy displayed a remarkable agility, but he fought a fight he couldn't win. A relatively untrained boy against two full nightblades wasn't a battle.

It was murder.

Eiji stopped and watched for a moment, not sure he accepted what he was seeing. In all his time among the blades, he wouldn't have believed even those he didn't care for would possess the necessary evil to harm a child.

The eruption building inside Eiji for the past two cycles finally exploded. He didn't care if the two nightblades had been close to killing him just moments ago. They didn't have the right to attack Isau.

Exhaustion fell from his limbs, and he darted forward with a confidence that bordered on certainty.

Distracted as they were, the two nightblades didn't notice him as early as they should have. Kosuke's partner sensed him first, turning just in time to block a decapitating strike. But the power of Eiji's attempt knocked the man off-balance. The nightblade stumbled but caught himself quickly.

It wasn't quick enough. Eiji's next cut sliced into the man's sword arm, and from that moment on the conclusion of the duel was inevitable.

The nightblade's eyes went wide, and he uttered something that might have been a cry for mercy. Eiji didn't hear it, his sword already making the fatal cut.

Kosuke turned at the death of his partner. His shock didn't last long enough for Eiji to take advantage of, and in a moment, the two blades were locked in combat once again.

Eiji's fears regarding Kosuke's strength turned out to be well founded. Once, cycles ago, they had been well matched. But the greatest warriors no longer lived in the Three Kingdoms. Eiji hadn't grown as a swordsman in his wandering through the past two cycles. At best, he'd maintained his skills from the island.

But Kosuke had gotten stronger, both with his sword and with his gift.

And he was angry enough to kill.

Not even Eiji's rage could break Kosuke's defense.

With every exchange, Eiji came closer to defeat. The difference between them wasn't great. Perhaps Kosuke could see some fraction of a heartbeat further into the future than Eiji could.

Not much, but enough.

Like Isau, Eiji's fight wasn't so much a matter of if he would lose, but when.

A yell pierced the smoke, and a weak energy attacked Kosuke from the side. Kosuke turned and deflected Chiasa's stab, but he sacrificed the advantage he'd built against Eiji in their exchanges.

Eiji pressed the momentary advantage. Chiasa couldn't kill Kosuke, not as injured as she was. She'd be dead if Kosuke turned his attention to her for more than a heartbeat.

Eiji denied him that time, forcing Kosuke back.

Right onto the tip of Isau's knife.

Kosuke's eyes widened in shock, and he turned around and backhanded Isau straight to the ground, the boy's body limp and unmoving. Eiji stepped forward and cracked Kosuke over the head with the pommel of his sword.

Kosuke's eyes rolled up in his head as he collapsed.

Eiji stared down at the nightblade. So much trouble, and for what?

"Can you carry him?" Eiji asked Chiasa, pointing to Isau. She looked uncertain, but nodded. Eiji helped throw the boy over Chiasa's good shoulder.

Then he started dragging Kosuke, even though Chiasa hissed at him.

His bloodlust had cooled, and now he refused to leave Kosuke behind to burn to death. A warrior, and a night-blade in particular, deserved better. Perhaps the day would come when he regretted this decision, but for now, he would give Kosuke one more chance at life.

50

I sau woke to a near-perfect darkness.

He scrambled backward, gasping for breath.

A familiar voice spoke softly near him. "Easy now. You're safe, boy."

Isau stopped scrambling. He heard bodies shifting, and a low groan came from a few paces away. "Eiji?"

"Yes?"

Isau slumped, realizing that once again he was with the rogue nightblade. Which meant the person groaning nearby was likely the woman, the archer who made even Yua think twice about attacking.

She didn't sound so dangerous now.

Memories returned, and Isau wished they hadn't. Fire and smoke, the look of satisfaction on the nightblade's face as he drove Isau back with powerful cuts. Eiji had emerged from the flames, as if a creature of smoke himself, to kill the nightblade's partner. Then Eiji fought the nightblade with eyes like his father, but Eiji hadn't been skilled enough. The woman had fought, and Isau had seen an opening, and he'd slid his knife into the nightblade just as easily as he had the monk in the village before.

Then darkness, and now here.

As his eyes adjusted, though, he saw that what he'd thought was perfect darkness was in fact just a moonless night. He saw the shadow of Eiji nearby, and the woman a few paces away, as he'd guessed. All three of them hid in deep grass.

Eiji had come back for him.

Yua hadn't.

Isau sighed and leaned back in the grass. Not even the stars twinkled overhead.

Smoke from the fire obscured the night sky.

He might as well be trapped in perfect darkness, though. Yua's betrayal tore him open, leaving him an empty shell.

What did any of it matter?

Eiji should have left him long ago, back when they'd first met. He never should have freed Isau from the monks. They'd all be happier.

Isau glanced over at Eiji. The nightblade had a knife in hand, and he drew it slowly across his forearm. "What are you doing?"

"Remembering."

Isau wasn't sure what to say. But he didn't like to see Eiji hurting himself. "I can heal that, if you want."

Eiji turned to him, doubt visible even in the gloom.

"Really."

"If you can, heal her." Eiji gestured toward the woman. "She saved your life as much as I did, and she did it wounded." The nightblade watched his arm as blood trickled into the grass.

Isau had seen Eiji's scars before, too parallel to be the result of battle. Now he knew what they represented. He didn't understand why Eiji carried so much guilt. What was the point of all this skill if he didn't use it to shape the world?

He knew better than to ask, though.

Lacking any real desire, but needing to do something, Isau crawled over to where the woman lay. She glared at him, but didn't push him away when he looked at her arm. The cut was deep, far more than the little scratch Yua had tested him with.

But Isau supposed the principles were the same. He put his hand on her arm and closed his eyes. His sense of the woman's internal energies came easier than Yua's. Perhaps it was because she didn't possess Yua's overwhelming aura, or perhaps Isau's skill had just improved. Regardless, he felt the flow of her energy, and the wound to her arm was as obvious as staring into the sun.

"This will hurt," he warned.

Then he began to work, rearranging the pathways of her energy using his own. After the events of the last few days, he found something resembling peace in the process. Right and wrong were easy to separate, and with every bit of energy he poured into the work, he sensed the result before him.

In the back of his mind, Isau knew he was spending too much energy on the archer, but he continued anyway. Sensing the change was its own reward.

He didn't stop until strong hands pulled him away.

"Much more and you'll never walk again," Eiji said.

Isau was too tired to argue, and he slipped into sleep.

WHEN HE WOKE, it was still dark, and quiet. For a few heart-beats, he thought he was alone, that Eiji and the woman had left him. But then he sensed Eiji nearby, even if the night-blade remained silent.

A soft snore came from the grass across from him. The woman, it seemed, was asleep. It didn't surprise Isau. He still felt as though he could sleep for a full day. Eiji handed him something, and Isau took it without question.

It was some dried meat, no doubt carried by Eiji for far too long, but at the moment, it tasted like a feast for a lord.

The two didn't speak. Isau, for his part, didn't know what he could say. He couldn't sort through his own feelings, much less explain them to someone else.

Only one thought made it past his confusion.

"I'm sorry," he said.

Eiji took a long breath, the type adults took when they had a lot they wanted to say, but refused to say it. "Me, too."

Isau finished the meat and looked up. The smoke hadn't cleared, but it had thinned. He could see through in places, the dim light of distant stars offering momentary glimpses of hope. "You shouldn't have saved me. Back when I was tied to that tree, and the monks were returning for me. You should have left me. I know you wanted to."

Eiji didn't deny it.

"Why didn't you?"

"I wish I knew. I think I was tired of turning my back."

It struck Isau then that Eiji possessed a quality he hadn't properly appreciated before. He didn't tell comforting lies. Eiji wasn't the sort of man who would tell you things would be all right as the world burned around you.

But he was the man who would walk through a burning village to pull you out.

Maybe leaving Eiji had been wrong.

But his time with Yua had felt just as right. And she'd taught him skills Eiji either wouldn't or couldn't.

Both his masters couldn't be right. If they were, they wouldn't be fighting one another. But Isau saw a path forward with each of them.

He also saw their flaws.

How did he choose, if the choice was presented to him?

Eiji noticed something else. His daggers remained in their sheaths, right where they belonged. A small thing, perhaps, but a level of trust Isau didn't believe he deserved.

Eiji swore, the curse of a doomed man.

"What?"

"She's looking for you," he said. "Making circles around the village, ever wider."

Isau tried to extend his sense, but he felt nothing. But he believed Eiji. And the nightblade's claim sent his mind spinning into confusion again. Yua had left him, but now she searched. Why? "Why hasn't she sensed us?"

Eiji's laugh was bitter and short. "She's far stronger than us. You barely have the energy to stand, and I'm not much better off. It's far easier to sense her, but we don't have long."

That harsh truth, once again put plainly.

Isau didn't have any problems imagining the near future. Eiji knew it, too. When Yua found them, she would kill Eiji and the woman. They couldn't fight her in their condition.

Isau didn't want that. Which left him only one choice.

"I need to go to her."

"No!"

"She'll kill you otherwise."

The protest died on Eiji's lips. "I didn't want this for you. I'd hoped, that by going to the island, you never would have known any of this."

It was the most of his reasoning Eiji had ever explained. If only he had made it back when it mattered.

And it made Isau's decision certain. He stood up,

surprised by how the ground wavered in his vision. He was weak.

Eiji's hand snaked out and grabbed his wrist. "You know I would have fought here for you, right?"

"I do." Isau was surprised to find he didn't doubt it, either. "And thank you."

He saw the low fires off in the distance. If he walked toward them, he'd soon find Yua. And an uncertain future.

It was an instinct he couldn't quite explain, but he turned to Eiji one last time. "We're heading to Stonekeep."

Then, suddenly feeling guilty for betraying Yua's confidence, he walked away, stumbling forward as fast as his legs and balance would carry him.

He had tears in his eyes again, but this time he couldn't blame the smoke.

51

T he fresh cut on Eiji's arm burned, a line of fire ants crawling across his forearm.

He welcomed the pain.

He understood it.

When the actual moment of killing had come, it came easily. Once the choice was made, his sword cut through flesh without hesitation.

Killing was easy.

Living after was not.

But at least the consequences were familiar. He expected the nightmares now, a fresh layer of muck added to the memories that formed the bedrock of his existence. In time, the fresh horror would blend with the old. It would harden, and in a cycle or two, if he lived that long, he wouldn't remember which memory was linked to which event.

That was why, more than any other reason, he didn't sleep this night. Let the new nightmares wait until tomorrow.

He looked off in the distance, toward the village, in the direction Isau had gone to meet with Yua. The boy acted so old, Eiji sometimes forgot how young he was. Isau had seen far too much, too early. Eiji had hoped to protect him, to act as a shield from the worst the world had to offer, at least for a time. He had failed in that, too.

Beside him, Chiasa stirred from her deep slumber.

Another surprise, there. Somehow, the boy had the skills of a dayblade. Perhaps even more than those of the nightblades. But the ability to use both, at all, was incredibly rare. In the records Eiji read, back on the island, only one nightblade had ever managed to make the shift. The manifestations of the gift were too different for one to learn both paths.

At least, that was what he had always thought. It was accepted as a truth on the island. Maybe, though, it deserved questioning.

The boy wasn't half bad, either. A dayblade on the island would have healed Chiasa far better, of course. But the boy had less than a moon of training. The fact he'd healed Chiasa at all was the greatest mystery of the past day, and it had been a day full of questions that had no answers.

Chiasa went from sleep to perfect awareness in a moment. Eiji sensed the change in her energy. She opened her eyes, took the scene in with a single glance, then grunted.

Eiji didn't think he'd ever met someone who could say so much without words.

She was disappointed, but apparently not surprised. "You let the boy go, didn't you?"

"Yua was searching for him. It wouldn't have been long before she sensed us. He wanted to leave so we could stay safe."

"He'll betray you."

Eiji shrugged. "Still alive, so he hasn't yet."

Another grunt.

"He also told me where he's going."

That got the hunter's attention. She sat up, winced, and looked at her arm.

"How does it feel?" Eiji asked.

She glared at him. "Like I got stabbed." She paused. "But far better than it should. His healing worked. Where's he going?"

"Stonekeep."

Chiasa cursed.

Eiji handed her the last of the dried meat he'd carried. The rest of their supplies were back with their horses, and although his stomach rumbled, he suspected Chiasa needed the sustenance more than he did.

She nodded her appreciation and attacked the food as though it had hurt a loved one. Eiji let her enjoy the meal in silence. His thoughts darted from worry to worry, like a bird flitting from flower to flower. When choosing which concern to focus on, he found that he had an overabundance of choice.

Chiasa noticed the fresh cut on his arm. Her eyes narrowed when she saw it. She was too observant not to understand.

When she finished the meager portion of food, he passed over the small waterskin he'd been carrying. It held little, and she drained the rest in a couple of gulps.

"I didn't think you had it in you," she said, referring to the reason why he cut his arm.

He hated the tone of her voice, the begrudging acknowledgment that maybe he was worth her attention now. All because he had killed a man.

Her attitude felt so... small.

He said nothing, not wanting to follow that particular

thread of conversation. The silence stretched as she focused all her attention on him.

When she spoke again, her voice had changed. It was softer now, more understanding. "It really bothers you, doesn't it?"

"Shouldn't it?"

"I suppose."

Another silence grew, interrupted only by the sound of the wind in the tall grass. Eiji wanted to speak. He wanted to make her understand, but he was more likely to hit a target with an arrow at a thousand paces in a stiff wind. A chasm separated their beliefs, and he didn't think anyone possessed the wisdom to build the bridge between them.

She swore. "You annoy me, you know that?" She swept her hand over the grasslands, encompassing the burning village and much, much more. "At every turn, you make foolish decisions. You won't defend yourself against Itsuki or me. And you claim to want to protect Isau, but if you wanted to save him, all you had to do was leave me behind last night. You should have killed me long ago. You won't say it, but I know you believe Itsuki is dead. If you kill me, no one will hunt you. I know you think so, and you know what?"

Eiji didn't respond. He couldn't. He hadn't realized Chiasa was capable of stringing so many words together at once.

At least, not without putting an arrow in someone.

Fortunately, she wasn't waiting for an answer. "I don't even worry about defending myself when I sleep. I know you're not going to harm me. Truthfully, I'm not sure I've ever slept as well as I have since I started travelling with you."

Chiasa swore again, and this time it brought a smile to

Eiji's lips. He couldn't deny it, but frustrating the archer brought him tremendous joy.

She growled, the sound coming from deep in the back of her throat.

Eiji laughed, and for a heartbeat, he truly thought she might try to stab him. He sensed her intent, but it never quite reached the level of manifestation.

He gave her a few moments to cool down. But he couldn't keep the smile from his face. When he was certain that she wouldn't kill him, he spoke again, standing up as he did. "So, to Stonekeep?"

She sighed and nodded, taking his proffered hand for aid. "To Stonekeep."

52

The essence of a good lie, Isau knew from hard experience, was to say as little as possible. The more complex a lie became, the more holes that could be poked in it. Saying little allowed the listener to fill in the gaps, to lie to themselves.

Saying little also provided scant evidence for a wary listener to seize onto.

So when Isau ran into Yua, all he told her was that he'd escaped the village, thanks in large part to directions an assassin on the rooftops had given him. He'd run and hidden for a while, then had been on his way back to the village to search for her when she found him.

Isau said nothing of the nightblades he'd fought, and didn't even think about mentioning Eiji and the woman.

The temptation was there. Yua would be proud he stood his ground against not just one, but two nightblades. And if she knew he had healed a deep cut on his own?

She might even grant him a smile.

But a simple lie was best.

And the truth was likely to kill him.

He couldn't tell if Yua believed him. Her face remained neutral as he told his tale. But even if she didn't, she said nothing. When his story ended, she nodded, then gestured toward the guardian village where their carriage waited.

Though Isau's feet carried him in a straight line, his thoughts wandered in every direction.

Chiyo had said her people would find another home. Not that she would build one. Her statement combined with the assassins' willingness to torch their buildings at the first sign of trouble, led Isau to suspect the village hadn't been Chiyo's to begin with. And yet everyone within had been an assassin.

It didn't take long for Isau to connect the facts and understand the fate of the original villagers.

The thought sickened him, but Chiyo and the others were assassins. What else did he expect? He'd always known the world was full of cruel people. Just because Chiyo had been respectful enough to him meant little.

He thought of Eiji and the woman he traveled with. They had saved him, at no small risk to their own lives. Isau couldn't lie to himself any longer. Eiji might have wanted to send him to the island, but it wasn't out of a lack of concern.

That realization painted everything from the past moon in a new light.

If he'd been wrong about Eiji, was he right about Master Ryota? Was he right about Yua?

They reached their destination as the sky turned gray above them. Smoke and memories were all that remained of the assassins' village.

Isau stood helpless as Yua discovered all that had transpired in their short absence. Men were dead, and the arrow wounds pointed to the culprit.

And Isau had healed her.

Another thought to twist his insides even more. He'd healed a killer no better than any other monk.

He just wanted one thing in his life to be simple and straightforward. He wanted something he could anchor his beliefs to. But whenever he found something promising, like the ability to heal, it revealed itself as more layered than he initially thought.

Yua went around the small village. In short order, she'd found someone to harness the carriage to the horses and find someone willing to act as their driver. Well before the sun was high in the sky, they were off, heading south and east.

Toward Stonekeep and whatever awaited them there.

Isau tried to sleep, but any form of rest eluded him. The same seemed true of Yua, though she displayed none of his discontent. She stared out the window, her eyes never focused on anything in particular.

"Tell me, Isau," she asked, "what would you die for?"

Another test.

Always another test.

He didn't rush to answer, knowing his life might very well rest on his response. He felt a tension between them that hadn't been there before. Real or imagined, caution was warranted.

A few days ago, he was certain he would have said Yua's name. Part of him still wanted to. She was strong and had shown him kindness. Perhaps the correct answer was Master Ryota, but although he respected his master, he wasn't sure he would die for the intimidating warrior.

When nothing came to mind, he realized he'd found his answer.

"I don't know."

Her eyes turned from the window to him. "It's a question

you must find an answer to, and soon. You've shown great promise, but to continue to train Master Ryota's secret technique, you'll need more than just skill and training. You'll need belief."

She paused for a moment, seeing if her words had the desired effect.

"Not many possess the actual skills necessary to use Master Ryota's technique," she continued, "but more do than most nightblades realize. What holds them back is a lack of belief, a lack of certainty in their path. The technique extracts a cost that only a true believer is willing to pay." Yua's gaze returned to the window. "Choose your path, Isau, and commit to it with your whole heart. I know you are torn between Eiji and your future, but the time is coming when you'll have to stand on one side or the other."

Though it wasn't explicit, Isau knew she referred to Stonekeep. He couldn't say why, but she viewed Stonekeep as an ending, or perhaps a new beginning. Maybe both.

And at the rate the carriage traveled, it wouldn't be long before they were in the capital of the Northern Kingdom.

He wanted more time. He was being forced into a decision when he didn't even know nearly enough.

"What will happen in Stonekeep?"

He didn't mean to blurt out the question. Some part of him knew that Yua wasn't supposed to tell him about it, but if she demanded a choice, he could demand information.

She never even looked at him as she answered, her voice colder than her aura.

"We kill the lord and lady of the Northern Kingdom."

53

Eiji and Chiasa retrieved the horses from the kindly farmer without difficulty. If the older man had any questions about the pillar of smoke in the distance or their own disheveled appearance, he possessed the wisdom not to ask them. They never neared the village where Chiasa had killed the two men, choosing to avoid any unnecessary trouble.

Eiji was grateful for the horses, but almost swooned when he smelled the store of food in his saddlebags. Chiasa's quick search of her own supplies also concluded with food in each hand.

They thanked the farmer, but Eiji saw the way the tension drained from the man's body as they rode away. The greatest gift they could offer him was their speedy departure.

Chiasa led them overland toward Stonekeep.

Eiji followed, amazed how quickly life returned to something imitating normalcy. The scorched village had been close to nothing else. Word of the disaster might spread slowly, a whisper passed between relatives, but there would be no scattering of the displaced. Eiji was convinced that town hadn't held a single innocent life.

Two long days of riding returned them to a world where other concerns remained paramount. No one would shed a tear for the lost village. The story was the same everywhere. People fought to survive. Food was scarce no matter how far one traveled. Most didn't have the time or heart left to be concerned about a small village that held no family or friends. Sympathy had been wrung dry throughout the Northern Kingdom.

Personally, Eiji believed the Northern Kingdom would soon recover from the worst of the famine. This kingdom was ruled fairly, and house Kita had done more in the early stages of the famine to protect and aid its people. Of course, many wanted more, but there was only so much to give. But in his own travels, Eiji found the citizens of the Northern Kingdom to be better off than their neighbors to the west or south.

It was an argument that brought no comfort to those still living on one bare meal a day, though.

Chiasa's behavior fascinated him.

The two of them were well supplied with food. Chiasa seemed to have a bottomless purse, and even Eiji carried more money than most citizens would see in several cycles. But beyond that, Chiasa and Eiji working together made an excellent hunting partnership. Eiji could sense prey, and Chiasa never missed with her bow.

Here, in some of the hardest hit areas of the Northern Kingdom, Chiasa gave most of their food away to the villages they passed. The action seemed so out of character for the warrior that Eiji asked her about it.

She shrugged and ignored him.

But eventually, he inquired again. The pieces of her didn't seem to fit together, and with nothing but time on the road, she was a question that demanded answers.

One day he finally worked up the courage to press her until she answered. He drew his horse even with hers. "Who were you, before you entered Lady Mari's service?" he asked.

"Chiasa," she answered.

When no further answer seemed forthcoming, Eiji tried again, undeterred. "What was your life like? Where are you from? What made you want to try to become one of Lady Mari's guards?"

"Do you always have so many questions?"

"No," he said, "but I'm rarely confronted by such puzzling people."

"Why do you want to know?" Eiji imagined Chiasa as a warrior standing guard at a gate of memories. The question was her drawing her sword against his inquiry.

"Because you interest me more than most."

His frank honesty disarmed her.

It took another hundred paces of riding for her to finally open up, though.

"I grew up near the southeast corner of the Northern Kingdom. Probably not more than three or four days' ride from the border with the Southern Kingdom. I still have family there. A much younger brother, mother and father."

She took a deep breath. "When I was younger, I also had an older brother. He was responsible for keeping us fed during the worst days of the famine. My father was injured in the Great War, and although he can maintain a small garden, he can't do much more. My brother hunted for us, bringing back game often enough to keep us going."

Chiasa's demeanor changed as she spoke. The sharp-edged killer vanished, and Eiji wondered if he was seeing something of who she used to be.

"My brother was the one who taught me the bow. I think he dreamed of a day when we might hunt together.

"It didn't come to pass, though. He got sick one day, though we never understood why. It happened right after he'd brought back an enormous deer. He was dead a few days later."

She paused her story. Eiji almost offered his condolences, but he suspected they wouldn't be welcome. He didn't know when he would get her to open up like this again.

"There was no choice. I took on my brother's mantle. He'd taught me quite a bit, and what was left I needed to learn on my own. There was a moon, perhaps, when I didn't think we would survive. I snared a few rabbits, but even though we ate little, I wasn't killing enough to keep us alive."

She smiled. "But I was a quick learner. I got better, and although it was never easy, I kept us fed. My hunting and our small garden were enough to keep us alive.

"Then the hunting became more difficult. There had been several cycles where everyone was hunting for food, and the animals learned and moved on. Hunters started hunting one another for the game we'd killed. I had a few experiences where I almost lost my life, all over a rabbit or deer."

She glanced at him, as though judging his reaction. "I knew it couldn't last for long, and this was about the time I heard of Lady Mari's recruitment of trained women. The rest of the story, you know. I keep most of my pay and take it to my family when I get the chance."

They rode on for a while longer in silence. Then she

smiled sweetly at him. "And if you ever tell anyone any part of that story, you won't live to see the next morning."

With that, she rode off, leaving Eiji with a grin on his face.

He hoped she never changed.

54

"You're going to kill Lady Mari?" Isau couldn't keep the disbelief out of his voice.

"Maybe not me," Yua said, her voice a calm contrast to his rising one, "but someone among us will." Her sharp eyes settled on him. "Does that bother you?"

"I thought Lady Mari was the ruler who fought with the blades during the Great War. That's what people always said back home. They didn't like her very much."

"You came from the Western Kingdom, so that's no surprise," Yua said. "She nearly destroyed your kingdom during the war, and she didn't do it many favors after, either."

Isau noticed that Yua hadn't actually answered his question. "Why kill Lady Mari and her husband? Aren't they friendly toward the blades?"

Yua gazed out of their carriage. She bit her lower lip briefly, then turned back to Isau, a decision made. "She is no friend of ours, though some now make the claim. At one time, Lady Mari was the staunchest supporter of the gifted. She stood by us when no one else would."

Yua's eyes unfocused for a moment, lost in stories of the past. "Of course, part of it was expedience. She was beset on all sides by enemies. Allying with the blades was the only way to keep her house lands intact. The question is: would she have allied with the blades if she didn't need to?"

Isau didn't know the answer to that question. The only history he knew was the stories told at night by his family and friends. They hardly made him a scholar.

"I don't think so," Yua said, answering her own question. "Master Ryota agrees. Because when the situation became difficult—when allying with the blades would cost her everything—Lady Mari exiled us. She was the primary architect of the treaty which allows the monks to hunt us today."

Isau's eyes were wide. If what Yua said was true—and he had no reason to doubt it—then Lady Mari wasn't a hero, but the worst of the traitors. "So we kill her for her crimes?"

"Partly, but also because both she and the Northern Kingdom are vulnerable." Yua paused, checking to see if he understood. He didn't, but he wanted to know, so he gave no sign of his ignorance. "Attaining power isn't just as easy as killing a leader and taking their place. Nobles, armies, and the citizenry must all be considered. All of which makes Lady Mari the perfect target for Master Ryota."

Isau didn't understand. He swallowed his pride and asked for her to explain.

Yua ticked her arguments off on her fingers. "First, her citizens are uneasy. The famine may be easing, but several hard cycles are behind us. Many people have gone hungry for as long as they can remember, and they point their fingers at Lady Mari."

"Why?"

"Because she is supposed to protect and feed them all,

and as the only woman with any real power in the Three Kingdoms, she's an easy target."

That didn't seem fair to Isau, but he didn't argue.

Yua continued her original thread. "Second, Lady Mari doesn't have the support of all her nobles. To keep her people fed, she's taken a tremendous amount of food from the nobles and redistributed it to the citizens. It's prevented the revolts the other kingdoms have dealt with, but a poor noble is an unhappy noble, and no small number of them wouldn't mind seeing her vacate the throne. Tomiichi, the noble whose land Master Ryota uses, is among several nobles who have created an alliance. If Lady Mari falls, order will be quickly restored."

Isau nodded along. He didn't quite understand, but what he knew was that Master Ryota had a plan, and powerful friends.

"Finally," Yua said, "the Northern Kingdom is among the strongest positioned in the Three Kingdoms. The population is low, but it has tremendous mineral resources. If the blades can seize control of the Northern Kingdom, we'll be well prepared to take control of the Three Kingdoms and unite them once again."

"That's Master Ryota's plan? To reunite the Three Kingdoms?"

Yua nodded. "Eventually. The lands won't survive split as they are. Only under the strong leadership of the blades can this land return to its rightful place. And Master Ryota will command the blades."

Isau leaned back against the cushions, amazed by the ambition of those he had fallen in with.

Everyone dreamed of a united kingdom, but it seemed more out of reach every day. Tensions between the three kingdoms were always high. But if anyone had a chance of making the dream a reality, perhaps it was Master Ryota. Isau began to wonder. Perhaps Eiji and Master Ryota weren't that different. Perhaps, in time, Isau's alliances wouldn't be torn in two.

Or maybe it was all wishful thinking.

"How did you meet Master Ryota?" he asked.

It had been an impulse, a question he'd had since they'd first met, but one he didn't dare ask. It felt too personal, too much like asking a friend to share their darkest secret. But he wanted to know, and some part of him hoped that in her story he might find some of his own answers.

At first, he worried that he had gone too far. Yua's stare was hard, and her aura chilled the entire carriage.

Then she answered. "There's not much to tell, actually. I grew up on a farm, much like you did. My father tended the land, along with two older brothers. We weren't rich, but we grew enough for us to live on, and some extra that we gave to neighbors in exchange for other goods. My youngest days are filled with memories of being busy, but happy. It was my parents, more than anyone else, who taught me the importance of looking out for those who couldn't protect themselves.

"Master Ryota found me when I was younger. I hadn't seen six cycles yet, but my gift was strong. I think my parents suspected, but they were always loving and kind. Master Ryota told them about the horrors of the monasteries, and told them he had a safe place where I could live. He gave me a final moon with them, then returned and took me to the village. I was among the first he found."

When she saw the look on his face, she smiled. "Not what you expected?"

"You were happy with your family?"

She nodded. "Very. I still write to them at times, just to

let them know that I'm safe, and that I'm doing well. I miss them sometimes, but what we're doing will change the world."

The world was never what he expected it to be. Knowing Yua, he'd expected violence in her past, but it sounded as though she had little but good memories of her childhood. So many blades seemed forced into violence, but she'd chosen it. Then a memory came to him.

"You said, when you started training, that you fought too often. Why?"

"I was the first girl Master Ryota recruited. The boys didn't believe Master Ryota's judgments about me, and they mocked me mercilessly. My first few cycles of training with Master Ryota were difficult. That was when I learned that if we want something, we need to fight for it."

Isau thought on that. "Does it ever bother you, doing what we must?

"It did once, but not for a long time. The world is a cold place for blades. I take no joy in my actions, but immense pride in what those actions might bring about."

She won him over again with those words. Like Eiji, she wasn't perfect, but he admired her efforts to change the world. In this, she was the greater master, and he thought he was willing to follow her to the ends of the Three Kingdoms.

55

E iji couldn't help but think of humid and steamy days. Such days were unpleasant, but the heat and moisture in the air portended something worse to come. Storms were likely, rolling banks of clouds that ripped the air apart with light and sound.

The Northern Kingdom had much of that same feel.

Perhaps it was imagination, fueled by the events of the past moon, but he didn't think so. The air was heavy, leaden with promises of violence. Scenes of starvation and struggle, common as they were, now carried a new weight.

What would be the spark that unleashed the storm?

Such thoughts troubled him. They led him to glance over his shoulder frequently, not because he feared attack, but because a vocal piece of him wanted to travel any direction besides the one he did.

He called that voice his voice of reason.

This wasn't his fight, and even his concern for Isau was overwhelmed by the enormity of what awaited them in Stonekeep.

Chiasa's shifting attitude didn't inspire confidence, either.

After the burning village, she'd marched eastward with grim determination. But the days of riding had changed her demeanor. He'd been around her enough now to notice the differences.

He suspected it had something to do with their frequent stops. Anywhere from three to six times a day they would rest, often at inns and taverns, but sometimes at random homes.

Eiji enjoyed a break as much as the next traveler, but given the nature of their travel, haste seemed appropriate. And none of their stops lasted long. He would just be getting settled when they would have to leave again.

A pattern soon emerged. Wherever they were, Chiasa would find a ledger, either in the possession of a person or hidden in places no one would look. Inside were notes written within in some cryptic text Eiji couldn't hope to decipher. Chiasa flipped through a few pages, scowled, then made her own notes.

Then they would ride on, the lines of concern etched ever deeper into Chiasa's expressions.

Eiji knew better than to ask for details. He could piece together the meaning of Chiasa's actions easily enough. The ledgers represented Lady Mari's vast web of informants, and whatever Chiasa sought, she wasn't finding.

They rode long days, pushing their mounts to the brink of exhaustion. Before long, they were just a couple of days outside Stonekeep.

This was new territory for Eiji. In his travels throughout the Three Kingdoms, he'd never dared come here. Part of it was the history embedded in the land, but the more pragmatic part of his decision was based on the large monastery, named Discipline, filled with monks that zealously patrolled most of the approaches to Stonekeep. Lady Mari's known history with the blades had dictated the creation of a powerful monastery near her home. Discipline was supposed to keep her bound tightly to the terms of the treaty. This was no place for a blade to be.

Which raised a question he didn't bother asking. Why would Yua bring Isau here? The monks might not be that threatening in small groups, but their numbers in the area were enormous.

Eiji didn't think their opponents were fools, though, which meant more was happening here than he understood.

And that worried him even more.

They pulled up to an inn for lunch, one of Chiasa's choosing, which meant that it held a ledger inside. Eiji didn't know if she'd simply memorized an incredible list of locations, or if she followed some signs invisible to his eye. Either way, they hadn't stopped anywhere that didn't have one of the books.

Sure enough, as Eiji waited for their food to appear, Chiasa vanished into a small room with the innkeeper. She returned just as their food arrived.

Despite the long day of riding already behind them, Chiasa didn't dig into her meal. She sat there, a vacant look in her eyes as she stared off somewhere only she could see.

She spoke of her own accord, a feat so rare Eiji wondered if he should make a note of it in one of her ledgers. "There should be more."

He didn't respond, largely because his mouth was full.

Her shoulders slumped. "I'm not going mad, am I? Something enormous is approaching Stonekeep."

Eiji agreed. He didn't know what, exactly, but they had

found a collection of blades hiding on a noble's property. Some of those blades had left, seeking out a village where apparently everyone was a trained killer. And now those same blades were traveling to Stonekeep.

Yes, something enormous was definitely happening. In his mind's eye, he saw the thunderclouds building, ominous on the horizon. He nodded. "I think so."

"There's nothing," Chiasa said. "Not even a whisper. I know that my message will reach Lady Mari. I ensured that it would. But there is nothing to back it up, no corroborating piece of evidence. I know what I've seen, but without something else to support it, I don't know that Lady Mari will have the information to take action."

"No one else has reported anything similar?"

"No. There are a few recent entries of pairs of strangers traveling through, and I suspect they are from our mysterious village, but they aren't raising enough suspicion to merit special notice. No one will connect them with my report."

Eiji wondered if it wasn't too late to turn his horse around and ride the other way. He wanted no part of what was coming.

Chiasa pressed her lips together in a tight line. "I think you should leave."

Eiji almost choked on his food.

A hint of a smile played across her lips.

Once he'd sufficiently recovered, he found his voice. "You'd let me?"

"I haven't been stopping you for a long time." She paused, and Eiji thought she looked like she was deciding whether or not to tell a secret. "But as we get closer, you won't have the chance anymore. You'll get swept up in all of this, and I know you don't want that. So you should go, now, after this meal."

Eiji glanced around to make sure they weren't being overheard. "You'd let a blade wander free?"

"No," she said, "but I'd let you."

Her claim brought Eiji's thoughts to a standstill. She risked her livelihood by offering him this chance. He would never have expected such a gift from her, but now he felt like a fool for not understanding her better before.

Eiji thought the choice would be easy.

All that he wanted was to put this behind him. He should have been out the door already, taking his horse and riding west as fast as the animal's legs could carry him.

And yet, he remained seated, and he couldn't figure out why.

Perhaps it was the hint of a promise Chiasa offered. Perhaps it was the boy.

Or perhaps he was just a cursed fool who possessed an incredible ability to always choose poorly.

Whatever the reason, he wasn't sure what path he would take.

They finished their meal in companionable silence. Eiji kept glancing toward the door, but he couldn't quite convince himself to leave.

If he left, he'd be abandoning Isau for good. Whatever was happening would swallow the boy up soon, and there would be no retrieving him.

It felt as though an hourglass was draining away. With every bite, the moment of his final decision loomed larger. They finished their meal and went out to their horses.

It had to be now or never.

Chiasa had given him the opportunity he'd been dreaming of almost since the moment they met.

She started down the road toward Stonekeep without even so much as a farewell, leaving him on his horse, choosing which direction to go.

He gave Chiasa one last, long look. She was a remarkable woman.

Then he shook his head.

Enough was enough.

He turned his horse west and rode away, leaving his problems behind.

56

I sau noticed when they departed from the well-traveled road heading to Stonekeep, mostly because the carriage began jolting and rocking. At times, he worried their conveyance would fall apart over the rough path. He looked to Yua, but she displayed no surprise, so the departure must have been planned.

He wished she would tell him more. After all he had done, he deserved more of her trust. Her gifts of information were rare, but he felt like a true part of their movement when she did. Most of the time, he felt more like a passenger being dragged along on a journey where he didn't even know the destination.

But digging iron out of the side of a mountain was easier than getting secrets out of Yua. Isau didn't even bother asking. If she wouldn't volunteer the information, it was unlikely she would answer a direct inquiry.

Isau contented himself with staring out the window. His brief stint in the mountains of Master Ryota's village had only whetted his appetite for more. After a lifetime of flat plains and fields, mountains now held an appeal he couldn't articulate, but couldn't deny. Although he knew they were just stone, he thought of them as majestic and noble.

The mountains here had a different character than the ones further north. Here, they were sharper, with jagged peaks and exposed granite. The mountains surrounding Master Ryota's village had been imposing, but these were intimidating. He'd heard somewhere that Stonekeep had never fallen to siege, and if it rested up in those peaks, he began to understand why.

Yua gazed out of the carriage with him, and it was she who ordered the driver to halt. Isau couldn't say what clue she'd spotted, but she opened the carriage door and dropped down. After she held a short conversation with the driver, Isau found himself alone once again with Yua, watching the carriage return the way they had come. The departure had an air of finality to it, as though he would never see the carriage again. After the last league, he wasn't sure that was a bad thing.

Yua watched the carriage go, and once it was out of sight led him up a small trail Isau hadn't even noticed before. The trail gained elevation quickly, and it wasn't long before Isau was struggling to breathe.

Fortunately, Isau soon sensed the end of the journey. Though he couldn't see it yet, he felt a gathering of blades, so strong he'd only felt anything like it once before. To his sense, it felt as though most of Master Ryota's village was here, packed into a small space. The thought of reuniting with so many friendly faces put a spring in his step that hadn't been there before.

Not long later he crested a ridge where he found Master Ryota's camp. As his sense had informed him, tents were crowded around a small mountain pool, fed by a trickling waterfall. The encampment looked out over a vast landscape, and at that moment, Isau didn't want to be anywhere else in the world.

He grinned from ear to ear as some of his friends from the village found him. Though barely a half moon had passed since he'd seen them, it looked like they had all grown more than a hand since he'd seen them last. Yua left them to their catching up, promising to return soon.

Isau's reunion with his friends didn't last long. It only felt like Yua had been gone for a few moments when she returned with a summons from Master Ryota. Isau's friends wished him well, but a lump grew in the back of his throat. Lying to Yua had been hard enough, but he wasn't sure he could to Master Ryota. He only hoped the master didn't have any questions about the village and what had happened there.

Yua led Isau to the edge of the encampment furthest from the path. Not that he couldn't have found Master Ryota on his own. Even resting, the man's aura was unmistakable. The master studied various documents, his eyes narrowed in concentration. He put it all aside when Yua and Isau approached.

Master Ryota directed his gaze at Isau, no doubt searching for lies. Isau's heart pounded in his ears. It was as he feared. Yua had seen through his deception, and now he would be called to account. Isau knew he was dead.

Master Ryota's voice was far gentler than Isau expected. "Will Eiji follow you?"

Isau gulped and searched for an answer. Fortunately, he suspected the truth would suffice. "Yes, master." It was a belief he'd developed in the last few days. Despite everything, Eiji would follow. Isau knew it to be true, and at times, even imagined he sensed the blade behind him.

Master Ryota glanced back toward his papers. His next

question was aimed at Yua. "How much of a threat is this blade?"

"He's persistent," Yua said, "and with that archer guarding him, hard to kill. But by himself he's not that strong, at least not for a nightblade."

Master Ryota took a deep breath. "When the time comes, I want you to kill him."

Isau hoped Master Ryota was speaking to Yua. He had no desire to kill Eiji, and hoped he never had to make such a choice.

But then Master Ryota was again staring at him, and Isau felt the pressure of the man's gift examining him. He nodded. "The boy is considerably stronger than when he left."

A fierce pride seized Isau, not just for himself, but for Yua. It had been under her instruction that he'd advanced so quickly. His advancement was hers.

Master Ryota seemed to think the same. "He will continue to train under you as we move. Every student capable of advancing before the attack is vital, even if he is so young."

Yua bowed, and Isau realized the only reason he'd been summoned was because Yua wanted him evaluated by the master himself. He looked down at his hands. He didn't feel that much stronger than when he'd left. But if Master Ryota claimed it, it must be true.

Master Ryota gave them his final instructions. "Now that both of you are back, we'll take one more night. Use the time to rest. Tomorrow we move and take possession of our new home."

57

S ome of the bloodiest battles were fought with only one warrior, whose only opponent was himself.

Self-preservation warred against Eiji's desire to save Isau. For the moment, self-interest held the higher ground, repelling assault after assault. But the fight ripped up the peaceful fields of his mind, tearing deep furrows in the land and coating his thoughts with the blood and broken bodies of his old ideals.

It wasn't his fight.

Eiji repeated the phrase like a mantra, hoping that repetition would make it true.

Or, at the very least, make it feel true.

It wasn't his fight.

And it wasn't. He didn't care what schemes Isau's new friends hatched. He'd been rejected both by the island where he'd been born and the Three Kingdoms where he'd die. What point, then, was wasting his blood or energy? Better to use that effort to create something of a life for himself here.

He railed against the guilt that built like a towering

thundercloud with every step his horse took. What did he have to feel guilty for? No one was asking for his help.

None of this had anything to do with him anymore. Chiasa had made the defense of the Northern Kingdom her life's work. Eiji only wanted to live in peace. And Isau had decided, time and time again, that he preferred Yua's company to his.

On the battlefield of Eiji's mind, Isau was self-preservation's nemesis. Like an enemy general, he launched small assaults on Eiji's conscience, finding weaknesses and exploiting them.

This fight had nothing to do with Eiji, but everything to do with Isau.

Eiji reined his horse to a stop. He had maybe only made it half a league. If he kept moving forward, he wouldn't stop. He would run to the edges of the Three Kingdoms, if that was what it took. Maybe even beyond. And he would live with his regrets for the rest of his life.

But at least he'd be alive to have regrets.

He turned his head, looking back at the mountains that still hid Stonekeep from view. This land had already seen plenty of blood, enough blood for hundreds of cycles. But more would soon be shed. Of that, Eiji had little doubt.

Where others saw majesty in the snow-covered peaks, Eiji only saw threat. Death waited in those mountains. It sat, patient as any predator, ready to let its prey walk right into its open jaws.

Chiasa had called him a fool, and maybe he was.

But was he more of a fool for leaving it all behind, or for returning to a fight that wasn't his?

In the end, his selfishness won out.

Eiji turned his horse around.

He had no desire to live with even more regrets. He

carried enough already, and if he could do well by Isau, then perhaps, when he rejoined the Great Cycle, he could point to something he was proud of. At the very least, perhaps it would ease this burden that crushed him little by little every day.

Eiji pushed the horse into a gallop. If he had any amount of luck, Chiasa wouldn't have gotten too far.

His luck, if it could be called that, held. He ran into her not more than a league from where he'd left her side. Given how little she'd traveled, it was almost as though she'd been waiting for him to return.

She didn't even turn her head as he came up beside her. "You didn't make it very far," she noted, a hint of satisfaction in her voice.

"Thought you might miss my company," he replied. "Didn't want you to suffer."

Chiasa made a sound that might have been a snort or a laugh. She shook her head, but her next words were more serious. "Some part of me had hoped you would accept the offer. I'm not sure Isau can be saved."

"I couldn't live with not trying."

They rode for a while, but for the first time since he'd met the enigmatic woman, Eiji felt as though they were riding together. No longer was she his captor and keeper.

"For what it's worth," she said, "I'm glad you're here."

He nodded, and they continued on.

It turned out they'd been even closer to Stonekeep than he'd realized. They turned a corner in the road and there it was, looming far above them at the end of the valley.

Stonekeep was a marvel of both design and location. It sat high up in the mountains, at the tip of a valley, accessible only by a single narrow road that hugged the side of the mountains to the north. Where Chiasa and Eiji rode, the valley was maybe a league across, but rapidly narrowed as one came closer to Stonekeep.

Eiji looked out on that valley. The road they traveled would eventually turn into the one that led to Stonekeep, and was high enough above the valley floor that he had a mostly uninterrupted view of the land.

This was a place where history had changed.

If he was being honest, he'd expected more. The final battle of the Great War had cost thousands of lives and had been the last time the Three Kingdoms had seen the blades go to war. In that battle, the blades had singlehandedly destroyed the ability of most of the noble houses to wage war with one another. They had laid the bloody ground-work for the treaty that now defined the Three Kingdoms.

And for all of that, Eiji had expected—something—he supposed. A monument, or some evidence of what had come to pass here.

But the valley was filled with farmland, the same as any other. Had Eiji not known where they were, he would have had no clue what had happened here.

He felt wronged. These had been his ancestors who'd given their lives.

But the land healed, and the people forgot. Faster than it seemed possible. Eiji shook his head. "It's like the battle never even happened."

Chiasa looked at him, then pointed out two children working in a field maybe two hundred paces away. "Those children don't care about the Great War, and maybe don't even know how much this land means to the Three King-doms. But they are happy, and don't fear for their lives." She paused. "Isn't that enough?"

Eiji wasn't sure it was. But maybe it had to be.

They rode on, soon coming to what was probably the

last inn before Stonekeep. Eiji felt an aura within, one familiar but long absent from his life. He looked at Chiasa, who had an enormous grin on her face.

"No," he said.

She turned and entered the inn, giving him little choice but to follow.

It couldn't be, yet it was.

He swore and wondered if it was too late to turn back. Chiasa's warning, that this was his last chance to leave, took on a different meaning now. She'd known. Her smile was evidence enough of that. Somewhere among all those ledgers, there'd been a message.

Eiji followed her into the common room, where an enormous man sat in the corner. He smiled when he saw Eiji and raised a mug of ale in his direction.

Itsuki looked as smug as ever.

58

I sau woke to the sounds of camp being broken. He blinked, doubting his hearing at first. The sun hadn't even risen yet, but from the quick movement of people outside his tent, Isau didn't think it would be long before the entire camp was prepared to leave.

The others in his tent were already awake, and he rubbed his eyes, rolled into a sitting position, and joined them in packing up the gear and passing it on to the porters who would move it when the time was right. Master Ryota's blades didn't travel alone. They had support from the villagers who served them back home.

Last night, Master Ryota had explained what today held for them all. As often seemed to be the case, Isau couldn't believe the sheer audacity of Master Ryota's ambition. Such feats had never been attempted, so far as Isau knew. And because it had never been attempted, it might just work. How could anyone defend against what they couldn't predict?

Master Ryota himself would join in this fight, and Isau was both eager and terrified to see him in battle.

Yua found him as he finished breaking his fast, as she had promised. She asked a silent question with her gaze and he nodded. "I'm ready." He wasn't sure if that was true, but either way, they would be marching soon. There seemed little point in admitting how nervous he was.

"We'll be near the rear of the column," she said.

"Why?"

"Because this is only the first battle of many, and the ones still to come are more important. We can't be risked if it can be avoided." When she saw the expression on his face, she cautioned him. "We might not be near the front, but prepare to fight regardless. Our battle will not be an easy one."

Once, Isau might have wanted to be near the head of the column. He dreamed of the hero he might become. But now that he had seen violence firsthand, his eagerness had faded. If being near Yua kept him safer, he'd voice no complaint.

The last part of his preparation was to don a white robe over his other clothing. It felt wrong, like wearing the skin of another person.

For many moons now, these robes had represented everything he'd come to fear, everything he wanted to overthrow. They felt scratchy against the bare skin on his arms.

Then he thought of what the robes would allow him to do, and a wave of strength flowed through his limbs. The very robes he'd so feared would serve as the tool to begin destroying the monasteries. He wasn't a monk, but an instrument of revenge. He clenched his fist. Today, the monks would pay a debt they'd been building for cycles.

Master Ryota's plan was simple, but Eiji had once told him that simple plans were often the best. Master Ryota seemed to be of a similar mind.

When all was prepared, the blades of Master Ryota's village gathered in a column, three across and over a dozen deep. Together, they began their journey from the hidden camp to their destination below.

Discipline.

A foolish name, but a trend the monks had started a few cycles ago. They named their monasteries after what they considered desirable traits. By all accounts, Discipline was the largest in the Northern Kingdom, and perhaps the largest in all three lands. For all Master Ryota's recruiting, he informed them they would probably still be outnumbered.

And yet Isau soaked up the confidence from those around him. There were nerves. He saw the way eyes darted back and forth, how many were a little too quick to laugh, too eager to hide their concerns behind a mask of joviality. No one was fooled, but no one spoke against it, either.

When Master Ryota ordered them forward, they marched, careful to maintain the formation of the column. They had about a league to walk, but Isau feared it would feel like far longer.

They hiked down the mountain, and it wasn't long before Isau saw their destination below. It was a stone fortress with thick walls and stout buildings. Had they besieged the monastery, Isau suspected it would have taken a small army and at least a moon of combat. Those walls could repel even Master Ryota.

Hence the white robes.

They possessed one advantage greater than any other. The monks were secure in their position. They believed themselves to be the strongest warriors in the Three Kingdoms, invulnerable to attack. It weakened them. Even now, only two monks patrolled the walls of their monastery, and their attention seemed to be everywhere but on their duty.

Before, Isau hadn't believed such a simple deception would work.

How did the gifted surprise the gifted?

By pretending to come as friends.

And sure enough, even as they approached, the monks on the walls did nothing to warn the others of their arrival. The gates remained open, welcoming the coming destruction. Isau looked up as he passed through, surprised by how thick the wall surrounding the gate was. Then they were in the courtyard, where a group of monks mingled together casually awaiting the new arrivals. Master Ryota didn't bother upholding the deception a moment longer than he needed. Without so much as a warning or a shout, he drew his sword and sliced across the neck of a monk nearby.

It was signal enough. All his students leaped into action. Swords were drawn, and a dozen monks returned to the Great Cycle within two or three heartbeats. The students advanced, spreading out from the column like a flower opening wide.

Isau kept close to Yua, as he'd been instructed. He would have done the same even if no one had given him the orders. She'd been part of the center column, whose purpose was to reinforce whoever needed help.

Isau had seen several faces of death, but he'd never seen so many happen so quickly. He felt it deep in his bones, his sense announcing the loss of each life, candles being snuffed out all around him.

The surprise was complete, but this was Discipline, one of the most important monasteries in the Three Kingdoms. The monks responded quickly, and soon the sound of steel clanging against steel echoed within the thick walls of the monastery.

Most duels appeared one-sided. The majority of the monks were armed with staffs instead of swords and lacked the martial skill to defeat the edged weapons. Isau watched as students delivered fatal wounds, then engaged in that complicated exchange of energy as the monks died.

There were exceptions. The monks armed with swords were better trained, and in some cases, were superior to the students. Isau watched familiar faces fall, and for a few moments, it seemed that the battle for the monastery teetered on the edge of victory and defeat.

Isau sought Master Ryota with his gaze, but saw nothing. He could sense his master, though, moving through the shadows on the far side of the monastery. He was completely unsupported, but that didn't seem to bother him in the least. Any ally near him was just as likely to slow him down as to aid him. Everywhere he walked, he brought death.

Off to Isau's side, a monk killed a student with a primal yell. His eyes fixed on Isau, and the young man's heart skipped a beat.

"Stay here!" Yua commanded. She stepped between the monk and Isau, breaking the line of sight between them. Isau immediately felt safer, sheltered from that gaze. Yua drew her daggers, and Isau was certain the monk didn't have much longer to live.

His sense alerted him to another danger. Off to his other side, a bloody monk emerged from a tangle of bodies. One sword was stuck through his side, which he pulled out with a roar that leaked blood from his mouth. He saw Isau and charged, leading with the point of his sword.

Isau froze for a moment, but remembered his training in time. He slid to the side, sensing the attack before it struck.

The monk looked confused, but before Isau could turn the tide to his advantage, the monk twisted his sword and cut again.

Isau dodged, but tripped and fell backward.

The monk didn't hesitate. He stepped forward, sword upraised, ready to make the killing blow.

59

Itsuki's grin faded as they joined him at his table. Despite initial appearances, the monk had changed. The smugness that had greeted them when they entered had been little more than a mask, a reminder of a past self.

In their time together, Eiji had come to understand Itsuki's confidence, born of a lifetime of victories. Among his peers he had no equal. But after meeting the mysterious man in the mountains, Itsuki now understood defeat. It lurked behind his eyes, a darkness that no smile quite hid.

Eiji couldn't sympathize. He'd never been the strongest, even among children his age. He didn't know the pain of losing that part of his identity.

More ale arrived at the table, and soon the exchange of stories began. Itsuki insisted they go first, and Eiji let Chiasa tell their tale of the past half-moon. His interest was in the monk. Itsuki listened to Chiasa with full attention, sipping at his drink as their story unraveled. He had few questions when she finished. Eiji was reminded again of the trust that existed between the two of them. There was so much they didn't understand, but Itsuki didn't poke at the unanswered questions. If Chiasa said she didn't know something, Itsuki simply accepted.

Eiji was envious of the two of them.

Mugs empty, another round was ordered. Itsuki looked like he needed the liquid courage to proceed.

He began his story unprompted.

"I should have listened to you, Eiji." He stared at his ale, then lifted his eyes to meet the nightblade's. Eiji saw how much the confession cost him. "I sensed his strength, but I think some part of me didn't believe it was real."

Itsuki took a long drink from his mug. He shook his head. "I've never felt the like," he confessed. "Up close, it was all I could do to focus on the battle. His aura makes him nearly invincible. It was like fighting within a fire, the flames hungry for my flesh. In two passes I knew I had no chance. Somehow I survived another two, but I never came close to cutting him." Itsuki paused, then took a deep breath. "I ran."

Itsuki's suffering took on a new meaning with those words. Eiji saw the change, plain as day, and realized he'd misjudged the monk once again. Itsuki wasn't distraught because he'd been beaten. He was haunted because he had found the limits of his courage.

That, Eiji well understood.

Everyone lived within a story of their own telling. Some painted themselves as the hero, others were content to call themselves merely honorable. Still others only told stories in which they were the victim, or perhaps even the villain. But few ever realized the stories were just that.

In Itsuki's story, he'd been the equal to any challenge.

His fight in the mountains had revealed a harsher truth.

Against an overwhelming foe, Itsuki would run.

Eiji didn't judge the monk. Most people ran, in his experience. Retreat was only difficult for those who thought they never would.

Itsuki continued. "He pursued me, and he was too fast. I couldn't even flee from him." The monk's hands tightened around his mug, to the point Eiji considered pushing his chair back a bit in case the mug shattered and spilled ale everywhere. "But I found a cliff, and I jumped into the waters below."

Despite himself, Eiji leaned forward as Itsuki's story continued. The monk's next few days had been one challenge followed by another. Hungry and cold, and pursued by the blades who hid in the mountains. The fact that Itsuki was here to even tell his story was testament enough to the man's skill.

He had survived, and beyond that, had learned something of the blades in the mountains.

"The man calls himself Master Ryota. He claims to have uncovered a secret technique that allows all who master it to grow stronger as they fight."

Itsuki noticed Eiji's expression at that. "I didn't believe it at first either, but now that I've had some time to consider it, it might be true. I can't think of any other way to explain the man's strength."

Eiji decided to ignore the question for now. The how didn't really matter. The strength existed, and it needed to be dealt with.

"They march toward Stonekeep," Itsuki said. "Ryota and most of his students left the village not long after our fight. Once I was certain of their direction, I ran ahead to warn Lady Mari and the monasteries."

Chiasa leaned into that information. "They know?"

Itsuki nodded. "I informed Lady Mari a few days ago. She said she would take action."

Chiasa breathed a deep sigh of relief and sank back into her chair.

"The monks were not so interested in my warning," Itsuki said. "I spoke with the abbot and he ordered me out of Discipline."

Chiasa's eyes hardened. "He still hasn't forgiven you?"

"It would seem not."

At Eiji's questioning look, Chiasa flashed a hint of a smile. "When Itsuki last visited Discipline, he ended up challenging the abbot to a duel. Of course, Itsuki humiliated the man. But that was cycles ago."

Eiji wished he understood the monk in front of him better. In so many ways, the man seemed to be the epitome of everything the monasteries stood for, and yet he was an outsider among them.

Chiasa asked the question Eiji also wondered. "What's next?"

Itsuki's gaze turned to Eiji then. Eiji met it, no longer afraid of the monk. Whatever answers Itsuki was looking for in Eiji's posture, he apparently found. "Tonight, at least, we rest. You both look exhausted, and there are plenty of rooms available. I chose this inn because any advance into Stonekeep must pass here, and there's no way for them to pass without me noticing."

"They also can't pass without sensing you," Chiasa said. "Even Eiji sensed you a few dozen paces away from the door."

"It's not a perfect plan," Itsuki admitted. "But I was also waiting for you. It might be wiser to move up to Stonekeep tomorrow. Perhaps Lady Mari can convince the monks at Discipline to increase their presence in the area, or we can convince her to close the gates for a time. Even Ryota and his blades can't take Stonekeep if it's prepared for them."

Eiji heard the plan, but he was largely focused on the "we." When Itsuki said the word, it had taken on a new meaning.

Eiji had become one of them. Not as someone they needed to escort or protect, but a member, or a friend.

Itsuki left them for a few moments to arrange their rooms for the night.

Chiasa spoke softly. "You regret not fleeing?"

Eiji frowned, realizing something inside him had changed as well. The argument that had been running since he'd first met Isau had faded. It hadn't even occurred to him until just now. But he was determined. He understood what he would do next, and had no fears about the outcome, even if he rejoined the Great Cycle. "Not one."

She smiled. "Good."

When Itsuki returned they spoke for a while longer, but Chiasa eventually claimed the need to rest. She stood up, locked eyes with Eiji for a moment, then walked to the stairs that led to the rooms above.

Which left Eiji alone with Itsuki, once again. He wasn't sure what to say to the monk, but he felt comfortable around the other man. They drank together in silence.

"It's good to see you again," Itsuki said.

A warmth spread through Eiji's stomach, and he wasn't sure it was just the drink. He nodded. "And you, too." He was surprised to find he meant it.

After a short pause, Itsuki continued. "You're still as thick as a stone."

Eiji frowned.

"Chiasa," Itsuki said.

It took Eiji a few more moments, but when he understood what Itsuki had meant, he felt as though he'd been slapped across the face. Dozens of interactions presented themselves in a new light. His eyes widened, and he looked to the stairs.

But a part of him still didn't believe.

Or maybe he was just frightened.

Either way, he couldn't quite convince himself to follow her.

Itsuki sighed. "I only got one other room, and I don't plan on sharing my bed with you tonight."

It was all the convincing Eiji needed.

60

Time froze in place. The monk stood over him, sword upraised, ready to strike. His face was twisted, almost inhuman, a mix of primal emotions that seemed perfectly matched with blood-spattered white robe he wore.

Then Isau felt as though a hot poker had been shoved deep within him. His stomach burned and his spine stiffened.

He was done with fear and uncertainty. Every adult he befriended forced him on a new path. And he followed, not because he wanted to, but because he was afraid what would happen if he didn't.

All that had led him here.

He was tired of it.

He wouldn't be afraid. Not anymore.

His sense came alive, and he saw the monk's future attack. A straight overhead cut, simple and effective. If Isau remained where he was, the monk's sword would stick in Isau's skull, and another blade would come by soon enough to kill the monk as he worked the weapon free.

But it would be too late for Isau.

The thought passed in less than the blink of an eye, and as soon as Isau saw the future, he knew he could change it.

Isau rolled from his back to his side as the sword came down. The cut struck stone, sending reverberations into the monk's grip. It had been a clumsy attempt.

The monk stumbled forward, the unexpected miss throwing him off balance.

Isau kicked out with his foot. Even if the monk sensed the attack, there was nothing he could do. He was too busy regaining his balance, and a body could only move so fast.

Isau's heel struck the man's left knee. He felt the joint give, and the man collapsed to the ground, landing hard next to Isau.

He didn't give the monk a chance to recover. The moment the man was on the ground he leaped on top and drove his dagger into the man's chest, the same way he'd seen Yua do so often. Isau knew where the heart was. The knife slid in, just nicking the monk's ribs.

The monk's eyes went wide, but he didn't have time to realize what had happened before he died.

Isau felt the moment it happened. The man's energy, so clear to Isau's sense, dissipated. The monk became part of the Great Cycle once again. Perhaps his next journey would be a more peaceful one.

Isau looked up, and for the first time in a few heartbeats, his surroundings extended beyond his own small duel. The battle, it seemed, was nearly over. Only two or three monks remained, and those were quickly killed by Master Ryota and the students.

Isau's eyes traveled around the courtyard, taking the bodies in. The ambush had been nearly perfect, but it hadn't been without cost. There were familiar faces among the dead, their bodies motionless on the ground. So many looked surprised, as though death had somehow snuck up on them.

Isau supposed most didn't go into battle thinking they would die. They lied to themselves, convinced themselves that no matter what happened, they would survive. Where else did they find the courage to draw steel?

He knew he should feel something more. He was supposed to weep and shout to see his friends gone, however briefly he'd known them. As the last sounds of the battle faded, they were replaced by some of the students doing just that.

Perhaps that grief would come, but at the moment, he couldn't find it in him.

All he felt was relief that it wasn't him.

He should probably feel guilty about that, too. But he didn't.

He was alive.

And right now, that was all that mattered.

Master Ryota explored the monastery and examined the carnage. The surviving students sat scattered around the courtyard, listless. Some attempted to clean the blood from their swords and clothes. Others just sat, empty-eyed. A few wept over friends, but fewer than Isau would have guessed.

Master Ryota gave orders. The dead monks were collected and piled haphazardly in a corner of the monastery. The fallen students were carried carefully to another side, their bodies lined up and covered with discarded white robes.

Isau wasn't big enough to help carry the bodies, so he collected the white robes and helped cover his friends. He did so until Yua came and pulled him away. "Others will want that responsibility," she said softly.

He followed her into one of the buildings where Master Ryota sat. The building was richly furnished, looking more like the home of a wealthy noble instead of the monks who lived here.

Master Ryota looked up from a sheaf of papers he'd been reading. "How are they?"

"Tired, but unbroken," Yua replied. "Do we move tonight?"

Master Ryota shook his head. "I still haven't received word from Chiyo." He sighed, and Isau frowned. He'd never seen anything but pure confidence from the man. "It's moving much faster than we'd hoped. I don't think anyone knows the full extent of our plans, but Lady Mari is no fool. She suspects something. The next few days won't be easy."

"But we're behind you, master."

The reassurance seemed to bolster his energy. "You are, and thank you for reminding me, Yua." Master Ryota looked through the papers again. "I think we can safely expect to remain here tonight. Hopefully by tomorrow Chiyo will contact us, and we can march up to Stonekeep." His attention turned to Isau. "How did you fare?"

"He killed a monk in combat," Yua answered.

Master Ryota stroked his chin. "Did you, now?"

Isau nodded, not trusting himself to speak clearly. Master Ryota's attention was almost too much to bear, even casually.

Master Ryota turned to Yua. "Teach him, tonight, if you can."

"Master?" There was uncertainty in her voice.

"It's sooner than I would like, but we might need every advantage we can get, and there is no harm in it, even if it fails. Just ensure there are no witnesses, and make sure it is far enough from here no one suspects."

Yua bowed. "As you command."

She turned and left. Isau bowed to his master as well, then hurried after her. "What was that about?" he asked.

She glanced at him and smiled. Even now, it still had the same effect on him. "Tonight, I'm going to teach you Master Ryota's secret technique."

61

B y the time Eiji woke the next morning, the bed next to him was empty. He wasn't surprised. Chiasa planned on scouting the city today. If something was amiss inside Stonekeep, she hoped to find it.

She didn't seem like the type to lie in bed all morning, no matter the circumstances.

Eiji stretched and rolled out of bed. He sensed Itsuki already down in the common room, waiting for him. For the first time, Eiji realized he was grateful for the company. He didn't know what the future held, but at the moment, he didn't much care. This was good enough.

Itsuki greeted him with his now-familiar smile. Eiji welcomed it. He poured himself a cup of tea and joined the monk in eating everything in sight. The food tasted wonderful. "What shall we do today?"

"I've arranged a meeting with Lady Mari," Itsuki said. "She's taken some precautions already, but now that we've combined our information, she must be made aware of the full extent of the danger. We can't stop this on our own."

"How do you plan on bringing me anywhere near the lady?" Eiji asked. "That sentences us both to death."

Itsuki grinned, and Eiji knew he wasn't going to like the answer. Itsuki reached down and pulled a white robe into view. "For the next few days, I think it's about time for you to become a monk."

Eiji swore. "If you think I'm putting that on—"

"Do you want to meet Lady Mari or not?" Itsuki interrupted.

The protest died on Eiji's tongue. Lady Mari was one of the only people in the Three Kingdoms who knew Koji personally. He'd never considered approaching her directly, for obvious reasons, but shouldn't he take the opportunity now that Itsuki offered it?

He glared across the table. The monk understood him too well. Once their temporary alliance ended, Itsuki would be impossible to outsmart. But the monk was also right. He did want to meet the lady.

Eiji reached out like a petulant child. "Fine."

Itsuki's grin broadened as he handed over the robes. "Welcome, brother!"

Eiji grimaced but bit back his sharp retort.

A full breakfast behind them, they proceeded to Stonekeep.

The hike up the side of the mountain exhausted Eiji. Though it didn't look difficult from distance, the continual uphill climb took a brutal toll on his legs, and the thin air prevented him from filling his lungs. He felt as though he was drowning on dry land.

Eventually, though, they passed through the open gates of Stonekeep.

Eiji noted the layers of protection. The most obvious was the geography of the surrounding land. Only one path led to

Stonekeep, and it was long and narrow. Besiegers would be bunched up and have the disadvantage of being well below the walls of the city. Arrows would rain down on any hostile advance. The gates were as sturdy as any Eiji had ever seen, and if someone did manage to push a force through those gates, the narrow corridors on the other side of the gate would continue to bottle up invaders while archers on the rooftops above had every advantage.

But the design of the city was only part of what he noticed. He also saw the walls loaded with soldiers. Good ones, too. It was all too easy to lose focus on a guard shift, but Eiji saw little inattention here. The guards stood alert, their eyes trained on the approach and narrow passages. The guards at the gate didn't just let them in, either, even with the white robes. They endured nearly a dozen questions before being allowed within the gates.

"Is it always like this?" Eiji asked.

"No. Much of this is due to our warnings," Itsuki answered.

Eiji swore up a storm when he learned their climb wasn't over once they passed the first gates. Stonekeep seemed almost as vertical as it was wide, and stairs and narrow passages were the rule rather than the exception. Eiji alternated between claustrophobia and vertigo. Who would want to live in a place like this?

Itsuki led them still higher, and eventually the castle came into view.

After a day of wonders, Eiji found himself disappointed at the sight of the castle. It possessed a thick wall and many of the defensive advantages one would expect. But it wasn't any larger than some of the largest homes they had already passed. The buildings in Highgate were much larger, and much more suited to the ruling family.

Gaining entrance to the castle took time, with several people needing to confirm that Itsuki was, in fact, expected. But Eiji was once again impressed by the efficiency of the guards.

How did Ryota plan on defeating these preparations? It seemed to Eiji to be hopeless.

Eventually, though, they were ushered into a small room within the castle, tastefully furnished. It was the sort of room that seemed posed, where every piece was in place to tell a story. A sword hung on the wall, and Eiji found himself drawn to it.

He was so distracted he didn't hear or sense her enter. "That's a sword with a lot of history," a strong female voice said from behind him.

Eiji spun around, as though he were a child caught stealing.

His first impression of Lady Mari was that she wasn't at all what he expected. On the island, everyone knew of her, and her life and actions neatly divided the blades. Most still viewed her as something of a hero, the lady who saved them from complete annihilation. She had stood by them when no one else would.

But there were a growing number of blades, most of them younger, who disagreed. They considered her the architect of their exile. They argued that Lady Mari had only used them to her own ends, then sent them away when that purpose had been fulfilled. When he was younger, Eiji had found himself swayed by those arguments.

After a few cycles in the Three Kingdoms, though, he no longer did. Of course she had acted to her advantage. Any ruler would. But he knew the hate most had for the blades. Lady Mari had stood against that.

Admire her or despise her, though, she had always been a figure of legend, larger than life.

In reality, she was anything but.

She was an old woman, with hair more gray than dark. But she held herself with the confidence of a warrior, and her eyes were sharp. She wasn't one to be underestimated.

Itsuki bowed, and Eiji followed suit. "My lady."

She looked between the two of them, then spoke to Itsuki. "You made a friend?"

The sharp disbelief in her tone made Eiji instantly respect the woman. Itsuki choked on his answer. "An ... ally ... my lady, for what is to come."

Lady Mari arched an eyebrow, then turned her attention to Eiji. "That's Koji's sword. He sent it to me, several cycles after he returned to the Three Kingdoms. He said he couldn't bear the weight of it any longer."

"My lady?" Eiji wanted to know more, but why had she told him this?

She shook her head. "There's no point pretending, Itsuki. You think I wouldn't recognize a nightblade?"

Itsuki's mouth opened, but no words came out.

Eiji looked between them. He didn't sense any threat from this woman, but she'd put Itsuki neatly in a corner. He laughed out loud, enjoying the discomfort on the monk's face.

"We've come to warn you, my lady," Itsuki said, attempting to regain his composure.

"More than you already have?"

"My lady, I believe you should close the gates and demand a response from Discipline. Whatever Ryota is putting together, it's well organized, and large. I'm also certain they know we are on to them. They'll move quickly, now. I would feel safer if we had all the help we could get."

"Even the other monks?"

Itsuki nodded.

"I've already ordered my guards to pull double shifts," Lady Mari said. "And there hasn't been so much as a whisper of trouble in Stonekeep. I haven't heard back from Discipline, yet, but I can send another messenger. Unfortunately, closing the gates will cut off the chain of supplies coming to and from the city, and people will suffer. I've scheduled a shipment of seed to leave in just two days."

"Can it be sent today?"

Lady Mari chewed on her lower lip and looked around the room. "You're that certain?"

"I'm that worried."

"I've heard nothing from anyone else, Itsuki. Even my own web hasn't reported anything beyond what I've heard from Chiasa."

It was a challenge, but all Itsuki could do was shrug. The monk had no answer beyond his own certainty.

She sighed. "I'll see what I can do. Perhaps something can be arranged. How long would you want the city closed for?"

Itsuki glanced at Eiji. "We're here with Chiasa. Between the three of us, I'm hopeful we can bring you Ryota's head within five days."

"That's too long," Mari said. "But I'll see. Our safety must be balanced with the needs of the land. I hope you understand."

"All too well, my lady. Thank you."

She gave them a slight nod of her head, then turned to go.

Eiji couldn't let the moment pass.

"Lady Mari?"

She turned back, looking like a patient parent putting up with a willful child.

"What was he like?" Eiji gestured to the sword.

Lady Mari's attitude changed at that. No longer did she appear in a rush to leave. "Why do you ask?"

Eiji hesitated. Every moment Mari remained near him endangered her. The treaty stipulated strict punishments for anyone who spoke to a blade, but that punishment was even more severe for nobles.

But she hadn't thrown them out or had them killed, so she was comfortable with some risk. She could deny the truth, because of the white robes Eiji endured. And he would never get a better chance to learn more about the blade he'd obsessed about for cycles.

"When I first came here," he said, "I had hoped to find him. He fought for the Kingdom, and even when he erred, he continued to serve. I hoped he might show me a new way forward."

Lady Mari was silent for a few moments. "He was a good man, although one torn by his beliefs. But I could always trust him to do what he thought was right."

She paused.

"He would have no answers for you." She looked to his sword. "I believe he's still seeking peace for the harm he's caused. The one lesson he never learned was that his purpose couldn't come from someone else. He had to make it himself." Her eyes settled on Eiji. "Don't make the same mistake he did."

She gave them both a slight dip of the head, then turned and left, leaving Eiji more torn than ever before.

62

Isau and Yua moved through the night, silent as wraiths. Darkness embraced him, hiding him from sight. Once they were well away from Discipline, they stopped to rest about two dozen paces away from a small road.

Yua held out her arm and made a small cut. "Can you heal it?"

Isau's heart beat faster as he reached for her arm. He closed his eyes, and found the process surprisingly difficult. The archer several days ago had been easier to heal, and her wounds had been much more severe. But he'd been practicing his mental focus when he could, and he found the injury and healed her in time.

"Good," she said. "When you heal, you use your own energy to assist in the process, right?"

He nodded.

"Do you think it could be reversed? Could you take energy from me, instead of giving me yours?"

Isau frowned at the thought. He supposed it was possible.

"Try." She held out her arm once again.

Isau latched onto it and repeated the process, except this time he imagined pulling her energy into him. At times, he almost felt as though it might work. It was like pulling on bread dough that refused to separate. It would stretch and bend, but the energy wouldn't quite flow from one body to the other.

Eventually, she pulled her hand away. "That's enough. It's not something anyone else has been able to do, yet, although Master Ryota says it is possible."

She took a deep breath. "Master Ryota's discovery was a simple one, but it was found someplace no one was looking. The technique isn't terribly difficult for anyone who can heal. It's just what I told you: the idea of pulling from instead of giving to. But life holds on dearly. There's only one time when a person's energy can be freely pulled."

Isau thought of the complicated dance of energy that happened whenever one of Master Ryota's advanced students killed someone. "When they die."

She smiled. "Very observant, yes. The technique has two parts. First, you must deliver a fatal blow. Then, you must pull at their energy at the moment of their death. When you do both, two changes occur. First, you gain an immediate surge of energy, one that only lasts for a few moments. But in that time, you'll feel strength like you never have before. Second, there is a lasting effect. It's more subtle, but you'll notice yourself feeling stronger, and your gift will be, too."

Isau considered what she said. On the surface, the idea seemed simple enough, but when he thought about the steps, it would be anything but. He thought of Master Ryota's instructions. "So, if we're going to train tonight—"

"We need to find someone to practice on," she said.

Isau noticed she didn't use the more accurate terms.

They had come out here tonight to kill. His stomach rebelled at the idea. "Isn't that wrong?"

"You need to move beyond the ideas of right and wrong," Yua said. She held his hands in her own. "You've sensed people die, right?"

He nodded.

"You know that some part of them returns to the Great Cycle. You've felt it."

He nodded again.

"We view death as an evil, but it's not. It's a doorway to another life. Hopefully, when those who die are reborn, they are reborn into a better world, the world we will create. We're not taking anything away from them, and in exchange, we earn the strength to make a world where our people can live without fear. Isn't that worth it?"

Yua's eyes lit up as she spoke, and he found himself moved by the strength of her convictions. Something about her argument didn't sit well with him, but he couldn't figure out what. He nodded.

"We'll wait here near the road for a while," Yua said. "If no one comes along, we'll go searching."

They fell silent. Isau used the time to practice with his sense, extending it as far as it could go. He'd been more diligent as of late, and he thought he could notice the difference. Already, he could sense farther than he had before. It wasn't much, yet, but in time, it would grow and grow.

They didn't wait long. Soon, Isau felt a lone traveler walking the road. Yua looked at him. "You know what to do?"

Isau nodded.

"Make the cut a slow death, like to the stomach. That will give you more time to get set. I'll be right behind you to ensure your safety."

Yua spoke with all the emotion Isau would have expected if they were attacking a practice target stuffed with hay. Isau tried to reach the same mindset. Death wasn't harm, and he would be stronger. In time, perhaps he could even be as strong as Master Ryota.

With that final thought echoing in his head, he crept toward the road. He found a patch of tall grass that mostly concealed him, and then he saw the man he was supposed to kill.

The traveler was older, and had seen perhaps sixty cycles. But he still moved well and carried a pack on his back with a firm step. He was by himself, whistling softly as he walked. Isau wondered what he was doing traveling alone, here, at this time of night.

Isau couldn't allow the questions purchase. His hands became weak if he did. He gripped his dagger tightly, and when the man was close, he leaped out of the bushes and plunged his steel silently into the man's stomach, just as Yua had told him.

The man's eyes opened wide with surprise and pain. Then he collapsed to his knees.

Yua emerged from the tall grass, her sword drawn and at the man's throat.

"Why?" the man asked.

Isau ignored the question. He grabbed the man's arm and held onto it tightly, as though the man might run away if he didn't. He reached out with his gift, and the man's energy was easy to find. A strong aura, it seemed, was more hindrance than help with healing. Isau's consciousness took him to the stomach wound, a mess of broken lines of energy.

Isau knew how to heal it. In many ways, it was like the archer's arm, but even more damaged. But Isau thought it was within his ability. It would take everything from him, but he could save the man's life.

He fought against the instinct. That wasn't why he was here. He was here to pull.

So he began, gritting his teeth as he did.

Time lost meaning. Isau crouched there, eyes closed, pulling with all his might. When he lost focus, he shook his head and began again.

Then the man died. Isau felt the moment. The energy, which had resisted for so long, suddenly jumped from the man to him. It felt like waking up from a long nap, but without the grogginess. He could run for days and jump high into trees.

He opened his eyes to see Yua smiling wider than she ever had before. "Impressive." She stood up. "Now, spar."

When he moved, it seemed as though she was playing with him. He sensed her moves well before she made them, and he landed three solid blows before she gave up ground. She came in again, and this time the match was more even. Then, two passes later, she punched him easily. Isau didn't understand.

"As I said," Yua explained. "Right after, you're stronger. But it doesn't last."

Isau thought he would do almost anything to feel like that again.

"But you are stronger, aren't you?"

He looked down at his hands. It wasn't like before, but yes, he did feel stronger. He felt lighter and faster.

"Come," Yua said. "Master Ryota will be most pleased."

And the two left the road and began the journey back to Discipline.

Isau didn't even think for a moment about the dead man they left behind.

63

E iji walked the streets of Stonekeep in a daze, his steps slow and uneven.

When he had left the others, he had claimed a desire to understand the city better. It was a thinly veiled excuse, but they let him leave without question. He appreciated their trust. He still wore the white robes, so didn't expect trouble.

Eiji wished his excuse was true. Stonekeep's steep construction and narrow passages created a city unlike any in the Three Kingdoms. Given the large number of monks who usually watched Lady Mari and her capital, he knew he would never have another opportunity to explore the city.

But he couldn't focus his attention on the endless vistas or the unique streets. His thoughts were turned inward.

Though her words had been gentle, Lady Mari's answers clawed at his heart.

He'd been a fool to expect anything else.

His whole quest had been nothing more than a dream written in sand, washed away by the first wave of the rising tide.

Perhaps he'd always known, but had just never been able to admit the truth. He wanted Koji to have answers, to give him a new direction to his life.

But no warrior, no matter their skill, could give him purpose.

Lady Mari's words had stripped him of his delusion. They exposed something wrong deep within him, a truth long buried.

In his own way he, too, was a coward. Not only did he run from enemies, but he ran from himself.

He had hoped to flee from the responsibilities of his own actions. Lady Mari had cut off his only retreat.

His decisions had always been his own. The path he chose next would be his own.

Eiji's wanderings eventually brought him to an overlook high in the city. He took a seat on a stone bench and stared out at the verdant fields in the valley far below. Here, at least, it looked as though famine might soon be nothing more than a memory, a warning passed down from elders to their grandchildren.

He hoped so. This land deserved respite from the endless cycles of suffering.

It took him longer than it should have to realize that Itsuki had joined him. Despite the monk's considerable aura, Eiji's distraction was great enough that a whole army of monks could have approached him without warning.

Eiji spared Itsuki a glance. The monk looked troubled, but right now Eiji couldn't find it in him to ask why. The two men looked out over the valley together.

"It's beautiful, isn't it?" asked Itsuki.

Eiji nodded. Itsuki had the air of a man who had something he wanted to say but hadn't yet figured out how to broach the subject.

Eiji didn't care enough to make it easy for him.

"What's wrong?" Itsuki finally asked.

Eiji considered this enigmatic monk who had somehow become a partner on his path. He didn't want to trust Itsuki. Their journeys aligned for now, but what happened when they chose to travel separate paths? What happened when he was no longer useful to the monk?

Eiji hoped they would part as friends, but that seemed unlikely. Their lives and beliefs separated them as cleanly as any cut. When their alliance ended, it would be with blood. Itsuki had never pretended otherwise.

So Eiji didn't know why he answered honestly.

"I would have traveled the length and breadth of the Three Kingdoms looking for Koji," Eiji confessed.

"No longer?"

Eiji shook his head. "She was right." He exhaled slowly. "I've been looking for meaning everywhere but the one place it can be found."

Itsuki looked like he understood, sparing Eiji from having to explain further.

A wind picked up, carrying the scents from the valleys far below. Eiji breathed them in deeply. It smelled of new life and fresh beginnings.

"What will you do?" Itsuki asked.

Eiji leaned back. "Save Isau, if I can. Then—I don't know."

"You could join the monasteries."

Eiji regarded Itsuki, wondering if his friend was jesting. But Itsuki appeared serious, with no hint of humor playing across his face.

The monk understood his skepticism. "I mean it," he said. "I understand how you view us, and I won't argue that the monasteries have a long way to go before I can say that I am proud, but we are trying."

Eiji didn't know what to say to that. He hated the monks, but it didn't seem wise to remind Itsuki of the strength of his convictions.

"For every monk who abuses the power granted them," Itsuki continued, "there are five that just want to do right. Your help would be invaluable. You're certainly stubborn enough to fight for the changes that need to happen."

Eiji cut Itsuki off with a gentle wave of his hand. "I'm sorry, but I will never be a part of a system that tears families apart and forces children into a life they didn't ask for."

Itsuki didn't take offense. He spread his hands wide. "Again, I understand. But remember that the monasteries are young. Our methods now are often crude, but the gift needs to be controlled. How else can we prevent battles like the one that took place in this valley, or the one that is coming, thanks to Ryota? I believe there are better ways, but the only way we find them is by searching together. Not fighting one another."

A small pang of guilt seized Eiji. He had forgotten that this valley was where Itsuki's father had lost his life. He didn't know how to answer Itsuki's challenge, so he said nothing. Participation in the system was as good as condoning it.

Eventually, Itsuki spoke again. "Have you come across any monks today?"

Eiji frowned. He hadn't thought of that, distracted as he was. He imagined his journey in his mind. "No."

"Me neither." Itsuki looked worried. "These streets are always crawling with monks from Discipline."

There could be only one conclusion.

"Ryota's coming soon, isn't he?"

Itsuki nodded. "I convinced Lady Mari to close the gates tonight. We should rest, though, while we still have a chance." Itsuki looked one last time at the valley and beyond. "I don't think it will be long before this city sees a clash of swords once again."

64

Isau and Yua returned to Discipline as the early morning sun rose over the horizon. As they approached, Isau saw new activity in front of the gate. Far more than he'd expected. It looked like monks were carrying one another through the gates.

As they got closer, Isau saw that many of the monks' white robes had dark stains on them.

Yua understood first. "Monks returned to Discipline last night."

Isau gave her a questioning glance.

She gestured toward one of the bodies, white robe stained, carried between two familiar faces. "A group of monks from Discipline returned from patrol last night. They might have been in Stonekeep, or somewhere else in the surrounding area. They must have realized something was wrong before they entered the gates."

He felt like a fool for not considering that their siege of the monastery the day before hadn't caught all the monks. Of course it hadn't. The monasteries were like the heart of a beating body, sending monks throughout the land to find and control the gifted. They didn't just sit within their thick walls, hiding from the world.

Yua didn't seem concerned, though, so Isau wasn't either. Those who carried the bodies didn't appear too distraught, so the attack must not have done much harm.

A hive of activity welcomed them into Discipline. In one corner, the bodies of the monks were being stacked with the others. The odor was already becoming overwhelming, which led him to believe that they wouldn't remain here long. If this was to be their new home, he expected Master Ryota would have found a more permanent solution.

Additionally, Isau saw several of his friends training, a sight which now chilled him. The dried blood that remained splattered across the courtyard stones reminded him of the truth of their training. In a clean courtyard, it was easy to forget the techniques they practiced were meant to kill. Here, among the bodies and blood, such a fact couldn't be so easily forgotten.

Yua led him past all the activity, straight to Master Ryota. As soon as the master's attention turned to them, she spoke. "He succeeded," she said, ignoring any preamble.

Master Ryota cast an appraising eye over Isau. Perhaps for the first time, Isau didn't flinch from that gaze. Master Ryota's power might be much greater, but he had done it!

He had learned Master Ryota's secret technique. He didn't have Master Ryota's strength yet, but he now possessed the key. The rest was just a matter of time. He had no reason not to meet the master's eye.

Master Ryota nodded, a gesture which almost made Isau's cheeks flush. "Well done, Isau. I knew your promise from the first moment I sensed you. You have certainly earned the right to join us in our attack on Stonekeep."

The master turned to Yua. "You will keep him near

during the assault," he ordered. "If more opportunities present themselves, they are for him. If you become uncertain you can keep him safe, leave him somewhere where he will be, and continue on."

Yua bowed. "Yes, master."

Master Ryota dismissed them, and Yua and Isau each found places within the monastery to rest. Yua took an empty bunk. Isau wasn't so comfortable among so many reminders of the recently deceased, and chose instead to find a comfortable shaded patch of grass near the main courtyard to sleep on.

He woke to a bell, ringing twice high above him. He needed a moment to regain his bearings, and then he remembered where he was and what had happened.

Isau knew the route to power, now. He would follow Master Ryota as far as he could. Soon he would be strong enough to change the world as he saw fit. He would have true freedom.

The bell summoned them to the courtyard. The students lined up in neat rows, waiting to hear their master speak. Isau stood proud among them. He looked around at the familiar faces. Many appeared tired from the effort of the last few days, but they all stood with their chests out and chins up. No one slouched, and no one wanted to.

He understood. He felt the same.

Their master came and stood before them. "I've never been much for words. I know how hard you've trained for this day. I know how much today means to all of us." He paused, and to Isau, it felt as though the whole world held its breath. "I have received word from our friends already in Stonekeep. All is ready. Tonight, cycles of planning come to fruition. By tomorrow morning ours will be the final voice in the Northern Kingdom. Tonight we take back what has always been ours."

Isau fought the urge to cheer. He was about to be a part of something great, to make his own legend.

Master Ryota looked them all over. "Get some rest today. We leave shortly after dusk, and it's a decent hike to Stone-keep. Be ready. Tomorrow, you will possess the power nobles only dream of. You'll get detailed instructions later, but for now, just know that we assault the castle of House Kita. Your task is to follow me inside and make sure that all who resist rejoin the Great Cycle."

Ryota grinned, a vicious smile. "That is, of course, if I leave anyone alive behind me."

There was laughter at that.

"Rest now," Ryota repeated. "Because tonight will mark the first day of a new era in the history of this land."

65

E iji stared at the ceiling, an undeniable peace settling over him. He knew the feeling was a lie, or more likely, a mask placed over his true emotions. Ryota and his mad students would make their attempt soon. Probably in the next day or two. Eiji didn't see how they could succeed, but no matter what, there would be blood.

And after?

He didn't have the slightest idea.

Isau had saved his life outside the village, but Eiji wasn't convinced it meant the boy wanted to be rescued. Ryota promised power. For a boy who had seen what Isau had, who had lived through what Isau had, that temptation would be almost impossible to resist.

Surprisingly, Eiji didn't worry much. The boy would choose. Eiji couldn't know one way or the other until they spoke again. The outcome was a mystery, but no amount of thinking on his part would change Isau's decision.

Another mystery stood a few paces from the bed, looking out their window into the city below. The moon, just rising, silhouetted Chiasa's lithe figure. Eiji felt a stirring of desire for her, despite the time they'd just spent together.

He knew better than to ask. Chiasa lived by her own desires. If they aligned with his, he could count himself fortunate. If not, nothing he did would change her mind. He suspected she would spend the night haunting the thick walls of Stonekeep. She didn't trust the defenses Lady Mari had put in place, significant as they were.

Although worries surrounded him, none penetrated his thoughts. He drifted in blissful acceptance, ready for life to unfold before him however it would.

Chiasa stepped away from the window, and for the briefest moment, Eiji had hope. But she began dressing, instead.

"Want company?" he asked.

"You'll just slow me down," she said. She didn't intend the comment as an insult, but it stung all the same. She finished dressing, grabbing her waiting bow from the corner of the room. "You should get some rest."

Begrudgingly, Eiji sat up, ignoring her request. The haze surrounding his thoughts began to clear. "I'm rested enough. Even if you don't want company, I should be out there."

If Ryota planned on somehow storming the walls, he would need the cover of night. Nightblades, able to sense the movements of their enemies, weren't restricted by darkness the way soldiers who relied on their sight were. Ryota would need the advantage.

Chiasa simply nodded, her hurry evident. She'd wanted to be on the walls by dusk, but their rendezvous had stretched longer than she expected.

Eiji smiled at that thought.

He climbed out of bed and walked toward the window where Chiasa had just stood. Thin clouds covered the moon, and a building storm promised more darkness soon. Stonekeep was quiet tonight, all citizens inside due to another order of Lady Mari's.

He had to give the lady credit. She took no unnecessary risks.

He took a deep breath, enjoying the view. Behind him, Chiasa moved to the door.

Something wasn't right. He frowned, not able to place it right away. The city below, although quiet, still thrummed with life. Cities were never pleasant places for the gifted, but Stonekeep was worse. The city was so vertical, he felt smothered any time he extended his sense more than a few paces.

He still risked it at the window. It was an instinct, to reach out with his gift to match the vista his other senses took in.

Tonight, life should have been relatively motionless. He expected to find most people moving within the confined spaces of their homes. And there was plenty of that.

But others were not. Some hurried toward the wall, like water flowing downstream. They ran around buildings, but their descent to the wall always continued.

"Wait," he said.

Chiasa released an exasperated sigh behind him. No doubt, she misunderstood his reluctance to let her leave.

He held up a hand for patience. Then he closed his eyes, pushing his sense as far as he dared. He felt them then, clearly. Pairs and trios, all rushing toward the wall with sure steps.

They weren't gifted, though. If not for every law-abiding

citizen trapped in their homes, Eiji wouldn't have noticed them. They slipped beyond the range of his sense as he observed them. He turned to Chiasa. "I think it's happening. Several groups are moving toward the wall."

"Gifted?"

Eiji shook his head, and she frowned. "I'll get Itsuki. Join us downstairs." She looked at him, still naked. "And hurry."

She left.

Eiji glanced at the white robes of the monk, lying on the floor of their room. After a moment of consideration, he ignored them and threw on his regular clothing.

He found Itsuki and Chiasa waiting for him downstairs. Itsuki took in Eiji's clothing choices with a glance but said nothing.

They left the inn, the innkeeper wisely remaining silent about their dismissal of Lady Mari's commands when he saw Itsuki's white robes. "Where?" Itsuki asked.

Eiji pointed to the southwest. "The groups I sensed headed in that direction."

Itsuki and Chiasa glanced at one another, exchanging concerned looks. Chiasa asked the question Eiji knew was coming. "The main gate is over there," she said, pointing to the northwest as though he didn't know that basic piece of information. "Why go there?"

"I don't know. I can only tell you what I sensed."

The decision was Itsuki's. Did they trust Eiji's sense? Or did they obey logic and head toward the main gate? Had Eiji been in Itsuki's place, he wasn't sure which he would choose. Either path presented opportunities and perils.

Itsuki didn't think for long. "We follow what we know. Better than guessing."

They made their way down the streets toward the southwest. Eiji kept his sense open, searching for that same movement he'd noticed earlier. When they didn't encounter any, he began to worry. Itsuki had trusted him. Had he led them astray unintentionally?

Chiasa climbed onto nearby rooftops. She returned a moment later. "Everything's fine. I even got a glance at a wall at one of the patrols. Nothing looked unusual."

Itsuki's look turned to Eiji. The nightblade didn't know what to tell them. He'd told the truth, and he'd assumed ill intent of whoever he had sensed. When he thought back on that moment, he still did. It couldn't be coincidence. Ryota's attack was happening tonight.

The air felt thick, and Eiji's stomach twisted. Off in the distance, thunder rumbled.

"We should continue," he said.

The other two looked uncertain.

"I know. Let's get to the wall, though. If we still haven't found anything, and the guards say the night has been quiet, at the very least we can still follow the wall to the main gate. It will be faster."

The two long-time partners shared another glance. Chiasa nodded.

"Fine," Itsuki said. "But quick."

Eiji took off quickly, trailed by the other two. How much longer would they trust him before Chiasa put an arrow in his back, just to be safe?

They found a stairwell that led up to the wall and took it. The spot on the wall where they arrived was empty, the patrols having moved on to different sections.

Everything looked quiet.

Had he imagined the movement?

Chiasa squatted down, running her finger along the stone beneath their feet. When she lifted it up, it was dark.

Itsuki immediately drew his sword. Eiji, always a step behind, didn't understand until Chiasa spoke.

"It's blood. And fresh."

66

Stonekeep loomed above Isau. To his imagination, the city looked like an aloof master, controlling its subjects from on high. It sneered down at the peasants below.

Until tonight.

Tonight, it would fall.

His legs ached. His rest through the afternoon had been intermittent, interrupted both by nerves and excitement. He focused on his footsteps, placing them carefully behind Yua's. Step by step, he followed her toward Stonekeep.

Yua and he were a pair, a decision Master Ryota had made before they left. They acted on their own. Yua's instructions to him before they left had been simple: follow her.

From listening to the others speak about their own orders, it sounded as though once they broke through the gate and the initial passages, they were to spread out through the city, and each make their own way to the castle. It diluted their strength, but it prevented a single well-laid ambush from killing them all. Over and over,

Master Ryota had reminded them not to underestimate their opponents.

Their targets were the lord, lady, and their family. Anyone who stood in their way also forfeited their lives.

The idea of killing the whole family didn't sit well with Isau, but he said nothing. Yua's explanations stuck with him. Some of the actions they took might feel wrong, but they were in service of a greater good. And the Great Cycle would reward those who deserved reward. Isau believed that.

As they neared, Isau's heart beat even faster, and it wasn't just due to the altitude. They were coming into range of the archers who walked the walls.

Isau looked down again at his white robes. Yesterday, he'd been uncertain about donning them. Today, he knew they were his best armor against falling arrows.

Would the guards be suspicious of such a large group of monks?

Probably, but Isau knew how the people of the Three Kingdoms deferred to the monks. He'd seen it firsthand often enough. The guards would hold their suspicions close until it was too late.

He and Yua walked near the rear of the column, along with the other advanced students. Though no one spoke of it, Isau understood the logic of Master Ryota's placements. It was the same as with the attack on Discipline the day before. If something untoward happened, Master Ryota was more willing to sacrifice less advanced students first.

The logic was heartless, but Isau agreed. All that mattered was reaching the castle and killing the rulers. Whatever acted in service of that goal was good. They were all prepared to lose their lives tonight. Their sacrifices would seed the beginnings of a new future.

The expected arrows never came. Isau kept looking to

the sky, although he wasn't sure he'd be able to see a falling shaft in the darkness. But soon they were well within range of the walls and nothing fell to oppose them.

When he found the will to study Stonekeep, he saw that the gates were closed. He swore. He knew that Stonekeep had never been taken by force. Even Master Ryota couldn't accomplish the impossible. They couldn't besiege the city. Such an idea was foolish.

But up ahead, Master Ryota's step never faltered. And just when Isau thought all was lost, the gates began to open, as if welcoming Master Ryota with open arms.

Isau looked up. On the wall, directly above the gate, stood a figure he'd seen before. It took him a moment to place her. He'd never expected to see her in the guard uniform of the Northern Kingdom.

But Chiyo was unmistakable.

She bowed to Master Ryota, who gave a short bow in response.

Then Master Ryota and his students walked through the gates, unopposed.

67

From where Eiji stood, the wall seemed calm. Guard towers were built into the fortifications at regular intervals. The space between the towers the three warriors occupied was currently empty except for them. Eiji expected more guards, but he didn't know what was standard. It could be a group of guards would emerge from the nearest tower in a moment.

But there was still the matter of the blood. That wasn't so easily explained.

Chiasa's gaze wandered up and down the wall, an arrow nocked in her bow. But no threat was apparent. After a few moments, Itsuki sheathed his sword. The monk and archer shared a glance, and Chiasa angled her head north, toward the main gate. Itsuki nodded, and all three made their way that direction. Chiasa and Itsuki, moving as one, took the lead. Eiji followed two paces behind, his gaze and his sense focused more on the wall behind them than ahead.

Eiji's sense of the area felt normal. Citizens were retired for the night, resting comfortably in their homes. The streets were calm. If not for the foreboding feelings squeezing his heart, it could have been any other night.

Their footfalls landed softly against the unforgiving stone of the wall. Eiji sensed movement a few moments before a pair of guards emerged from the guard tower ahead. The guards startled when they saw the hulking form of Itsuki less than a dozen paces away.

"Hold there!" came the command.

Eiji blinked. Hairs stood on the back of his neck. Something in their bearing, or in the heartbeat of delay between their discovery of intruders on the wall and their order, seemed wrong.

Still, he doubted his sense when it warned him the guards would attack.

That delay between his gift and his reason nearly cost him his life.

Knives spun through the air, thrown with practiced speed and precision. One was aimed at his chest.

Eiji twisted away, losing balance in his hurry to avoid the twirling steel.

In front of him, Itsuki had listened to his own sense. Not only was he in motion before the knives flew, but he shouldered Chiasa to the side, keeping them both from harm.

Eiji caught his balance before he fell, transferring his falling momentum forward. His sword leaped from his sheath, in front of him almost before he was aware of it.

The guards' quick reactions revealed their considerable skill. More knives cut the air between the forces, but Eiji no longer doubted his sense. He sidestepped and raised his sword across his body, deflecting one of the knives meant for his heart.

Then he was upon them. The first guard drew a short

sword, and his reflexes were incredible. The shorter, lighter weapon, combined with the warrior's well-honed instincts, challenged Eiji. Three times he turned aside Eiji's attacks. The defense was almost perfect.

Almost.

Eiji knew he might not be the most proficient swordsman on this section of wall, but he'd learned one lesson the hard way on the island.

When skill failed, sheer relentlessness could overcome.

It proved true tonight as the moon broke through a gap in the clouds. Eiji pressed his assault, never giving the guard a moment to catch his balance. His cuts were strong, each attack forcing the guard back another step. Finally, Eiji opened a gap, and his sword reached through to drink the man's blood. The guard fell with a snarl as his life drained from him.

Eiji turned to the second guard, but there was no need. It looked as though Itsuki and Chiasa had raced one another to kill him. Judging from the cut across his chest and the arrow sticking through his skull, it was difficult to decide who had won.

Eiji looked down at the two guards, and for the first time, he thought about what had just happened. He blanched. "Did we just kill—"

Chiasa shook her head, cutting off his thoughts. "These were no guards."

She kneeled next to them and sliced through the guard uniform with a knife. Dark clothes lay underneath.

"Assassins," Itsuki said.

Then Eiji understood. He felt blind for not having seen it before. The village. Those who had lived there had come to Stonekeep first, and they meant to clear the way for Ryota and his students. Not being gifted, they could enter the cities in pairs or small groups and never raise an eyebrow. But now that they were here...

Eiji looked north at the same time as Itsuki, both swordsmen reaching the conclusion at the same time.

Itsuki swore.

Seeing the distress on the confident monk's face caused Eiji to freeze. That, more than anything else he'd seen, shook him. Part of the peace he'd felt earlier had come from the certainty they had done enough. They'd foiled Master Ryota's plan. The Northern Kingdom was safe.

That certainty had fled.

No orders needed to be given. The three warriors ran as one toward the main gate.

They encountered one more pair of false guards on their way. Chiasa put an arrow in each before they'd even had a chance to draw a knife.

Eiji felt sick. Who could they trust, if anyone in a guard uniform might be an assassin? Or worse, what if they killed an actual guard?

Their pace left him no time to answer these questions.

Eiji came to a stop first. His sense, slightly stronger than Itsuki's, warned him before they came too close to the danger.

Itsuki and Chiasa, running by his side, stopped a moment after he did. Eiji shook his head, the words not quite spilling from his lips.

Finally, they did. "We're too late."

The worst had come to pass. Though he could only catch the vaguest impressions of what happened to the north, he sensed enough to piece together the rest. The warriors from the village had opened the main gate, and Master Ryota and his students had come through.

Eiji sensed the students. They were a mass of energy, just now finishing their journey through the passages into the heart of Stonekeep. Thick walls and narrow passages meant nothing if your enemy walked unchallenged through them.

The mass of students came closer, and Itsuki sensed them then. His face turned pale. Ryota was there, too, as much a challenge as the rest of the students combined.

"You two look like you've seen your dooms," Chiasa said.

"We have," Eiji answered.

As he spoke, the large mass of students broke into smaller groups. Eiji thought he sensed three, but at this distance, he couldn't be certain.

Itsuki looked to Eiji. "I've never seen you move the way you did against those first guards. Are you with us now, truly?"

Eiji hadn't thought much of the fight. The assassins had been trying to kill his friends. Now they threatened the Three Kingdoms. For once, his decision was simple.

"I am."

"Good." Itsuki closed his eyes and extended his sense. Eiji felt the man's awareness expand. When he opened his eyes, Eiji saw resigned certainty. "I know where Ryota is. I'll follow after him." He paused. "And I'm taking Chiasa."

The two men stared at one another. Chiasa, they both knew, could very well mean the difference between death and survival in this upcoming battle. But Itsuki's judgment was correct. Ryota mattered most. If their leader died, this foolish coup might end.

Eiji nodded. "I guess I'll take the rest, then."

It felt like a moment when they should say something to one another. Eiji looked to Chiasa, whose face had become an expressionless mask. What was there to say, though?

Eiji rolled his shoulders back, then turned away from them.

He silently wished them well as they ran their separate ways.

68

After Master Ryota's students passed through the gates, they advanced as a group up the narrow passages on the other side. Every other step, Isau looked up at the imposing walls that squished them together. Had those walls been lined with archers and guards, this advance would have been a bloodbath.

His imagination needed little help. He thought of the arrows raining down on top of them, or stones or flaming pitch dumped from above.

Waking dreams of fire and blood filled his vision.

Nothing could be further from the truth, though. Their passage was nearly silent, with no other sound than the soft rustle of cloth. Chiyo and her assassins had performed admirably. In some places, trickles of slow-moving dark liquid ran down the walls.

As they exited the passages into a small square, the groups began to split as they'd been ordered. Isau followed Yua, who moved with calm certainty.

They didn't make it far before they ran into trouble.

That trouble took the form of a lone man, stumbling through the road.

When he saw them, he perked up. "About time I found someone!" he practically shouted. He lurched toward them, and Isau was surprised the man kept his feet. Even from a dozen paces the smell of piss and alcohol was overpowering.

The drunk must have been very deep in his cups to ignore their white robes.

Isau imagined the man was trying to walk a straight line toward them, but he weaved down the street, effectively blocking their passage. When he got closer, his eyes widened. Perhaps the man had finally realized he was looking at monks, but Isau was surprised once again. Their white robes still evaded the man's attention.

"Well, aren't you a pretty one," he said to Yua.

Yua froze in place, and the man came within a few paces of her, arms outstretched.

Isau stepped forward, intending to stand between the man and Yua, but he was too slow, too surprised by the man's unexpected actions.

Not that Yua needed help.

A dagger flashed once, flinging a dark splatter across the street. She'd aimed low, a fatal but slow cut.

The man collapsed to the stone street, appearing more confused than surprised, like he couldn't figure out why he was on his knees before this woman. Isau watched as the man's insides leaked from him, but the drunk seemed oblivious.

Yua turned to Isau. "He doesn't have long. Finish him and give his life some meaning."

After a moment's confusion, Isau stepped forward and drew his own dagger, the one Yua had given him. He put his left hand on the confused man, searching for the drunk's energy with his sense.

It was easier this time than before. Still, he hesitated.

This man was no model citizen. Given the state of his clothing and general behavior, killing him might actually be a mercy. And he was already dead. Yua had made sure of that.

Rationally, Isau believed he acted as he should.

So why did he resist?

He grimaced and drew his dagger across the man's neck, hastening the drunk's departure for the Great Cycle.

As he did, he pulled, and after a few heartbeats, the man's energy flowed into Isau.

At just that moment, a group of four guards turned the corner and spotted him and Yua.

They were confused for a moment on account of the white robes. But a man was dead, and the murderers were clearly before them. The soldier in the lead stepped forward and Yua leaped into movement.

Isau followed her. The guards' sudden arrival left no time for thought. He wanted to hurt someone, and they had conveniently arrived. His feet flew, and he was among the guards almost before he realized it.

Their slaughter was quick, the deaths of the guards coming too fast to take advantage of their fleeing life forces. Isau's own rush of energy faded as the last of the guards fell.

His heart pounded, and his limbs trembled with savage joy.

He was stronger and faster than ever before, and would only become more so.

He would rule over others.

And he would make his family and village regret turning him over to the monks.

Isau looked down at his disguise, now covered in the blood of his enemies.

He felt sick.

But this was how it should be.

His eyes locked with Yua's, and he knew, deep down, that she understood him. She felt the same.

Together, they would be unstoppable. He saw their future, creating a world where every gifted soul could walk the land in peace. That future was closer than it had ever been.

Together, they would change the world.

69

Eiji paused on the rooftop of a house, looking out over the labyrinthine streets laid out below him. He'd opted to stay high, running across the tightly packed roofs to remain above the advancing students. Now he used the height to his advantage.

He sensed two groups nearby, and while they took different routes, their final destination was easy enough to guess.

Lady Mari's castle.

Stonekeep itself was a treasure, but the jewel was the lady. No conquest of the Northern Kingdom could happen without her defeat. She'd proven that in decided fashion during the Great War, and had only improved her standing since then.

Knowing their destination made intercepting a group an easy enough task. But Eiji remained still, a thought tickling the back of his mind. He focused on his breath, giving his thoughts space to run. Something about tonight bothered him.

It was too quiet.

Dozens of Ryota's students were inside the walls. From his vantage point, Eiji should hear the distant sounds of battle as students clashed with patrolling guards.

Stonekeep didn't even realize the danger it was in. Their enemies were already inside, but few people were aware.

He needed to warn the city.

There were bells stationed throughout Stonekeep, a standard precaution among towns and cities of the Northern Kingdom. If he could find one, he could alert other guards. He couldn't believe the assassins had killed even a majority of the guards stationed here. They had to have focused only on the walls and main gate.

Eiji continued along the rooftops, searching now for one of the bells. He remained close to Ryota's students, following in their wake. At the very least, he ensured that his route always brought him closer to the castle above. Ringing an alarm would be far more effective if it was near trouble.

He discovered a guard station in short order. It wasn't much—a small stone building built near a major intersection of streets. Two guards stood watch outside, the bell behind them. Eiji studied the guards from a shadowed perch. If they were true guards, they were among the best trained he'd ever seen. They barely shifted their weight.

For all his study, though, Eiji couldn't uncover any explicit evidence that identified them as assassins. Lady Mari's guards were well trained, and it wouldn't be a stretch to assume that those closer to the castle would be among the best.

Still, something about the guards unsettled him.

If he wanted, there was a path along the rooftops that allowed him to drop down behind the guards and take them by surprise. He rubbed at his chin. If he was wrong, he'd be killing innocent guards. But it almost completely ensured his safety.

After another few moments of deliberation, he dropped to the street from his perch. He couldn't take the chance of being wrong. He couldn't add the uncertainty to the already weighty burdens he carried.

Eiji tested his sword, ensuring it slid from the sheath with ease. Then he took a deep breath and stepped forward before he could second-guess himself. After all, he was still a nightblade. He shouldn't have any problems against two assassins.

Eiji adopted a nonchalant attitude as he strode into sight of the guard post.

Too late, he remembered that all of Stonekeep was supposed to be within their homes. He didn't break stride, though, and continued toward the guards.

He sensed the guard on his left almost draw a knife and throw it. The intent had been there, but reined in at the last moment.

That was evidence enough for him. A real guard's first instinct wasn't to throw a knife at an approaching stranger.

"Turn around and go home," the man on the right commanded.

Eiji bowed, as if in acknowledgment, but continued his approach. He kept his sense focused on the two assassins, alert for the smallest twitch. At about fifteen paces, the assassins became suspicious. At a dozen, Eiji knew he had no more time.

He plunged forward, drawing his sword and shifting to the side as he sensed both men reach for knives. Eiji reached the first before he could throw. The assassin's reaction was quick. He dodged out of the likely path of Eiji's cut, a dagger ready to exploit the opening.

But Eiji was a nightblade. He sensed the evasion a moment before it occurred and adjusted his cut in response. The whole exchange lasted less than two heartbeats and was simplicity itself. The assassin collapsed, a look of surprise frozen on his face.

The second assassin threw a knife, but Eiji, warned again by his sense, wasn't there.

Dodging the throw cost him a step, though, and it gave the assassin a chance to draw his own sword.

It did him no good. The assassin didn't realize who he fought, and although his swordsmanship was excellent, Eiji's advance knowledge of his strikes was an advantage too large to be overcome. Eiji exploited an opening in the first pass, and the second assassin died just as surprised as the first. Steel hadn't even met steel.

Eiji opened the door to the guard post, looking for anything that might help him and his allies tonight. All he found, though, were four dead guards, the smell of them already filling the room. Eiji gave the bodies a short bow, then closed the door quietly. Their fellow warriors could honor them more properly after this night was done.

Then Eiji reached up, took a deep breath, and rang the bell with all his might. It would alert the other guards, but it would also make him a target for any students nearby.

He rang for several more heartbeats, then paused to listen, hoping the alarm had been taken up by any of the other posts.

The night remained silent.

Eiji rang the bell again. Who knew how long it would be before someone came for him? Even now, an assassin could be hiding in the distance, drawing a bow just as Chiasa would. If they were far enough away, Eiji would never even sense the danger. He waited for his end to come.

But it never did.

He rang and rang, and eventually, he stopped to listen again.

Still nothing.

He slumped against the wall of the guard post. Had the assassins already penetrated so far into the city?

Eiji suddenly felt very alone, and every shadow looked eager for blood.

Then he heard the sound of another bell, up higher, closer to the castle.

Then another.

Soon bells were ringing through several parts of the city.

Eiji grinned. Maybe now they at least had a chance.

The moment his hopes rose, they were dashed by his sense. He stood up straight and squared his shoulders.

Four of Ryota's students, all wearing white robes, came around a corner into the light cast by the guard post's torches. They sensed who he was, just the same as he had sensed them a few moments ago. And they were angry. As one, they drew their swords and charged.

70

I sau and Yua weren't far from the bell when it began ringing. It brought Yua up short, cursing.

The bell rang for an impossibly long time. It woke citizens and alerted guards. It warned of the danger lurking in the streets.

The bell rang because of them. It sent a chill down Isau's spine.

Yua appeared indecisive, glancing between the direction of the bell and that of the castle.

Then the alarm stopped. After the last echoes died, Isau listened for an answer from elsewhere in the city. When none came, he released the breath he'd been holding. All was well. Chiyo and the other assassins had no doubt put an end to the matter.

Then the bell began again, and Yua took an involuntary step toward the sound. She turned to Isau. "We need to stop it."

He followed after her, but she abandoned the effort when the sound of other bells reached their ears. Yua's face fell. One bell, they might have managed. But that no longer mattered. Speed replaced stealth as their greatest necessity. Yua turned away, her steps now aimed squarely toward the castle.

Isau wasn't more than a pace behind her. She moved with a quick step, forcing Isau to run at times to keep up.

They didn't make it far.

A group of wary guards intercepted them. They called for Yua to halt, and when she didn't immediately comply, they drew their swords. No doubt, the blood on Yua and his white robes gave away their intent.

Yua crashed into the guards like a wind-driven wave against a rocky shore. They retreated against her ferocity, but no amount of lost ground could keep them safe from her daggers. By the time Isau had reached the fray, it was over. Yua stood tall over the corpses, a fierce grin on her face.

Isau had never seen anything so terrifying and yet beautiful.

Their triumph didn't last long. Another group came onto the street, but these were no guards. It appeared to be a family of men, from the grandfather to the father to two sons. From the way the grandfather and father held their swords, it looked like they, at least, had some training. The sons weren't much older than Isau, and they carried wooden practice swords.

Isau stared, not understanding what the group hoped to accomplish. Four guards lay dead on the street, all clearly the victims of Yua's skill. What hope did this family have?

Isau's lack of belief didn't deter the family, though. With a yell, the father led them in a brave but foolish defense. Isau almost yelled at them to stop. He didn't only because he knew it would do no good.

For a moment, Isau thought Yua might spare them.

But that hope died before it had a chance to take a single

breath. Yua cut down the father and grandfather with ease. The two boys froze at the loss of their family. Isau reached out his hand and tried to yell, but the words caught in his throat.

They were boys armed with nothing but wood.

A heartbeat too late, the boys turned to run, but Yua plunged her daggers into both.

Isau could do nothing but watch in wide-eyed horror as the boys fell, their short lives already over.

Then Yua was beyond them, walking up the street in the direction of the castle, eagerly searching for the next fight. Her aura hummed brighter than it ever had before. He didn't detect so much as a trace of uncertainty.

Whether she had forgotten him temporarily or just expected him to follow, he didn't know, but she didn't give him any orders as she walked away.

Isau took a few shambling steps forward, but he felt nauseous. He stared at the bodies of the family, seeking an understanding that eluded him. How could something so right feel so wrong?

Yua's argument raced in circles in his head. If death was nothing but the path to rebirth, then nothing was taken, and everything was gained as they built the new world, a better world. He understood every step of her argument, but when he looked at the faces of the dead boys, he kept imagining his own face upon them.

They'd come to fight, yes, but they'd been no danger. She'd stabbed them in the back as they ran away.

Yua's argument felt hollow. Isau couldn't say why it felt so wrong, but he no longer believed her.

He wanted to. As he stared at Yua's retreating figure, all he could think was of the future they could build together.

But now that future presented itself more sharply to his

imagination, and he saw the rivers of blood that might need to be spilled for such a vision to come true.

If this was right, why did he feel so sick?

He swallowed, pushing the nausea down. Answers would come, but Yua was walking away, and he refused to leave her alone.

Isau took one last look at the corpses, desperately hoping for an answer.

But the dead provided nothing.

With a grimace, Isau turned away and ran after Yua, deeper into Stonekeep.

71

The hesitation that had once plagued Eiji was gone, a memory he couldn't even recall. Past and future, regret and worry, had all faded away. His awareness and focus fell firmly in the present moment. Colors, sounds, and the indescribable gift of his sense all sharpened, honed like a well-crafted sword.

Ryota's students only required a heartbeat to reach his position, but in that heartbeat, Eiji sensed their weakness.

It wasn't that they lacked skill with their weapons. Their training, as near as Eiji could tell in that brief span of time, had been competent enough. Even at a full sprint, they remained balanced and prepared to react to him. He could almost feel their confidence.

But their strength was brittle.

Their confidence was their undoing.

True strength came from the hard lessons of defeat.

Loss taught flexibility. It taught resilience.

These young warriors had none of that.

Eiji sensed it.

Their intent burned brighter than any torch, their

first cuts as clear as day. The four of them, working together, formed a pattern that they no doubt had practiced.

And it was a beautiful pattern, where the first cut from the first in line served as little more than a distraction. Fatal, if ignored, but easy enough to deflect. An enemy was supposed to react to the first attack, then get cut by the succeeding ones.

But Eiji sensed the trap before it could be sprung. Instead of the traditional deflection the first student expected, Eiji stepped into the cuts early.

It threw off the rhythm of the line. The others, already committed, cut at the place where they had expected him to be.

Then their weakness revealed itself to them.

They had only prepared for the one move. They had expected it to work.

After all, Eiji suspected they'd been trained to believe no one was stronger than them. They had never prepared for failure. When Eiji still stood after their first pass, they weren't sure how to react. For a long breath, they stood there, uncertain.

For three of the four, it was their last mistake.

Eiji twisted the sword in his hand so he cut with the blunt back side of the weapon. It ruined his balance, but he couldn't miss. Three blows sent three students to the ground, unconscious.

He couldn't bring himself to kill them, but it wasn't the old hesitation on his part.

They were too young. Most of them only had a handful of cycles on Isau.

He wouldn't kill a child for being misled.

The last student standing backed away from Eiji. Shock

dominated his expression. He didn't understand how his friends had fallen.

It took time for a belief to die.

More time than Eiji had now.

"Where is Isau?" he asked.

The student looked confused, but Eiji wasn't sure if it was because he didn't understand why his friends were on the ground, or if he didn't understand the question.

"Where is Isau?" Eiji repeated.

The young man shook his head.

Eiji swore softly to himself and attacked the student.

The student recovered just before Eiji reached him. One against one, and perhaps realizing he wasn't as invincible as he'd imagined, the student fought fairly well. But he had still been unbalanced by Eiji's actions, and in two passes, Eiji had knocked him out as well.

He checked briefly on all four students, ensuring they were all still breathing. Satisfied that he hadn't done permanent harm, Eiji continued toward the castle. Even if he didn't know exactly where Isau was, that was the direction to take.

The sounds of battle began to echo in the streets. Assassins, students, monks, guards, and citizens created a confusing and ever-shifting landscape.

Ryota needed to be stopped, but that wasn't Eiji's responsibility. He trusted Chiasa and Itsuki in that, at least.

He needed to find Isau.

Steel rang against steel not far from where Eiji stood.

He swore.

It was going to be a long night.

72

Yua and Isau made solid progress up the steep incline of Stonekeep. At least once, Isau sensed a pair of assassins fighting guards, but most of what he sensed were his brothers and sisters fighting their way toward the castle.

Master Ryota's plan was coming together. Groups of students advanced on the castle from different directions, dividing the defenders' attention. Combined with the general chaos of the night, he and Yua didn't meet with any organized resistance.

But the city still fought, in ways that he didn't expect.

He'd been prepared for the guards. They had a duty to protect the city, an oath they had sworn to uphold.

He hadn't expected so many citizens to also rise to the city's defense. They had nothing to lose by allowing Master Ryota's students to pass. Isau was certain that Master Ryota would rule the Northern Kingdom well, treating all of his subjects with the respect they deserved.

But the citizens gave him no time to make that argument. Fathers, sons, and even a surprising number of women attempted to block their way. They emerged from their homes as the alarms were raised and word spread about the assault. The white robes that had protected them until now had become the target the citizens aimed for.

Not only that, but when the citizens attacked, they fought with anger flashing in their eyes.

It took Isau a few of these clashes to understand.

It was the robes.

How had he not seen it before?

The people hated the gift. Here, overlooking the valley where so many lives had been lost, history still lived in the minds of many. The monks were tolerated, a necessary evil, but they were still gifted. And the gifted would never be welcome. Now that Master Ryota's assault had given them a reason, the citizens were unleashing the built-up anger of generations.

Yua saved his life more times than he cared to count. Her daggers dripped blood, and she didn't suffer from the same compunctions that held him back from fighting ordinary citizens. Her kills were quick and clean, leaving no time to tap into the energies returning to the Great Cycle. And a great number of lives had made that journey tonight.

She kept pushing them forward. At times it didn't seem so, but then Isau would look behind him and see the trail they'd left. Dead and dying marked their ascent to the castle.

They weren't more than two hundred paces from the walls of the castle when Isau's world tipped on end.

Yua turned a corner after defeating a pair of guards, and for the first time, the main gates of the castle came into view. A battle, larger than any Isau had seen yet, raged at the main gates. The guard stationed there, warned by the bells, established a strong defense. From the glance Isau got, though, it appeared as though they were losing ground against Master Ryota and the other students. Assassins were there, too, picking off guards with bows.

Isau didn't have time to see much more. They ran headlong into a group of three guards running to join the battle for the castle gates. Yua killed two of them before they realized the danger she presented, and Isau struck one in the back.

Their short battle was witnessed by a man standing at the side of the street. Isau couldn't say why, but something about the man drew his attention. The citizen looked old enough to be Isau's father, if perhaps a little older. He carried himself with the air of a man who had once been a warrior. His stance was solid, and the tip of his sword never wobbled. The citizen made no move to help the guards. He'd planted himself in front of a door to a home.

Isau extended his sense. In the home beyond were several other lives, all huddled together.

The citizen protected his home. He protected his family.

The way a parent should.

Yua angled toward the citizen.

Isau opened his mouth to warn her away, but the words died before they left his throat.

She had no need to attack him. The father had no desire to involve himself. Had they walked past, Isau was certain the man would do nothing. But Yua's steps were relentless.

The fight between the two lasted as long as every other fight against Yua did. The man displayed excellent skill, but against Yua's gifts, he had no chance. He fell for the defense of his family.

The way a parent should.

Isau felt cold, frozen daggers stabbing into both limbs

and torso. He blinked rapidly and mouthed his disbelief silently.

The struggle that he'd wrestled with for so long finally ended. He couldn't condone Yua's actions this night, no matter what reasons she gave.

As much as he wanted to believe, Yua was wrong.

Yua moved on, her expression showing no more concern than if she'd stepped on a bug in her kitchen.

Isau's legs moved of their own accord.

Despite her actions, and his disagreement, he would still follow her.

Yua was his family now. He'd chosen her, and in all of the Three Kingdoms, there was no one left. Family made mistakes, but you still didn't abandon them. He would follow her and protect her, and when all this was over and the world was at peace, they would talk. He would make her understand.

Together, they would build a better world. And he would insist they do it a better way.

But never before had it felt so far away. The vision slid from his imagination like a dream upon waking. The more he grasped for it, the more elusive it became.

None of it mattered.

He wouldn't abandon Yua the way his family had abandoned him.

He held onto the thought.

Given the labyrinthine nature of Stonekeep, it came as no surprise that Isau sensed the man before he saw him. Isau's stomach clenched tightly.

Eiji came around a corner. Isau met his gaze, expecting a fiery anger or bitter disappointment.

But he saw neither. Eiji's eyes shone brightly as they gazed upon Isau.

Understanding felt like a slap across the face.

With that single look, Eiji split his loyalty to Yua like wood before the axe.

She wasn't the only family he had left.

Ahead of him, Yua settled into a fighting stance. "You again," she said.

And then the battle between the two people he was closest to in the world began.

73

E iji breathed in deeply, then slowly released it. Isau, at least for now, was safe.

The young man's white robes were stained in several places, though it looked like none of the blood was his. He held himself differently, though, and it took a moment for Eiji to place it.

Isau held his head high now, not glancing left or right or down at the ground as he used to. Since the last time they'd crossed paths, it seemed that life had not treated the young man gently. But then, it never had. Isau had grown, though, one step closer to the man he would someday become.

Eiji wanted to see that.

Only the woman, Yua, stood between them. But she was enough. Eiji well remembered her speed and strength. In both, she was his superior. If it came to a fight, he held out little hope for his chances. And she looked eager for a fight. Her daggers dripped blood, and Eiji had sensed the murder of the man just a few moments earlier.

On the island, he'd heard stories of warriors who became consumed with bloodlust. The rush of combat and the thrill of survival, the incomparable feeling of besting an opponent. For some, it was too much to control. Once unleashed, all they wanted was more. Eiji had never come across such an individual until now.

Eiji left his sword sheathed. He didn't believe it would stop her from attacking him, but this fight wasn't about her. He held up his hands. "I've only come for Isau."

The young man started at that, as though he'd just been prodded by something sharp.

Before Isau could reply, Yua laughed. "He's one of us now, nightblade. And we'll never abandon him the way you did."

She wanted his attention on her. She wanted to anger him, to get him to attack. Her cruel words lashed at him, but he ignored them. Instead, he focused his gaze on Isau. "You know that's not true. I only wanted you to escape all of this," Eiji gestured to the chaos around them, the attack on Stonekeep putting a point on his argument, "and I could not join you. As much as I wish I could."

More words threatened to come tumbling out, but Eiji forced his lips closed, damming them up. With Isau, less was often more. The young man would have to make his own decision. That had been one of the mistakes Eiji had made before.

If Isau chose him, Eiji had no doubt he would continue to make mistakes. But he swore to himself they would at least be new ones.

Isau shifted his weight back and forth, one moment leaning toward Eiji, the next toward Yua. Eiji waited. It was both the wisest and safest course of action.

Yua didn't share his patience. "Enough," she snarled. She ran at him.

Eiji drew his sword, holding it in front of him, keeping it

between them. Yua slapped at it with daggers and her armored forearms, intending that he lose his line and allow her to finish him.

Eiji sensed the attempts well enough in advance, and he had no qualms with giving up ground to keep himself out of reach of her daggers. He circled at a gentle angle, ensuring he never got trapped in a corner.

Yua's anger at her lack of immediate progress was almost victory enough. When her first and second attempts to gut him failed, she growled and swung wildly at his sword. He avoided the cuts easily and sensed a small opening. He stabbed at her.

She sensed his attack and avoided it without problem. Eiji almost followed with a series of cuts, but then he noticed how she settled into a defensive stance. Memories of their first duel were still too fresh. If he attacked, she would counter and kill him in a heartbeat. Eiji disengaged and opened some space between them.

His mind raced.

Eiji held no delusions. Yua possessed greater gifts and greater speed. But for the first time, she had cracked. The opening hadn't been much, but it was more than he'd seen from her before.

Yua didn't give him time to solve the riddle. She came in again, this time more controlled.

Unfortunately for her, Eiji was fast enough to keep distance between them. He refused to let her close, always giving up ground. He felt no pride at his tactics, but they kept him alive, and he much preferred breath to honor.

Yua's expression darkened with every attempt to close. Finally, she broke and attacked with a flurry of cuts, doing everything in her power to penetrate his guard. She almost succeeded, but Eiji just kept himself beyond her reach. He sensed several small openings, but none were tempting enough to risk.

Yua broke away again, swearing. "Fight me!"

Eiji shook his head. "I'm not here to fight you. I only came for Isau."

"You're a fool. He'll never come with you."

Behind her, Isau twitched.

Calmness descended upon Eiji, then confidence. Not that he would win. That was far from a given. But certain in his actions. His grip was firm but not too tight on his sword. His stance was relaxed, ready for an attack from any direction. "That's for him to decide."

Yua's nostrils flared. It wouldn't be long before she attacked again, and Eiji suspected this next exchange would be their last.

But he knew how to defeat her, now. Instinct and recent experience illuminated the path.

Yua was far stronger, and more experienced, than any of the students he'd fought yet. But she shared a similar weakness. She considered herself better than her opponents. The world had given her little reason to believe otherwise. Eiji's continued resistance wore away that brittle confidence.

He saw the way she flexed her fingers. Her knuckles were pale from gripping the hilts of her daggers too tightly. With every beat of his heart, his life battered at her belief.

That was how he would break her.

Not by skill, but by survival.

He might not be the strongest warrior, but he would keep fighting long after everyone else had given up.

He smiled, knowing it would stoke the fire raging within her. "Surrender, Yua. Isau respects you, and I don't want to hurt you. But if you attack again, you will die."

Eiji hoped he sounded certain. He was anything but. His

idea might work, but simply surviving a full assault from Yua would require more than a little luck. Despite his bravado, he didn't underestimate her. If his guard fell even for a moment, he would die.

It worked, though. Perhaps better than he would have wished.

Yua shouted and attacked, and Eiji saw his death reflected in her eyes.

74

Isau watched his former master the way prey focused on a predator in the distance. Something in the night-blade had changed. Isau couldn't find the words to describe what he sensed, but everything about Eiji's presence unsettled him.

Part of his discomfort came from Eiji's tactics. Isau had never imagined a nightblade would fight more as a coward than a hero. Eiji refused to stand his ground, refused to meet Yua on even terms. He always evaded and retreated, using the far greater length of his sword to keep her away.

No, there was nothing honorable in the way Eiji fought.

And yet, he was here, again. The story repeated itself, demanding Isau's attention.

Isau thought of the now-dead father standing in front of his home, protecting it against warriors far superior to him.

As Yua attacked again, thoughts of the father blended with the sight of Eiji fighting desperately to survive Yua's deadly daggers.

Eiji wasn't the warrior Isau wanted him to be, but he was here.

Was that enough?

Isau didn't know.

When he watched Yua, he saw her strength. Her anger lent her blinding speed. The nightblade could barely give up ground fast enough.

Yua fought the way a warrior should. Her strength and speed were worthy of envy.

The two combatants were like broken halves of a complete warrior.

Isau's eyes broke from the fight to look ahead to the castle. The battle at the gate was over, and it appeared Master Ryota, his students, and the assassins had won. Why else would the gate be open and undefended?

It was only a matter of time before this battle was over. Master Ryota couldn't fail, not after making it this far.

Eiji was here, and Isau respected that, but he'd chosen the wrong side. The nightblade was dead, no matter what happened in the next exchange.

Isau couldn't convince his body to move. He should be helping Yua. Against them both, Eiji wouldn't last for more than a heartbeat or two. And maybe Isau could plead for mercy for his former master.

But his feet were heavy as stone. They didn't even shuffle forward.

The duel before him could fall either way. Yua's cuts were ferocious, and a few wounds had appeared on Eiji's arms, but nothing fatal. And Yua was tiring. She was giving everything to break Eiji's stubborn defense, but he refused to let her past his guard.

When the ending came, it was almost too fast for him to see.

Eiji lunged forward, the first time he'd reversed direction in the entire prolonged exchange. Yua reacted and tried to deflect, but her daggers were too far out of position. Eiji's sword stabbed deep into her, and then the nightblade was retreating again, his weapon freshly coated in blood.

Isau blinked, not quite believing what he thought he'd seen.

Yua roared and attacked, all semblance of control a distant memory.

If ever there was a time for a decisive stand, it was this moment. Yua swung wildly, with little more control than a child throwing a tantrum. But Eiji still refused to close with her. He backed up, even faster than before. Isau expected Yua to follow. She did for several steps, then faltered. She fought a battle with her own body, and she was losing.

That, Isau understood. He wanted to run to her, to wrap his arms around her and heal her. He would give all his own energy to save her.

But he was the greatest coward on the field of battle. Even greater than Eiji.

Through it all, Isau could do nothing but watch. His body betrayed him.

Yua dropped to her knees, staring down at her torso as though she didn't understand.

Too late, the ice fell from Isau's limbs. He started toward Yua, a halting, shambling advance that slowly quickened into a run. He slid to a stop beside her, wrapping his arms around her, seeking her energy with his sense.

He could still save her.

Yua offered him no final words. She didn't even turn to look at Isau as she died. As near as Isau could tell, she spent her final breath doing the same as she'd done for the last several dozen. She glared at Eiji, eyes filled with venom.

Then they went blank and she pitched forward, face first, onto the street. Isau, consumed by the search for her energy, couldn't stop her fall. But he felt the moment of her passing.

Isau imagined himself as one of the statues within the wealthy neighborhoods of Highgate, a man made of stone. In the moment of Yua's death, Eiji took his hammer and chisel and with one strike, shattered Isau, scattering the pieces of him to the corners of the Three Kingdoms.

Eiji killed Yua.

The thought was both everything and nothing. The moment of her death played on an endless loop in his mind, but it felt hollow, like a play being performed without an audience.

Isau stared at Eiji. The nightblade was gesturing, and his mouth moved, but Isau neither heard nor understood.

He looked toward the castle and the open gates. Master Ryota fought there, bringing about the dream he'd spoken about. The dream that Yua had just given her life for.

It didn't seem like a choice. The castle was the only direction he could go. Master Ryota was the only person who could help him understand. He was the only one who could give Yua's death meaning.

Isau ran.

75

Eiji reached out for Isau as the young man bolted, but he was too slow. The fight against Yua had pulled everything from him. His limbs felt heavy with disbelief. He had resigned himself to death, and his rebirth left him weary.

For all Yua's skills, she should have killed him.

But she had been too fragile.

With better control over her emotions, Eiji knew he would be the one lying motionless on the ground.

He wasn't, though. He stood, his sword dripping Yua's blood onto the street next to his feet.

Isau ran up the thoroughfare, and he could only have one destination in mind. The castle gates were open and unguarded, but the battle wasn't over yet. Eiji sensed the fighting, faint but unmistakable to his gift.

Eiji turned to Yua.

It was a waste. She'd been so talented. To have her life ended like this was worse than meaningless.

Anger warmed his deadened limbs.

Ryota.

So many of his students were so young. He caught them early and sold them a dream. He told them everything they wanted to hear.

They would be meaningful. They would change the world.

Eiji felt sick. Cycles ago, he'd made the same argument to his fellow blades on the island. He hadn't understood the pain in the elders' eyes when he spoke. Now, for the first time, he did. They had lived through the Great War. They'd seen the outcome of his arguments long before him. Perhaps he hadn't been that different from Master Ryota.

He shook his head. He'd believed in his vision, but he never would have gone this far. This was too much destruction in the name of progress.

Eiji wished Yua's essence a safe trip to the Great Cycle. The sentiment wasn't much, but it was all he could offer. Then he turned back to the castle. It would end there. He wanted to fight Ryota even less than Yua.

But he would.

This madness had to stop.

His first step was the hardest.

Each one after came a little easier. He walked with a steady stride, his sense alive.

Little else was. These streets had filled with guards when he'd rung the bell, and they had fought to defend their rulers and their land. Blood soaked the cobblestones as it trickled down the hill. Eiji stepped carefully, ensuring his feet wouldn't slip as he climbed the last few hundred paces to the castle.

The vast majority of the dead were guards. But not all. A few appeared to be everyday citizens, and Eiji mourned those more than the others. This wasn't their fight. Or, at least, it shouldn't have been. But there were several white-robed figures among the corpses. Eiji made a brief study of each.

On average, they were young. They were mostly men and boys, but he counted three women as well. Most were old enough to serve in the army, barely, but not all. Eiji's stomach knotted a little more with each one he passed.

Could he have walked this path as one of them?

He hoped the answer was no, but he couldn't be so sure. If Ryota and he had crossed paths several cycles ago, Eiji might very well have followed just as eagerly.

The thought almost brought him to a stop, but he pushed forward.

Isau needed him. And even if Isau turned away again, Eiji still intended to kill Ryota.

Near the gates, he came across another white-robed corpse. This one caught his eye because she had an arrow in her back, a perfect shot. Eiji would recognize that fletching anywhere.

He took a long breath before crossing the gates. Now that he was closer, he sensed the battle more clearly.

The outer sections of the castle had fallen. At least, Eiji couldn't sense anyone. Which meant either outright defeat or retreat to even more defensible positions.

He'd been in the castle, though. It was all built with an eye to defense.

If the battle was deeper within, it meant defeat.

Eiji walked faster, alert for surprises.

The castle reeked of death, and the trail of corpses continued. Eiji passed a few survivors. Some might live through the night, but others were dead men breathing. He wanted to stop and offer what aid he could, but his duty was to the living. He apologized as he walked past.

Beyond the castle walls, Eiji would have said that there

were five or six guards lying still on the street for every one of Ryota's students. Here, that number looked even worse for the guards. Bodies could be found in every hallway, but few of them wore white robes.

He supposed that was reasonable. Although a few strategists had developed techniques to take down nightblades, the most common approach was still to simply overwhelm them with numbers. It was a bloody strategy, but effective.

Within the tight walls of the castle, the strategy broke down. It was more difficult for defenders to surround the invaders, and they paid a dear cost.

It didn't take him long to find the outskirts of the battle. His sense warned him of a pair wandering the halls. Unfortunately, his gift didn't have the ability to determine which side of the fight they were on. Eiji backed away from the intersection, giving himself enough space to react to whatever happened.

When the pair turned the corner, chaos reappeared.

They were wearing the uniforms of Lady Mari's guards, and Eiji's initial reaction was to relax.

His gift warned him otherwise, though. He sensed them reaching for knives, the weapon of an assassin. Earlier in the night, Eiji might have hesitated, but no more. He jumped forward as knives cleared their sheaths.

His sense proved to be advantage enough. The two assassins fell without a sound.

Eiji gave his heart a few moments to stop pounding in his chest. The familiar surge of excitement passed, as did the relief at living through yet another fight. But the crash of guilt didn't come. The assassins had chosen their path.

Eiji continued on, pausing not long after in a room where the scene was even worse than those he'd already witnessed. Almost a dozen men had fallen in this one room alone. But there were no white-robed figures. Every corpse was a guard, and not a single body drew breath.

It was the ferocity of the slaughter that caught Eiji's attention. He crouched next to the bodies. Backs of skulls were caved in where they had been smashed against walls. The cuts on the bodies were deeper than most swordsmen would make. They cut through bone as often as flesh. Eiji shook his head. The amount of strength needed to do this boggled his comprehension.

This had to be Ryota's work.

Strangely, the sight before him didn't frighten him. Instead, it strengthened his resolve. This amount of power, held by a man with such a casual disregard for life, couldn't be allowed. Even if it cost Eiji his own life, the cost was well worth it.

Eiji stood up, his shoulders back and relaxed.

He could sense Ryota. The aura, which he'd once thought was a group of people, was unmistakable now.

Eiji followed it deeper into the castle.

Isau's world was filled with blood.

Everywhere he looked, he saw the vital liquid. It was splattered against the walls of the hallways he walked and made the ground slippery underneath his feet. It trickled from the newly dead and hardened around those who had joined the Great Cycle some time ago.

And it soaked his memories.

He sensed the battle, still in front of him. But regardless of desire, his pace had slowed to a walk. At times he could hear shouts, or the now-familiar sound of steel against steel. But he was the only living creature in the hallways he walked.

He stopped at the sight of a familiar face. A young man who had seen no more than a cycle or two more than him. One of Master Ryota's other students. He'd been killed by no less than a dozen separate cuts. More the work of an angry mob than a skilled warrior.

No doubt, a whole unit of guards had attacked him at the same time. Skilled as they were, even one of Master Ryota's students wasn't invincible. Given the number of dead guards that surrounded the body, the student had acquitted himself well.

But Isau couldn't remember the student's name.

He should be able to. The student had been one of the first to welcome him into Master Ryota's village. He'd been at that table where Isau had first eaten.

And yet the name eluded him.

The young man was no more than another dead familiar face.

That was when the grief struck.

It hit with the force of a landslide, burying him under layers of loss. A hole opened up in the pit of his stomach, because for the first time he realized that he wouldn't ever see his friends again. This nameless student, who had shown him kindness when he needed it most, would never do so again.

The same was true of Yua. He would never feel her cold aura again, strangely comforting as the world burned around him. He would never again earn one of those all too rare smiles. Eiji had taken those futures away from him.

He didn't mourn their deaths. He believed in the Great Cycle. He mourned for himself, because he would have to go on without them.

And at this moment, a life without Yua was devoid of all meaning.

He sank to his knees, the white robes he wore eagerly mopping the blood from the floor.

Isau had no tears to cry. Crying implied that he was filled with sorrow, but he wasn't filled with anything.

A void grew within his heart, consuming his emotions and leaving him hollow.

His breath, which had been rapid, slowed. A deadly peace fell over him. He wondered, briefly, if this was how

Yua's aura had become so cold. Had she, too, been overpowered by a grief she couldn't fight any other way?

He felt a brief pang of sympathy. Hopefully, she would find a more lasting peace in the Great Cycle.

Isau looked down at the young man. His end had not been pleasant, but he wished the same for him as well. They deserved an end to the violence.

Isau didn't know how long he knelt in that hallway. There were no windows to track the progress of the moon overhead. No one disturbed him. All he knew was that when he stood, hardened blood cracked around his knees.

He needed to find Master Ryota. Not because of any strong desire, but because he didn't see any other paths in front of him. He would serve Master Ryota as well as he was able, for what else was left for him to do?

His sense stretched out through the castle. Several groups of gifted fought deeper within the building, most of them arranged against clumps of guards. The battle, he believed, was nearing its crux. The narrow hallways of the castle meant much of the fighting would be close in and brutal.

That thought scared him no longer.

Master Ryota, of course, was easy to sense. He burned so brightly that even dozens of paces away, Isau could feel every cut the man made. He was a human storm, blowing through everything in his path. He and the two students who followed him were closest to the heart of the castle.

That was where he needed to go. He felt compelled, as though he was a moth attracted to flame.

Isau drew his own daggers and advanced.

He sensed the guard before the woman was in sight. She was running, away from another group of Ryota's students. She turned the corner and stopped, less than a dozen paces from him. Her eyes widened when she saw his bloodstained white robes.

She was unarmed and wounded. Blood trickled down her right arm, and from the way it hung limp from her shoulder, Isau guessed she couldn't make use of it.

In short, she was no match for him. He saw the same knowledge haunting her gaze.

In a heartbeat, her fear became resignation.

Isau had no desire to fight her, though. The void within him had no lust for violence. It possessed no wants at all.

He would fight if needed, but only then.

Isau stepped to the side of the hallway, angling so that it would be easier for her to pass.

She glared at him suspiciously. It wasn't much of a trap, though. She was already stuck between him and another group of Master Ryota's students.

The only question was if she would accept the offer or attempt to fight for her lord and lady.

Fighting would be pointless. The battle for Lady Mari's life took place deeper in the castle. The guard couldn't beat him. If she attacked Isau, the guard might maintain her honor, but it would be an empty gesture.

The guard came to the same conclusion. She nodded and walked slowly toward him.

Isau focused his sense on her. If anything, his decision put him at greater risk. He allowed her to close with him.

She walked past him, stopping about two paces behind him.

"Thank you," she whispered.

Isau nodded. He didn't want her gratitude. He just wanted her to leave.

She did.

When he was sure she wasn't going to double back on

him, he went deeper into the castle. Even though he could easily sense Master Ryota, it didn't mean the man was easy to find. The castle's design kept pushing him in different directions, and it took him far too long to find his master.

When he finally did, though, his relief was palpable. Master Ryota stood with two students in a small chamber, the floor filled with bodies. Isau stepped carefully so as not to trip. The guards, it seemed, had made this chamber one of the places where they would make a final stand.

Master Ryota was painted in blood. Not a single patch of white remained to be found anywhere on his robes. He studied Isau briefly. "Yua?"

Isau shook his head. Master Ryota nodded, but gave no outward expression of grief. Even his aura remained constant. "I'm sorry," he said.

The words rang hollow.

Master Ryota gestured toward the door opposite the one Isau had entered. "They are gathering beyond. There is nowhere left for them to run. Are you ready to watch history be made?"

Isau couldn't find the strength to nod, but Master Ryota had already moved toward the door, Isau forgotten. This close to the end, all that mattered was killing Lady Mari.

And she was behind the next door.

77

J ust once, Eiji wished that someone would have the courage to build something straight in Stonekeep. He could sense Ryota and a few of his students nearby, but reaching them was proving to be an obnoxious challenge. The castle was as much a maze as the city that surrounded it.

At one point, Eiji was certain he was within fifteen paces of Ryota. The man's energy blazed brightly, but thick walls separated them. He cursed and continued on, following the path even though it led away from the master.

He took the first turn that he found, then stopped in his tracks.

There were three people not far in front of him. He guessed they were around the next corner. One was gifted.

He'd only sensed them as he retreated from Ryota's presence. Just being near him was like being trapped in a one-man city. But the gifted wasn't fighting with the others. They were waiting, together.

Which meant one of Ryota's students with the assassins.

The battle for the castle wouldn't last much longer.

Ryota was near the center, and from the number of bodies Eiji had already found, it wouldn't be long before Lady Mari ran out of guards to defend her.

Eiji threw caution to the wind. As he neared the intersection of hallways, he sprinted, his tired limbs requiring two extra paces to reach his full speed.

He took the corner too fast, but as the throwing knives passed harmlessly behind him, he knew he had chosen well. Eiji leaped, kicking off the wall to redirect his momentum.

A sword flashed as Ryota's gifted student cut at Eiji. Eiji sensed the attack, and sword clashed against sword. Then Eiji's momentum sent him sprawling into the heart of the group.

The four combatants were a tangle of bodies, and it was all Eiji's sense could do to keep up with the attacks all aimed for him. He twisted and cut, avoiding daggers while slicing at enemies. But the assassins nimbly avoided his attacks.

In truth, the assassins proved to be more dangerous than Ryota's student. The student was young and only attacked when he was certain Eiji couldn't counter. He was frightened of Eiji.

The assassins didn't share his fear, and though they weren't gifted, they were well trained. They reacted quickly to Eiji's movements and were relentless in their own attacks. Eiji's sense kept him alive, but not much more. The hallways didn't give him as much space to isolate his opponents as he would like.

In the end, victory required sacrifice. Eiji sensed the moment, and it presented him a choice. He could accept an injury and end this cleanly, or he could fight on and hope for a better opportunity.

The student's sword sliced across his side as the student

lunged. Eiji felt the edge of the blade, a razor-hot burning sensation along the side of his torso. Eiji twirled and cut, sending one of the assassins staggering back from the force of the blow. The second assassin couldn't take advantage of Eiji's momentary imbalance because the student's lunge carried him between Eiji and the assassin.

But the student wasn't fast enough to make the cut fatal. Eiji used the openings the student's wild lunge provided. A flurry of cuts brought down the off-balance student and the assassin behind.

Eiji turned as the final assassin drew a dagger to throw at him. The two raced, Eiji's sword against the assassin's throw. Eiji's cut won by a hair's margin. The assassin had thrown the knife, but hurried as he was, he missed.

Eiji grimaced against the pain in his side. It had been a difficult fight, and a harder one remained.

He glanced back at the corpses he'd left behind. The sickness he usually felt was nowhere to be found. These three had been on the wrong side of the fight, a side that promised little but death and suffering if they succeeded.

Eiji turned and went deeper into the castle.

78

Everything came down to these next heartbeats. Though Master Ryota said nothing more, Isau felt the import of the moment deep in his bones. The air felt heavy and he found it difficult to breathe. A mass of warriors had gathered ahead of them, and while a few small battles waged in the corridors beyond, this was where the ruling family of the Northern Kingdom planned on making their final stand.

Master Ryota took one final look at his students. Was it pride Isau saw on his face?

Isau couldn't be certain.

Master Ryota nodded one more time, then kicked at the door.

It didn't budge.

Master Ryota kicked again, and the door shuddered. The door itself didn't appear to be that sturdy. The remaining defenders hoped to make the most out of this last barrier.

The door couldn't last long, though. Master Ryota's students joined in, and against their combined strength, the door began to shatter. With a squeal, the hinges finally gave, and Master Ryota and his students plunged into the hallway beyond.

Master Ryota's energy sent Isau to his knees. It was so overwhelming that he had no other choice. He clutched at his head, wishing for the pain to subside. Fighting nausea, he looked up to see Master Ryota collide with the wall of guards in the hallway.

In all his young life, Isau had never seen anything like it before. Against such numbers, even one such as Master Ryota shouldn't have a chance.

But he did. Not only did he survive, he pushed the guards back, unbelievable as that seemed. Unlike Yua, Master Ryota preferred the sword, and in his hands, it was a weapon suitable to take down an entire kingdom. The guards fought valiantly, but Master Ryota couldn't be beaten. His sword blocked every cut, and his own took a life whenever it lashed out.

The students behind Master Ryota weren't so fortunate. Both fell in the storm of swords.

Master Ryota didn't even notice.

Isau forced himself to his feet, the world spinning around him as he did. Hands on knees, he stabilized himself for a moment before standing straight.

At that moment, as if by unspoken agreement, the fighting stopped. Master Ryota retreated three paces, and the wall of guards before him didn't pursue. Isau looked closely and understood why.

There, at the end of the hallway, stood an older woman. Isau, not the best at estimating age, figured she had seen somewhere between fifty and seventy cycles. Her hair was gray, but her eyes were lit with a youthful energy that belied the wrinkles around them.

Though he'd never seen her before, Isau had no doubt

that this was Lady Mari. Her presence acted as a calming influence over the entire hallway. Even Master Ryota seemed somehow lesser compared to her, like a belligerent child before their parent.

She fixed Master Ryota with a steady gaze. To Isau, it appeared as though she took his measure with a single glance and found him wanting. "You must be Ryota," she said, her voice laced with disappointment.

Master Ryota didn't respond, and Isau wished he could see his master's face. What emotions played across that surface now? Here he was, face to face with his greatest enemy.

"What do you hope to accomplish here?" the lady asked. "I don't believe you are a fool, so you must know becoming ruler of the Northern Kingdom requires far more than just killing us."

For the first time, Isau saw a man standing behind Lady Mari. Lord Takahiro. He stood tall, though somehow had seemed almost invisible beside his wife.

Master Ryota finally found his voice. "Killing you is just the first step. Even as we speak, my allies move toward Stonekeep."

Lady Mari shook her head, a sad smile on her face. "You shouldn't put any faith in Tomiichi."

Even from behind Master Ryota, Isau saw the surprise cause him to falter.

Lady Mari continued, her words succeeding where so many swords had failed. "He's an opportunist, not a leader. Yes, he's supported you and given you land, but he will never send you the support of his house troops. At best, he hopes you'll kill me so that he and his supporters can attempt a new coalition. But he'll never sacrifice anything on your behalf."

"You lie!"

Lady Mari shrugged, and it was that casual dismissal, more than anything she'd done before, that convinced Isau that she spoke the truth. "Believe what you will. But my children are gone and safe, so my line will remain unbroken. I have always been willing to give my life for my people. Are you willing to do the same?"

With that, a servant handed Lady Mari a bow.

At first, Isau almost laughed. But when the lady nocked an arrow and brought the bow up with practiced ease, he realized Lady Mari meant to fight beside her troops. None of the hardened warriors who stood between her and Master Ryota seemed concerned in the least about her aim.

And Isau remembered the stories that had been told of Lady Mari.

And for the first time, he believed them.

When Master Ryota answered, it took Isau a few moments to realize it was actually his master. His voice was pitched slightly higher, and his retort came out faster, as though his tongue raced to get the words out before his mind forgot them. "You are nothing, Lady Mari! Your name, and the name of your family, will become nothing. No historian will mention you, except as a failure. You have lost, Lady Mari! You have lost everything!"

Lady Mari's expression never changed, even as Isau looked upon Master Ryota, amazed and disgusted by what he heard. It sounded so personal. The difference between the Lady and Master Ryota was stark, and Isau found himself disappointed to be standing behind Master Ryota.

Though her expression never shifted, her actions spoke loudly enough. She released her arrow. It sliced between the heads of her guards, aimed straight for Master Ryota's heart. Master Ryota must have sensed the attack, because he had already shifted to the side, even before she released. The arrow split the air of the hallway, and when Isau looked back to Lady Mari, she already had another arrow nocked. Age, it seemed, had not dulled her skills in the least.

Isau wondered why Master Ryota didn't attack. Standing as he did in the hall, he was nothing more than a standing target. Then Isau sensed another presence and he understood. A monk came around the far corner, next to Lady Mari. It was the huge monk, Itsuki. Half a step behind him followed the woman. Itsuki spoke loudly enough for all to hear. "Lady Mari, the path to the armory has been cleared. Very few of his followers remain. Your men should go arm themselves with spears, in case we fail."

"You heard him," Lady Mari said.

It was all the order her men needed. They retreated quickly as Itsuki pressed forward. Isau didn't know how far away the armory was, but he couldn't imagine it was too distant. They wouldn't leave Lady Mari for long.

There was a moment, perhaps a heartbeat long, where Isau thought Master Ryota might attack. Lady Mari still had her arrow trained on him, but with the guards retreating, her shot wasn't clean. The same was true of Itsuki's companion. The only real threat was the monk.

Master Ryota stepped forward, as though he was going to take the opportunity, but then he hesitated.

Then the moment was gone. He was bracketed by the two women and their bows and Itsuki's incredible mass. The monk practically filled the hallway.

Isau took an involuntary step back.

In that moment of hesitation, he'd seen the impossible.

Master Ryota was afraid. Afraid of two women and a lone monk.

The master snarled, and Isau wondered if it was at himself or at his enemies. Then he stepped toward Itsuki, and the final battle began.

79

When the battle between Itsuki and Ryota began, Eiji swore it could be sensed for leagues. The sheer intensity of Ryota's energy was beyond understanding. Itsuki couldn't hope to match his opponent's strength, but there was a certain quality to his stand that was difficult to quantify.

When Eiji sensed Itsuki, he thought of a sturdy but unadorned shield. It couldn't compare to the dazzling forces arrayed against it, but time and time again, it turned the blows meant to destroy it.

When Eiji finally found a hallway that led to his destination, he ran. He turned one final corner to see Lady Mari, a man he assumed was Lord Takahiro, and Chiasa, all holding position at another intersection of hallways. Both women held bows, and Chiasa released an arrow down the hallway just as she came into view.

Lady Mari saw him, her aim swiveling slightly in his direction. Recognition flashed in her eyes, and she returned her focus to the hallway where the two warriors were locked in their final battle.

Eiji accepted her gesture as invitation enough and joined the others. He sheathed his sword, not wanting to die as the result of simple confusion. Though Takahiro had never seen him before, the lord accepted his wife's judgment and stepped aside to allow Eiji among them.

Eiji stopped in mid-stride when he caught his first glimpse of the duel in the hallway. It was a battle both physical and mental, and in each arena, Eiji found himself in awe.

The speed of the two swords was almost too fast for Eiji to track. Limited by the narrow hallway, the two masters didn't have the space for big swings and powerful blows. They relied more on stabs and quick short cuts, utilizing their swords in ways they hadn't been designed for.

Moves and counters built upon one another, a crescendo of masterful swordsmanship.

Their battle was made even more impressive by the expression of their gifts. Eiji sensed the way in which their attacks and defenses shifted subtly in response to one another.

Ryota intended a stab at Itsuki's heart. Itsuki sensed the intent and moved to block it. In response, Ryota, sensing the block, shifted the aim of his stab. Thriving in such a battle was difficult, but both Ryota and Itsuki were masters of this type of duel. Eiji knew if he was to so much as approach he would be cut down in moments.

This battle was a masterpiece of ability, and he was ashamed that he was the only one who truly understood what passed between the two warriors.

Movement at the far end of the hall, on the other side of the battle, caught his attention. Isau stood there, watching the battle with the same awe-filled expression Eiji suspected he wore on his own face.

The boy was still covered in blood, but he didn't look any worse than he had when Eiji had fought Yua in the streets. He was alive, at least, and that was something. Eiji couldn't even begin to guess what the future held; he wished the best for the young man.

Somehow, Ryota found an even deeper reserve of strength and speed. He pushed Itsuki back, forcing the monk to give up one step at a time to avoid falling to Ryota's cuts.

Eiji barely believed Itsuki still stood. While Eiji could mostly follow the action, he knew he would be worse than useless in such a fight. For all his own gifts, he was nothing compared to them.

Itsuki couldn't match Ryota, either, but he didn't have to. He had Chiasa and Lady Mari behind him. Whenever they believed they had an opportunity, they would release one of their arrows. Ryota had to evade their arrows as well as Itsuki's sword.

Fortunately for the rogue warrior, Itsuki's bulk in the narrow hallway shielded him from most attempts. The archers evened the battle, but they hadn't yet proved decisive. Eiji thought he sensed Itsuki attempting to push Ryota closer to the walls of the hallway, so that Chiasa could have some clean opportunities, but Ryota refused to be pushed around. Neither archer ever had more than the briefest of moments, and every time they fired, Ryota was already moving away from the arrows.

The battle, when it turned, did so in a moment. The two mighty warriors had been evenly matched for a while, but then Ryota found some flaw, some opening, in Itsuki's otherwise impeccable defense. He launched himself forward, and Ryota's speed was beyond all belief. His sword cut like lightning, and there wasn't a warrior in this land who could stop the advance.

Eiji watched in horror as Itsuki gave up ground, faster and faster. For the briefest of moments, he hoped that Ryota would make an error as his victory loomed. It was often at the end of the journey that one made a fatal mistake.

But Ryota refused to be that warrior. Even in his final offensive, he ensured that he remained behind Itsuki, using the monk as a shield against the two archers.

Time slowed.

Off in the distance, a large group of guards was returning. Eiji sensed them, but also knew that although they would be here soon, they would be too late. Lady Mari had three, maybe four heartbeats left to live.

They all did.

With that realization came sudden clarity. No matter what he did, Eiji wasn't leaving this hallway alive.

His eyes met Isau's. It appeared as though the boy had just noticed him. With the two warriors assuming so much attention, it was no surprise. Given how untrained Isau still was, he probably couldn't even sense anything beyond Ryota's immense energy.

There was so much Eiji wanted to tell Isau. He wasn't a sage, but he saw so much of himself in the young man. He didn't want Isau to make the same mistakes that he had. If he could ask for nothing else, he would ask for that.

He didn't think he would get the chance, though.

There wasn't any time left to waste. Eiji couldn't win the battle on his own, and Itsuki was only a move or two away from losing it all.

His mind, holding tightly onto the promise of life, resisted. But there was no real choice. If Ryota won here, it wouldn't just be Isau's life that was destroyed. It would cause suffering on a scale Eiji didn't want to imagine.

The Three Kingdoms deserved better.

Isau deserved better.

It wasn't much, but there was only one thing he could do.

And as much as it pained Eiji, the enormous monk was the best chance Isau had at a future.

Eiji sprinted forward, his movements feeling sluggish compared to the speed of the warriors he approached.

He thought he heard something behind him. A gasp perhaps, or someone whispering his name. He hoped it was true. He wanted Chiasa, at least, to remember him well.

Eiji leaped at the wall to the left of Itsuki. The monk was too large to simply run around, but Eiji planted his foot about waist high on the wall. His momentum held him to the wall for a brief moment, and in that moment, he leaped at Ryota, drawing his sword as he did.

It was a beautiful cut.

Perhaps the best of Eiji's life.

But of course, Ryota sensed him coming. Eiji couldn't hide his intent from the sense.

Ryota had no choice but to respond. He ducked his weight low and stabbed up at Eiji as Eiji's own cut passed harmlessly over Ryota's head.

Eiji had hoped his cut would take Ryota's life.

But he supposed that was too much to ask for.

Ryota's sword cut deep into Eiji's stomach. A burning lance of pain exploded in his gut, as overwhelming as Ryota's energy.

Ryota attempted to withdraw the sword, but he wasn't quick enough. His sword was lodged in the nightblade. Eiji's momentum forced Ryota to turn to hold onto his weapon.

With a shout, Ryota pulled the blade free. Eiji tumbled, unable to control a single limb.

Ryota spun to meet Itsuki once again, but for once, the man was too slow. Itsuki's sword stabbed cleanly into Ryota's chest. Two arrows followed suit moments after.

It was the last thing Eiji saw before he hit the ground headfirst.

80

The whole fight happened so fast Isau could barely follow it. Master Ryota's skill was everything that Isau imagined.

This was what he could be someday, if he fought hard enough and trained as Master Ryota instructed.

The initial clash of swords seemed to almost be evenly matched, but Isau had a hard time telling. Itsuki was as strong as he looked. He stood toe to toe with Master Ryota, and Isau imagined that the monk was the only one alive who could.

Then Isau noticed that Eiji had shown up beside Lady Mari and the others.

Again, Eiji was here, someplace where he had no need to be. With every appearance it was harder to believe in any other explanation but one.

Eiji was here for him.

But again, what could Eiji do? The two warriors who separated the sides were far stronger than him. If Eiji tried to fight, he was just as likely to get in Itsuki's way as he was to somehow help.

And Eiji had killed Yua.

Isau couldn't forget that, but he was surprised the knowledge didn't bother him more.

The sight of Eiji should have angered him. It should have enraged him. But he didn't know what to think anymore.

Master Ryota began his final advance, and Isau knew it wouldn't be long. He overpowered Itsuki, and while the monk hadn't fallen yet, it was only a matter of time. Lady Mari's words wouldn't matter once Master Ryota finished his task. Perhaps the road ahead would be long and difficult, but Master Ryota had already come this far. He wouldn't be overthrown by weak political manipulations.

Isau caught Eiji's gaze, and again that same sadness was there, the emotion Isau couldn't quite understand. Why did the nightblade feel that way?

Then Eiji was in motion, his leap off the wall carrying him around Itsuki and directly at Master Ryota.

It was suicidal, and at the last moment, Isau realized that Eiji had known that all along.

One moment, both his past and current masters were alive and well. The next, they were both dying in the hallway.

"Master!" Isau yelled.

Of the two, Eiji's energy faded faster. Master Ryota's wounds were fatal, but it would take some time yet for the warrior to die. Itsuki had backed up several paces, well aware that no opponent was more dangerous than the one who had nothing left to lose. Just behind the monk, both the woman and Lady Mari looked as though they were just waiting for an excuse to release another flight of arrows into Master Ryota.

In a single moment, Eiji had changed everything.

And it had finally cost him his life.

Isau didn't understand. Master Ryota might have allowed Eiji to live, so long as the nightblade promised to serve.

Why?

Why would he sacrifice himself like that?

He knew the answer Eiji would give.

The sacrifice had been on his behalf.

But it couldn't be true.

People didn't die for other people, especially not someone like him.

It couldn't be true.

Yet all the evidence was right before him.

Isau ran forward, not sure if he was running toward Master Ryota or Eiji. Now that Master Ryota's energy had faded, Isau sensed the others more clearly. Itsuki gestured for the women to hold their arrows, but all three remained wary, watching the scene like hawks. Beyond, the guards were returning from their trip to the armory. Soon they would surround Lady Mari and whatever small opportunity still existed would vanish forever. They would all watch Master Ryota bleed out, unless he somehow found the strength to stand. Then he would be shot with arrows and stabbed with spears, still unable to achieve the goal he'd dedicated his life to.

Isau fell to his knees next to Master Ryota, whose eyes were wide, staring at the ceiling.

When Master Ryota saw him, a spark returned to his eyes. And with that life, determination.

Master Ryota stared at him. His voice was soft, but the hallway was small enough everyone could hear him. "I know you have the skill, Isau. Yua believed in you, and I do, too. We can still win."

Master Ryota's gaze was meaningful, as though he was trying to communicate something with his stare. But Isau didn't understand.

"With your sacrifice," Master Ryota said, "we can still make a better world."

And then Isau understood. Master Ryota wanted healing. Isau looked down at the wounds. Severe as they were, Isau knew one fact for certain. To attempt the healing would cost all the energy he possessed. Master Ryota knew that as well.

A stark trade, but easy enough to understand. His life for that of the dream they shared.

Isau's life would mean something. It would change the course of history.

Isau laid his left hand on Master Ryota. He searched for the man's energy.

Like Yua, it was difficult to get beyond the external manifestations. Master Ryota's internal energies were even more difficult to sense.

As Isau searched, his eyes rose until he saw Eiji. Somehow, the nightblade was still alive, but wouldn't be for much longer. If Isau healed Master Ryota, it meant that Eiji's sacrifice would be for nothing.

Isau paused his searching.

In all their time together, Eiji had never asked for anything from Isau. He'd just shown up, time and time again.

Isau thought back to his very first meeting with Eiji, with him bound to the tree, abandoned by family and friends both. Eiji cut those bonds and had set him free. And this was how Isau had treated him.

Isau knew he should have died long ago. He should have died when the monks returned to his village. Every day, every experience he'd had since that day was thanks to Eiji.

Isau looked again at Master Ryota. Compared to Eiji, what did he promise?

He promised that the life Isau had been given by Eiji would matter.

Isau connected with Master Ryota's energy. He sensed the power flowing through him yet. He felt the wounds Master Ryota had taken. Master Ryota's time was running short.

So why did he hesitate?

He swallowed the lump forming in his throat. He knew what he wanted, but could he follow through? Could he sacrifice his master?

In one smooth motion, Isau drew the dagger from his hip, the one that Eiji had bought for him in Highkeep. He stabbed the dagger into Master Ryota's chest, straight into the heart.

Master Ryota's eyes widened, but that was all he had the energy for. Even as his heart stopped, he couldn't believe that one of his students had betrayed him.

When the energy hit, Isau felt as though a horse had run him over at full speed. Once he recovered from the initial shock, though, the strength he felt defied description. He looked down at his hands, not sure that they were even his own anymore.

Isau didn't have long. This surge of energy could only last for a few moments.

He ran over to Eiji, who hadn't stirred since his suicidal attack on Master Ryota.

Isau searched for Eiji's internal energies, afraid for a moment that he had made his decision too late. He bit his lower lip until blood flowed. Then he felt Eiji's life, barely holding on.

Isau sensed the wounds, and knew that even with Master Ryota's borrowed energy, this healing might be the last he ever performed.

The young man was comfortable with that, though. Once, several moons ago, Eiji had saved his life.

Now it was time to return the favor.

Isau focused and pushed the energy from his body into Eiji's, reconstructing the broken pathways and filling them with new life.

The attempt was far beyond anything he had tried before, but he understood the principles well enough. Healing felt intuitive, a making right of things that were broken.

He enjoyed the practice.

Isau felt the stolen energy slipping away from him. The surge, brief as it was, had managed to seal up most of the wounds, but there was still more to be done.

Isau kept pushing, kept rebuilding his former master's body, even though it cost him.

He began to feel weak, too weak even to open his eyes and see if he'd succeeded. But Eiji still hadn't been completely healed, so Isau pushed harder.

Until he felt a hand on his wrist.

Fighting drowsiness, Isau opened his eyes, and he found himself staring into Eiji's.

The nightblade's voice was hoarse. "You've done enough."

Isau wasn't sure he agreed. Eiji's wounds weren't completely healed, and Isau had more to give.

So Isau continued to heal, but Eiji's grip tightened. Once again, their gazes met.

"Isau."

It wasn't his name, but the way that Eiji said it, that stabbed deep into his heart.

Eiji refused to accept Isau's sacrifice on his behalf.

He wanted Isau to live.

The gesture was enough to shred the last remnants of Isau's focus. He couldn't heal the nightblade any more even if he wanted to. His eyes rolled up in his head and he collapsed onto Eiji.

81

Isau sat in the common room in the inn, reading a book describing the history of the Kingdom, a time that seemed lifetimes ago, but was in truth only a few dozen cycles ago. He devoured the words with a surprising eagerness. There were many he didn't know, but he was able to read enough to grasp the outlines of the story. The book had been a gift from Lady Mari, though she'd never explained why she gave it to him.

He found it fascinating, though.

To him, history had always been a family story. He didn't often think about the history of entire kingdoms.

With every page, knowledge found purchase in his heart, like a seed that would bloom many cycles from now.

If nothing else, flipping through the pages, treating each one as though it were a treasure, was a far more entertaining pastime than staring at the wall. He'd been kicked out of the room without ceremony, and there wasn't much else for him to do.

In time, he sensed them coming down the stairs. He carefully put the book away in his pack, wrapping it in layers of clothing to protect it from harm. Books were rare enough, but to have one from the lady herself was something else entirely.

Chiasa, of course, led the way down the stairs, Eiji not far behind.

When Chiasa saw Isau, she went over to his table. She didn't sit, and Isau figured that it wouldn't be long before she was gone once again. "I wish you well, Isau. Watch after one another."

Isau nodded, and Chiasa bowed deeply to him. Isau stood and returned the bow.

Such deference still unsettled him. He didn't deserve their respect, and yet everyone he'd met in the past few days had shown him nothing but. It felt like a dream that he should wake from, but hadn't yet.

Chiasa turned to Eiji, but Isau suspected the two had already said their goodbyes in their own way. Chiasa gave the nightblade a quick nod of the head. "I hope to see you around sometime."

"Will you be trying to kill me?"

She shrugged. "Hard to say."

Eiji shook his head. "I'll miss you."

To that, Chiasa had no reply. With another quick nod of her head, she turned around and left the room.

Isau wondered if they would ever meet again. Somehow, it seemed unlikely, and that made him sad in a way he couldn't describe.

Eiji glanced down at him. He already wore his pack, and he had every appearance of a man ready to leave. Isau stood, shouldered his own pack, and nodded.

Together, the two of them began their journey out of Stonekeep.

After everything that had happened, it seemed

somehow anticlimactic. The streets were quiet, not due to curfew, but to residents voluntarily deciding to remain indoors for a few days as efforts to clean up the city were undertaken. When people did leave their homes, it was with hesitation, as though disaster might befall them at any moment.

Like Eiji, the city was healing, but it would take time before it was whole again. Despite Isau's efforts, Eiji still moved gingerly, and his hand unconsciously drifted to his stomach time and time again, as though his body still didn't believe that it was alive.

For a while, Isau thought that they might leave the city completely without notice, but he felt a familiar aura as they exited the main gates.

Eiji felt it, too. Isau could tell from the way his shoulders tensed up. But the meeting was as good as inevitable.

Itsuki stood at the edge of the road in a place where it widened just a bit. He stared off into the valley below. It appeared to Isau that the monk was looking for some meaning within the vista that he couldn't find.

Itsuki turned to them, not bothering with polite conversation. "Your decision is final, then?"

"It is," Eiji replied.

"You'll be hunted for the rest of your days."

"I knew that when I first came here."

Itsuki sighed. "It's no way to raise him."

Eiji glanced at Isau. "He's made his own choices."

Itsuki grumbled under his breath. "You put me in a difficult position."

"If you ever see me after today, I won't hold any of your actions against you."

Itsuki grimaced and shook his head. "I had hoped we could live as friends."

Eiji grinned at the monk's discomfort. "We still can. Friends disagree all the time."

"If we meet again, honor dictates that I will have to fight you. And we both know how that will end."

"With your pride damaged?" Eiji said.

"You mock me."

"You're just realizing that?"

Itsuki glowered.

Eiji softened. "I'm sorry, but I have no guidance to offer, Itsuki. You will have to choose your own path, just as we have chosen ours. But I will not raise my sword against you. I will fight if needed, but never against you, and hopefully, never against anyone ever again."

Itsuki didn't have an answer to that, but he turned to Isau, no doubt hoping to change the subject. "Although I disagree with your choice, I still wish you the best. I'm not sure traveling with him is wise, though."

"I'll keep a close eye on him," Isau replied.

"See that you do."

Isau knew that Itsuki and Chiasa planned to travel north, back to Tomiichi's lands. They would bring Lady Mari's justice to Tomiichi, no doubt delivered at the point of one of Chiasa's arrows. Itsuki would search for any remnants of Master Ryota's movement. His orders were to kill or convert them to monks.

Isau wasn't certain how he felt about Itsuki's orders. Those that had remained behind in the village were mostly young. He wished the monk and archer well, but refused to make the problem his own. He had done his piece, and now the rest was up to others.

They bowed deeply to one another, and Eiji and Isau began the hike down the mountain, which was much easier than the journey up. After they'd walked for a bit, Isau broke the silence. "I wasn't sure he would let us go."

"Either was I."

"Where should we go first?"

Eiji shrugged. "Wherever you want. You're the healer, now. I'll follow you."

Isau grinned.

It was time to travel the Three Kingdoms and bring what peace they could to the land.

WANT MORE FANTASY?

As always, thank you so much for reading this story. There's an amazing number of great fantasy stories today, and it means so much to me that you picked this book up.

If you enjoyed this story, I also have three other fantasy series, filled with memorable characters. My first fantasy series is called *Nightblade.*

Links to all of my books can be found at www. waterstonemedia.net

THANK YOU

Before you take off, I really wanted to say thank you for taking the time to read my work. Being able to write stories for a living is one of the greatest gifts I've been given, and it wouldn't be possible without readers.

So thank you.

Also, it's almost impossible to overstate how important reviews are for authors in this age of internet bookstores. If you enjoyed this book, it would mean the world to me if you could take the time to leave a review wherever you purchased this book.

And finally, if you really enjoyed this book and want to hear more from me, I'd encourage you to sign up for my emails. I don't send them too often - usually only once or twice a month at most, but they are the best place to learn about free giveaways, contests, sales, and more.

I sometimes also send out surprise short stories, absolutely free, that expand the fantasy worlds I've built. If you're interested, please go to https://www.waterstonemedia.net/newsletter/.

With gratitude,

Ryan

ALSO BY RYAN KIRK

ABOUT THE AUTHOR

Ryan Kirk is the bestselling author of the *Nightblade* series of books. When he isn't writing, you can probably find him playing disc golf or hiking through the woods.

www.waterstonemedia.net
contact@waterstonemedia.net

 facebook.com/waterstonemedia

twitter.com/waterstonebooks

instagram.com/waterstonebooks